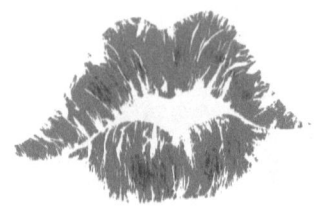

EVERNIGHT PUBLISHING ®

www.evernightpublishing.com

Copyright© 2019

Allegra Grey and Emily Sloan

Editor: Karyn White

Cover Art: Jay Aheer

ISBN: 978-0-3695-0070-0

BROKEN WINGS

DEDICATIONS

From Allegra:

To my mom, for encouraging me. To my stepdad, who let me read romances even when she said "no". To my dad, who always told a good story. To my stepmom, who handed me a truckload of Harlequins and talked about them with me. To my husband who puts up with my obsessive writing habit and explains military mysteries. And to Natalie, Selah, Sharona, Amy, James, Christa, and all my friends who answer strange questions, willingly read rough drafts, and tell me when things are messed up. Oh, and Selah, don't worry: I haven't forgotten your alien requests.

Also, to my co-author. I literally wouldn't be doing this without you, lady.

From Emily:

To my mother, for teaching me that anything worth having is worth working for. To my father who never quite understood my hobbies but supported me anyway. To my brother who forced me to read the classics when I was young and helped develop my love for literature and writing. To my sisters who have been my best friends and anchors. To Jess and Janelle who have always make me feel loved and accept me without judgment.

And finally, to Allegra: You have taught me so much about myself, my writing, and about life in general. Thank you for being you.

BROKEN WINGS

BROKEN WINGS

Storm Crows MC, 1

Allegra Grey and Emily Sloan

Copyright © 2019

<>•◆•<>

Chapter One: May 1

Oak Grove, IL

Does hell have fans? Joker groaned, rubbing his face until his contacts shifted the world into focus. Overhead, a squeaking fan spun molasses-heavy air to no effect but a nerve-shredding counterpoint to the buzzing from his nightstand. The glistening brunette tangled in the black sheets beside him didn't move. He slid his arm out from under the girl and reached over her to grab the stupid phone. A familiar number blinked across its screen.

Shit. Six missed calls. His companion inhaled and rolled over without missing a beat. A long weekend ride and longer parties lay behind them both, and he didn't blame her for knocking out. *Might as well leave her to it.* He pushed the sheet off his legs and dropped the phone on the pillow. Better to get moving and say he hadn't heard the ringtone on the bike than admit he slept through it.

Joker stumbled to his feet and reclaimed his clothes from the floor—boxer briefs, Kevlar jeans, and a black t-shirt—so he wouldn't wake the girl by rummaging around. The crow insignia's weathered eyes looked reproachful as he lifted his cut from the doorknob. The sun-faded leather felt like wearing a flak vest these days thanks to a black-lettered, sharp-edged badge with the words "Vice President". He draped it over his arm instead of slinging it on, ignoring the twinge of guilt. *I should have been up earlier. Should have stayed at the clubhouse.* The endless list of things a better VP might have done ran through his head.

He eased the door shut behind him before he walked down the hall and nudged his roommate's door closed on his way by—no snoring, no tapping keyboard, meant Grim wasn't back from his run. Flipping on the bathroom light, Joker dropped his boots on the tile floor and choked. A fake apple stench assaulted him from the potpourri bowl on the towel cabinet. His nose twitched. *Does that shit have some kind of nuclear half-life, or is Grim refilling it?* He could just about imagine his best friend buying it, if the salesgirl was pretty enough.

He turned the water on, splashed some onto his face, and blinked until the contacts moved again. His reflection glared back at him, red-eyed and shaggy as a stoner hobo. *Fuck, that's impressive. No wonder you get pussy so easy, asshole.* He ran his hands over his jaw, scratching at the day-and-change stubble. Shaving would end the itch, but wearing a beard took the edge off his sharp features and—more importantly—hid the damned dimples. *No inspection at 0500 these days. Screw it.*

Donning his cut, he took a pack of Marlboros from the left pocket. He stuck one between his lips and lit it to spite the potpourri phantom. *I'm dumping a case of Febreze here next paycheck. Reagan's gone, and her stupid scented bullshit's gotta go, too.*

Joker trailed smoke through the house and out to the garage. Standing on the threshold, he swiped his hand at the wall-mounted button just inside and watched with a reverence polite society reserved for churches as silver moonlight poured past the rising bay door, casting an ethereal glow behind a divine vision of chrome and black: a 1992 Low Rider Sport, 582 pounds of steel and twin-engine perfection customized so she was all his, right down to the stylized wings painted on the fenders. After hunting her down for three years, he'd spent the last two getting every last part just right, achieving every spec he'd dreamed up out in the Iraqi desert.

Standing beside his baby, he lit a fresh cigarette, savored the cool night air, and looked out at the silent street. Frogs and crickets practically drowned out the occasional sounds of traffic echoing from the main road.

Forgotten by the world outside, Oak Grove—like the rest of Pharaoh County—belonged to another era, a fact that suited the Storm Crows' original chapter and its national president just fine. Taking a last, slow drag, he checked his watch and calculated what level of bullshit might be waiting. He'd left the rest of the crew neck deep in pussy and booze, so probably a bar fight. Unless it wasn't.

He tossed the cigarette butt, crushing it with the tip of his boot while he slid his gloves on and flexed his fingers to stretch the leather. He ran his right hand over Baby's fender to pay his respects before he straddled her. The usual thrill lifted his soul—feeling her purr to life beneath him lit him up in a way nothing else did these days. Her engine rumbled, eager for the road. He grabbed his helmet and locked it in place before answering her call.

He took his preferred route—the long one—

toward the clubhouse, reveling in the empty roads up north of town that wound through endless seas of grass and early spring crops. The cool spring wind in his face and the open road always cleared his head. He needed that tonight. A few cars passed, and he had to look out for deer—always a bitch of a hazard, but no worse than an IED. At least the deer were visible beforehand. He checked his watch at a stop sign, sighing at the time before he made the turn to head back west. *Tree's going to rip my nuts off if I'm late again...* He gunned it on the straight, revving to eighty in a fifty-five until a headlight shone in his mirrors. Another glance revealed one light, not two: a bike. He moved into the right out of courtesy. So did the other rider.

Fucker.

About twenty feet behind him, the stranger slowed to maintain the distance and flashed high beams. Signaling. *For what?* Joker squinted at the mirror again, but the darkness revealed only the headlight. *Is it one of the guys?* Too late, he realized his phone was back in his bed.

Why would Dad send somebody out to wave me down? His question unanswered, he accelerated. The tail could ride behind him to the clubhouse and tell him there. The guy matched Joker's speed. And gained. Concern became irritation, became nerves. *This don't smell right.* He adjusted in his seat, more aware of the Glock in the back holster beneath his cut—he didn't even remember putting it on, but the habit was too engrained for thought.

He turned off the highway onto an oil-and-gravel road that skirted the edge of Oak Grove over to Ravenwood. Shit to ride on, but his shins could take a few rocks. And his baby could take the turn faster than whatever junker the asshole behind him rode. The distance between them grew. He checked the mirror and kicked down a gear—he didn't need to spin out on loose gravel. Baby's front end wobbled from his shifting weight and the uncertain road. He looked ahead, praying for a passing car. Something. Anything to knock the fuckstick off until Joker could get steady enough to outrun him. Or pull his gun.

A set of matching white lights gleamed in the distance. A house. If he could get there, maybe asshole would get off. Witnesses fucked up these games... The light behind him flashed again. A set of headlights turned into the road. A few hundred yards and closing fast. *Shit.* Steadying Baby with his left hand, he reached for his gun with his right. A darker shadow loomed in the pavement ahead.

He swerved around the pothole—plague of southern Illinois roads—and turned back.

Crack.

Shrieking, rending metal. Chrome on gravel. The world slowed and tilted, everything going weightless. It didn't hit him until he hit the ground: he'd been thrown. The pain slammed through him, taking over his body with excruciating pressure, crushing and tearing him apart at the same time. More snaps, crunches. Not his bike, but bones. The assholes after him were shouting, but the pain roared in his ears. Darkness claimed him without even the flash of a gun.

Raindrops hit his cheek instead of shrapnel.

For a delirious second, he imagined he'd dreamed it all while passed out in the clubhouse yard, gotten caught in the rain. He opened his eyes. Bone hung out of the skin on his left arm, yellow, white, and vicious red-black in the starlight. Body turned to meat. He spent the last of his strength pushing himself onto his back with an aching but usable right arm. He tried a scream, but his lungs betrayed him. There wasn't enough air in the world. The pain dulled, even cooled. Maybe it was the rain. His eyes took in the storm-darkened sky, glaring at the inconsistent stars.

Was a bullet too-fucking-much to hope for? The dark yawned and the stars wavered. *Guess it could've been worse: Got laid, got to ride Baby the way Harley intended, laughed with my brothers.*

But going down like this?

Bleeding out on a dark roadside, gravel in his back, and rain spitting in his face. Alone. No buddies calling in a chopper, no friend taking his tags. Just a bunch of fucking cowards who ran off before they even finished killing him. At least he had his cut on, and the bright light heading his way. *Won't be alone for much longer.*

****

Ashlyn

A wet ribbon of patched blacktop wove through fields and pastures lit by the waning moon and her Miata's headlights as they prowled along hairpin curves and blind corners. Ashlyn ignored her engine's purring invitation to speed and fun: two herds of deer had already crossed their path, leaving her knuckles so white they all but glowed against the black steering wheel. *This is what we get for leaving the main roads. And the 21st century...*

She cranked the volume and sang along to her latest favorite song as she negotiated another turn, taking her car from the blacktop to an oil maintenance road—a shortcut to Oak Grove, little used. Yet another hill followed. At the crest, a high beam scorched her retinas. Her voice flew sharp into a scream, the Miata's tires screeching to a halt alongside with her heart and Taylor Swift's chorus. She braced for impact.

Nothing happened.

Ashlyn eased one eye open. The beam hadn't moved, so she opened the other and allowed herself to breathe. Assess. The offending light shone out of the ditch further up the curve, explaining why she'd thought it was in her lane. Several yards past it, something lay crumpled and motionless at the edge of the right shoulder.

Great, more kamikaze deer.

She threw the shifter into park and grappled her cell phone out of her oversize, overcrowded purse, only to wince at the screen's messages. One measly bar of service—guaranteed, by the miracles of technology, to mean the same thing as no bars. *Of course. Why would you need service in the middle of nowhere? Why would you even be in the middle of nowhere? That's a place crazy people go, obviously...*

She opened her door and hit her phone's flashlight app as she got out, only to belatedly duck back in and hit the emergency blinkers. Outside, the Illinois night pulsed with life. June bugs and cicadas sang their crackling tunes, frogs and crickets adding another melody while the wind whispered through the grasses and trees beyond the fence row. Somewhere in the darkness, a rain crow called, and she could just about feel her hair frizzing in answer to it.

With her headlights, flashlight, and the foreign headlamp all lit, a forest of shadows rose up beyond the cyber-age LED's, writhing and receding with every crunching-gravel step to reveal the heaped, twisted wreck of a motorcycle. She raised her glowing phone up like a shield, turning its beam to survey the damage. Black paint and chrome gleamed here and there, but deep gouges showed along the side facing her. A busted Harley emblem lay a couple yards away from it. *No rider.* She frowned. Considering the shape of it and the worrying smudges along its side… *Why'd they run off and leave the headlight on like that? Is it stuck?*

"Hello?" She called into the night. "Hey! Anybody there?"

A rumble of distant thunder answered her. Then something rustled. Close. Ash's stomach jolted, and visions of coyotes and dire-wolves danced through the shadows as she turned her phone toward the lumpy thing half-hidden by the road's slanted shoulder and overgrown ditch. Her blood chilled.

Not a deer.

"Oh no… No!" She clutched the phone tight and ran. The tarp wasn't a tarp: it was leather, shredded to pieces by the oil-and-gravel pavement. Mud from some earlier downpour coated the person. Man, she amended as she knelt—huge frame, and the badly broken leg didn't look feminine. *Hell, that doesn't even look human… Swelling must've set in? Maybe that means he's alive?* She searched her memory for any lingering remnants of Girl Scout First Aid. A helmet and cracked visor masked his head, but he had to be mostly road rash or dirt beyond that.

"I don't know if you can hear me, but I'm calling for help. Okay?" Ash reached for the man's left arm, only to find the bone far too visible through his torn leather sleeve. She stopped before her fingers made contact. *So much broken stuff, where am I supposed to touch him?* "Shit-shit-shit don't be dead." Like pleading would make a difference. She decided to try his neck, just under the helmet. A little bit of skin not stretched over a bone. *Not cold means not corpse, right?*

Her tentative fingers brushed over his neck as lightly as possible. The rider's clammy skin felt kind of warm, so she let out a breath and pulled her phone's keyboard up. 911. Send. *Come on, networks. Don't let me down.* The call connected as she got up the nerve to touch his throat again, this time daring to press against his damp, unconscious flesh. He had a pulse. Not strong, but present. The call dropped. "Fucking *merde, sheit,* hell, dammit..."

Two more tries. First, the call dropped before it even rang. The next connected, buffered by the steady stream of frantic curses. "Please, you've got to hurry. It's a bike wreck, and he's... I don't know how long he's been here. His leg's busted, and his arm's pretty bad, too, and his helmet's still on..."

The 911 lady sounded less than patient. "Well, can you tell me where you are?"

"No, I can't!" she hissed. "My phone's got GPS. Can't you just find me?"

"The county hasn't upgraded yet."

Of course. Of fucking course. Why would Pharaoh County ever leave 1957? Panicked tears stung Ashlyn's eyes, straining her voice. "I'm on the ... County Maintenance 20 ... North of Oak Grove."

"How far?"

"I—I don't know. A little bit after Route A..."

"Is that where Ryman Dumbrowski's farmhouse burned down?"

"How would I know? I don't know a-anything about this place! Google won't load, and I just ... just drive out along Route A, take County Maintenance 20. White Miata in the stupid road! I put the flashers on. Please!"

Powerless to move the ambulance, she fumbled his visor up, half recalling some Girl Scout leader talking about airways, and checking them. The guy made a pained, grunting noise. Ashlyn choked back a sob. *I moved him, and now he's dying. He's dying now. God, why is this even real life?*

Inside the helmet, his face was a bloody mess, but most of it seemed to be coming from his nose. And he kept breathing. Worst—or best?—his swollen eyes moved. Hard to tell if the slits were blinking or not, but she opted for yes.

"Shh, it's okay." She softened her voice, barely touching her fingertips to his neck again—the only bit of skin both visible and not shredded, sliced, or over obviously broken bones. "Y-you... Can you talk? Your name? What's your name?"

His eyes, both of which were almost hidden in bruises but might have been brown or black, darted around for a few seconds before they locked on hers. "Nathan," he said in a raw, rough whisper. The headlights kept his ruined face mostly shadowed, but she smiled, hoping to encourage him.

"Nathan. Okay. Don't move any more. You had a pretty bad spill, but help's coming. Um. Eventually."

Nathan winced and his eyes shut. "Might ... be faster ... to go to them..." He sounded like he thought this idea did not belong to the same order of likelihood as Mr. Tumnus running out of the nearest oil well.

"Right. Yeah. First, um..." *What do they do in TV shows? Shit, come on, what would* Grey's Anatomy *say?* "Tell me if you can wiggle your toes. Um. Your right ones. The left leg's ... kind of broken. Let's not move it." She figured that would take him a minute or two. He had long legs and probably a concussion, so it seemed like a big job.

Thunder rumbled again, and Ashlyn cringed, looking at her tiny, two-seater convertible. She focused on his legs. Big, much longer than hers, plus all the blood and swelling. *Crap. Should I take his boots off, or does that make it worse? Oh God, I should probably tourniquet something... But what if I tie the wrong bit?*

Didn't someone say those were bad now?

"Moving." He didn't sound convincing, but if he thought his toes were moving, why argue?

"Okay." She relayed the information into the phone. More syllables cut up into unintelligible nonsense answered. She took a deep breath, tried not to look completely terrified, and got off her knees to settle down onto the road beside him, ignoring the gravel biting into her hip and the unpleasant chill of wet dirt on her bare, shorts-clad leg. *Do I keep him talking? If he has a head injury, he'll die if he passes out. But he was already passed out once... Why the fuck didn't I get a nursing degree? Where is Google when I need it?*

Nathan's head tilted back in the helmet, or maybe it settled into the mud. "Th-think ... they're gonna make it?"

She glanced at him but a second later, her gaze rolled to the sky as fat raindrops landed on her arms and then the top of her head. *Of course.*

"They'll be here, Nathan. Hold on." She ran to her car, frantically tossing through the stuff piled in the passenger seat and floorboard. Her fingers closed around the Hello Kitty umbrella just as the sky opened up. She raced back and dropped next to him with a muffled shriek at the cold water rolling down her spine. *Cold-as-hell rain would be Mother Nature's choice today. Why not?*

"I ... I can't believe ... I'm gonna die here..." His mirthless laugh turned into a moan.

"Shut up. You're not dying." The words came out harsh to forestall any further argument. After two fumbled attempts, the umbrella blossomed above them, shielding Nathan from another mouthful of rain.

"Well..." His gaze swept over her as he exhaled. "There ... there are worse ways to go..." She glanced down to find her light pink shirt clinging to her bra and managed not to roll her eyes. Barely.

"At least your vision's survived." She switched the flashlight app off—the headlights were bright enough. Better not to see Nathan's injuries while she attempted to keep him conscious. The bone in his arm (or out of it, more importantly) was making her queasy. Eternities dragged by. At the end of the universe, sirens wailed like a blessed choir of distant angels. Ashlyn sagged in relief until she realized they were still alone.

"Hey, they're here!" She squeezed Nathan's right wrist and touched his neck again to find his pulse. Weaker, but still there. He didn't answer. She dropped the phone and tapped his cheek. When that didn't work, she pulled the umbrella up and over so the rain hit his face. He twitched. "Hey, eyes open, Mister! Wake up! You are not dying on me. I don't have those paddle-thingies. Come on!"

"'M... here..." He slurred.

Shit, does he have a brain whatever? Nononono...

"Wake up. Wake. Up. Eyes up here. Hey! Eyes on my boobs? Go ahead. No, seriously. Please, come on..." The next few minutes passed with her tapping his cheek and forcing responses until the ambulance's wail drowned out both their voices.

The two paramedics hauled ass from their vehicle, and Ash found herself politely (and thankfully) pushed out of the way. She watched them from a safe distance until a guy in a Pharaoh County sheriff's car helped her into his back seat to get warmed up. He and an officer from the State Police filled out forms and took down her information. She stuttered out a few numbers and hoped they were the right ones.

PhaCo Deputy Zack Gebbert had blue eyes and

an easy manner, even lending her his cell phone so she could call her grandparents, who'd waited up and were about to call the sheriff themselves. He continued quietly putting down information until she hung up, probably making sure she was who she claimed. Ash didn't blame him. She doubted her grandfather mentioned her at Council meetings. Or ever. *No one brags about family disappointments, Deputy.*

She handed the phone back with a shaking hand. Zack must have noticed because he turned on the heater. She wiped a water droplet from her forehead. It took more effort than she anticipated. Her eyes drifted from Zack to the patrol car's windshield. Before, the scent of blood and rain had kept her focused. Now, the fog settled in. Running on two hours sleep and already exhausted emotions, her thoughts scattered. A corner of her head wondered if she could even touch the deputy sitting across the console. *Is he real? Nothing feels real... We've already done this, and it's a long time ago...*

"Are you sure you can drive, Miss Davis?"

"I ... I'm just tired."

"We can pull your car off the road, and I'll take you into town if you want. There's no sense risking another accident tonight." Deputy Gebbert's earnest gaze held hers. She wrapped her arms around herself under the blanket. Someone had put it on her shoulders. When? Was there a blanket last time a cop sat with her? She thought there had been, but maybe that was a paramedic and not a cop at all...

"Yeah. Yeah, okay. Can you? I'm kinda woozy." She held out her keys. Zack took them and got out into the rain.

Soon enough, her Miata was backed off the roadway at the entrance to somebody's pasture, and they were on the way to Oak Grove, where her grandmother waited with a hug and fresh cookies. Her grandfather discussed the evening's events with Deputy Zack in the front room, and their voices faded to a dull buzz behind a haze of cookie scents. Grandma Bonnie fussed around the kitchen until she pressed two pills into Ash's hand and ushered her to bed. None of it felt solid until her cheek hit the pillow.

I hope Nathan lives... But she couldn't get the words out before the sleeping pills caught up to her.

Chapter Two: May 10

Ashlyn
Oak Grove

Stranded in Oak Grove, Ash found herself tiring of its chief occupations: eating pie, and gossip. First, it wasn't pumpkin season. Second, she didn't know enough people to care about the gossip that Grandma Bonnie's friends so generously shared. In ten days, Ash had attended three brunches, two church lady socials, and one Rebekahs meeting—spending all of them with eyes smiling and soul cringing while Grandma expounded her selling points like a new car someone's grandson ought to have the good sense to win (or possibly buy). Still, there were worse places to live. And then her phone pinged.

Megan: **Nate's home!!! Party tonight! Storm Crow. You're coming. You can't plead fear of hospitals now.**

Ash stared at the message. Wrecked-Nate had ended up being identified as her cousin Megan's best friend/almost-foster-brother—and that meant Megan had been at the hospital every night. Now there was a party. But she'd never been allowed to meet most of her cousin's friends when she was younger, and then with college—and everything else—she'd mostly communicated by phone and text. *I won't know anyone.*

Ashlyn: **It's Tuesday?**
Megan: **... And?**
Megan: **U got something better to do?**

Then again, it isn't another church social. And the drinks will probably be cheap.

Ashlyn: **Is anything even open on Tuesday nights??**
Megan: **SC Clubhouse is. U in?**
Ashlyn: **... What are you wearing?**

Megan took too long to answer, so Ash dropped her pink-encased Galaxy onto the white chiffon bedspread and studied her closet. *At least I left Mom's with all my clothes still packed.* She eyed a black satin bustier top with attached choker. *On the other hand, this ain't Oz anymore, Toto. Some substitution required.* She took the miniskirt hanging with the bustier and held it up to an orange tank, grimaced and replaced it. Time became a haze of clothing combinations.

The door creaked open. Even muffled by the thick carpet, she recognized Grandma's slow tread. In the middle of a choice between a green peasant blouse or a blue cold-shoulder tunic, Ash didn't have the energy to do much more than smile over her shoulder.

"Ashlyn Marie, what on Earth? You fixin' to bury those clothes or wear them?" Bonnie Tilden stopped at the foot of the four-poster bed, her green eyes flaring at the size of the clothing pile and Ashlyn's thunderous expression. "My, that's a frown. You'll give yourself wrinkles."

"Megan wanted me to go out with her tonight." Ash sagged onto the bed by the mountain of discarded apparel, twisting a lock of blonde hair around her finger.

"Honey-child, if the choice is goin' to a party or not goin' to a party... What are you going to do otherwise? Stare at the TV all night? Or worse. Let your grandpa and me drag you off to the club for a rousing hand of bridge?" Bonnie's smile warmed, and she sat next to her granddaughter. Her soft, manicured hand covered Ashlyn's.

"The TV isn't so bad, you know." Ashlyn gripped her grandmother's fingers, hesitating before she added the actual explanation. "It's a Storm Crow party." Bonnie's smile creased into a tired sort of worry.

"They're different over there in Ravenwood. If

you go, you stick close to Megan, hear me?" Her lips thinned. "It's a rough crowd."

Ashlyn's eyes rolled, and she stood up to get to the closet, where a pink sundress waited. She considered her grandmother's caution, though not as intently as the dress. "I've been weirder places." She wondered what her grandmother would do if she ever listed them. *Maybe they think it was all a bad dream, too. They never ask, do they?*

Bonnie's left brow rose, but she didn't speak. Ashlyn waited in obedient silence for whatever lecture would start. It didn't take long. "Ashlyn, honey, I know you're a grown woman now, but we still worry. You know you can always call us, don't you? If you have any troubles." Ashlyn's shoulders stiffened. An unspoken "again" hung the end of her grandmother's sentence.

"If I need it, I promise." She examined her mismatched blue-and-coral painted nails, still gleaming under the top coat she'd put on that morning. *Should I match my outfit to them?*

"It's no trouble, honey. Keepin' you … safe."

Ash pulled a purple floral print dress off the pile of clothing. *Matching colors are for wimps.* Better to think about fashion than her grandmother's meaning. "I've survived frat boys and St. Louis parties. It's not a problem. I just wanted to let you know where I'd be." She held the dress up and examined herself in the antique silver mirror over the mahogany vanity. *Too prim.* She put it back and tried a striped tunic, but her grandmother's fingers caught her arm. Bonnie watched her with bright eyes.

"Well, get yourself all dolled up. You can't let those local girls go outshining you tonight. Not that any of 'em have half a chance." She stood up and wrapped her fragile arms around Ash before leaving a light-as-air kiss on her cheek. Ashlyn didn't exactly relax in her grandmother's grip, but she stayed still and accepted. Acknowledging the sullen response, Bonnie laughed. "You do look so much like your mama sometimes." Her spider-silk hand cupped Ashlyn's cheek. "I happen to think underneath you got a bit more a' me an' my side of the family."

That made Ashlyn laugh. *Thank the universe for small favors. And yet...* "I wish I was more like her. At least I might know what the heck I want to do."

"I bet you've got a better idea than you think you do."

"Would you be disappointed in me, Grandma?" Ashlyn couldn't quite hold her voice steady. "If I said I wanted to paint pictures or sew or something? Or if I didn't know?"

Bonnie kissed Ash's forehead. "This world needs all kinds of people, baby. Just 'cause your mama knew where she was aiming from her first steps on don't mean it's the only way to do things. You keep walkin' 'til you sort it out." Bonnie grinned. "And if you want to start sewin', your grandpa's got a mess of gardening pants could use some help."

Ashlyn's nose wrinkled. "Are you suggesting that to punish him or me?"

"Two birds, one stone," Bonnie laughed. "You can do it tomorrow when you're pleading out of goin' wherever he's intended to drag you off to on account of the hangover I predict in your future."

"I'm a little freaked out by the fact you know about hangovers."

"Honey-child, your grandpa and I threw a party every weekend for thirty years or close enough. Where do you think your mama always got her booze? Raidin' Grandpa's liquor cabinet downstairs." The dry tone drew

Ash's side-eyed gaze.

"There are moments when I think I'm a horrible child. Then you mention Mom, and I realize the spawn of Satan is always a disappointment."

"Pish. Your mama wasn't that bad. A girl's gotta have her fun while she's young enough to survive it. You should know that." Bonnie selected one of Ashlyn's lace miniskirts and a draped top. She held them out. Ashlyn's eyes narrowed, but she took the offered outfit.

"And what do you know about fun, young lady? You stayed home reading."

Bonnie sniffed. "Oh, yes. That's exactly how I got your grandpa's attention."

"Fine. How *did* you get Grandpa's attention?"

"Batted my eyelashes real pretty until he asked if he could take me for a ride in his convertible. And ignored him for a month just to annoy the piss out of him."

"Grandma, are you telling me you turned Grandpa down?"

"Lands sakes, girl, of course I did. Don't let nobody tell you any different: men think they want simple, but they die young of boredom iffen they get it." Bonnie spoke while sorting through Ashlyn's jewelry box.

"Mom's boyfriends must all be immortal by now."

"And yours?" Bonnie's brow rose again. "You haven't heard from Dr. Matt lately, have you?"

"I think he's in Borneo or something, so no." Also, she hadn't checked her messages. Just in case.

"You really ought to give the boy another chance, Ash. He was so nice." Even Bonnie sounded wistful when it came to him, but Matt's perfect smile and flawless manners floated through Ash's mind and out again with all the substance of dandelion fluff.

"He's going to be just fine. Some Pinterest blogger will patch up his bruised ego with kale chips." Ashlyn scrunched her nose at the mirror and pulled off her top to try the one her grandmother suggested. If she couldn't take Bonnie's boyfriend advice, at least she could accept fashion choices.

"One of these days you'll find one you can't walk away from so easy."

"Or maybe I take after Mom after all. I'll just continue her massive database of exes." The bitterness hung so heavy in her voice that Ashlyn shut her mouth. She stepped out of her pajama pants before wiggling into the white lace miniskirt and turning her attention to the jewelry. Bonnie watched her from the bed.

"Well, your mama always wanted her husband to match her purse."

Those simple, laconic words knocked the air from Ash's lungs. An earring dangled forgotten from her right hand as she turned on her grandmother. *"Husband" is a long-ass leap from "boyfriend".*

"You know."

"Now, Ashlyn…" Bonnie didn't pretend to be confused. Not one, tiny bit. A single option remained. Ash almost gagged on the realization.

"You *all* knew."

"Honey, it's not—" Bonnie rose, but Ashlyn lifted her hand like the earring was a talisman to ward off evil family members.

"And you—all of you—couldn't even bother to tell me? Didn't want to set off another one of 'Ash's little episodes'? Jett's been my every-day dad since I was nine! He *is* my dad. More than Dad is. And once some stupid paperwork has their signatures, he's nothing anymore!" *Just one more thing that isn't real after all…*

"You've had enough pressure with school finishin', and we didn't think…"

Ash wiped at her cheek but the emotions closed her throat. *Oh, you thought. All of you thought! And you talked, and you schemed. Even Jett…* She shut her eyes, willing herself to wake up and turned away.

"He ain't gonna disappear on you, honey." The plea in Bonnie's voice only solidified Ash's resolve, and she cleared her throat to cut her grandmother's speech short, squaring her shoulders with the mirror. Her reflection wavered as she blinked back tears. *I won't cry in front of them again. I won't.*

"I need to get ready." She put the earring in and pulled her hair to the side. *Calm thoughts, self.* "I'll probably stay at Megan's tonight."

Bonnie watched her for a few moments before she walked out. The soft click of the latch cut the imaginary strings holding Ashlyn upright. She melted into a lace-clad lump on the floor and thumped her head against the bedpost. *Stupid. So, so stupid.*

****

Barely four miles separated tiny Ravenwood from less-tiny Oak Grove, but the smaller village occupied a world of its own. *Like going from Rockwell's Saturday evening dreams to David Lynch's,* Ashlyn thought with a sigh. Gravel streets and ancient cobblestones ringed Ravenwood's collection of sagging, bulging houses and two rotting storefronts out of an Old West movie. The anachronistic carcass of a Pepsi machine—its '80s-era logo all but vanished into the fading plastic— had beached on the stores' rickety porch eons ago, and served as Ash's cue to turn onto her cousin's street. She drove past meticulously mown—if patchy and browning— lawns and clean-swept doorsteps until she reached Megan's place. Like the rest of Ravenwood, it had seen many better, brighter days, but its white paint was spotless, if peeling here and there. Even the lawn looked healthy. Ash pulled her Miata in behind Megan's ancient blue Honda, breathing deep before she got out. She grabbed the brown paper bag out of her passenger seat and walked up to the front steps just as the warped door swung inward.

A curvy young woman, several inches taller than Ashlyn, stood on the other side, a smile on her pouty lips. As cousins only by incomprehensible degrees, their family ties didn't extend beyond a similarly ivory complexion: Megan McClay's elbow-length hair grew darker and straighter, her lips were fuller, and her face bore a much more classic look beneath the thick eyeliner and contoured makeup. Even her green eyes were a darker emerald, inherited from her long-departed father.

"You're early." Megan's familiar, husky voice was as much a relief as seeing her. Ash grinned in answer to her cousin's greeting and held up the paper bag, unveiling an unopened bottle of Jack Daniels with a theatrical flourish. Not at all a bribe.

"Can I stay with you tonight?"

Megan's brows rose but she took the bottle. She eyed it, then stepped back to let Ashlyn in. "Sure." Her head canted to the side as her eyes swept over Ashlyn's gladiator sandals up to the lace skirt and draped blue top. "Did you bring jeans?"

"I think so. Maybe." She'd stuffed a bag of things before rushing out of her grandparents' house. Ashlyn crossed her arms instead of sitting down on the well-beaten sofa. The scent of Febreze didn't quite mask the whiff of mildew in the air, and she cast a suspicious look at the unfamiliar, almost-neon green chair sitting near the kitchen door. *Megan and her dumpster rescues.* "Why?"

Fortunately, Megan didn't notice Ash's skeptical

eyes on her new prize. "Go get them while I make the drinks," she said as she broke the seal on the whiskey. "I'm not taking you in a skirt."

"That's what he said." The joke only earned a snort. Ashlyn followed Megan into the kitchen—an immense distance of ten steps across threadbare olive carpet, past the dark wall paneling and into the brown and orange kitchen area, which still had mottled tan carpeting. *Because the '70s didn't care about hygiene*, Ash thought with a dubious glance toward the stove and sink.

"Just promise me you're not wearing a thong under there." Megan took down two cups from the cabinet and poured generous shots in each before she pulled a bottle of Coke from the fridge. "We might end up on somebody's bike. That don't mix with miniskirts, kiddo." She shoved one of the cups toward Ashlyn.

"I didn't think about that." *I should have. I'm an idiot.* She gulped down some of the mostly-Jack-Daniels elixir while Megan took a drink and set her cup aside. She leaned in closer to study Ashlyn's face.

"You've been crying. Did your ex call or something?" Another oversize gulp let the Jack burn her throat.

"No. It's … it's nothing." Megan only blinked and crossed her arms. Waiting. After a moment Ash relented. "My family decided not to tell me Mom's divorcing Jett. I guess they intended to say he went to a big farm to live with nice people. Like Rover the Goldfish."

"So how did you—"

"The movers were there when I got home from school. Mom must've forgot what day I moved out of the apartment." She managed a defeated shrug and one more drink to banish the knot in her stomach. "All his clothes were already gone, and the papers were on her desk. Maybe if I'd gotten through college faster, he could've gotten out sooner. Who knew I fucked up everybody else's lives again?"

"Did he say that?"

"No. But he bails right when I'm graduating instead of three years ago, when he could have … I don't know. Not paid for stuff?" She cringed and drank. The whole county didn't contain enough Jack Daniels to face that timeframe. *They were splitting up back then, and I screwed it up. That's what I do.*

Megan nodded with regrets in her eyes. "I get it, babe. I liked some of mine, too. I even miss a few of them." Ash raised her cup in a salute—she'd long since lost the ability to keep Megan's stepfathers straight. "You can stay here a few days."

After celebratory hugs, Ash retrieved her bag along with her laptop, tablet, and purse—all of which got dumped on the dubious couch so she could dig through the bag for jeans. She discovered one pair at the very bottom and carried them to the bedroom for Megan's approval.

"Is the big thing tonight just Nate—er, Joker getting out of the hospital?" she asked once Megan's head emerged from a black tank top.

"Just." Megan rolled her eyes. She took her drink from the chipped nightstand and carried it into the bathroom while the nightstand wobbled on its magazine-pile stilts. "He's the VP, sweetie. They take it kinda hard when a founder's grandson gets hurt. And he's hot, single, and a whore. Expect the entire female population of Pharaoh County to be in attendance."

"You make them sound like vultures," Ash muttered. The bruised, bloodied face under the helmet still didn't connect to the handsome, grinning tough-guy in any of Megan's pictures. She finished pulling up her jeans and adjusting her top before she followed Megan. "So what about you and him? Is that secretly why we're going? Childhood sweethearts, near-death moments?" Ashlyn asked from the bathroom doorway.

Her cousin shot her a look capable of felling a tree.

"Ew. That's like dating my brother..." Megan hesitated and added a swipe of mascara to her eyes. "Look, Joker's pretty, but he's kind of a dick, too. I like guys who show signs of actually possessing a heart."

"Mmhm. So explain how you married Asswipe again?" They'd long since agreed not to utter the names of their worst exes. Megan only had one He-Who-Must-Not-Be-Named: her dearly despised ex-husband.

"Asswipe has a heart. It's brain capacity he lacks. And self-control. And maybe a soul." Megan tossed her dark brown hair over her shoulder before fixing her eyeliner. "Anyway, I don't even want to hear your sass, Miss Never-Dates-Same-Man-Twice."

"I date lots of them twice! Hi, just got dis-engaged over here. Remember?"

"Did your mom like that one?"

"She loved him. So did I. So did the whole world." *That's what creeped me out.* Ashlyn busied herself by going through Megan's make-up bag instead of looking at her cousin. Megan spun around with a superior smirk on her glossy lips.

"And why do I not know this paragon?" Megan's brows wiggled. She leaned in to whisper, "Is he why you're here? Did you bury him in your basement?"

Ashlyn fidgeted with her turquoise bracelet and slid it off her wrist to grab another one from the small collection in her make-up bag. "I sort of, um, broke up with him after he left the country. You know, so he couldn't come back and be satanically charming at me. It's—"

"You did what?!" Megan put her hand over the bag so Ash had to look at her. "But he's a doctor, Ash! A *doctor*. What is wrong with a medical degree and actual income?"

"I wanted to marry a Russian oligarch." Megan's eyes bugged, but Ashlyn continued. "Have you ever met someone so perfect at everything that standing next to them turns you into a disgusting slob? He's probably better in *bed* than me. On top of his general sainthood, I couldn't deal."

"Poor you. A man too good in bed? The horror!" Megan lifted a hand on her forehead. "What's his number? I want to be his rebound. And his soulmate. Or his mistress."

"He'll be back to the States in a few months; I'll hook you up. I want him to be happy. Just … with someone else. Far away where I don't have to be nauseated by their combined divinity. South Africa, maybe. Or Mars."

"Uh huh." Megan's hips swayed as she sauntered out of the bathroom. "Get your warpaint on, brat. We'll find you a rebound yet. He'll be awful in bed and have the brains of a water buffalo, just the way you like 'em."

Glancing after Megan's busty silhouette and painted-on tank top, Ash felt the cold certainty of invisibility but drew a deep breath and focused on her own eyes in the mirror. *You can do this.* "And you've got a full bottle of Xanax if you can't," she added under her breath.

****

Joker
Ravenwood

The fact he couldn't fully participate in the fun

stung almost as much as the raw stripes of flesh along his sides, but for the first time since the wreck, Joker could breathe easy. His brothers surrounded him, their friends and women close at hand. Life was good—long as he didn't count the pins and plates holding his bones together.

He closed his eyes and focused on the moment, trying to ignore the aches and irritation. Hickory logs burned in the firepit, filling the cool night air with warmth and wood smoke. All around him, people laughed and shouted. Joker stayed quiet, appreciating the familiar, echoing voices and the hum of noise coming from the clubhouse, where a rowdy celebration rolled on, despite its guest of honor's (his) absence.

I'm in a cast, not fucking maimed. This is temporary. If he kept repeating those words, eventually he'd believe them. It didn't help that his favorite fuck-buddy had chosen his hospital stay as the opportune moment to discover her maternal instincts—so much that he'd told Dragon to stick Ari behind the bar for a while. He needed a break from people volunteering to fetch and carry things he didn't want anyway.

Joker brought a cigarette to his lips but didn't retrieve the lighter from his pocket. Wood and canvas creaked as Grim dropped into the chair beside him and leaned in until their arms touched. The sharp scent of Jack Daniels hit Joker's nose and brought a familiar pang to his bloodstream. *Why can't some damn oxy-dosed doctor come up with a way to be high and drunk without the risk of dying?*

"Any reason you're glaring at everybody?" Grim asked, his speech slow. Joker raised his brow without answering. Grim snorted. "Oh, right. Resting bitch face. Too bad they didn't fix that with your nose. Look, man, I got you this." Grim handed him a cup full of Crown on ice. "Don't tell the prez."

"If he finds out…" Joker let the words hang as he stared into the whiskey's golden depths.

"Hey, I said not to tell. If I knew you were gonna be such a bitch about it—Fuck it. Changed my mind. Give it back." He made a grab for the cup, but Joker pulled it out of reach and took a grateful sip. A sweet, beautiful burn hit the back of his throat. He smiled.

"Thanks. Any idea where my dad is?" Grim shrugged and leaned back, putting one foot up on the chair next to Joker's cast. "Oh, by all means, make yourself at home."

"Shit, look at you gettin' all territorial. My bad, man. Next time, I'll bring you some Tampax."

"Be less of a pain in the ass for once. Try that." Anybody else would shrink under Joker's glare. Grim laughed without even pretending to give a shit until his eyes darted toward the clubhouse and stayed. The smile vanished.

"Aw, shit. Ariel's slithering back." Joker's answering groan set off more laughter. "I'll head her off. You sit here and nurse that drink, princess." Grim hauled himself upright and knocked into the side of Joker's chair as he sprinted away.

God damn drunk elephant…

Joker and his cracked ribs hissed at the abuse, so he took a much-needed sip of the Crown. Then another. The whiskey seared some of the edges off his perceptions. Tommy, the club secretary, emerged from the clubhouse with a woman on both arms, each dressed in just as little as the other—and neither one of them was his Old Lady. Envy pinched Joker's gut. *Too many painkillers and too much road rash for that game right now.* He'd be suffering a couple more weeks without pussy. Ice called it penance. Joker considered it hell. At least there was no sign of his father yet. *Probably fucked off with one of the "dancers" he hired. Gotta keep the Viagra-peddlers rich.*

Like he'd been summoned, Tree emerged from the clubhouse door. His eyes fixed on Joker and on the cup in his hand. Joker took a couple more sips before setting it aside. *Thirty-three years, two tours: still cowed by a look from Dad. Jesus, Grim's right. I should get some fucking Tampax.* He lifted his arm higher in his sling to pull his new leather cut over his shoulder.

"Prez," he said with a slight nod of his head. His eyes drifted toward Dragon, their sergeant-at-arms, trailing just behind Tree, then swept over the girl on his dad's arm. Most people looked small next to his 6'7" father, but she came up well over a foot short, and with Dragon's bulk right behind them she might as well have been a kid. Which she kind of was. Way under the age his dad went for while sober, at least. *And that face… Did I take her home one night? Must've been drunk as shit. Think I'd remember fucking a piece who looks like the angel on a Christmas tree.*

"See, what did I say? Surly asshole. Mixing narcotics and alcohol like a professional fucking idiot." Tree didn't miss a beat, and his deep voice held an alien note of warmth. *So, he's on the charm offensive for this one. He's gonna be real happy if he finds out I've already been there.* Joker picked up his drink. Maybe he could piss his old man off enough to abandon the attempt on the girl.

"Bad form to waste whiskey. Think you taught me that."

Tree shook his head without taking the cup away. "Crack a smile, Joker. You should remember this young lady."

"Oh?" *Fuck me, when did I nail her?* He checked

the girl out again, even eyeing the jeans and drapey, uneven top for familiar cues. Mid-size breasts, nice hips, probably a sweet little ass. All appealing, none of it ringing any bells above his waist.

"I'd think so." His dad's knowing smirk didn't relieve Joker's concern. At all. "Son, meet Ashlyn Davis. She scraped you up off the pavement the other night." Tree patted the girl's shoulder. She winced a little at the touch and tucked a piece of hair back. Her silver earrings glinted in the firelight. A memory stirred. Fleeting, gentle fingers on his throat, his hand, and a worried presence at his side... He raked a hand through his sandy hair; his fingers served as the only comb he'd used in a couple of days.

"I just called 911," the girl said. "You did the hard stuff by not bleeding too much." Her voice was the soft, velvety kind that could talk an Eskimo into buying ice. *No wonder I didn't die, with that next to me.*

"There's no telling when the next person would've come by. Thank you."

"Then, um, you're welcome." Her eyes lowered.

He forgot he should say something until his dad made a quick hand gesture: talk. The blonde—Ashlyn—must've seen, too, because her head twisted Tree's way. Dad let his hand fall to his side and gave her a grin just as Joker cleared his throat to reclaim her attention. "It's good to meet you, hon."

She laughed, startled into meeting his eyes. Her slow smile belonged on the girl next door in an after-school movie. *How old is she? Shit, I should've asked for ID too...* "It's nice to meet you too. Uh, again."

"She's Amos's granddaughter," Tree put in quickly, like he could hear Joker's thoughts. Joker blinked at that news: last he knew, the club's old lawyer had a son who had one kid—a boy. Definitely not the kind with long, bet-she-likes-it-pulled blonde hair and tits made for wet dreams. *Maybe this one was adopted?* Not that it mattered, considering Amos had personally pulled Joker's ass out of the fire more than once. Even if it landed him in the army. *Don't fuck with her. Got it, Dad.*

"Please, have a seat," Joker told Ashlyn while his dad and Dragon had a quick, whispered exchange. "I at least owe you a drink."

"Sounds great—"

A furious, pained bellow echoed from the clubhouse door.

"I'll let you two get settled," Tree announced while Dragon took off ahead of him. "You need another drink, send a Prospect in for it." He directed the words to Ashlyn, but he shot a heavy look at his son with a quick dart of his eyes. Joker nodded to show he caught the message: *don't put a Tilden in the middle of a brawl.*

Ashlyn's brows gathered. Her gaze followed Tree's departure before swinging toward Joker. Her shy smile returned, and she took a sip from her cup before she folded her denim-clad legs into the chair beside him. "Um. What am I supposed to call you? Sorry, I know there's, like … biker code? But I wasn't sure when the names get used?"

"No need to be sorry, sweetie. Call me whatever you want." *A face like that, you can call me a lot of shit.* He could see her better once she sat next to him, but the shifting firelight disguised the color of her eyes. Not that it mattered, but he wondered all the same. "Officially, we use the names for club stuff. Off duty, it's usually Nate."

"So … Joker? Is that a comic book reference, or were you super funny?" The girl blinked. "Wait. Am I supposed to ask? Sorry. I, uh, haven't done this scene before." She looked like she was having trouble switching gears. He felt his lips turn upward. His Prospect days felt dusty, the memories dim and dull behind walls he didn't want to touch. He drew a breath, considering how to explain, and caught a whiff of something floral and sweet beneath the bonfire's smoke. *Sugar all the way through. Bet she even melts on the tongue.*

"Don't know what it was for anymore. Never thought of myself as all that funny. You smoke?" He tilted the pack toward her. Ash waved it off with a grin.

"Plain cigarettes? I expected all joints all the time in a bar like this. I am disappointed, Joker."

"If you like weed, there's plenty around."

"Nah, I don't smoke it either. I prefer mine in brownies." Ashlyn shrugged, but her gaze lingered on the cigarette he held. He considered rolling it between his fingers to give her ideas, but held it still instead. "Your, um, your lungs are ok?" He raised a brow at that, and she grimaced. "It's just that night you were... I thought you might've punctured one or something. But you heal fast, right? Super villains do, from what the movies tell me."

"All super villains need a vice." He felt another smile tugging on his lips. "I cracked my ribs, but not that bad. My leg and arm got the worst."

"Seriously. That was pretty ugly. Way ugly." Ash drank from her cup, and her nose wrinkled. She set it on the seat between her legs, shaking her head like she could escape the flavor. His smile widened.

"You want another?" He looked around as he asked. They weren't exactly in the center of the action out here, but a couple of the Prospects lurked off toward the far side of the yard. Nominally it was sentry duty, but they'd fetch and carry for members, and show they could stay out of the bar.

"Yeah, I should go get a new one." She rose to

her feet. He found himself looking at her tight, worn jeans—specifically the hole in the knee and the sliver of porcelain skin showing through it—before catching up to what she was saying. "I don't hear any more breaking glass, so it should be good, right? Sure you don't want pop or something? I—"

He caught her wrist in his good hand, cutting off the question.

"You don't need to go yourself." He could hold both her wrists in one hand and still have room for a beer. No way could she handle herself near the former commandos mixing it up in the clubhouse. His brothers might not aim for her, but accidents happened.

"Well, there's no remote ordering services out here, so unless you've got the tablet hidden in your pants." Ashlyn's eyes turned from the leg cast up to his face, but for once he didn't rise to innuendo. Cursing the sling, he let go of her to raise his hand, motioning to nobody in particular. The hovering Prospects started toward them just as Grim meandered up from the far reaches of the yard, beer bottle in hand, waving off the Prospects.

"I'll just..." She trailed off. Joker glanced sidelong at her blank-eyed gaze. Grim seldom had to do much more than wink at most chicks, but the effect wasn't usually this immediate.

"What's up?" Grim asked, smiling at Ashlyn and giving Joker the kind of look that asked "Is this seat taken?" Joker gave the barest shake of his head.

Bad idea, brother. On way too many levels to count. Not that Grim ever listened.

"Um, I was going to go grab a drink?" Ashlyn looked to Joker, confusion showing more in her voice than her face, with a slight hesitation between her words. He clenched his hand to keep from reaching for her wrist again. "I didn't know if you wanted Dr Pepper or—"

Grim's dilated blue eyes caught with Joker's. "J-man here'd drink diesel before Dr. Pepper." His gaze ran over Ashlyn, slow and interested. Joker's jaw clenched. "So, a Coke for him … and for you, hon? What's your poison?"

"Same. But I got it. It's no problem. I'm not the one on crutches."

"No worries, girl. Be right back." He waved her back toward her chair and clapped Joker's bad shoulder. Joker grunted and kept a white-knuckled grip on his cup until the throbbing faded while his unconcerned best friend disappeared into the clubhouse. His scowl eased as he focused on the pretty blonde still hovering next to him. He leaned sideways in his seat and picked the cigarette up from the side table, rolling it between his fingers. She stared off after Grim.

"So where are you from, Ashlyn?"

"Hm?" She blinked before her eyes returned to him. "Oh, I live most of the time in Carlesby." His brows lifted at that revelation, but he kept quiet. She'd landed on the wrong side of the river as well as the tracks. "But that's Mom's place. Dad's in Nebraska, my stepdad winters in Miami, and then my grandparents are in Oak Grove, so, uh, I'll probably be moving around some now I'm graduated. What about you?"

He watched the bonfire, picking his words. *Graduated what? High school? Better give the PG version.* "Born and raised here," he said at last. "You're staying with your grandfather?"

Ashlyn's pert nose wrinkled. "It sounds so lame, 'staying with Grandpa'. Like I'm twelve… But I'm actually staying with Megan right now."

And how long ago was twelve? Five years? No, she has to be over twenty for Megan to bring her. Maybe.

Where the hell's Megan? Asking her would be a fuckload less awkward than carding Ashlyn, but the dark terrace proved better camouflage than he expected—he couldn't make out Megan's voice from the surrounding conversations, and couldn't see her in the shadows. He considered sending a Prospect to track her.

"How do you know Legs?" he asked, using Megan's nickname.

"Cousins. Somehow. I never can keep the tree straight." Another twist of hair around her finger, and she looked toward the clubhouse.

"Family gets complicated." *Some boyfriend coming to pick her up? Or is it Grim? That'll be one hell of a drama with Megan.*

"Blood and water and all that, right?" She sat back, biting her lower lip. "But some blood seems thicker than others. Ever notice that?"

He regarded her in silence as his thoughts slid back in time to when he'd counted his own family as a little larger. His jaw tightened. *Not the time to take a trip down that damned road.* "Sometimes."

Ashlyn's momentary seriousness ended in a laugh. "Sorry, I was just thinking vampires would fix blood problems. And they'd always be able to keep track of bloodlines."

"But they drain the life right out of you," he answered without missing a beat. Life with Grim and the club's wilder hangers-on had long since immunized him to left field conversations. "Kind of like life. Wake up one day and realize you got old." He made a face to get her to laugh. Obligingly, Ashlyn giggled and clapped her hand over her mouth; she looked like one of those animes Grim liked. *Damn, I need more whiskey.*

"Happens to the best of us according to Grandpa." Her delicate fingers fiddled with another lock of hair.

"But I hear motorcycles help you age better. Are you getting a new one?"

His amusement died. *My poor baby.* Luckily, Grim stumbled toward them, offering two cups of cola from hands glistening with spilled syrup.

"Crowded as hell in there." Grim gave Ashlyn the cup with less soda running down the side, which she took with a quiet word of thanks. Joker grabbed the other one. A gulp of the half-flat contents washed away the lump in his throat. Grim scratched his nose and straightened up, proud as a conquering general. He pulled a beer out of his back pocket and popped the top.

"So, you're Megan's friend?"

"Cousin," Joker corrected. Ash's smile returned, focused on him for the barest moment.

"She's the reason I stay sane whenever I visit my grandparents. You're … um, Grim, right? She's talked about all you guys before, but I've only ever seen some old pictures."

Funny, Legs never mentioned you to us. Joker kept his eyes on his cup, but Grim perked up with the expression of a puppy spotting a tennis ball.

"Escapades? She didn't tell you *all* of them, did she?" Grim's smile returned, full-on 1,000 megawatts meant to drop panties on sight. Ashlyn's brows arched.

"Something about girls in the clubhouse painting the walls with their boobs one time?" She trailed off with one of those porn star giggles. "And an attempt to go mudding with motorcycles? Or maybe stolen crotch rockets? Wait, maybe that's somebody else—"

"Nope, that was us," Joker said slowly, looking into his glass. Despite telling himself they wouldn't, the memories rose from the back of his mind, twisting something in his chest. Reagan clutching tight to his waist and laughing, hair slicked in black mud. He could see her tackling a younger Megan, the pair of them rolling in the field. They'd all been so young then—the war was someone else's problem, and the future held dreams he couldn't even remember. "A long goddamn time ago."

"A couple of years or so," Grim chuckled. "And they weren't stolen. We gave them back, so that's technically borrowing."

"Sure. I bet the cops saw it that way, too," Ashlyn said.

"They had a depressing lack of imagination." Joker forced the next smile. "But they couldn't run for shit. We got down in the creek and hid."

"Had to call Booboo to come get our sorry asses." Grim shook his head, no doubt remembering Booboo's heavy frame leaning out a dirty van window, cussing them all and threatening instant death if they hurt the upholstery.

"Hey, boys!" Ariel's honeyed call snatched Joker from his thoughts. He sat up as she sauntered over. Her coral lips turned in a too-wide smile when she reached them. "Your dad said to find you, Joker. He's got a call in the office."

"Damn it." Joker groaned. "Fine." Before he could try levering himself up, Grim came around and got hold of his good arm. Ari's attention had already drifted.

"You're Megan's little cousin, right? She always talks about you." She held out her hand to Ashlyn, their quiet greeting taking up the moments until Joker gained his feet. Ariel moved at once to his other side and slid her arm around his waist. Joker winced, sharply aware of her hip and the side of her breast against his body. Her floral body-spray combined with the smoke made his eyes water. He looked over her, but Ashlyn was typing on her phone.

"Is Megan inside?" she asked Ariel with barely a glance their way. "She's not answering my texts."

"Probably can't hear her phone, but she'll be right out. It's getting pretty hot in there."

Joker frowned. "Grim, you coming in?" He made a tiny motion sideways with his head, hoping Grim wasn't too drunk to notice.

"Nah, brother." Grim flopped into Joker's abandoned chair, propping both feet up and reclining as best he could without tilting backward. "I almost melted getting you those drinks." He fanned himself like an old maid in a corset.

"I'll help you in," Ariel said to Joker. "I gotta go back anyway. Break's almost up."

Joker nodded to Ashlyn as she glanced up from her screen. "Later," he informed her. She waved her hand before the phone reabsorbed her. He turned and Ariel came with him, her arm still around his waist and body tight to his.

He looked back from the door: Ashlyn and Grim sat where he'd left them, lost in some animated conversation. A twinge caught his chest. Grim had a way of getting along with anybody. *Even when you'd rather he didn't.*

"You sure you're okay?" Ariel whispered, her breath warm on his ear, her arm squeezing him. "We could go around the front if you want." Joker hated himself for considering her offer. But he hated a lot of things lately: the weakness that refused to leave him, the frayed nerves he got in crowds of people. *The list of shit wrong with me is getting too long.*

"No," he grunted, taking the crutch from her. As they stepped into the packed clubhouse, Ariel's warm hand settled at his back; an anchor to focus on if nothing else. She kept it in place until they made it through the gauntlet of drunk friends and visitors and stood at the entrance to the sanctum—the back room where the club's officers met. Storm Crow tradition held the Oak Grove sanctum as sacred space, where the founders drew up the original charter on its heavy wood table with his grandfather at the helm. The mantle passed to his war buddy, then to his son. Under Tree, the organization had branched out far beyond the Midwest and found contacts across the sea through a maze of private military organizations and underworld markets.

"I'll wait for you," she said with a soft smile. He took her lips for a lingering kiss—thanks for her help, and a way to get his head off an untouchable bit of fluff. A taste of tequila greeted him with her velvet tongue. He put his good hand on her silky hair, willing himself back to the present. Out of his own head. Ari was good for that.

"Don't," he whispered when the kiss ended. "I'll find you when I'm done." *Or not.* He crossed the threshold and closed the door on her before facing his father.

Tree sat at the head of the deserted table with a cellphone lying in front of him, his broad shoulders bowed, a hand over his face. "It's the cock-sucking Heathens."

Without Ariel's help, he had to rely on the crutch, and it took him too long to hobble across the bare room. He kept his face stony, his eyes cold, and didn't say a word until he was in the chair by Tree. The fingers on his right hand flexed into a fist, instincts calling for him to use it. "How do you know?"

"Bauman got hyped up with Scott Harding, started sniveling about it." Tree lowered his hand to the table. His eyes met Joker's. "Guess it's his way of proving himself to Brandt."

Landon "Scratch" Brandt led the Heathens chapter just north of Star Hollow—an upshot support group of an eastern club. Newer, smaller, and needing to make a name for themselves, they had alliances with some other regional players wanting the chunk of river and I-67 corridor the Storm Crows held. Crows had rules about things passing through their territory: no one dealt meth or human flesh through southern Pharaoh county in particular unless they wanted to lose their teeth and fingernails. Every other illegal shipment paid its passage, or ended up in Storm Crow hands.

"On Brandt's orders or because he's a gutless dipshit?"

"I'm assuming both. Brandt's only entertaining his dickless, two-faced ass to piss us off. Figures he'd push Bauman into making a gesture."

"We should've killed that bitch when we had the chance." Throwing Megan's ex-husband out of the club remained one of the easiest votes of Joker's life. The crutch slid from the arm of the chair and clattered on the hard wood floor. He stared at it without reaching down.

"We can always make another chance. But we'd still have Brandt." Tree tapped on the solid oak table, forcibly drawing Joker's attention back.

"Brandt can be isolated. Just a matter of time 'til he shows his colors to the Italians or whoever he's in bed with. We get rid of him, Bauman will be easy to sniff out. Hell, the others'll hand his ass to us on a platter to keep their heads." Joker watched his father. "But you know all that, so what's the play?" *You ever going to stop testing me, old man?*

"Just letting them know we got their message." Tree's lips curved in a strange, placid smile. "You got enough hands left to make a few toys?"

"I can manage." He'd walked Grim through det

cord knots and assembly before. Exercising his own demolitions training might even brighten this shitshow of a week.

"Good." Tree's eyes lit with a fierce joy—the way his dad always looked when a fight started. "How do you feel about some old-fashioned justice? A few bikes for a bike."

"Sounds like a good deal."

"Rig some small charges. Something we can get to the Heathens' clubhouse. We go early, hit the bikes outside. Maybe light up the clubhouse a bit."

"I'll have them done by tomorrow afternoon." He knew his expression matched his dad's, but for once he didn't care.

Chapter Three: May 12

Joker
Ravenwood

He ignored the first knock at his office door. And the next five minutes of knocking. Grim called through the door, so Joker turned up the volume and adjusted his headphones. No point in talking. His brothers were going, and he had to sit out the game. That they carried charges he'd put together didn't help—even that required Grim's assistance. *If I ever feel like more of a pussy than right now, I'm shooting myself in the head...*

Joker stared at the monitor in front of him and counted under his breath until the sound of motors faded. Once the noise died out, he pushed back from his desk and yelled for Frog.

"Hey!" He poked his head out into the shop, ignoring the milling Prospects and mechanics until he caught sight of his designated driver. "Need a ride."

Frog nodded and ran for the keys.

"What d'you want us to do about the Johnsons' car?" Case called as Joker limped out of the office and across the sun-warmed concrete lot.

"Whatever Dragon told you to." He glared at the Prospect. Case stood close to Joker's 6'4" height, was built like a brick shithouse, and damn good in a fight. He'd get his patch soon, but he didn't have it yet, so Joker left him to figure his shit out and limped on toward the van Frog pulled around. They spent the cage ride to the house in silence, broken only by the local radio station.

Back in his own house, he kicked Frog out rather than endure more help. A shower might have helped, but he made do with shedding his shirt and using a pile of baby wipes. *Just like good ol' Iraq.* Afterward, he sat in his oversized easy chair and flipped on the TV. There wasn't shit on, but he didn't need it—he had his own entertainment.

He got the recliner leaned back and his leg elevated, then popped the top off a pill bottle and dry-swallowed his next dose of painkillers. Instead of putting it down, he turned the bottle in his hand. Three pills rolled out onto the side table.

What else is a slug going to do? Laid up when your brothers face a battle because you were too much of a bitch to go straight to the meeting. Even the voice in the back of his head sounded like his damned dad.

The house's silence loomed over him so he cranked the TV volume. That only made it worse. With the extra pills, he'd have a stretch of absolute oblivion until Grim got home...

Fuck it.

The doorbell shocked him back to the present with the narcotic halfway to his mouth. *Grim and his damned Amazon habit.* He abandoned the pills on the cement-block side table and pushed himself up. He got the crutch under his arm and maneuvered his unwieldy body and thumping cast to the door, cursing Grim the whole slow, clomping way.

He reached the dingy, worn-out door before he realized that anyone on the other side wanting him dead could've already shot through the stupid thing. *Then again, maybe they're sadists.* That thought was almost cheerful. The peephole revealed a gleaming white convertible at the curb. *No UPS, no hit squad. Damn.* His eyes turned downward, to a mop of shiny, blonde-streaked hair. *Not a Heathen then.*

The mail slot rattled just as Joker edged sideways and pulled the door open. A startled, porcelain doll face turned up toward him with reddened cheeks. Ashlyn

Davis, he discovered, had green eyes.

****

Ashlyn
Oak Grove

What did I expect for not texting first? Sighing, she pulled the DVD out of her purse. *I'll put it through the mail slot. That's polite, right? I should put a Post-it on it. Do I have a Post-it?* Uneven footsteps on the other side of the door froze her hand on the mail flap.

The ancient door swung inward, leaving nothing but empty air between her and a crutch-wielding Joker. Who'd forgotten his shirt. She fell half a step back as her cheeks ignited. Her vision narrowed to a flawless six pack and miles of sculpted, tattoo-and-bandage-bedecked chest. *How does being shirtless make him taller? No, focus, self. Focus ... not there, not there!* She coughed and tried to keep her eyes on his face.

"Oh, hi! Sorry. I was just leaving this for Grim? He said he'd be home this afternoon." Ash's weight moved from one foot to the other, and she pushed some hair off her face. Joker stared at her. *Maybe I shouldn't have put on eyeliner. Is it too much? Or not enough? God, why isn't there a small town survival how-to?*

"He'll be right back," Joker said with a lip-twitch she assumed to be the closest he got to smiling around annoying, unwelcome strangers. Ash nodded, ready to make her escape until Joker shuffled backward, the cast hampering his steps, but the intent plain. "Come on in."

Dubious, but conscious of etiquette, Ash hesitated. *Not like he's going to be hard to outrun*, she reminded herself as she stepped through the doorway. A messy front room greeted her—clean but host to a scattered host of magazines and papers drifting out from under a ragged futon and over a plastic coffee table. Two big easy chairs faced a massive TV hanging on the other side of the room. A particularly hideous lamp/table combination sat beside the far chair, and both had cement blocks masquerading as side tables. Her eyes caught on the wide picture window, where a faux-silk sheer curtain hung from a decorative rod. That, combined with the greige paint on the walls… *So not a complete bachelor pad. Huh.*

She edged past her host to give him as wide a berth as possible, while he stood back obligingly with the door in his good hand. It was, of course, only in the interest of avoiding contact that she sucked in her tummy. *Better to treat the injured person like lava than risk knocking him over, right? Touch him, you're definitely burned. But those tattoos though…* Armor covered his left shoulder and upper chest, drawn to appear engraved with a military-looking skull and Norse runes. He turned and the top of a Storm Crow logo peeked at her from under the bandages covering what she suspected was road rash—while another tattoo of a skull in a helmet crossed his ribs on the left side. All in all, a lot of ink on a big, well-built canvas.

"What movie is it?" He closed the door behind her and looked at the DVD in her hand.

She averted her eyes. *Yes, this is very interesting carpet. I am very interested.*

"Oh, it's, um, *Nine Queens*? It's an Argentine *Ocean's Eleven* kind of thing. Grim said he's into caper films, but he hadn't heard of it and I had it with me."

"Yeah, I don't think there's a lot of Argentinians around."

"One of my friends has, um, a major film fixation. We—" She dug her pinkie nail into her palm. *Stop. He doesn't need real stories.* "We basically spent an entire semester watching Spanish language movies."

She turned toward him. A mistake. The armor

tattoo spread across her field of view. How could she not stare? Ash's design obsession overwhelmed common sense, and she leaned in closer. The armor showed a realism only available from an expert artist, depicting skin torn away to reveal a metal pauldron embellished with Norse symbols, from Thor's hammer on his chest to the skull on his upper arm. Above the hammer, four runes curved towards his shoulder, and she tilted her head to get a better look. "Does the *Futhark* spell something?"

He didn't answer at first, and she looked up in time to see his eyes narrow. She shrank back, doing her best to look apologetic. *Are you not supposed to ask a biker about his tattoos?*

"The ... what?" Joker's frown remained.

"Um, the runes." She cleared her throat. "Sorry. I had a huge obsession with this TV show about Vikings. It's called, shocker, *Vikings*. Maybe you've seen it, too?"

"Oh." He glanced down at his shoulder, and she got the sense he was filing away the word for future Googling. "Don't know. It looked cool. The artist said it's a spell of power or some shit." Those unreadable brown eyes settled on her again. "Wanna sit down? We've got iced tea or something in the fridge."

"I'm fine." She headed to the futon. "Where'd you get them done? The armor's spot-on 3D. I almost want to send your artist a fangirl letter."

"I got my crow here. The other two I got in North Carolina." Joker's eyes didn't leave her, like he expected weapons to show up out of her cut-off shorts. "The kitchen's in there if you change your mind." He nodded across the room to an open doorway before limping to one of the two big chairs facing the giant TV.

Without meaning to, her gaze followed his cue, and she looked around at the mix-and-match furniture of multiple decades, then back at the weirdly designer window treatment and Pinterest color scheme walls. Worst of all, those sheer curtains diffused the light streaming through the picture window, softening the world—especially Joker's chiseled, imposing features. The effect basically turned him from MMA poster boy to a movie-star pirate with the kind of body meant for climbing. *Damn it.*

"Your house is adorable. I kinda expected more early-frat boy decor. You're missing the pizza box chairs." She pulled out her phone to check for a nonexistent text so she wouldn't get caught ogling as he settled into the chair. *Bad enough to run around shirtless! Who said dudes like you are allowed to flex?*

"Got rid of the last one over the weekend. Not enough back support." She laughed as she dropped onto the edge of the futon.

"There's a pizza place that delivers here? The Grove's moving on up."

"The gas station does carry out."

"Think they need a waitress?" Ash glanced at him from the corner of her eyes. His disbelieving gaze caught hers.

"Figured you were hiring on with one of the local lawyers."

"Yeah, I'm trying to find an alternative." Her cheeks felt hot again, and she pulled her hair over her shoulder like that would hide it. "But writing a travel blog and bouncing around the world doesn't build a 401k, right?"

"Got a gypsy streak, huh?"

Stop blushing, face. This isn't okay. She shook her head, clearing out the Etch A Sketch. "Maybe it would be different if I had the whole life-friends-family thing you guys have going on. I can't imagine you ever ran off to join the circus."

Joker's eyes sharpened a little. "This wasn't always my thing. I've been around."

"But for real leaving? I mean, not like army-leaving. Just wandering around the world, forsaking it all for *la vie boheme*?"

"Maybe not," he admitted with a shrug of his good shoulder. "Got a pretty decent gig here."

"No selling paintings on the beach? Starting a bakery?" His answering laughter shocked the hell out of her, not the least because the striking change to his features. From deadly pirate to charming rogue. *Wait, does he have dimples under his beard? Oh, no wonder the whole county fell into his pants. Puppy eyes, dimples, and badass—all the deadly sins in one convenient, jungle-gym-sized package.*

"I could make a *mean* eclair."

The asymmetry of that image was irresistible. "Could you?"

"Yeah, sure." Joker coughed, shifting in his seat. "Probably."

"I'm just saying, I have a deep love for eclairs, and there's a tragic shortage of them around here." Her smile returned full-force. "I'm totally willing to assist you if it means I get one."

Joker blinked. "I should Google it."

"Here, I've got my phone." She opened the browser and held it out. His callused fingers brushed hers as he took the Galaxy. This close, she couldn't help but watch his darkened cinnamon eyes—too dark. *Wow, his pupils are gigantic.* He scanned the screen and she looked around them, fixing on three abandoned pills and a big script bottle on the table. Right in reach of his chair. *Shit.*

"Probably don't have half of what we need…"

"I can go to the store," she offered too quickly. Joker laughed—a real one, rich and soft. He glanced up at her with a killer Hollywood smile. As long as you didn't look at his eyes... *Yeah, he's way too high to have another dose sitting out.* A familiar weight settled on her, and the nerves fled. *I know this game! Right. Let's play, big boy.*

"You're no help, sweetheart."

"I'm lots of help! See, me right here. Helping. I'm hungry, too, so come on..."

"You can't run my errands," he snorted. She gave an enthusiastic grin and hopped up, one hand extended toward his.

"You okay to ride in a car? Or, uh, be squished into one? They didn't have you in mind when they designed a Miata."

"If I don't fit, guess you could always strap me to the top." He handed her phone back and rose unsteadily, but without help. "I'll grab a shirt. Meet you at the car?"

"All right, I'll see you outside." Once he was moving, she fled to the front step. She needed to text Megan almost more than she needed to breathe. Maybe not as much as she needed to stare at Joker's chest, but that wasn't a good idea for anyone. Ever.

Ashlyn: **Going to store w/Joker. Need anything?**

Megan: **... Ur what with who?**

Ashlyn: **Grocery store. Joker.**

Megan: **Pics or it didn't happen.**

Ashlyn: **I'll get one when he puts his shirt on.**

Megan: **... GURL YOU DID NOT.**

Ashlyn: **Didn't what?**

Megan: **U PUTTING ON CLOTHES TOO??**

Ashlyn: **OMFG NO. He didn't have on a shirt when I got here. Pretty sure he's doubled his pain**

meds. I'm sticking around til Grim or whoever gets back.

Megan: **I'll leave pizza out for you. Floozy.**

****

Joker

A grinding pain ran up and down his right leg; it started when he got out of the motorized cart/wheelchair combo they'd requisitioned at the grocery store. The last few steps to the kitchen fanned it to a jaw-locking flare. He leaned on the table next to the grocery bags he'd wrestled from the car, counting the stars behind his eyes. He hadn't been anywhere but the clubhouse or physical therapy in weeks, and the distance between driveway and kitchen had to be double what he remembered. He abandoned the bags without a second look and made his way to the cabinets.

Two years humping a hundred pounds around the fucking desert. Now, a handful of groceries screws me up? The mighty have fallen.

"So, which one is the saucepan?" He called the question over his shoulder as Ash arrived in the kitchen with another set of bags. Something about her shiny hair and lace-edged shorts threw the room's flaws into sudden, stark contrast—the kitchen's smudged walls and chipped Formica countertop, the empty space where a dining room table had never materialized, the sliding glass door's stunning patio view of a gleaming grill next to a grimy blue bucket filled with beer bottles and crumpled cans. *I need to get a fucking curtain.*

"That smallish one with the handle? That's also not a skillet." She stopped putting the eggs away to shoot him a playful smirk. "Wait, why are you assuming I know? Are you being sexist?"

"You went to college. I assume college people know things." He took the pan out and set it on the stove.

And I've never been happier to know one thing. Twenty-three hurt his brain a hell of a lot less than nineteen.

"Ok. You got us. That's what we college kids do. We drink, and we know things." For some reason, saying so made her laugh. He let the mystery pass and watched her instead, tired and pained and finding some comfort in the view. Odd as she was, nobody could deny Ashlyn was cute. And efficient. She set up the cutting board and ingredients on the kitchen's spindle-legged table and a process emerged: Ashlyn fetching, him directing. The first batter formed in the mixing bowl before Ash stopped and put down the flour she'd measured. For the first time, she lingered next to him instead of retreating. Ash's forehead creased, and her eyes didn't quite meet his when he looked up from the mixer. "Hey, are you due for another pill any time soon?"

Instead of telling her to fuck off, he shook his head. "I've got an alarm. Couple hours off. I won't need any 'til then if I keep off my leg."

"Grim's not going to kill me for not knowing your schedule before we went out, is he?"

"Doubt if he knows it. But he'd have to answer to Legs, so don't worry."

"So he does like her? Why doesn't he say anything?" She dropped into the chair next to his with a wide, expectant look. He caught the scent of her perfume again—different from the one she'd worn before. More like straight candy. *Down, boy. Down. Shit.* The images of her and candy didn't need to be mixing in his head.

"A few reasons," he said, trying to whisk without knocking the bowl off the table—a rough challenge with one working hand. Flour erupted from the bowl and powdered his gray t-shirt. "Come on, doesn't Megan know? The whole fuckin' town does." *Why the hell am I telling some chick about Grim's business? Narcotics? Or tits.* His focus slid to the side, confirming that Ashlyn's top showed a distracting amount of cleavage when she leaned in.

"You'd be amazed what a girl can manage not to notice." She took hold of the blue ceramic bowl. He found himself watching her slender fingers and chipped, mismatched nail polish. Not the kind of nails he expected on a rich girl, but then again, she didn't behave much like one either. *And how does a rich girl act, dumbass? You don't know jack shit about society chicks. For all you know she's writing this afternoon off as a charity act.* "You should tell him to grab her shoulders, look deep into her eyes, and tell her 'I want to put my penis in you.' She might get the message."

Jerked out of his distraction, laughter all but doubled him over, ribs and bandages be damned. The image of Megan kicking Grim's ass for that was just straight-up gorgeous. He got control of himself and wiped his eyes. *How long since I laughed that hard? Damn, these drugs are good.* "Fuck." He stared at the batter. "I don't know what comes next."

"Read the next step, Snowball." Ash pushed her tablet toward him. "If you can fix an engine, pretty sure you can manage dessert." He glared at her but started reading the instructions out loud.

They fell back into the motions, and the easy conversation continued. Topics ranged from his favorite movies to vacation destinations, normal, silly bullshit that he hadn't talked about much the last couple years. Joker cast a sidelong look at Ash. *When was the last time someone besides Grim mocked me over loving* Roadhouse?

Oblivious, she breezed away from the table and deposited the filling on the stove. She snagged the flour and turned back toward the table, mouth open to make some sarcastic retort about Alaskan vacations—until her foot landed in a smear of spilled milk. She skidded sideways. Her hand flew up toward the cabinet, missing the wood but knocking a bowl off the counter. Flour, Ashlyn, and the plastic bowl all met the floor in a sickening crash. Ashlyn yelped, coughed on airborne flour, and flopped backward with a high-pitched whimper.

Joker scrabbled up from the table, moving to her side as fast as his cast and throbbing leg allowed. "Shit, girl! You okay?"

"Um, yeah..." Ashlyn levered herself into a sitting position before her fingers wrapped around his outstretched hand. Holding tight, she adjusted her weight using her legs so he served as a pivot point instead of leaning on him—a move she managed with considerable grace. She kept her head bent, eyes cast downward. The pose didn't hide her bright pink cheeks.

"Hey, you sure you aren't hurt?" he asked again. Flour streaked her blue shirt and down one side of her lacy jean shorts. He balled his hand into a fist, lest his itching palm reach down to wipe it away. No matter how perfect the curve of her thighs was. *Off limits,* he reminded himself.

"I'm surprisingly bouncy. It's a talent." She cleared her throat before she grabbed the towels and edged around him. "I can even fall down stairs without major injury." The smile she shot his way busted his resolve. His fingertips found her cheek, rubbing away the flour. She froze in her tracks, not flinching, not pulling back. He lowered his gaze so he could think, but ended up watching her lips instead. Her very pink lips, that matched her soft skin so well...

"What the fuck is going on in here? That goddamn Frog, told his sorry ass not to—motherfucker!"

Grim's shout rattled the cabinets. The door slammed for emphasis as he stomped in. "I *just* cleaned the kitchen!"

Joker greeted this with a cold glare that dropped in temperature as Ash skittered away.

"We all didn't get to play macho man today," he muttered, though fortunately Ash's voice carried over the top of his.

"Hey, Grim! We're, um, making eclairs?" Ash wiped at her cheek—the same one Joker had touched—while Grim stared at him over her head.

"What. The. Fuck?"

Joker heard the unspoken question: *Could you not come up with a better line, bro?* He answered by lifting a brow and shrugged it off. "They're gonna be fucking delicious." *And what the hell does it matter? What else was I doing with this wasted motherfucker of a day?* He couldn't say any of it, so he tilted his chin and dared his roommate to push him.

"How many pills did you take, jackass?" Grim's attention settled on Ashlyn as he stalked into the kitchen. "How many was it, Blondie? I'm calling overdose before I believe he's telling me about baking."

"N-none. Since I got here…" Ashlyn's hands flew up in surrender. The rest of her shrank from Grim until her back hit the counter. "Look, the first time I met him, his bones were on the outside. I have no idea what he's supposed to be like." Her voice was too soft, green eyes too wide. The mad instinct to get between her and Grim wriggled at Joker's conscience, and he took a half-step toward her before his own logic kicked in. *Shit, she's scared of him?*

His eyed his roommate, more curious than concerned. *She's good with my ink, so it's not his tats.* Grim's black hair and sharp, tanned features contrasted hard with his bright blue eyes. *I never saw Pretty-Boy freak out a girl.* Grim must've sensed it, too, because he stopped moving and gave her some space. When he answered, he kept his voice down a few decibels.

"Moody, silent asshole about sums it up. Pretty damn sure he don't know an eclair from a donut."

Ashlyn's head swiveled to Joker.

"Then he took … a lot?"

Joker smirked and put a hand on her arm. She didn't flinch, so he kept the contact. "Nah, the company's better than my usual asshole roommate."

"Feeling weak yet? One more joke might lay you out, brother."

"Or maybe you. Start the glaze, Ryan." Joker picked up Ashlyn's tablet and held it out for his roommate. Maybe laying off the road name would help her out? "Here. Instructions."

"You're actually doing it? Fucking *Twilight Zone.*" Grim took the tablet, reading quickly, then gathering the materials he needed with a methodical air. "Gonna be the best fucking glaze to ever grace a pastry. Just you watch."

His display of domestic competence must have distracted her because Ashlyn's hands stopped shaking after a few turns of the mixing bowl. While Grim separated egg yolks like some iron chef contestant, Joker caught Ashlyn's eye. "Told you he watched HGTV."

"I bet he knows where to keep pans, too." Her sarcasm returned, and his shoulders relaxed.

"Under the oven?" Grim's glib answer earned a glare from Joker. "Unless you live in *this* house and follow Nate's particular way of doing things. Finding shit in this kitchen is like accepting a search quest in Warcraft. Which I could be playing right now, by the way."

"You cook. I clean. That's—" Joker stopped

himself and shook his head. "Fuck. We sound married."

"And it's super cute. But one of you should probs tell Ariel. Let her down easy." Ash skipped backward to avoid a spoon Grim swiped at her arm. Whatever her earlier bad reaction was, she looked comfortable.

"As if I'd let that bitch anywhere easy," Grim snipped. "'Course, I wish more of us would be willing to let her down at all."

Joker groaned, waving off the retread conversation. They'd had that argument too many times.

"Don't feel threatened, Grim. *She's* never helped bake shit."

One of Ashlyn's blonde brows rose. "She looked pretty serious about you the other night."

Is she asking if I've got a girlfriend? He risked a look from the corner of his eye. Ashlyn fiddled with the dough, ignoring him. "Ariel likes to play mother hen." The answer didn't get him so much as a glance, and Grim pushed the conversation on with a question about Dr. Who. Apparently, her favorite doctor was a matter of some importance. *What kind of name is Ten anyway? Nerds.*

The eclairs mostly ended up on the sheets with only a few on the ground. Grim celebrated by pulling whiskey out of the cabinet and rum from the garage fridge for Ashlyn.

"Spiced, m'lady." Grim held the bottle up before handing it to her.

"Truly, Lord Bacchus, thou art a god among men." She hopped off the counter to take the bottle and yanked the top off with impressive speed. "Where are your cups?"

"By the fridge," Joker answered. She got onto her toes as she reached for one, her blue shirt riding up to expose a wide strip of creamy skin above her shorts. He met Grim's knowing smirk with a tilted beer.

"A Mickey Mouse cup?" Ashlyn held the ceramic thing in front of her, laughing as she turned around to them. "Not the fandom I expected to find around here."

Joker's face—and thoughts—blanked for a full heartbeat. *Reagan and her goddamn Disney fetish. Must've missed it when I boxed up all her shit.* He gave Grim a cautionary look but shrugged. "Probably a gag gift."

"Those are always fun. Oh! I brought the movie you said you hadn't seen. *Nueve Reinas*. It's on the futon." Ash stirred the Mickey Mouse rum with her index finger.

"Cool. Thanks, babe." Grim stopped with his own cup halfway to his lips. "You carry around a lot of obscure DVDs?"

"I hadn't unpacked everything from school before I came down." She busied herself with pouring more rum into the cup.

"Are you living out of your car?" Joker's question shocked Ashlyn into staring at him across Mickey's ears.

"What? Oh. No. Mostly I'm staying with Megan and avoiding my grandparents." She slumped back against the counter. "How long before pastries are ready, kind sirs? A lady could use an eclair to complete her sugar rush."

So, she doesn't want to talk about her living situation.

With their desserts timed and baking, Joker got ushered out of the kitchen to cue up Netflix while the others cleaned. He chose *Archer*. By the time the eclairs came out, Ashlyn and Grim were shouting insults to an imaginary butler. Then they scrounged a tray from some forgotten closet and performed butler impressions as they served—and devoured—the eclairs. Maybe the secret to becoming a chef would be keeping his clientele drunk.

Joker remained in his armchair, and Grim took up the other one while Ashlyn sprawled, bounced, and flopped around on the futon, even after Joker pointed out it probably looked worse than Archer's couch under a black-light. Grim answered that remark by humming "Under the Sea" until Joker punched his arm.

The next round of drinks saw Grim taking control of the remote and putting on *Buckaroo Banzai*. Matters devolved into Bruce Campbell-as-Chuck-Norris jokes before Ashlyn passed out. Joker let it go until the credits rolled, giving Grim time to grab an actual sheet for his bed instead of the shredded flannel blanket Joker had used the last few weeks. He hefted himself up out of the chair and limped over.

"Hey, sweetheart, come on. Time for bed." He squeezed her shoulder, careful not to grip too hard.

"Oh. Ok." She blinked, but her gaze stayed glassy. A confused smile formed. "I—I'm sorry. I, um, don't think I should drive. Are there Ubers here?"

"Yeah, no. Come on. Megan's out with the girls tonight, and you're not heading back by yourself." He helped her stand up before ushering her toward his room, ignoring her protests about staying on the couch. Minutes later, he watched her climb into his bed and disappear under the covers. A mop of gold hair gleamed on the pillows before he turned off the light.

Joker avoided Grim's eyes as they met in the hall. For once his roommate didn't poke the bear.

"Went pretty well down on Route 9 tonight." A slight hook in Grim's voice betrayed his unease about raising the topic. Joker's posture hardened and he lifted his chin.

"The charges?"

"You're a wizard. As ever." His eyes glinted in a

wolfish smile. "Scratch's bike is toast, among others. And half their clubhouse."

At least I'm not a total waste of flesh. "Anybody get hurt?"

"Nah, couple bruises here and there, but they didn't even get a shot near us."

"Good."

"So, Ashlyn—"

"Is sleeping." Joker cleared his throat and glanced back the way he'd come. "Can you, uh, look into her?" It wasn't a standard request. The club's friends in local cop shops specialized in finding information when they needed it. When Grim dug shit up, he went deep.

"You really that paranoid?" Grim's voice flattened.

"She graduates some fancy ass college and comes out here where there hasn't been a job worth having in decades? Seems ... off."

"Think she might bring trouble?"

Joker shook his head. "I think she might need help."

"Are you trying to tell me you're worried about a chick who just conned your ass into baking?"

"Maybe." Joker kept his eyes on the closed door.

"I'll see what I can find out." Grim sighed. "But I'll tell you what I'm gonna find for free, brother. She's not in trouble. She's going on walkabout, living with the natives before they ship her off to get a PhD in women's studies or some bullshit."

"And I hope you're right." He patted Grim on the shoulder and made his solitary, clumsy way back to the easy chair. Despite the pain pills—now a couple hours overdue—sleep took a while.

Chapter Four: May 26

Ashlyn
Oak Grove

Unknown: **Get out bitch.**

Ashlyn shoved her phone into the console the second she parked, slamming the lid on top of. *Maybe the screen will melt before I get back.* Megan watched from the passenger seat, a brow cocked. Ash made a show of getting out and hurrying to help with the trays occupying her cousin's shapely lap, her lips sealed tight and a glare warning her cousin not to ask.

It's Memorial Weekend. I'm not dealing with it today. Not with the car, not with psychos, not anything. I—What the hell? Did Meg get the wrong address?

She stopped halfway around the car, dumbstruck by the house in front of her. They'd parked at the east edge of Oak Grove, nearly back into the farm country, halfway to Ravenwood. A large, two-story Victorian rose before them—testament to the days when mine bosses and railroad managers still called Oak Grove home—painted white and black with a wide front porch and cobblestone path. The lawn, like every other in town, was freshly cut and vibrant green. Nothing indicated a biker lived there except a wrought-iron crow in flight fastened above the porch steps. *Joker grew up here?* The whole thing looked far more idyllic than what she'd imagined. *Wow, I am a bitch. Check your privilege, self.*

"That's Tree's house?" She couldn't help the disbelief in her voice. "Like, for real? He doesn't just keep it as a rental or something? I thought this was the old Scholl place." Megan laughed as she shoved the trays into Ashlyn's distracted hands and climbed out of the car.

"Oh yeah, it's his house. He bought it from the

estate, I think, forever ago. Even before he got married."

"Wait. Tree's married?"

"Only once. Joker's mom." Megan's unhelpful answer got a frown.

"Where is she?"

"Moved to California when we were little. Died in a wreck … fifth grade, maybe?" Her cousin shrugged, but Ash's thoughts kept swirling.

His mom just … left him? But she couldn't ask that out loud, and Megan wasn't pausing for conversation.

"Come on, let's get this stuff inside." Megan took the top Saran-wrapped tray off Ashlyn's arms. Ashlyn followed her across the flawless lawn and up the broad wooden stairs. The door flew open before they even got to it, disgorging a cut-clad but shirtless Ice, one of the club members who frequented movie nights at Joker's place.

About the same height as Joker, with a trimmed goatee enhancing his smile and twinkling blue eyes, Ice looked more like a Viking god come to life than a real person—complete with tree-trunk arms meant for throwing mystic hammers. Laughing, he pulled Megan into an enthusiastic embrace. Ashlyn dove in to save the pink plastic tray from disaster.

"Hello, Legs! And you, too, half-pint." Ice's rosy cheeks and shining eyes marked him as at least halfway drunk. Megan laughed, wiggling free of his grip— resulting in Ashlyn being seized in her place. She yelped and tried to get out of it, but Ice had other ideas, and once Megan rescued the trays in turn, she ended up held against a sculpted side.

"Guess what, Dragon? I found two hotties! They're mine now, you slow-movin' ass!" He yelled into the house before draping an arm around each of them. He ushered them through the door at an angle to accommodate their combined widths. "Hailey! I have spare wives!"

"We brought Jell-O shots!" Megan called over the top of the last pronouncement, though Ashlyn doubted Megan was concerned about her lifelong bestie being upset.

The interior's centrally-conditioned air eased the sweat off her brow, and Ash relaxed in relief. Their footsteps echoed on a hardwood foyer floor boasting an intricate inlay pattern that mirrored the delicate, carven swirls on the crown molding. Ice pulled them through another towering door into a wide room with built-in shelves. Three large bikers and a couple kids lay sprawled over two tan leather couches and coordinating floor pillows, all in the thrall of a NASCAR race displayed on a massive television hung over a fireplace. Ashlyn's eyes caught on the tiles around the hearth: actual shepherdesses and pipers danced in relief.

Because why wouldn't there be original Victorian motifs? I'm in Wonderland...

"Tree's out there." One of the bikers—Grease, according to his patch—pointed toward the far side of the room where an open archway led to a formal dining room serving as a further entertainment annex. Ahead, another set of doors showed glimpses of gleaming white appliances. The scent of brats and beer wafted across Ashlyn's nose when Ice escorted them into the kitchen, stole two Jell-O shots off Megan's tray, and dashed out the back door. Conscious of her floaty white skirt and peasant top, Ashlyn picked a more careful path through the kitchen, keeping close behind Megan.

"Hey, girls!" Ariel's voice reached them a second before the screen door slammed open and the leggy brunette stepped up from the back porch. "Let me put some of those in the fridge. You can take the other half on out back. They need some cooling off." Ariel's cheerful smile caught for half a second as she looked over Ashlyn's outfit. "I hope there's something clean enough for you to sit on out there." Ariel laughed. "It's gotten pretty grubby for white."

"No worries. It's washable." Ashlyn moved to help Ariel clear counter space while Megan grabbed a smaller tray from a cabinet. *At least someone knows their way around.* The thought felt strangely bleak.

"If there's any emergencies, don't worry. I've got a spare t-shirt in the car." Ariel grinned. "How are you doing? I heard you've interviewed a couple places."

"Yeah. Not that I got the jobs." Ashlyn's nose scrunched. "Either too much education or not enough experience. I'm considering taking up street theater at this point."

"Tell her not to worry, Ari. Someone's bound to take her." Megan piled half the shots onto the new tray with practiced ease as she spoke. She patted Ash's shoulder and picked up both trays with a practiced flourish. "See you out on the field, babes." She hip-checked the back door and all but waltzed out, calling to others in the yard as she went.

Ariel made a sympathetic noise while she moved the remaining Jell-O shots into the crowded fridge. "You'll find something. Jess and some of the others are out back, too. You should go say hi. I've gotta run to the liquor store, but I'll be right back."

"That sounds like a fun errand. Need any help?"

"Not this time." Ariel tilted her shoulder with a mischievous smile. "I've got a couple Prospects riding shotgun. Need to see if I like them."

Ashlyn laughed. "Happy hunting, Ariel."

"You, too." She waved before she walked off.

Ashlyn wandered out the back door. The yard spread out behind the house, green and lush as the front, save for a chunk absorbed by an outbuilding that looked suspiciously like a carriage house-turned-biker-garage. A unique monument to changing passenger conveyance. Ash got barely a second to think about that before someone yelled her name.

"Over here!" Megan's voice carried across from the far end, where a group lounged in a motley collection of webbed lawn furniture and wicker chairs beneath a shady pop-up pavilion. Megan sat next to Katie and Jessica, a pair of her friends Ashlyn recognized mostly via Facebook interactions. Dragon and Grim sat next to them. Across the way, Joker reclined in a larger chair with his cast propped up in front of him. Paper shot glasses already littered the ground.

"Hey, guys!" She waved at the others before focusing on her cousin. "You piglet. Didn't you save me one?" She feigned a pout. "And after I helped make those things."

"You have the other half!"

"And Ariel wisely put them all in the fridge."

Katie laughed. "We aren't *all* the way through them!" She pulled a quarter-empty tray out from under Megan's chair. "See?"

"I take back my insinuations." Ash grabbed a blue shot and tilted her head back to slam it, finishing by licking the rim out of bar-borne habit. "You're not at all alchies."

"Oh, but I'm still a piglet?" Megan's lower lip curled outward.

"Like you haven't called me worse for eating the last chip."

"Hey, Ash. Good to see you made it!" Grim stood up and wrapped her in a hug, having apparently decided to stop their brawl before it got started. Her shoulders stiffened, but she returned the hug.

He can't help the fact his eyes look like someone else's. It's not his fault. If she thought it enough, maybe she'd get over herself.

"Thanks. I wouldn't have missed it. I did promise, didn't I?"

"Come over here. You're going to end up with Jell-O on that skirt if you sit too close to them." As he spoke, he pulled her across the circle. Somehow this maneuver ended with him pushing her down onto the arm of Joker's chair. "Cleanest seat in the house. Right, Joker?"

Ashlyn glanced at Joker. Sunlight made his eyes look more gold than usual, and his expression didn't seem that festive, considering the holiday. "You aren't hiding any shots under this chair, are you?" At least her question got a half-smile...

****

Joker

Grim deposited Ash on the arm of Joker's chair so fast he almost offered his best friend a biscuit for learning a new trick. Luckily, Ash distracted him. "You're more than welcome to look."

Ashlyn's teeth caught her lower lip, and those bright green eyes turned from the chair's feet to his face. Something about the tilt of her head and the way her eyes moved up caught the worst parts of his imagination. *Baseball. Dad hungover. Engine numbers...*

"I'd hate to risk getting you hurt again," Ash said. "Facing your PT guy is scary enough when he likes me."

"You've gotten me out of worse spots."

"Only if I have a cell phone and an emergency crew *en route*." Ashlyn twisted a little and overbalanced. She grabbed for the back of his chair just as he put his hand on her waist. Her cheeks reddened. "How are you doing the last couple days? I, uh, haven't seen you."

Two days. He'd been clearing out paperwork at the garage and helping Dragon prep for the club's ride, she'd been on job interviews—the longest he'd gone without seeing her since they met at the clubhouse. *Pretty damn sure I shouldn't know that.*

"You could have texted. Don't you always have a phone?" His thumb moved against her back, noting the curve just at her waist and the body heat radiating through her gauzy shirt. His fingers itched to slide lower, but he didn't let them. "I thought it came attached."

Ash pulled up the brown leather bag she wore slung over her shoulder and opened it, tilting for him to inspect. A flat-line wallet with a pin-up girl design, a pack of cinnamon gum, and a bottle of Advil occupied the limited space. "It's not quite that attached."

"It's in the car, isn't it?"

"Maaaybe," she said, eyes sliding away guiltily. He laughed, and she sighed. "All right, you caught me."

"Still, that's yards away. Do you need to lay down?"

"I'm kinda faint, but I think I might survive with the right amount of alcohol applied." Ashlyn sat up, dropping her purse onto the grass and pushing her hair off her face. "Are you going to tell me you don't have your phone on your person, Mr. Badass?"

"Are you kidding? I'd die without the damned thing—learned that about a month back." He levered himself up and turned to face her as she chuckled. "Let's find you a drink." He held out his hand.

"And what are you drinking?" Her palm pressed into his as her feet touched the ground, but she took a second to find her balance. "I thought your dad had an official ban on alcohol for you."

"Only 'til I stopped the pain meds." Leaving his crutch behind—the PT guy said it was good to go short distances—they started up to the back porch. He navigated the steps by leaning on the rail. Ash stayed at his side, her hand hovering behind his arm without quite touching. "So … how have you been?"

"Bored mostly." Ashlyn darted ahead and hauled the door open for him. "Trying to make friends and be sociable. And not get dragged to Grandpa's club every day. A girl can only take so much golf at a time."

"I don't think I've ever played."

"A wise life choice." His cast hit the linoleum with its usual thud. She looked down and put an arm out to steady him. "How are you for real? You can get all juicy detail now that nobody's around," she teased as he reached out for her in turn, steering her to turn toward the fridge with his hand at the small of her back.

"Ready to get the hell out of these casts. The sooner they say I'm good, the sooner I can pick out a new bike. Take you for that ride I promised."

Her eyes widened. "Then I'm on your side."

I'd rather have you on something else, baby. Ashlyn stood back against the counter, the thighs he'd just been thinking about bared beneath that damn skirt. He turned to one of the taller cabinets where Tree hid the better booze, retrieving a bottle of Kraken rum that he'd sent Frog two counties over to find. He poured some into a pair of red Solo cups, adding Coke from an open two-liter on the counter. He handed the first one over to Ashlyn. "You ever convince Amos to try that barbecue place?"

"Not yet. He's too busy golfing." Ash shrugged off the question and glanced out the kitchen window as two more members pulled up the back drive on their bikes. "Have you been using your desk time wisely?" she asked. "Picking out new Harley things or … maybe a new helmet? Whatever accessories go with bikes in general."

"I got new gloves. Haven't been able to find any of my old pairs." His smile returned, but didn't stay. "As long as we're talking juicy details, how'd those interviews really go?"

She winced. "Okay. Ish. I … could probably land the one at the Dollar Tree, but it's almost no hours."

"Listen, if you need a job, I know where one or two could be found." A lot of people owed the Storm Crows or would welcome the chance to have the Crows' VP owe them.

Her smile tightened, but she let out a breath, setting her cup down. "I think that's where I'm supposed to say I'm all independent and fierce … but honestly, I'd appreciate it."

"How do you feel about bartending? There's an opening at the clubhouse." He took a gulp of rum as soon as the words were out of his mouth. *Fuck. Dragon's going to choke. This is a bad idea. Or the best...* The Crows' Nest had operated for decades as a private club— the legacy of some ancient Illinois booze restrictions— and by now the charter just figured it into expenses. Plus, a cash-only operation made a good cover. "I could find something else if you're not up for that."

"A-at the clubhouse?" Expressions flickered through Ash's eyes too fast for him to read. "Isn't that … I mean, is that even a thing?"

He shrugged. "Members do the honors some nights, but when we throw a party, they ought to get some time to enjoy it. And the guys all work different hours—gotta keep the clubhouse open for them when day shifts have to sleep." Of course, staff in the members-only bar was usually Old Ladies, or members' kids needing a job—half of it paid under the table. "It's not a lot of hours, but I bet you'll do all right on tips at the party nights. It ain't a lawyer's office, but if you're wanting out of the ordinary, I don't think it gets much further than us."

"I'm pretty sure I could tend bar." Ashlyn's expression turned sheepish, and she tugged on a piece of her hair. He recognized that habit and smiled. "I haven't, but I probably could? My only legit non-campus job was at Abercrombie one summer. I quit because the automatic perfume-sprayer gave me migraines."

"Abercrombie?" He remembered Reagan wearing that brand back in high school. Joker feigned an exaggerated leer at her boobs. "Poor you in all those miniskirts." Ash in a prep school polo and a miniskirt too short for anything but porn? *Good way to land a guy or two in jail. Maybe me included.* Her ass distracted him too much as it was. "You put your hair in pigtails, too?"

The curve of her lips belied the glare she shot his way. "Ha. Ha. Easy to joke when you don't have the Smell-O-Vision horrors to go with it. But if, um, if you're serious, I'll do it. I assume you guys don't order a lot of super complicated mixes, right? Or do I need to study up and start practicing drinks on you and Grim?"

"Simple men with simple tastes. But it might be good to make sure you practice a bit." *Not at all for the excuse to have you around the house.* He finished his cup and reached for the bottle only to meet her wide, innocent eyes and stop short.

"I don't have to dress like a Hooters girl or anything?" *I wish you would.*

"Dress however you want, Ash. They'll still stare. Beautiful girls attract attention." He set the rum down, realizing too late what he'd said. He grabbed the Coke and added considerably more of it to his cup, but he saw Ash's brows lift before she schooled the shock from her face.

"Well, thank you. Flattery will get you a waitress in a miniskirt, maybe."

Tempting as the idea was, he couldn't smile. "That might be borrowing trouble, baby."

"So far your friends aren't any worse than the average frat party. And a lot better than some of them." There—the flash in her eyes. Fear? Sadness? Her posture shifted, and she looked away.

"My friends aren't the best of people, but they aren't all dicks."

"Except for the bar fights?"

"You worried about flying beer cans?"

"It's a lot easier to worry about brass knuckles than keeping track of who might roofie who." She shrugged. He tried not to frown.

"You've led an interesting life, babe." *Which might be why you seem to raise twice the questions you ever answer.*

"Uh huh," she sniffed. "Are you hoping if you keep flattering me, I'll forget to charge you for drinks?"

"Would it work?"

She pursed her lips. "You'd have to try a lot harder to see any statistically significant impacts."

"And if I were to tell you that it's honesty?"

Ashlyn's green eyes raked down his body and back up to his face before she shook her head. "I appreciate you trying to, ah, up my badass cred and all, but I'm boring as beige."

"You manage to stomach your way through my cooking. Maybe you don't think that's tough, but you've got me convinced." He smiled wider when she giggled and patted his arm.

"Your baking's way better than my old

roommates' vegan cakes."

He set the cup down so he could put his hand on her cheek, pushing some loose hair back behind Ash's ear. *Fuck, even her ears are looking cute. What the hell was in that rum?* The move must've startled her—she jerked her head up, her eyes wide and blank. Until she covered with a nervous laugh.

"The only worse thing was her gluten-free cake. Which might have been mislabeled wallpaper paste, to be honest…" She swallowed and turned her head, drawing back just a shade. He let his hand fall.

"Want another drink?"

"That would be great." She drained the Solo cup. "Two days of country clubbing, I'm ready to drink for realsies. Hashtag First World Problems."

"Now you sound like a rich girl." He poured more rum into her cup and added a hefty amount of soda before handing it back.

"Something about too many playdates as a child and nannies who don't hug you enough and … oh, the trials of having a birthday when your friends are in San Moritz?" Her nose scrunched. "God, even I'm grossed out. Just dump me in the nearest mud puddle for that."

"Nah. I don't see that ending well. I happen to know what you look like in a wet t-shirt." Demons on his shoulder must've been talking—or the rum—but Ashlyn laughed.

"Of all the things for your brain to record after a nearly-fatal wreck, it's *that*?"

"Yeah, well. I'm hardwired for *that*."

"For remembering drowned rats? You should talk to a biologist. Get rewired."

"You need to get some self-confidence, sweetheart," he told her as he reached for her arm.

"Don't go positive-reinforcement on me now, J.

I'm not as egotistical as I seem."

He leaned even closer, lowering his voice for her. "You seem a lot of things. That's not on the list."

She tensed under his hand, and her jaw set at a familiar angle: defensive.

"Oh?"

Who taught you to be afraid? Someday soon he'd have to ask. He'd wondered about it often, from the times when Grim inexplicably sent her running, or Megan yelling at Frog broke Ash into tears she swore were PMS. He settled for a compliment. "You seem like you know who you are."

"A-and who is that?"

"Wish I knew. But…" He stayed close, inhaling the scents of rum and her candy perfume. "Maybe someday you'll let me?" Their gazes remained locked, except those few seconds his dropped to her lips as she licked them. His blood ran hot, pushing everything else out of his head.

"I'm an open book, Joker." It was a whisper. And a lie.

"Hm. That mean you'll answer a question for me?" He knew her well enough to sense lowered defenses. Feeling like the big bad wolf, he stayed still instead of giving her the space he always had before. His hand strayed toward her, but he didn't touch her. *Don't knock her off balance* .

"Sure. I mean, most questions. There are probably a couple I'd rather not. You know, in case of oversharing." Her gaze stayed on her drink. "Take your best shot?"

The demons on his shoulder crowed for action, and even Joker's better nature couldn't hold back. "What would you do if I kissed you right now?"

Ashlyn's luminous eyes flared so wide they

could've popped out of her head. "There are people here." He *saw* her thoughts catch up to her mouth by the shade of pink hitting her cheeks. "A-anyway, I don't think we have the kind of friendship where you randomly kiss me at a party at your dad's house."

"And if we weren't at my dad's house?" He couldn't help but smirk.

"Then I wouldn't object. Unless you're high, or way more drunk than I think you are." She cleared her throat but didn't look at him. "See? Open book. New question."

"All right. What if it wasn't random?" He touched her cheek, letting his fingers trail along her jaw and gently turn her head toward him. Her breath hitched, so his movements slowed as their lips neared. He paused barely a breath away, eyes still on hers just to be sure. Her pretty green gaze lowered, eyelids closing...

"There you are!" Hailey's voice kicked him upright. The brunette strode into the kitchen followed by Tommy's old lady, Lana, a bottle-born redhead with raccoon-style eye makeup. Hailey wore almost none in contrast, and a pair of shorts and a t-shirt. Lana wore a microscopic skirt and tank. Hailey eyed Ashlyn's white skirt and top without comment and settled against the counter with a telling raise of her right brow. "Ice's been lookin' for you outside."

Ash jerked backward. Her expression morphed into a pleasant facsimile of a smile—and with it, his one chance at getting past those goddamned defenses evaporated. He put his hand on the counter instead of on Ash's waist.

"Figured his drunk ass would be happier finding you, babe." Joker didn't bother making his smile look convincing. "Hailey, you've met Ashlyn, right?"

"Nope," Hailey said with heavy sarcasm. "I've

never met anybody my best friend's related to." Her gray eyes rolled as she took a drink from her beer. "Ash, don't let the cast fool you. You can still hit him."

"Very funny," Joker snorted. "Ignore her, Ash. Hailey was raised by wolves."

"Only way anybody's crazy enough to work in the Illinois school system these days," Hailey retorted. "So, you found any good jobs? Not that I'm planning on stealing it out from under you … unless it doesn't involve students."

"She's going to take Sandra's spot at the clubhouse," Joker said. Hailey's jaw dropped.

"Seriously?"

"Yeah," Ash answered with a nervous cough. "Joker was nice enough to offer and—"

"Karli's gonna fucking flip," Lana crowed. Her husky voice spoke of heavy smoking, and Joker almost choked on the scent of tobacco and cheap marijuana that hit as she walked over and put her arm on Ashlyn's shoulder. "C'mon, girl. I gotta introduce you to Karli." He watched her steer Ashlyn outside and turned to find Hailey's brows sky high and a knowing smirk on her full lips.

"Go get your husband sobered up." He made it sound like an order. Hailey's lips curled upward, but she moved toward the door. Slowly.

"You know I've walked in on you doing way more interesting—"

"Hailey. Go."

Her laughter lingered long after the door slammed behind her. He downed a straight shot of the rum.

Chapter Five: May 27

Joker
Oak Grove

Shortened shifts at the garage and no solo transportation meant weeks sitting on his ass with a bottle of Vicodin and daytime TV in between PT appointments. Facing that reality didn't do shit for his already frayed temper. He knew that, even when he threw a plate at Case's head, or yelled at Megan for calling him on his crap. He knew it when he bitched at Grim and sulked in the recliner. Those first days were rough.

Now, Ashlyn popped up in the afternoons with pie from Tim's Place, or begging for "sanctuary" from her grandma's social luncheons (or both). As often as not, they ended up on movie marathons, joined by a revolving cast of Crows and Prospects. Megan brought in pizza when her waitressing shifts ended, or they'd send someone for food and a handful of people ended up drinking and arguing over bad movies. Joker caught himself giving the clock funny looks if he didn't get a text or a knock at the door by 2 PM as one week turned into two, and then some. Worse, he got used to going places with Ash. Even PT. Even shopping.

With Reagan, ten-minute grocery store runs turned into two-hour scavenger hunts that filled two carts and still managed to miss what they'd come for. Ashlyn always had a plan. Thanks to the painkillers, *he* ended up being the one who filled the cart with random stuff. Today provided another lesson in that last embarrassing fact when Ashlyn drove him to Ebert's Grocery in search of dinner. Somehow the lasagna he promised to teach her (from a recipe he found the day before, during the party no less) now included frozen chocolate pie and two packs of gummi bears. *If I don't end up the size of a walrus by the time I'm cleared for the gym...*

"You didn't have to pay for it," Ash said as they walked out of the store. He shot her a quelling look. They'd had the same argument a few days before. He suspected they'd have it again. Maybe tomorrow.

"Grim and I will be the ones eating most of it. I'm picking up shit for tomorrow anyway."

"You are not picking up tomatoes for tomorrow."

"Fine. Consider it a thank you for keeping my grouchy ass company." He nudged her with his elbow as he hobbled along beside her. She hadn't mentioned yesterday's near-kiss but hadn't seemed awkward about it, so he didn't think she'd mind being teased. Maybe she'd written it off as the rum. He didn't mind. Plenty of time to handle that when he wasn't negotiating around crutches and opiate side effects.

"Oh, yeah. It's a real test of will." She lifted the key fob and popped the trunk—or, as he liked to think of it, the misplaced glove compartment. Her Miata had good points (according to Ashlyn), but the trunk space didn't make the list. Nor did the fact he had to fold his bendable leg up like origami to get inside it and accommodate his cast. *If she'd just damn well take Grim's Nissan without freaking out.* He reached over to help her load the grocery bags.

"Stop it!" Ashlyn's snapped command brought him up short. She pointed at the crutch. "No." He scowled. *One of these days she's going to figure out I'm not her damned puppy.*

"One of my arms still works," he explained through gritted teeth before he saw an angle she might appreciate. Joker smiled. "Thought I could put it to use. Wouldn't want it to go all weak and ruin the concept of that biker-chef blog."

Ashlyn side-eyed his arm and handed him the lightest bag as though salad and croutons might overwhelm his balance. "Good point. But if you fall over, I'm YouTubing it."

"Eventually I will have two arms, you know."

She answered his warning with a laugh and handed him a head of lettuce. With the groceries loaded, he grabbed the trunk lid before she could and made a show of shutting it. "I can still close a damn door."

Ashlyn huffed and stuck her tongue out before admitting defeat and pushing the cart back to the return pen.

Righting his crutch beneath his arm, he limped toward the passenger side but stopped short when the pavement crunched under his foot. He looked down and heaved a sigh: A mess of shattered plastic gleamed where a taillight should have been. *A parking lot hit and run. Damn.* He edged around the car toward his door. A vicious line of gouged paint marred the car's gleaming side panels from front fender to the tail light.

"Ash, can you come here?" Maybe the narcotics were scrambling his brain. Maybe he'd been distracted by her tank top. It did offer a luscious view, and the purple color looked tasty against her skin. *Maybe the damage was there all day?*

"Huh?" Ashlyn stared at him across the Miata's black ragtop roof.

"Looks like somebody keyed your car." He put his fingertips against the rough, broken paint. No hope of security cameras catching the offender. Ebert's idea of security was a lock on the door. Oak Grove didn't require much else, unless someone took up masochism as a hobby. *Probably some kids messing with an out-of-town car.*

"What?" Confusion turned to disbelief. She

dashed around the car. "Are you fucking kidding me right now? Is this even real life?" She raked her hand through her hair and stared down the street like she expected someone with a guilty sign to step out from behind the nearest pickup. "I don't... Why would somebody... Who does this? Seriously?" Her voice caught, and then a soft stream of curses continued under her breath. Joker supposed he couldn't talk. Not like he qualified as innocent of wrecking other people's shit. *But Ashlyn?* He watched her face—paler now than moments before—and put his hand on her shoulder. *Please, don't cry.* He let his grip tighten.

"Hey, it's not that bad."

She groaned and rubbed the back of her neck. "I guess ... I'll have to call my insurance. And Grandpa. Shit." He could almost see the dollar signs behind the tears gathering in her eyes.

"Don't worry. You've got friends with a body shop, remember? We'll get it handled, Sunshine."

Ashlyn blinked up at him. "That's practically a whole paint job, Joker. You can't." She shook her head. "Paying for groceries is one thing, but we're talking a lot more than a dinner."

"If you wait for the cast to come off, it'll give me something to work on now I don't have a bike to screw with. Any idea who would have done this?"

She fixed her eyes on the taillight. "I can't think of anybody."

He could have sworn her voice changed. *Maybe Grim's right and I'm getting paranoid.* His brows furrowed. People didn't normally resort to keying cars if they were just miffed. *And I still don't know what brought her here in the first place.*

Something heavy settled in the pit of his stomach. Joker's eyes stayed steady on Ash while they got into the car. *Or how long she's going to stay...* On the other hand, Grim's initial searches hadn't turned up anything more than speeding tickets and a car wreck. Still, he couldn't ignore the way her chipped nails dug into her arms as she walked around towards the driver's side. She slumped into the driver's seat and closed her door softly, like it might break itself, too, if she jostled it.

Getting into the car—carefully, after the last two weeks of practice—he settled into the undersize seat and caught her slender wrist before she could hit the ignition. "Maybe it ain't even about you? Tilden's a name around here. I know he's been out of the game a while, but your Grandpa was a pit bull in the courtroom..."

"But wouldn't they just key *his* car? Maybe I can ask him that anyway," she muttered. He wondered if she realized she was talking out loud. "He might help me pay for it." She caught her lip again. "Fuck. No. No, it's not worth that. I'll just ... see if Karli can get me a slot in that other bar she works at. You'd give me a reference, wouldn't you?"

"I would," he said, his brow rising, asking a silent question she didn't catch because her eyes were fixed out on some horizon way past the parking lot. *And how to say it out loud without pissing her off?* "What's wrong with asking him?" He expected her to deflect with another question, but after a long heartbeat, her eyes flickered his direction and her shoulders lowered.

"He'll want to know why I don't use the trust, or a credit card, and Mom froze all of those. Then he'll fight with Mom. Mom will offer to unfreeze it, if I just do what she wants. Then Grandpa says she's being reasonable, why don't I just act reasonable, too, and I end up back..." Ash's quiet voice trailed off. This time her teeth sank into her lower lip so hard he almost put a hand on her chin to keep her from drawing blood.

Back? Back where? Back home? He wanted to ask—wanted to keep prying into a life he had no business prying into. People's lives were their own unless it somehow affected the club. Hers didn't. But the more he didn't know, the more he needed to.

"Baby?" The prompt startled her out of whatever she'd slid into.

"It's an old routine. I don't want to dance for her this time."

"What does she want you to do?" His hand found its way to her shoulder, resting beside the purple shirt strap. He didn't remember reaching for her. Beneath his fingers, her shoulder trembled ever so slightly.

"You'll laugh if I tell you." Ashlyn's head moved to the side, and she went still before putting her hand over his. He felt the touch like a brand.

"I wouldn't. I pretty much never laugh."

"You do. All the time." She couldn't meet his eyes. Her hand fell away from his.

"I don't." Joker clenched his jaw. *Unless you're around.* "I wouldn't laugh *at* you, Ash."

"It's nothing," she said with a heart-wrenching quaver. "Poor little rich girl. Mom wants me in grad school, interning with one of her friends, with Matt's ring back on. I'm supposed to beg for his forgiveness, get the wedding date set... I even sound like a pathetic brat, don't I?"

"No," he answered. "You sound like someone who wants their freedom."

Ash nodded without looking at him. "Anyway. That's why I'm broke. At least I've done it before, and this time I got a job. If it wasn't—if you hadn't let me work for you, I'd already be picking out dresses. Thank you, Joker. The job, helping me cook and stuff..."

He gave her shoulder a squeeze and let go, but he

watched her more closely. *Done this before?* But she was already drawing away, not a good moment to push. "I'm the one who should be thanking you. Keeping my grouchy ass company? Dealing with my moods? I ain't easy to get along with. I make no bones about that, but you've been there for me and you don't have to be so I'm here for you, too."

Ash's face crumpled into a sob that she hid behind her hands. Joker's guts twisted. *Fuck. How do I... Shit, shit, shit!* He half turned, ignoring the way his body rebelled against the movement, and he got his arm around her bowed shoulders, pulling her in for an awkward hug. He didn't know what else to do except hold her and wish his arm was free to do more. "It's okay. Honey, it's all right."

"I-I'm sorry. I didn't mean to unload on you. L-look at me, trying to do all this self-sufficiency crap, and I just end up w-whining. F-feel free to shoot me. Still better than ... crawling home..."

"Being self-sufficient doesn't mean you never freak out. Baby, look at me. I've unloaded on you plenty. All the PT sessions, everything, and you never once held that shit against me, did you? Please, sweetheart? You *can* talk to me. I promise I ain't here to judge you. Let me help."

"You h-have helped. So much. I just..." Despite the uncomfortable angles, several seconds slid by before she coughed and straightened up, easing his arm back across the console, though her hand lingered on his wrist. "You've got a lot of people who lean on you, Joker. I don't want to add on the weight. You've given me a job and having friends here ... it's made the world seem way less empty. I'm never going to forget that."

Sounds like a goodbye. Fuck that. "Then you should know I don't mind being leaned on. I *want* to be here for you. I'll do whatever I can to help you with the car and anything else you need. Someone told me that's what friends do for each other. They help."

"No fair turning my hippy-dippy speeches around on me." She laughed through the sniffles and scrunched her nose. "You're supposed to be so out of it after PT you don't remember exact phrases, damn it. I bet you even recite back what people say to you during sex."

Joker sat back in his seat and let his eyes close for a second. *Engine numbers. How to assemble an M-16. Anything* but Ashlyn's husky voice begging for him to fulfill her every fantasy.

"Only if they request it."

"Always polite." She flipped the visor down, wiping blurry eyeliner out from under her eyes. "It's okay. Everything's fine. I'll pick up extra hours someplace. Plenty of dive bars around, right?"

His hand flexed on his thigh. He wanted to wipe her tears, not let her walk into a bar full of strangers on her own. "I'll talk to Dragon and Karli. If you're going to work in a bar, let's try to keep it one where they respect women." *And no one will get any ideas about groping the new, sexy-as-hell little bartender.*

"You worried about my honor, Joker? Guess chivalry isn't quite dead after all." She let out a shaky breath and shifted the Miata into drive. "We could go get ice cream, if you want. Discuss your concerns about worker safety in local establishments."

He chuckled. "Let's go, sweetheart."

Chapter Six: May 28

Joker
Ravenwood

By Saturday, Memorial Weekend hit full swing. The previous night's party had ended early, with only a few brothers crashing in Tree's spare rooms and the clubhouse before the club went on the day's ride. Joker stayed behind with the Prospects, Ice, and a couple others to oversee clean-up of the clubhouse and compound: hedges trimmed, fences touched up with paint and a couple new boards, everything down to the toilets washed and shined. This was everyone's home from time to time, and had to be treated as such. And Prospects had to prove themselves willing to help.

Megan and Hailey showed up to take the sheets from the back bedrooms—used by the Nomads and occasionally local brothers—to the laundry. Joker took special amusement in making his sponsored Prospect, Case, fix the beds and sheets after the girls brought them back. Next time bed duty would look like fun, when the kid would be cleaning the urinals. Despite a solid stream of bellyaching, the clubhouse was clean before the first riders came back, and the party kicked off.

Soon enough, the club was back and the sun sinking over the horizon. Joker lounged next to the crackling bonfire with a beer in his hand while Ashlyn and Grim roasted marshmallows and fought off a thieving Ice. Ash spun away from the big guy with a triumphant shriek, marshmallow and chocolate smeared across her left hand and right cheek, brandishing a sleeve of graham crackers like a weapon until she'd skipped back far enough for Grim to jump in. Laughing at their antics, Joker sent Case for a fresh round of beers while Hailey and Grease broke up the wrestling match. Grim and Ice were already yelling about "that time at state finals".

Dragon seized his opportunity and shut everyone up by launching into some story Joker didn't listen to because Ashlyn sat down on the arm of his chair, putting her chest at eye level. He forced himself to stare into the flames. *Do not go there, man. Not yet. When the casts come off and the Heathens are finished, I'll figure it out.* A promise he'd repeated a lot recently.

"Sure. If you live in the *Dukes of Hazzard*," Ashlyn giggled in reply to something. The sound dragged Joker's reluctant gaze back to her. She wore tiny jean shorts and a white hippy-girl top, her blonde hair braided in some kind of halo around her head. *Christmas Angel at Woodstock,* he thought with a smile. *She'd be fucking hysterical at Sturgiss.*

"All right, what the hell's that?" Dragon scowled.

"What's... Oh." Ash's voice trailed off as a dull, motorized growl filtered through the noise around them. Bikes. Up the road. Joker flashed through the faces and headcounts for the day. They usually had a couple stragglers running errands, but that was way too loud.

The rumble grew into thunder. *Dad never said he called another charter in. Nomads, maybe?*

The bonfire's dancing shadows writhed across moving people, wreaking havoc on his vision as he searched the darkness beyond the fences. He reached down for a weapon that wasn't there—his Sig remained at the back of his chair, hanging under his cut. He edged forward in the seat, his good foot braced so he could stand. His cup tumbled over, the Coke soaking into the grass while he wrestled himself upright.

All around, other Crows turned to the noise. Guns of various makes and models appeared in a few hands, but most conversations continued and the more inebriated guys and non-members remained unfazed. Grim moved to Joker's side, hand already under his vest. Dragon stood up, posture far more alert. He nodded at Joker and strode back to the clubhouse. Joker didn't have to ask to know the sergeant was looking for his dad.

"Trouble!" A sentry yelled from the farthest position.

"Wait here," Grim muttered before winding his way through people on his way to the fence that hid the terrace from the outer road—the sentry positions along it would show him the roadway. Headlights dawned over the hill outside. Three steps from the fence, Grim stopped, turning toward the clubhouse, but it was too late. The bikes were on them. And something flared in the road.

Shrieking laughter sharpened, morphing from joy to fear between one heartbeat and the next. Hysteria became panic and the sound of breaking glass. Male shouts, yells of incoherent fury and the drumbeat of running feet, rushing bodies, revving bikes all crowded the night as a yellow light flew over the fence. *A firework or a burning torch?* The object crashed into the paving stones by the firepit and flames spilled out, racing across the ground as the bonfire shot up into the sky. *Molotov.*

Shit.

Joker shoved Ash backward, pivoting on his good leg and using the crutch to take an oversize hop-step before falling to his working knee. Ashlyn hit the ground with a startled scream, but she was angled behind him, he hoped far enough. He drew his Sig from the back of his seat and took aim at the fence while people rushed the opposite way, further into the compound. The area between him and the perimeter cleared while his brothers marshaled their weapons and Grim ran for the fire extinguisher on the south wall. Joker kept his eyes trained on the fence while Grim sprayed down the edge of the bonfire and the first Molotov's flames.

"Ash, stay down!" He'd meant to order her to the clubhouse, but there wasn't time. Gunshots from above screamed a call to action, and people dropped behind cover. Boots thundered on the ground, men shouted as they mobilized... He started to get up, but the cast caught the ground with a hollow thud, trapping him on his right knee. He cursed, his stomach writhing and hands shaking as he fought to keep the gun level. *I will not let this control me.*

"What the fuck is that?" Ashlyn's shuddered question bit right through what calm he'd scraped together. She'd landed far too close to the smoldering fire, with a hand on her ankle. He set the gun down and reached for her. Ignoring her whimpered protest, he dragged her toward him as another flaming bottle arced overhead.

The stench of melting plastic blossomed, one of the lawn chairs going up in smoke and toxic fumes. Joker tightened his hold on Ashlyn—instead of fighting, now she scrambled for him.

"You hurt?" Joker kicked his chair to the side with his cast-bound leg so it stayed between them and the road. Ashlyn didn't answer or look away from the fence line. "Hey! You hurt?" He shook her.

"Not—"

Gunshots cut her off. Some of the Crows were out of the main compound, up by the wall and on the roof, shooting over the fence. Considering the training of the men on that roof, he didn't doubt a few Heathens were bleeding in their buddies' arms, but that didn't erase the danger to the rest of the compound. Joker's good arm wrapped around Ashlyn, and he pushed her down, letting himself fall over her—the cast kept him from doing much else while the return volleys deafened them.

Fucking casts. Fucking Heathens. Light them all up. Let the devil sort the assholes out.

"Keep down, you two." Grim crouched next to them as he spoke, shoving the table over. He tilted it so the wooden top blocked them from the fence—even added to the chair it was shit protection, but if the bullets hit the fence first, it might take the worst of the heat.

Better than nothing, Joker thought with a dark look at his best friend. Ashlyn curled up under him, her breaths becoming little more than an unsteady puff of warmth on his chest. She cringed with each shot while he kept still as possible. *Just don't start screaming, sweetheart…*

The gunfire stopped. Joker counted to ten to be sure before disengaging his arm from Ash. He sat up and scanned their surroundings, pressing her back to the ground until he was sure the danger had passed. Starlight and headlights filtered through a few new holes in the perimeter. Smoke billowed from the far side of the clubhouse. Screams, yells, and victorious howling echoed over it all, but no more shots. Ashlyn pushed his hand off her midriff and scrambled up to stare at his sling.

"Are you…" She touched his arm. He caught her wrist and squeezed.

"I'm fine. You?" At her nod, he raised his voice. "Grim?"

"Pissed as fuck," Grim answered, already on his feet and stalking around the table. "Looks like I'm not alone there."

Tree's booming voice arrived a few moments later over the roar of revved engines and retreating bikes. "Hell of a party, son."

Dragon, Frog, and a couple others walked in Tree's wake, but Joker watched his bright-eyed father.

"Reminds me of my twenties," he answered as he picked up his Sig and checked the safety. Grim helped him stand while his father watched his balance like an Olympic judge. *Of all the goddamned times to be laid up...*

With Joker settled, Grim got Ashlyn up and dusted off her back while she watched them all in quiet horror. The white, flowing top looked exactly like she'd been rolling around in the dirt, and pieces of blonde hair had escaped her braids to fall haphazardly around her pale face. *At least she's not crying.*

Storm Crows trickled toward the wall or down from the rooftop sniper positions. Those attendees who'd hidden poked their heads up to survey the chaos while a handful of Prospects and members took blankets and extinguishers to the two remaining fires in the yard. Someone called for a medic, and Booboo lumbered out the door toward the yells.

"Get my crutch." Joker pointed Frog to where it lay in the grass, barely two feet from a scorch mark. "I think you should find Megan," he told Ashlyn.

"Good idea," Grim agreed. He took the crutch from Frog and helped Joker check its adjustment. Ashlyn nodded but didn't move. Her dirt-smudged right hand rubbed her left wrist until Joker put his hand over it. He tried not to meet her eyes. If she kept looking like that, he'd forget a whole lot of shit he needed to do right the fuck now. *Soon*, he promised himself.

"She's in the clubhouse. Frog, help her find Legs." Tree barked the order without waiting for Frog or Ashlyn to comply before moving off to yell at someone else about the smoldering chairs.

"Here, honey." Frog reached for Ash. Joker tried

not to notice that she reached back.

"*Joker*! Ohmigod!" Ariel streaked toward them in a blur of dark hair and heavy floral perfume, knocking Ashlyn into Frog's side hard enough that Joker heard the contact. Ariel threw her arms around him, blind to the damage in her wake. Her body pressed close, warm and familiar, yet Joker's gaze hung on Ashlyn disentangling from the Prospect. Frog still had a hand on her back.

Joker hugged Ariel with his good arm, reassuring her he was fine while his father rejoined Ash and Frog. *She's having trouble with her ankle.* Frog's hand slid around her waist as she limped with him to the clubhouse. Joker's arm tightened on Ariel.

"Where the hell were you? What happened?" Ariel's spiked tone pulled him back to his immediate surroundings as she laid into Grim, who scratched his cheek and leaned his weight onto one foot in a deliberately nonchalant pose.

"Don't you have somewhere else you need to be?" Grim's eyes glinted in the uncertain light.

"The only place I need to be is right here! Where you *should* have been."

Grim's eyes rolled. "Run along, little girl, and hide under your covers. If there's room under them."

"Don't you dare," Ariel spat. "I was helping tend bar. I thought you were keeping an eye on your VP." Grim's face twisted, but the voice answering her accusation didn't come from him.

"Ariel." The iron in Tree's eyes betrayed his slow, easy paces. "Enough."

Joker looked over Ariel's head at his father and let go of her to holster the pistol under his cut. He nodded toward the fence. "I'd say that's the declaration we were waiting for."

"Or retaliation. Come on, VP. We're going to

Church. Grim, nobody leaves alone. Get it done."

Ariel's full lips pouted, but she pressed close to Joker. "You need anything, hon? I can have it waiting when you get done." Her voice sounded baby-soft now, but her luscious pink mouth and perfectly lined gray eyes inspired little more than an exhausted ache in his leg.

"Thanks, babe. I'm good." He braced his hand on the crutch before hobbling after his father. "I'll text you later," he added over his shoulder.

Grim joined Joker but turned back to Ariel. "Go home and grab a shower, Ari. I can smell the desperation from here."

"Give her a break," Joker said quietly. Grim rolled his eyes again.

"When she earns it."

****

Ashlyn

"There you are!" Panic still laced Megan's voice as she yanked Ash into a hug. "Are you all right?"

"Yeah." The clubhouse interior had transfigured into a safe-haven at some point in the last eternity-long half hour, but she clung to Megan as the most familiar face in a sea of crazy. "I'm fine. Does … does this happen a lot here?"

While others seemed as shaken up as Ash felt, many Crows sauntered through the clubhouse without any apparent concern—even the handful sporting bloody bandages. Ash's eyes caught on Joker's Prospect, Case, chatting up a wide-eyed brunette while Hailey wrapped a white bandage around his bleeding hand. *Maybe it's a bar fight, maybe it's fucking warfare! They should stick that on their napkins.*

"Not so much," Megan admitted. "Maybe in the bad old days. But not now."

She clutched Megan's arm and tried to hide from

her own thoughts while her grandfather's lectures on all the less-than-savory area history played in the back of her mind: old unions and the anti-union mine bosses, the Italians and the Irish, even farmers' feuds and religious strife from God knew when, the usual angry-rednecks-with-guns, the totally-not-Klans that still remembered the bad old days with whitewashed nostalgia. *Or idiots on meth. Never underestimate idiots on meth.* That cheerful idea drove her to look at the bar, where Frog and an unfamiliar biker passed a bottle between them. *Likelihood of convincing one of them to open a bottle of Jack?*

"It's weird…" Megan's attention flashed towards the back entrance a second before Grim came into Ash's line of sight. Whatever path he'd intended on, he veered to lay a hand on Megan's bare shoulder.

"You both good?" Grim's quiet voice sounded an octave lower than usual, and much rougher. Megan nodded but his hand lingered on her skin. Ashlyn kept watching Grim. *Come on, Buckaroo.* "Don't leave yet," he added. "I'll find somebody to take you home."

"That's not … you don't need to…"

Grim started walking before Megan finished her protest. She shook her head and pulled her phone from her black faux leather purse. Her fingers only stopped moving when Hailey walked up, towering over them both from her 5'10" height and extra four inches of heels.

"Do you have a safety pin?" Megan asked instead of greeting her best friend.

"Probably." Hailey dug into her purse—one of the "mom" breed that had enough room for a small kitchen sink and most of Lithuania. "Here." Sure enough, Hailey drew out a zippered make-up bag blazoned with the Clinique logo. A couple seconds' search inside produced a safety pin daisy-chain. Megan thanked her and grabbed it, turning her attention to the ripped side seam at the bottom of her blue tank top. The pins lent Megan's smeared makeup a post-apocalyptic punk look that blended beautifully with the general chaos.

Around them, wooden tables and old-style metal chairs lay overturned and forgotten—even the pool table rested on its side, with five guys struggling to right it. Ariel drifted toward the heroes, smiling and offering drinks. No matter what Joker said, Ariel Donarski didn't look or act anything like a random hookup. She swanned through tables and haphazard furniture, picking up bottles and debris with the unconcerned perfection of a model on a location shoot. She knew where everything went and who to talk to, where to put the trash and how to arrange the chairs. Even a gangland crime left her with little more than an artful smudge on her cheek. Ash put a hand up on her own falling-down braids and sighed.

The rising nausea is only adrenaline. Totally, entirely adrenaline...

"She's about a nightmare, huh?" Hailey said with a dry laugh. Where Ariel looked like a runway hit, Hailey had the 1980s-supermodel body, thin instead of waifish but with definite hips and a gorgeous rack—more Liv Tyler than Barbara Palvin. Megan sniffed and grabbed her cup off the table.

"She's insecure. It'll pass." Megan's pronouncement made Hailey laugh again.

"What's Ariel insecure about?" Ash asked. Her cousin shot her a look but ignored the question.

"Hails, use your magic Old Lady powers?" Megan suggested. "We need drinks."

Hailey walked off to collar Frog. She returned a minute later with a tray of shots and two open bottles of generic cola. After two hits of Jack Daniels, Ash checked Megan over, grinned, and pushed the left tank strap down before holding up her phone for a giggly joint selfie.

"The running eyeliner kinda makes you look like you're cosplaying a Grounder."

Megan slapped Ash's wrist and pulled her strap up. "Stop giving the brat shots. She's speaking Nerd."

"Like you're…" She trailed off with an exaggerated eye roll. There was no way to explain *The 100*. "Fine. Like you're auditioning for a part in *The Walking Dead*?" Surely even Megan watched that. *Hmm, Bikers and zombies? Daryl Dixon would fit right in.* The fantasy played in her head while Hailey and Megan fell into discussion of clean-up and the next week's schedule. Grim interrupted before Ash could quite work out how to talk Daryl into giving her crossbow lessons.

"Hey, ladies." He leaned on the table, his unnerving eyes solemn. "Hailey, Skull and Fluffy can run you and Lana home."

"Thank God. This blew my early night plans to hell," Hailey groaned and grabbed her bag.

"Text me!" Megan waved as Hailey rushed off, but didn't look up from fixing another newfound rip in her top. Neither did Grim, as it happened. Ashlyn watched him watching Megan. *Bet he'd give her crossbow lessons…*

"Legs, you and Blondie mind waiting a bit longer? We're short on guys, and Tree's gonna kill me if I send you out by yourself."

He'd called her that name before, now her mind was on it, but there'd been other names, too. Better ones, that weren't grossly generic. *I'm so beige, even other people can't make me sound cool. Wow, I need more shots. Or less? Nah, more is better.*

"I'm getting a drink. Meg, I think Grim wants to help you with your top," Ash chirped. She bounded to her feet, handing him the safety pin and sticking her tongue out before sashaying toward the bar—or the limping, tipsy version of sashaying, because her ankle wasn't drunk enough to forgive the twist she'd given it earlier. *Slow is ok,* she told herself. *Grim needs a couple minutes anyway.*

At the shiny, cherry-wood bar, a cheerful, older member named Two-Bit poured her a Jack and Coke and they fell into conversation. When she decided enough time passed, Ashlyn turned to look. Megan remained in the same spot, now playing on her phone, and Grim nowhere to be found. "Seriously? He just *left*?" She didn't realize she'd spoken until Two-Bit started laughing.

"Hon, it'll take a lot more than a few fire-bombs to get that brother's tongue loosened up."

"So, why use his tongue? Just lean in and kiss her. If she knocks his teeth out, at least he tried."

"No such option, baby girl." Two-Bit leaned on the bar, eying Megan before he looked toward the door Ashlyn recognized as leading to the back offices—where she assumed "Church" happened. "She was a brother's Old Lady."

"He got booted, didn't he? So how does that even count?"

Two-Bit's bulky shoulders rose in a shrug. "And her daddy was a member."

That bit of information knocked her between the eyes. "What?" Ash remembered her mother saying Megan's dad died in "a wreck", but the topic featured prominently on the familial List of Things-We-Don't-Discuss. But her dad being a Crow would explain Megan being at Tree's all the time when they were kids... *Why didn't I notice that before? I* am *the actual worst.*

"Mmhm," Two-Bit confirmed. "Her granddaddy was an Original, too. Like Joker's. Damn good men, both of 'em." He shook his head the way Grandpa did when the past tugged at his thoughts. "Come on, let's get you girls home. Me and Case are on duty to get you back to Legs' place."

Ash gave him a blank stare. "How? I'm drunk, and she's ... also drunk."

"I'll drive." Two-Bit put a hand out. "Come on, girly."

****

Joker

Joker clapped Dragon on the shoulder as he entered the sanctum before taking his usual spot by the head of the table. The others filtered in or roamed the room. Tommy and Tree bent over a ledger, whispering. Ice expounded his tale of heroism to Dragon—bodily shielding Hailey and one of the club girls from flying glass and terrible flames—oblivious to the way Dragon's eyes continued scanning over the room and the hallway to the bar. Joker didn't bother engaging anyone; he was too on edge to talk. His father finally sat up straight and cleared his throat. Conversations ended.

"Close the door," Tree directed. Dragon complied, and the last sounds from the bar vanished, leaving uneasy silence. Tommy set his notebook on the table and clicked his pen to begin his task as secretary. On Tree's other side, Grease set a burner phone in front of him in case they needed to call up a chapter head. Geiger had his own folder of records and flipped it open for a last-second check. Ice, Blackie, Spider and Jingle occupied the remaining seats, leaving only Dragon's empty. Everyone kept a gun in front of them.

"So, the Heathens wanted to say hello," Grease announced, leaning over the arm of his chair. "Couple of the boys made their bikes as they ran 'em off. I sent Shade and Mud as tails."

Ice's pale eyes flashed as his lips split in a grin at the Road Captain's words. "'Bout time the cocksuckers stopped licking their own balls. I was starting to worry shit would stay boring."

"They have to do it today, though?" Spider sneered. "Fuckers got no standards."

"They knew we wouldn't be expecting it." Dragon still lurked by the door, but he pitched his voice low. "Are they trying to get us back for their bikes or are they finally claiming responsibility for your wreck, VP?" Tree shot him a look and motioned to the chair. The sergeant-at-arms exhaled but moved to obey.

Joker rubbed his cast under the table, offering a shrug instead of an opinion.

"Brandt's been fidgety lately," his father said. "No secret he wants our access to the I-67 corridor, and the river. And he's never liked me much." Tree's smile was a flash of white. "Can't imagine why."

Joker sighed. "So, another push for territory? Isn't he tired of losing?"

"Whatever it is, I just drained some capital into the sheriff's department to shut this shit up." Geiger grunted, an exasperated sign of large numbers vanishing from his carefully tallied accounts. "We gotta wait for another shipment before we do anything expensive." He shot a look at Joker and Tree. "If we want to keep the reserves healthy."

"That gives Grim and me some time to dig," Spider said. He and Grim made up the IT section of the national charter. "We gotta know what the fuck's going on up north before we roll out."

Tree nodded. "Pulling this bullshit means that they've got a reason to be so damned sure of themselves. Brandt's good at a lot of things, but keeping anything quiet never made the list."

"Get Grim on his computer," Tommy said, tapping a finger on the table. "Fluff and I can poke around on the north side of Hollow. Those tweaker bitches always cross the line to go party with the Heathens. They might know something."

Joker's scowl remained. "The Heathens don't have the weight to take us on again. Who's backing him?"

"What if they're not after territory?" Dragon threw out. "What if it's something else?"

"We'll find it out when we're looking under the rocks the next few days," Tree answered with an easy shrug. "I'm less worried about what he wants than the heat he thinks he can bring. We need to keep shit wrapped tight—I don't want the new buyers spooking. But if we can't do quiet, we can damn well make a good show of force."

"Why don't we just target Kaminski?" Grease asked, putting his elbows on the table. "They hit our VP, we hit theirs. Fair game, brothers. He goes to Jezebel's every night and gets himself shit faced. Let's beat the dogshit out of his worthless ass when he shows."

"There's an idea." Joker finally smiled. The decaying strip-tease joint lay well north of Star Hollow, but the women working it had benefitted from many Storm Crow parties over the years. He could name at least one or two who'd turn over Kaminski in a heartbeat.

Tree leveled a hard look at his son. "Whatever we do, you aren't on the run." Their eyes met in identical glares. Joker felt the twitch in his temple.

"I'm not in the hospital anymore."

"And you aren't on a bike anymore either. You can't ride, you can't ride, son. There's time for you to break skulls when you get your bones back together."

Squaring off with his dad at the table would get

them in a mess nobody needed. *But goddamn, it would be just about worth the pain.*

Red and blue lights bathed the room, and the tension skyrocketed. Silence returned, and everyone reached for the guns, sliding them into holsters and under cuts.

"Thought you said you paid 'em, Geiger!" Blackie's protest broke the initial freeze, but earned him a snarl from the Treasurer.

"Fucking cops. Never can trust their sniveling asses. Sorry, Prez, it must be that goddamned deputy." Geiger slammed his books shut and stomped toward the far side of the room where a false-backed cabinet waited.

"Dragon, Grease, get the Nomads called in tonight. You head home, Joker. I'll deal with this," Tree said without missing a beat. Joker opened his mouth to argue but shut it when his dad's eyes narrowed. *Count back from ten. Don't lose your shit.*

"Anything I can do at all?" he asked as the others filed out. He'd get in the way with the cast and crutch if he tried to go with them. Tree studied him for a full five seconds before shaking his head. He walked out with Dragon and Tommy. *These casts come off, I may kick your ass, too, Dad.*

"Come on, brother. Let 'em feed the pigs. We'll grab a drink." Ice's hand landed on his right shoulder and squeezed. Joker nodded but couldn't speak past the sour knot in his stomach.

One more week as a cager. I've lasted out worse.

He followed Ice to the bar and took a cup of water rather than the straight vodka he wanted.

"Easy, man." Ice leaned on the bar next to Joker, eyeing the casts. "We've all been there. Hailey locked me in our damn room after that wreck last year. I tell you that?"

"I recall you bitching about something."

"Locked in and nagged to death. One of the drawbacks to keeping a woman around."

"One of them?" Resentment hung heavy in his voice; the water did nothing to wash it away, any more than it erased the image of Reagan's messy chestnut hair and big, red-rimmed honey eyes. Not that she'd cried when she left. He turned and snapped a finger at the Prospect tending bar. "Vodka."

"Sir?" Tyler slid a double shot of vodka to Joker with a shaky hand. Joker nodded and waved him off. *No point in socializing with the one who won't last the summer,* he decided.

"Hailey ain't so bad," Joker said after his first, grateful swallow of liquor. "You got one of the good ones."

"Hell yeah, I did. She even managed not to get hit by anything tonight. For a change." Ice shook his head. "Should've known she had shit luck when she shacked up with my sorry ass."

"Can't argue with that." Joker's humor faded into a warning glance at Tyler, who wilted back toward the other side of the bar.

"Actually, figured she'd have called when she got home tonight..." Ice pulled his phone from his pocket and frowned.

"Must be hard not to be the full-time center of her world."

Ice opened his mouth to answer, but his eyes shifted from Joker to something over Joker's left shoulder. The quick, light steps announced Ariel even before he turned. Her make-up had come through the fire and chaos mostly untouched. A faint smudge across her cheekbone only emphasized her sculpted features while inviting guys to imagine wiping it away. He wondered if she'd drawn it on.

"Joker, babe, I got the car around if you're ready to head out," Ariel cooed. She leaned in and kissed his cheek, allowing an incidental glimpse down her lopsided shirt—pink bra, gorgeous breasts. All on offer. "Grim's gonna see us at the house. He decided to follow Megan and her cousin home."

Joker glanced from her to Ice, and came to a decision. He set his elbow on the bar and stared at the flat screen on the wall behind it, where the Cardinals were locked in combat with somebody, bases loaded. He suspected Two-Bit had stopped taking cover long enough to pull a shelf in front of it when the shots started—the man had priorities and they all included Cardinals games.

"I'm gonna be here a while longer. Need to make sure Dad doesn't lose his shit with Schneider's new deputy." He swallowed some vodka and welcomed the burn. "Make sure one of the guys follows you back to town."

Ariel's jaw flexed, but she nodded. "Right. I should go check on Trish and some of the others. Text me." She kissed his cheek again before she hurried off. Ice watched her go and let out a low whistle.

"Brother, you *must* be banged up if that don't get you hard to go home."

"Yeah. Must be the Vicodin." Joker wiped at his cheek to erase any lingering lip prints.

"Uh huh." Ice's brows wagged, and Joker grunted. "Vicodin have pretty blonde hair and big green eyes these days?"

"I got nine more days with these casts, brother. And I'm keeping a list of who needs their asses beat."

"Nine days, you're gonna be busy with somebody's ass. And it ain't mine," Ice cackled. "Hey, Tyler! VP needs some more vodka."

Joker knew he should refuse, but the words didn't make it out. Instead he checked his phone. A text message waited.

Grim: @ **Legs place. Girls ok & eating magic brownies. U need a ride?**

The idea of an empty house didn't kindle the relief he expected. Joker frowned and added onto Ice's orders. "Double it. I want to get some fucking sleep tonight."

Chapter Seven: May 30

Joker
Ravenwood

Only bugs and crickets buzzed among the whining power tools and humming electronics. The guys' conversation usually drowned out the spring choir of insects and night birds, but tonight their exchanges came in terse whispers, silenced when the shifting breezes buried them all in the acrid scent of their charred clubhouse. Ice and Dragon concentrated on an old, blue Ford F-150, brought in a few days before. Jingle rolled under a '04 Chevy Monte Carlo while Case and Drifter dealt with tracking down the short circuit in a 2013 Ford Fiesta.

Working late hours on a holiday sucked, but they needed as much of the legitimate business as possible cleared away so they could use the bays for new shipments from their eastern contacts and outside charters. Joker kept an intermittent eye on the progress as he delivered batches of paperwork from the front office to his dad's back room lair. Tree didn't bother looking up from his screen, so Joker left the printouts on the desk and retreated.

The last documentation delivered, Joker slumped in his chair and stared at the invoice for a damage estimate on the new English teacher's ancient Crown Vic. Considering how best to phrase "total waste of time and money", he picked up a plastic fork and angled it into his cast toward an unreachable itch.

Fucking thing. That's about enough of this bullshit. He propped his good leg up on the desk and reached into his pocket. *What's a week or so ahead of schedule?* He drew out his favorite switchblade, flipped it open and pressed the knife to the plaster. Half an inch into the cut, heavy, running steps blew Joker's concentration. He swept his leg off the desk. The cast slammed into the floor and his whole leg reverberated, but he brought his hand up, blade out, drawing back for a throw. Grim stumbled through the door.

"Son of a bitch!" He slammed the knife onto the desk, gouging the wood instead of his best friend's torso. "Grim! Fucking knock!"

"Dude!" Grim waved a flash drive before dropping it next to the knife. "You don't even want to know how I got that shit, but who came through? I did. I came through. Me. Drinks on you tonight, sucker."

Joker snatched the drive. "That depends. What am I looking at?"

"Kaminski's personal hard drive."

Shit.

"*How* did you get this? *When* did you get this?"

"I said you don't want to know." Grim's face assumed a bland, dumb look he probably meant to be innocent.

"See, that's the thing. I don't," Joker growled. "But I have to. What did you do to get this? And will they find out you did it? Jesus, do they already know?"

"Don't see how, bro. None of them made it home last night. At least not the ones Brandt keeps close. Too busy rubbing their dicks over that bitch-ass stunt." His face contorted in revulsion. Memorial Day Weekend and a semi-public function: two taboos blown up with one set of Molotovs. "And this morning, Frog told me that they were all over at Huck's up on Braemer Road. One of their old ladies was talking about heading over to Odessa for that new bar opening."

Don't stab him. Joker drew his hand further from the knife to keep temptation at bay. *So what the fuck were they doing at Huck's? A group that big in our territory? Protection run? Meeting with suppliers?* They weren't supposed to be past the county line with cuts on. Technically Star Hollow's north side was a gray area because gas stations were getting harder to find in the boondocks, but it stayed gray by Storm Crow graces, and the Heathens were a long way from graces of any sort.

"All of them?"

"Well, a lot of them. Kaminski and a few others." Grim eyed the door. "Figured it was worth the shot, so I dropped in and gave the house a once over while he was out. The wife and kids were gone so…"

"So, you showed yourself in." Joker's voice stayed flat, but Grim lit up.

"You'll be happy about it later, man. I planted some tricks in his computer. Here on out, I know everything he does right down to his favorite porn site." He shrugged. "I admit, this batch's mostly mail. I gotta get to his phone for a real look—probably keeping the specifics over text or some shitty app, but I got into the charter emails. Vague, but they're moving something. And I'm betting they ain't supposed to be moving it through our county."

Joker rubbed his chin. *I need a goddamn drink.* "We already know they're moving something."

"No, listen to me." Grim put a hand up and shut the door before continuing: "With his computer comes the network. I can get to his tablet, and his phone in a few days. He's their VP, Nate. Whatever he looks up, whatever he sends out—if there are relay keys or locations on a website, we'll see it. I have his phone log, too, so we'll know what numbers to trace." He turned back to meet Joker's gaze with a reckless grin. "A few weeks reading their shitty code words, and I'll know all their pansy-ass moves."

"All right. You did good, brother," he admitted

with the ghost of a sigh. "You're absolutely certain nobody's going to catch on to this?"

"Positive, Joke-man. My hand to God, I left no sign." He even put up his hand in the Boy Scout pledge. Joker settled against the chair, ribs aching and thoughts turning.

"I'll take it to Tree. Any idea what the hell they were doing out there?"

"Frog said they were there for a while. Parked and talking. A few of their old ladies were along." Having the women with them should have meant it wasn't club business—but Brandt just fucked the club codes sideways. Without the rules of engagement, this fight got a whole lot bloodier. Joker nodded and picked up the flash drive again, turning it between his fingers.

"Go help Ice with Farmer Kotas' truck. Some kind of electrical gremlin—he's been chasing it all day."

"Sure thing." Grim knocked his knuckles on the desk. "Oh, by the way, I think the girls are coming by the house. Ash texted about what to bring."

"You know I don't care."

"Don't you?"

Joker's glare could have frozen vodka. *One more week...*

He allowed Grim's retreat while he opened the drive. A cursory glance through the folders told him more than enough. He cursed under his breath: either Grim didn't check what part of Kaminski's shit he took, or decided to include a bonus because right near the top he found "Taxes 2009". He all but heard Ash arguing: *Who says that's a porn stash?* Joker smiled at that thought, but thinking too hard about Ashlyn and porn in the same sentence...

He ejected the drive and tucked it into his pocket. Getting to his feet took less effort than usual. *I'm getting used to crutches. Someone punch me.*

At Tree's office, he stopped by door and knocked. His father remained oblivious. Two more knocks also failed to raise a response. "Prez?" He called through. Nothing. "Hey, Boss?" Nothing. *Only one option.* Joker sighed. "Dad?"

"Huh? Come in."

Joker pushed the door open, and Tree made a wild, vaguely inviting gesture without looking up from the keyboard. His lips moved as he typed, not forming a single greeting to his son. A full minute passed before his fingers stopped dancing across the keyboard and he faced Joker, who took the cue.

"Talked to Grim. He's got some intel from Kaminski. Nothing earth shattering, but turns out we're not chasing our dicks. I think we need to get Booboo and Ice some back up. They can't follow them all the time, and we need to get eyes on this."

Tree folded his hands across his stomach and looked at a point above Joker's head. "From Kaminski?"

"Apparently, there's something you can put on a computer—some spyware thing. Grim got access to Kaminski's and lifted some files. Figured you or I could look at it closer tonight, see what kind of weird shit old Frank's into." Joker slid the drive out of his pocket and put it on the desk.

"I need to worry about this bug getting traced back to us?" Tree didn't sound concerned.

"I figure so long as the bastard doesn't have hidden cameras all over, we're good. But we'd know if he was that kind of crazy. He's not Brandt."

"All I care about is that when shit hits the fan, we're all protected. The details beyond that? I trust you to make the right call, son."

"And about getting more people on the recon

detail? You trust my call there?"

"Ice's the one you'll have to convince. Seems pretty sure that he and Booboo can do it all."

"Right."

"Do what you got to do, VP." Tree reached for the keyboard.

A familiar popping explosion froze Joker halfway to his feet. Until the second round. A thousand nightmares railed through Joker's head, but his body dove for cover on reflex, stumbling against the desk. Shouts and more shots echoed off the cement walls outside.

"God fucking damn those jackasses..." Tree seized the holstered Glock slung across his chair without missing a beat in his swearing. "Stay here!" With that single, snarled order, his dad sprinted out the door.

Joker stared after him, caught with his leg in the plaster trap, too clumsy to keep up and too pissed off not to try.

****

The handgun's grip imprinted itself on his palm. Three shots left. *What were the first ones?* Good questions. No answers sprang to mind. The training had taken over, and adrenaline kept him moving. He stood in a tide of shimmering glass shards, facing out the front of the building to the dark road. Holes dotted the opposite wall. The computer monitor he'd stared into earlier spat sparks and whirred its death throes, most of its left side gone. He pressed his back against the wall and peered out of the window. A head emerged from behind a car across the street. He lifted his gun, breathed out, aimed. Two shots, dead on. The person howled and fell back with a new hole in their shoulder.

Fucking cast. Should've taken his head off...

His father's commands boomed from the garage, dissolved to meaningless growls under the ringing in

Joker's ears. Another scream broke through. Someone down, two yards beyond the door. Not moving.

"Grim?" He took a step, but—again—the cast caught him. He pitched forward, accompanied by a tingling shower of glass from the last windowpane and a bullet whizzing through the space his chest had occupied half a second before.

Dragon loomed over him, returning fire before grabbing the back of his cut and hauling him away from the window. "Behind the desk. Now!"

Joker rolled up and lifted his gun to fire his last shot across the street.

"Quit wasting bullets! Get!" The handgun didn't have the distance—he knew it as well as Dragon. Engines roared and tires squealed as the two SUV's peeled out.

Run like cowards, die like cowards.

"They're leaving!" Ice called as he appeared from behind the Ford—now decorated with holes along the hood and windshield. "Tires! Aim at the fucking wheels!"

"Are you hit?" Dragon asked. When Joker didn't answer and instead tried to limp into the garage, Dragon pulled him back, stepping in until they stood nose to nose. "Hey. You hit, Nate?"

"No!" Joker growled. "Get the fuck off me." He shoved away from Dragon to reach Grim, who lay in the same position as when Joker spotted him moments— hours—ago. Ice knelt by his head with one hand on Grim's hair and blood smeared across his fingers.

Joker got down as well, his cast clunking on the cement. He scanned his friend for any further signs of trauma. Breathing regular, no other blood. Heart rate elevated but not erratic, the list scrolled in his head as he held onto Grim's wrist. "Grim? Ryan? Come on, talk to us."

Grim didn't answer.

"Stunned," Ice whispered. "Cut along the temple. No skull fracture I can find, might need an X-ray for that."

Didn't rule out a concussion but could mean he caught his head on the wall or something instead of a bullet. Joker let go of Grim's wrist, drew his hand back and slapped him hard across the cheek. That got a blink.

"I ... I-I'm fine..." Grim muttered, voice weak. His eyes darted from face to face before focusing out toward the bay doors and narrowing. He put a hand to his forehead and glared at the blood left on his fingers. "God fucking damn it!"

"Sit up. They missed your face, so don't freak out," Joker advised as Ice bent and slid his own arm under Grim's shoulders.

"Here." Blackie tugged a mostly clean rag from his belt and handed it off on his way by. Grim's hand trembled as he pressed it against his head.

"He'll be all right," Dragon said.

"Anybody else hurt?" Joker called to the room at large.

Case and Drifter staggered back into the garage with their guns out. He heard his dad and the others outside. Bullet holes peppered the walls, a few of the cars. The Crown Vic looked like a poster for a Kabul Travel Agency.

"You're knocked around yourself." Ice's quiet reminder won a snarl from Joker, but what could he say? *Ignore the casts and stitches and the fool I made of myself in the front office just now? Yeah. Right.*

"I'll get Tree." Dragon ruffled Joker's hair and walked away while Ice rose to his feet and hoisted Grim up by his arm. Joker stood as well, though far more clumsily. He followed them into the office where a row of chairs remained upright and strangely untouched along one wall. Ice let Grim collapse onto the end seat and Joker watched his friend's eyes—the lack of focus, the vacant stare.

"You're all right," he said quietly. "You're here. You're fine."

"Fine?" Grim dropped his hand to his lap, staring at the rag. It wasn't as red as Joker expected, but Grim's mouth twisted. He tossed it away. "I'm a lot of things, Nate, but I sure as fuck ain't fine! Do you see *this*?" He pointed to his temple. "That was a fucking bullet. Half an inch over and you'd be mopping up my goddamn brain. Don't fucking tell me I'm fine!"

Joker sighed and checked the pistol he'd shoved in his belt, inspecting the chamber. "All right, man. I get it. Come on. Let's get you a drink."

"I don't want a fucking drink," Grim spat. "I want to end those motherfuckers. They just drove the fuck away! We're gonna sit here and let them?" He shook his head and looked down at the floor between their feet. "I want to see my daughter." That part came out a lot quieter.

"Deep breaths, get yourself centered." His eyes cut sidelong toward Grim and away. "We'll go see her." *With any luck, a stray bullet landed in your ex's head. But I shouldn't be hopeful.*

Sirens wailed in the distance just as Tree stormed through the bullet-riddled front door. Joker caught his dad's eyes, but Tree's steps didn't slow. "Balls to the walls, boys. Neighbors called in the cops." Tree hissed the words.

"It's only the sheriff." Spider hurried to keep up with Tree's longer strides. "You got that under control, Prez." He stopped to wipe some flaked paint off his cut and stared at Grim and Joker. "Shit, G, you look like you need a drink."

"So I've been told," Grim spat.

Whatever conversation that sparked, Joker didn't hear; his eyes fixed on the compound's entry. The car pulling into the lot outside bore the Pharaoh County sheriff's logo, but it wasn't Eldon Schneider who climbed out and ambled toward the garage's main bay.

Joker limped toward Tree and the newcomer as fast as he could. Deputy Zack Gebbert still looked like the Marine he'd been until an IED ended his military career—Tree's similar history turned the pair explosive, so leaving them alone in conversation ended in disaster the club didn't need tonight. And right now, Zack stared at the garage like a man planning to make a fuck-up into a shit sandwich.

"You all that's comin'?" Joker called to Zack.

"I'm all they can afford, Wronski. Unless you got somebody bleedin' in there."

"Just some kids pulling a prank." Tree crossed his arms as he spoke. Zack pointed toward the garage's shattered front windows.

"Lot of bullet holes for some brats out to prove their balls dropped."

"Nobody said they weren't vicious little shits."

"Uh huh. You want a report filed?" Zack craned his neck to see the bullet-speckled car in the second bay over Joker's shoulder. "You're gonna be doing a ton of cover-ups for free on those cars."

"We'll figure it out, Zack," Joker said, rather than letting his father's patience get much thinner. "Sorry they pulled you off your rounds. Can we get you some coffee or anything?"

The deputy's dark eyes met Joker's. "No, I think you got plenty to get done around here as it is." Zack hooked his thumb in his belt loop. "Try to keep the noise down, will you? Old Mrs. Kiehlman is about to have a conniption over these extra ... fireworks."

"No problem, deputy." Joker smiled. "I'll see you for breakfast at Tim's on Thursday. Tell you all about it." *Time for the monthly cash hand off to the local authorities anyway.* Zack nodded and smiled before he climbed back into the car and drove off.

"You and Grim head out, too." Tree put a hand on Joker's arm. "I'll get the guys cleaning up this mess tonight." Joker nodded. The dismissal stung, but Grim wasn't in any shape to help, and with one arm working, Joker would be more useful in watching him than working on a car.

****

Grim put his Nissan into park at the first stop sign. He hunched over the steering wheel, shoulders tense and breathing heavy. Joker counted to five before he spoke.

"Ryan?"

"What the fuck, man?" Grim's face stayed buried on his forearm, muffling the words. "I've seen plenty of shit. All the fights, hospital visits... Fuck, even yesterday. But for some goddamned reason, this time, all I can think..."

"I know." He didn't need to hear what Grim thought of. His kid, or his ex-wife, or Megan. He'd heard all the versions of those stories after other battles, from other mouths. "It ... gets quieter. In your head. Kinda numb. Breathe through it."

Grim's head rose. His pained, disbelieving eyes searched Joker's in the dim light. "How long does that take? How many bullets?"

"I don't..."

"No, come on! How many times did we almost

bury you before you stopped giving a shit? That's what this is, isn't it? You don't freak out because you don't care anymore." Joker's hand dropped from his friend's shoulder, and he withdrew to his side of the car. Waited. "I'm sorry." Grim exhaled, rubbing the heel of his right hand against his eyes. "Dick question. I … I'm being a fucking pansy-ass prick." He took a deep breath. "I'll see Diana in the morning. She's probably sleeping anyway."

So he hasn't totally lost his shit. Good. Joker nodded.

Grim shifted the car into gear. They drove in silence until Grim's phone buzzed. He glanced down at the screen, then held it out to Joker. "Shit. I forgot the girls are waiting. Just send 'em home… But tell Ash to leave the booze in the garage. I could use it."

Ash: **So much booze! You earned it!**

He didn't bother scrolling up to see the earlier messages. His thoughts lingered on the house and the hours of silence if he and Grim were left to their own devices, sitting in a dark room. Thinking. "No," he said. "Stop in at Huck's and we can grab some Coke."

Grim's head turned, but in the darkness Joker didn't see his expression, only the answering nod.

****

Several hours later

"Should I wake her up?" Ashlyn spoke just loud enough to be heard over the credits of some impossibly stupid fantasy movie. He couldn't even remember what they'd picked. Joker tore his eyes away from the TV to follow her question—Grim had passed out upright, bandage-wrapped head slumped back on the futon, his leg serving as a pillow for a sleeping Megan.

"Nah." He rolled his shoulders to get himself moving. His body felt like lead. *So this is what old bastards feel like; your aches get aches.*

Ashlyn's blue pajama pants rustled as she uncurled herself from Grim's recliner and set her rocket-shaped cup of rum and Coke on the cement blocks. "I think I'm good to drive to Megan's. I'll head out." Her words were softened, just this side of slurred. He grunted.

"You are not. Stick around." He smiled. Ashlyn only stared at him. The light softened and shadowed her features, but a frown line showed on her brow as she pushed her hair away from her face. He flexed his hand against his cast. *Whatever she's about to say, I ain't gonna like it.* "Go on back to the bedroom."

"I'm not taking your bed, Joker."

"Ryan's is open, too. It don't matter."

"Or Grim's. You've both had a terrible night and you need to get some sleep."

He relaxed while she tugged at the hem of her black t-shirt—a flimsy thing that continually slid off her right shoulder and always revealed a hint of her berry-red bra. He rubbed his neck and looked away. It didn't help. He shook his head. "The bed's free, baby. I won't be sleeping."

"Why not?" Her brows drew closer together. "Do you need something? I can—"

"Just wired." He settled further into the chair and watched her pull the shirt up her shoulder.

"Then I'll stay up with you."

"No. One of us ought to get some sleep."

"Do you…" Her voice faltered. She coughed. "Does it help … if someone is with you? I mean. In the bed. The room. N-not anything else. Just, um. There, you know? Some people relax easier that way. I'll share with you. If it would help."

Am I hallucinating? He couldn't help the blank stare on his face. He'd had girls ask him into bed but never in that tone of voice.

"Ash, that isn't…" *how I want you in my bed.* He shut his mouth on that near-disaster.

"I trust you," Ashlyn continued. *Thank-fucking-God she can't read minds.* "And I think you should lay down. At least try it?" Her voice sounded like she might cry. "I just … you need to rest, Joker. Please?"

He squinted, trying to read her. *Is she … scared? Of me, or did tonight freak her out? Maybe she doesn't ask men into bed that often.* He looked back at the empty TV screen. *What movie did we even watch?* His memory shorted out right at Ashlyn suggesting he get into bed with her. *And one of these days she's going to use my actual damn name, right?*

"All right." His voice sounded distant even to him. "Worth a try, I guess." He braced his weight on his good arm and pushed himself to his feet, half turning to hold his hand out for her. She took it. He expected her to let go once she found her balance, but those slender fingers remained wrapped around his. And she didn't start for the bedroom.

"You can talk about it if you need to." Her voice was stronger, and he saw the faintest glimmer of a smile on her lips. "Grandpa probably has some nondisclosure agreements laying around. I can sign one."

He laughed around the hollow pit in his guts and nudged her toward the hallway. "Never been good at putting shit into words. Even writing them down doesn't make any sense." She squeezed his hand and stopped walking.

What did I say wrong now? He turned to her, bracing for whatever was about to hit him, but slender arms slid around his waist and a soft form pressed against him. His breath stopped. Thoughts spinning around a proverbial drain, he set his arm around her shoulders with the grip of a man holding spun glass.

"You'll be okay," Ash whispered. His skin was tight, hot where her breath warmed his chest. "The right words can take a long time to find. I'm here either way, Joker." She stepped back, leaving him to sort through … everything. Not to mention the lump in his throat.

"Careful, baby. I may take you up on that."

She smiled and tugged him along with her into the bedroom—an image he expected to bank on for a while. "Let's go sleep. Circles under your eyes make you look old."

"Thanks," he muttered before closing the door behind them. Sleep might be a pointless chase, but lying next to her meant he knew where she was. That seemed like a good thing in the moment. A distraction from the familiar, creeping knot in his belly.

He lumbered into the bed, watching Ashlyn slide in under his covers and stretch like a kitten before curling up on the far side. Not that a full-size mattress gave much room for distance. Once he lay down, her body grazed his with the slightest movement. He breathed deep, recognizing her vanilla perfume. *Tonight might be the only time I don't mind being too lazy to buy a new bed.* She whispered good night, and he answered her in kind before settling onto the pillow to stare up at the ceiling.

Despite his doubts, exhaustion slammed his eyes closed and dragged him into his dreams. The world turned to darkness and sand while gunfire rained down. Men groaned and raged and sometimes wept in a dozen languages. Bright red blood spread across a concrete floor and blackened sand. Smoke choked the air. Bile rose as his stomach became a writhing snake-pile. He raised the gun, but ghost-light fingertips touched his shirt instead of his rifle's barrel. He jerked back, fighting for breath.

"Joker?"

The silky voice softened, and the hand lay flat on his chest. He seized the attacker's puny wrist. *Fuckers and their kid fighters...*

"Nate? Nate, wake up."

Ash. He was in bed with Ashlyn, in his own house. He bit his lip and turned his head into the pillow, releasing her wrist in the same instant. *"Don't ... I can't go..."* Hard to say who those words were meant for. Her? His goddamn useless head? His eyes burned.

"You aren't going anywhere. You're right here." She stroked his neck beside his pulse. "See?"

"Yeah." When he turned back, his nose brushed against hers. She'd gotten so much closer.

"I'm glad you're here." Her satin fingertips graced his jaw.

His hand shook, but he laid it over hers and pressed a chaste kiss to her lips. Just to feel something— to think of anything but the place his mind kept sliding into. She didn't pull away. Ashlyn squeezed his hand before she twisted hers and changed her grip so their fingers intertwined.

"So. Very. Glad." Their lips touched again with every word.

She's drunk.

He put their linked hands on her hip and edged closer. The shadows hid most of her features, but her green eyes gleamed. He filled in the rest from memories: the pink cheeks from the bonfire party, the smile she gave him when he told her she was beautiful. Letting out a ragged breath, he leaned in, his tongue gently tracing the line between her lips. Her mouth opened. Then she moaned, and a rush of heat arrowed right to his dick, evaporating all good intentions. Until Ash's leg bumped his cast instead of his hard-on. *That has got to go...*

She pulled her head back and scooted away, leaving a cold, air-conditioned void. *Back to reality.*

"Joker?" Her voice held a tone he didn't like. "Oh my God, I'm sorry. I'm so sorry." He reached for her arm, but Ash kept talking. "I didn't mean to do that. You— I'm so drunk. And you're drunk. And hurt. And you had a really, really, really bad day. And I'm not that bitch who does that. This…" She put a hand over her face.

Bless drunk logic.

He pulled her hand from her eyes and brought her knuckles to his lips. "It's all right." Guilt gnawed at him, burrowing deeper when she laid her palm against his cheek. "I kissed you first."

She graced that with a full two seconds' thought. "You have more of an excuse." Ash sighed and flopped onto her back. "I won't be that girl who uses somebody's—I don't know, moment of weakness or whatever. Friends don't do that."

This friend crap needs to be addressed. Soon. And sober. Joker closed his eyes, hoping she didn't see his frown. *Might as well be honest.* "I think about kissing you a lot, sweetheart."

"That's because you're a straight boy and I'm a girl." Ashlyn patted shoulder and sat up. "I need some water." She wobbled as she got out of the bed and thumped against the wall.

"Careful." He opened his eyes to check her progress and won a glimpse of her bare midriff before she pulled down her t-shirt. She made a face and continued along her uneven path. He relaxed into the pillow as best he could, trying to ignore the throb between his legs and the way her pants clung to her ass. *God damn it. Down, boy. Tonight is not the time.* "You sure you don't want me to go?"

"No. You're still broken."
Baby, you have no idea.

Chapter Eight: June 1

Ashlyn
Ravenwood

Amber and spices, and hints of metallic smoke suffused Joker's pillows. The scent chased her through steamy, disorienting dreams until she woke up. In his bed. In his room. A teensy bit drunk. And maybe a lot distracted by a warm ache between her legs and memories of his lips on hers and his hand sliding over her... *Damn it, I am so not doing this.*

Ash flung herself upright and stared at the bed. No Joker. She kept suspicious eyes on the bathroom for a minute, but no sounds of life emerged. *Right. I'm alone. Of course. Good.* She fell back into the bed and dragged the black cotton sheet over her head. *Life was easier when boys smelled like sweat and Axe body spray.*

"Hey, sleeping beauty. Want breakfast?" Megan's chirpy, cheerful voice filtered through the black cover, interrupting the morbid dirge Ash was composing for her own poor life choices.

If I hit her with a brick, will that make her stop being a morning person?

"I want Pepto. And water. And maybe coffee." Ash rubbed her eyes and pushed the blanket back off her head.

"Bad night?"

"I did wake up with all my clothes on. So there's that."

Megan's brow twitched upward. "Is that ... bad or good?"

"I have no idea." Ashlyn propped herself up on her elbow. Her cousin already wore a fresh t-shirt, and her newly-auburn hair hung in damp tendrils because *of course* she was already up and productive. "How about you? Grim have a post near-death lust experience?" She waited for Megan's laugh.

Silence.

"Wait… Did you?" She scrambled to sit up, but Megan gave a tense shrug.

"Not exactly. He … ugh. I don't know. He wasn't himself anyway." She cleared her throat. "Come on, I have Pepto tabs in the other room and *Animaniacs* on Netflix."

Ash smirked but allowed the subject change. "And if we're good, Mom, can I go to McDonalds for a toy?" Despite the sarcasm, she took Megan's hand and got hauled to her feet on rough, ancient carpet.

"Not with that attitude." Megan smiled as they headed down the hall to the front room. She produced the promised chewable pink tablets and handed over two before disappearing into the kitchen while Ash collapsed on the futon. She lost her thoughts in *Animaniacs* until Megan reappeared with a pile of toast and strawberry jam.

"Where are the guys?" she asked with one hand already reaching for the food. She snagged a piece and spread some jam across it with one of the plastic knives Megan piled on the plate.

"Called in early. Clean-up at the shop, probably cops' reports and stuff. Gotta deal with drunk hunters or whoever was shooting along the road and all that jazz." Megan munched on a piece of jam-smeared toast. "So, are we still pretending you don't like Joker?"

"Of course I like Joker." Ashlyn added more jam to her toast.

·   "You know what I mean. I saw your face at the party the other day when Ariel wriggled all over him. And you just spent all night … what? Cuddling? That man doesn't do cuddling."

"You're projecting your Grim issues. Stop." Ashlyn nibbled the toast and turned to sulk against the back of the futon while the Warner kids tormented their erstwhile psychiatrist.

"Grim's been one of my besties for years. It's different."

"And I can't be friends with Joker?"

"You go spooning with your friends that often?" Megan challenged.

"Oh, shut up. Any touching was totally incidental and because he's too gigantic for the stupid bed!" Ashlyn finished the toast and reached for a new piece. *Time to eat my feelings.* Good thing they had jam to take away the bitter aftertaste of rejection.

"So not even a little bit on-purpose touching? Come on, chica, you can dish." Megan waggled her eyebrows.

"I hugged him. We went to bed." Ash waved away the incident afterward, willing herself to ignore it as a vodka-induced dream. "He was drunk and tired and dealing with a terrible night. Did *you* get a kiss, Miss Prissypants?"

"A goodnight one." Megan slumped. "Or a few. But … it's different. Like you said, bad night. Besides, he's still hung up on his ex."

"Uh huh. Pull the other one, it's got bells on."

"What?"

"Sorry." Ashlyn's laugh turned sheepish. "It's what Grandpa says instead of 'bullshit' in front of Grandma." She licked some stray jam off her hand. "We should clean up the kitchen before we go."

"Yeah. One more episode. They won't be back 'til way late, and this TV kicks ass."

"So, you don't want to be here when they get back, huh?"

"Don't pretend you *do*." Megan's lips mirrored Ash's in a superior half-smile. "Come on. Just admit it: you made out."

"One kiss, High Inquisitor."

"Aha. I knew it had to be something if you're volunteering for clean-up. So, talk to me or I'll tie you to that futon and leave you here to deal with him. I'm bigger than you, brat. And I know more knots."

"What's there to talk about?" Ashlyn swallowed a too-big bite and coughed. Then coughed again. She plucked her cup from the table and took a desperate gulp. "A super-hot guy had a moment of drunken weakness. Then we passed out. The end."

Megan, still sitting in Grim's chair, leaned toward Ashlyn. "So? Was it a good kiss?"

Her cheeks flamed. "Dumb question." She put a hand on her abdomen, waiting for her stomach to finish flipping. "He's ... freaking amazing at kissing."

"But?"

"But it's not like it's going to happen again any time soon." She heard a thump from the chair as Megan flopped backward in theatric exasperation.

"You know he likes you."

"You know *he* likes *you*." Ashlyn's voice sounded tight as her throat felt.

Megan made a scoffing sound. "Now who's projecting? I'm friend-zoned so hard with Ryan that's not even the same game."

"So Grim makes out with his friends a lot?"

"He's never been stellar at keeping it in his pants. Most men aren't. Especially under stress."

Ash ignored the stink-eye her cousin aimed her way. "So, it came out of his pants last night? Is that why you're cranky? Or did it piss you off by failing to emerge from the pants cavern?"

"Ashlyn Marie, I am not having this conversation."

"So you definitely didn't have an orgasm is what I'm hearing. Funny, I thought—Oomph!" A bedraggled throw pillow slammed into her face.

"Go get laid. You'll be less annoying. Nate would be happy to help with that."

Ashlyn tossed the pillow back and sat up to fend off further attacks. "Hey! He has a chick, and her name is Ariel. He's just playing with a new shiny toy until he's ready to cope with that. I may have to be here a little while, and I'm not getting in the middle of that drama-train." This perfectly reasonable explanation earned a giant snort.

"Bullshit, kiddo. Nate likes *fucking* Ariel. That's not the same thing." Megan's dark green eyes narrowed. "Are you still pining over Doctor Perfect? Or is it that guy you went out with last week?"

"Chris? He's cute." Ashlyn shrugged, choosing to discuss her date rather than her ex-fiancé. "I may go out with him this weekend. I don't know yet." Their one date had been fun and quiet: a movie and dinner and general conversation. They'd parted with a kiss, which had been fun and quiet, too—nothing like the full-body buzz that Joker's lips elicited. Or like almost getting barbecued in the eruption of a gangland war... "Probably," she decided aloud. "Stop looking at me like that! Just because you don't ship Joker-Ariel doesn't mean I have to agree. He's not that into me. We could make a fucking movie."

"Right. That's why he's hanging out with you here all the time, and got you a job at the clubhouse. Because he doesn't like having you around." Megan shook her head. "You ready for that tonight, by the way? This weekend didn't freak you out too much?"

Ashlyn relaxed and licked some jam off her plastic knife. "Please. I'm used to parties that randomly explode, and nobody survives clubbing in Kansas City without a drive-by or two in the neighborhood. But can you help me pick out what to wear? Something in non-flammable material."

"Hell yeah I can. Try stopping me." Megan grinned. "Maybe if we go natural fibers it'll make them think you're a vegan, and they'll all leave you alone."

"That ... seems surprisingly plausible, considering the audience." Ashlyn climbed off the couch and gathered the dishes, jelly, and abandoned cups from the night before.

****

Later, Storm Crow Club House

The bare-walled closet that passed for the main Crows' Nest bathroom smelled of disinfectant and Windex, with notes of fresh paint wafting in from the building's front section. She still didn't know why the Crows used license plates for wallpaper in the main area, or why the hell dollar bills got stuck on between the plates, though she had a guess about why bras dangled from the ceiling. She barely understood the rules of anything, and the weight of too many unknowns drove her hand deep into her mini purse where a bottle of Xanax waited. She broke one in half and dry-swallowed one part, stared at the other, then took that, too.

Money's important, right? And this is a job. Paperwork and everything. If you say it often enough it might even be true.

Ashlyn looked in the mirror for the third time in as many minutes, yet again questioning her trust in Megan's cosmetic advice: smoky shadow ringed her eyes, and her face was framed by hair so volumized she felt like an extra in a Hollywood strip club scene. Cut off jean shorts, combat boots and a green, lace-trimmed tank with a black scarf-turned-vest completed her look—it showed a lot of skin, but it was too hot not to. The air conditioning wouldn't keep up with the crowd, and she wasn't about to risk wearing sandals around drunk, Viking-sized males in work boots. *Stage make-up on, game face ready. I can do this.*

She took one last swipe at the mirror with her paper towel, dropped it into the trash can and headed out to face the other bartenders. *At least the place started this evening clean.*

Charred scents hung heavier in the air of the main room, where late afternoon sunlight seeped through the cracks of a boarded-up front window. She tried not to think too hard about the holes in some of the license plates. Karli, the more-or-less head bartender, swore most of the holes were old, made ages ago before the plates got hung on the wall, and not from the previous weekend. Ash hoped it was true. Not that it mattered— she needed the job, and she needed to train before a big night, because life without her credit cards had ceased to be exciting.

Mid-week the crowd was thinner so she'd have an easier training, but facing Karli and Dragon she wasn't sure that helped. Built like a '40s pin-up girl, Karli's skin displayed retro-style tattoos to match, and she wore a bustier top guaranteed to stop traffic. Even Ash had trouble looking up from Karli's chest.

"Try not to stare, baby girl. You're gonna get them thinking you're a virgin and look out for that." Karli laughed and pointed at the bar. "Dragon, you teachin' her how to do the tabs?"

"You got something better to do?" Dragon's bearded, weathered face creased in a dangerous grin. Broad across the chest, his wide shoulders were always raised as if he expected a fight. His long, reddish hair hung in a loose ponytail, and his green eyes were alert and predatory even when he smiled. As far as Ash could tell, he might be fifty or thirty, and it didn't matter because he'd still beat you into a bloody pulp and/or charm your panties off, depending on your sexual preferences. His patch read "Sergeant-at-Arms", which she took to mean "big, red-haired button nobody should push".

"Unless *you* want to get that keg line straightened out?"

"Hmph. Come on, Trouble." He waved Ashlyn over.

"Figures," Karli muttered as she swanned off toward the back. Dragon winked at Ash.

"Pretty basic, but mostly indestructible. Cash per drink, or tally up at the end of the night." He dragged out a stack of old-school carbon paper tickets. "You'll get to know most of us by name pretty soon. Members will keep their cuts on, Prospects get name patches, too. Any of the girls, if you don't know 'em yet, ask or get down a description real quick. Me or Karli will know who it is."

"Um. Prices?" She asked when no clear signage materialized among the license plates and graffiti-covered dollar bills papering the walls. Nor did the assortment of bras hanging over the bar appear to contain any menus.

"Price list is down here." Dragon pointed to a curled, yellowing piece of paper whose original print had been scratched out so new prices could be scrawled beside it. "Jiggers are over there, not that you'll get a chance to use them much. Go by God and guess, best as you can. Most nights members and Prospects drink on the house. Paying is for guests and the fundraisers."

"Who gets real glasses?" Ash's expression

remained dubious as she looked from the bottles at the back to the glasses and stacked plastic cups.

"Just decoration. If somebody gets a glass, I'll serve 'em."

The general instruction continued for a few more minutes while the first couple guys drifted in, off early from their shift at the aluminum plant over in Zenobia. Dragon introduced them as Spider and Jingle though she couldn't see why either earned those names. Spider possessed an average build, average height with nothing arachnid about him. Jingle was rangy and lean, a few inches taller with a solemn face and weary brown eyes. His patch read "Tail-Gunner", and she wasn't about to ask about it.

"Beer for me, honey," Spider ordered.

"Same for me. Budweisers," Jingle added, having caught sight of Ashlyn's eyes widening at the countless labels stuffed in the fridge. Not just Bud and Natty, Michelob and Heineken—bottles of small-time breweries, local stuff and a few other imports all appeared. *New Question Not to Ask Dragon: Do you stock by request or whatever falls off passing trucks?*

"Right." She bent over to grab the Bud from the bottom. *They better tip*, she thought to herself before straightening up and turning around with a grin. "Anything else, guys?"

A dollar appeared in the tip jar, soon followed by others as she brought more beers. Jingle discussed the shift at the plant, their idiot supervisor, and his ex-girlfriend's lack of sanity. Spider didn't talk much except to chime in about work. A couple more members walked in, but they sat in the new benches over by the front window, so once they had their beers she returned to the bar where Jingle and Spider remained.

"Hey, honey." Spider waved her over, holding up

his empty bottle. "So, what's a girl like you doing 'round here?"

"Handing out booze and looking for jobs." She passed him a new beer, then wiped down the bar for the sake of something to do.

Spider chuckled. "Ain't gonna find a rich sugar daddy in this joint."

She shot him a grin. "I'd rather have my own money and an army of cute cabana boys."

"Feminist, huh?"

"Or hopelessly romantic."

"Romantic?" Spider looked skeptical.

"What's more romantic than having an army of minions to do your bidding?"

"Bidding? That's what they're callin' it these days?" This from Jingle, who she rewarded with a wink.

"Jingle, don't be silly. You can't have affairs with *boys*."

"So, who could you have one with?" Spider leaned in, though Jingle only laughed.

"That's the hopeless part, I guess. I can't seem to find anybody." Ashlyn sighed and grabbed another rag from the metal sink. She turned away while she wiped the cooler down.

"I suspect you ain't been looking too hard."

"Mmhm. You got a list of likely suspects?"

"I can think of one or two."

"Write them down, and I'll review it later." She nodded toward there door where another trio were walking in and went off to catch their orders.

Spider's eyes followed her the next couple hours as business picked up and took her out from behind the bar more often, while Karli claimed her attention to train on various intricacies of mixes or stocking. She didn't think anything of it until she walked into the back to change out the pop boxes for the mixer gun and heard voices and steps on the other side of the door.

"Hey, brother. What's the problem?" Spider asked.

"You help her with the boxes means you help her with the boxes," answered Dragon's voice, low and emphatic.

"I'm not doing nothin'—"

"Ain't about that."

The rest of the conversation proved inaudible. She finished unsticking the hose from the last box and attached to the new one, then kicked the old carton so it clattered across the floor as a warning. Outside, Dragon and Spider stood much further down the hall. She smiled at them as she shut the door. Spider kept his distance as she walked by.

At the end of the (mostly successful) night, she finally got a chance to ask Dragon what the hell happened. He looked at her she'd spoken a foreign language.

"You into Spidey?"

"No." She frowned. "And I am glad you looked out for me. Thank you, Dragon. Seriously. But what did you say to get him to back off? If there's a magic line, I'd like to know."

"You honestly got no idea?" His skeptical brow-wiggle jangled on her last nerve.

"That I've got herpes, maybe?" That sounded petulant. To make up for it she stalked off and shoved a couple wooden chairs onto tables. Dragon snorted

"I gotta admit that's pretty good for a 'magic line' if you need one."

"I'm still not hearing your answer."

"Don't worry about it, Trouble. Just get the last tables wiped down and you can head out."

Chapter Nine: June 6

Ariel
Ravenwood

Ariel's hand shook so bad she could hardly light her joint. She fumbled the button, but the window rolled down a couple inches before she took the first slow, deep drags. She needed something stronger. *After,* she promised herself. *You need your head together.* The image of Joker wrapped around the brat kept replaying behind her eyes, so she made herself focus on a bike in the lot up ahead. Faded paint, dent on the back fender, ape hangers…

Is this shit for real? He took one of the spares instead of going straight to the dealer. Does he even know who he is sometimes? God, I gotta get this cunt packed up. Thanks to Ariel's clientele at the shop and their never-ending fountain of gossip, she had the right intel for the job. Brandt would finish it whenever he got off his ass, but she might as well lessen the impact where she could.

The clubhouse itself didn't look too much worse for wear: Prospects and members milled around outside, finishing off the last repairs. Fresh gray paint gleamed on new siding—picked to match the shop across the way. The front windows shone like Windex diamonds despite the blackout curtains that kept anybody from seeing inside. Even the privacy fence had new paint and well-trimmed grass along its length. Almost like nothing happened. Back to how it should be.

Once the joint burned down to almost nothing, she pinched it out in the truck's ashtray and tucked it into her box before shoving the whole thing to the bottom of her purse. She checked her make-up in the rearview mirror, reapplied her lipstick, and got out. She picked her way carefully across the lot to the body shop at the far side. Heels and gravel didn't mix, but she had to look good right now. And she did. Her dark hair shimmered in a meticulously carefree fall of beachy waves to show off the few lighter streaks to the best advantage and frame her features, her jeans fit like they'd been sewn for her, and the purple tank top highlighted her cleavage without being too low-cut. She embodied what men wanted. Especially Joker. *He always says I look good in purple. Let's hope it works.*

Inside the front office, Dragon sat behind the computer going over who-knew-what. His massive bulk transformed everything around him into a toy destined to be broken—computers more than most other things.

"Hey!" Ariel smiled when he looked up. "Is Joker around? I need to talk to him real quick. It's important."

Dragon's gave her an approving once over. "Back there." He jerked his head to the door behind him—not the one to the garage but the back offices. Fresh paint and spackle didn't quite disguise the bullet holes, but at least they hadn't let a bunch of blood get scattered around. *Insurance companies must be loving Tree right about now.*

"Go on," Dragon said, oblivious to Ariel's quick-turning thoughts. She thanked him and rushed past.

Her heels clicked too loudly to let her surprise Joker, but he didn't raise his eyes from the papers in his hand when she came in. Like Dragon, he sat behind a desk today. At least she hadn't caught either of them looking at porn. Unless she counted the old pin-up calendars papering the office.

"Nate?" She grinned, relieved to see only jeans-encased legs in the gap between the desk and the floor, and two strong arms braced on either side of the paperwork. His sandy hair was tousled but clean, and his eyes didn't have circles under them for the first time in a while. "You got a minute, sweetie?"

Joker looked up. She hadn't expected surprise, but his chiseled features showed no emotions at all. Though that wasn't so rare with him since he came back from the army. "Sure."

"You got free of the cast today! Congratulations." She smiled and let her eyes linger on his arm. *Mm, the things he could do with two good hands again…*

"About time." He lifted his left hand from the desk and turned it as if he questioned its freedom, too. His eyes warmed as they turned back to her. "But thanks. What's up, Ari?"

She stepped in and closed the door. "Probably nothing."

"Uh huh. That's usually what gets you to drive all the way out here of an afternoon." His faint smile drained more of the tension from her.

"I hope I'm being dramatic, but I thought I should talk to you." She made a show of dropping her head, hesitating before she explained herself: "It's about Megan's cousin. The new bartender."

Joker's lips flattened, and his shoulders lifted. He was on guard. "All right."

"Look, it's just that I met her out the other night at Piggy's BBQ in Star Hollow. With Chris Michaels." His jaw tensed as she said the name—Chris had hired on with the Oak Grove PD a year before, the youngest of the three full-time officers and the one most eager to make a name for himself. "Which probably doesn't mean anything," she hurried to add. "Only I worried about it, because Megan and I were talking about her car getting keyed a couple weeks ago, and if she's getting into dating drama with a cop…" Ariel gave a helpless shrug.

"Doesn't Michaels have a girlfriend?"

"Not for a while. I think they broke up pretty bad, but she wasn't from around here, so I never got details." She fidgeted with her hair, but his eyes were glued to the damned desk. She wrapped her arms around herself to accentuate her breasts. *Maybe I should've worn a padded bra? Halter top?* "Look, I figured you ought to know. And if you already do, I'm sorry for repeating it. I wanted to be sure the club has all the information."

"Thanks." He flipped the top page on his file and focused on it.

I'm getting fucking dismissed? Ariel forced herself to smile. *This isn't his fault. He's stressed.*

"Any time," she said to recall his attention. "So, any chance of a celebratory ride this week? It's been a minute since we went out for a spin." She crossed her arms tighter, making the most of her cleavage on the off chance that he looked up. A quick glance was all she got, but she knew his eye for detail. He saw.

"We'll see, Ari. I got a lot of catching up to do."

"I know. But if you get some spare time, let me know? I miss you." She kept her voice quiet and a little sad. "And I'm real sorry I can't make it to the party today. Mom made me promise to help with the shop books."

"Shit." Joker grimaced. "Forgot about that." Ariel didn't bother asking how he knew about his own surprise party. She just smiled.

"Have extra fun for me, ok?" She reached for the doorknob as she spoke, ducking her head and hurrying out as though embarrassed to have said as much out loud. He appreciated restraint—he'd take the bait sooner or later.

****

Ashlyn
Oak Grove

Ashlyn heard the motorcycle turn up the street and abandoned the screaming group in the back yard to their continued assault on the giant waterslide. Grim could (probably) keep them all alive. She rushed into the house, stopping only to turn down the volume on the speakers before meeting Megan in the gleaming, food-laden kitchen to help lift the cupcake platter and walk it from the table to a patch of open countertop closer to the garage door. Ash stood back from the counter, glaring at the desserts.

"You sure he's into cupcakes?" The words even *felt* repeated.

"They're *cupcakes*, girl. Who doesn't love cupcakes?" With a glance at Ash's face, she relented. "Give him some whiskey, he'll love the shit out of whatever's in front of him."

Grim stepped into the kitchen wearing a wet t-shirt, grass stains across his bare knees, and a madman's grin. "Legs, you should try Karli's vape. That shit she bought in Colorado is cool as hell."

"I'll be there," Megan answered with a smile. "You better go warn Nate to look surprised."

Ashlyn's smile fell. "He already knows?"

"Prince of darkness power, chica." Megan laughed and swatted Grim's ass as he walked by them on his way to the garage. He winked at her but closed the door behind him.

"Boo." Ashlyn picked up a cupcake with orange icing from the platter. Hailey stopped in from the patio to make a face at her.

"Hey! You said no eating those!"

"That's when he didn't know about the party." Ashlyn sighed and hefted her calorie bomb toward Hailey. "They're fair game now."

"Well, we can't leave it unbalanced." Hailey

picked up a black iced cupcake from the other side of the arrangement. Her blue eyes danced as she tapped it against Ashlyn's like a toast. "Now, come on, you didn't…" Ash continued pouting, and Hailey's sympathy crumbled into laughter, joining Megan's. "Aw, you are such a newbie." Hailey patted her hair, talking like she would to a puppy. "It'll be ok, baby. You'll get used to it."

Ashlyn scrunched her nose before biting into the icing.

****

Joker

Grim's smile vanished when he stepped into the garage. He pulled the door closed behind him, then double checked it before walking over. Joker watched him from the Harley, his hand still on the ignition.

"Shit. You're in a mood already?" Grim paused, then took Joker's silence as permission to keep talking. "I don't know what's set you off this time, but can we not right now? It's just a party, Nate. It makes them happy. Fake a smile and suck it up 'til you're drunk." He pointed to the fridge waiting by the door. "You don't even have to get through the door first."

Joker's eyes narrowed, but he took off his helmet. "I'm thinking."

"Looks painful. Want some ex-lax?"

"Imagine how you're going to look if you keep mouthing off." He swung his right leg up and off the bike, placed his helmet on the seat. Then let his hand linger on it. A familiar tension crawled up his spine, and he cast a sidelong look at his roommate. "I'm not in the mood for this shit."

"Wow. And I thought I was kidding when I called you dramatic." Grim walked to the other side of the loaner bike. *Just out of arm's reach.* "I know you like being surly and antisocial, but come on, bro. Hot girls, waterslide? Did they take off your leg cast and put one on your dick by mistake? Because if that shit was waiting for me, I wouldn't be out here sitting on my ass."

"Grim."

"Damn it, Nate!" Grim stretched his arms wide. "You're going to make me hit you. And then you're going to hit me for hitting you. Then we'll fight and get blood all over, and Ash's gonna go ape-shit because she took some kind of Martha Stewart pill this morning, and I haven't gotten her to eat the brownies yet."

Joker's stomach clenched at the mention of her, and he turned away, running a hand through his hair. The thoughts inside his head stayed right where he didn't want them. "There's too many people, and *she's* here and I just— I need some fucking space."

"She?" Joker didn't dare look at Grim, but he didn't need to. Grim exhaled a very loud breath. "Christ. You picked today to remember you're an asshole? Fine. What's the deal with Ash being here? And you better make this one believable."

"She's fucking a cop." He spat the words, hating the weight of them on his tongue. The feeling of it. The images with it. Grim's eyes flared. *Good, let it stick someone else.*

"Nah, don't buy it," Grim announced after a second.

"I don't care if you do."

"Uh huh. Where'd you get this intel? Operation Deep Throat, maybe?"

"I'm not having this conversation." Joker groaned, turning to the bench where his toolbox sat open. "Tell them I've gotta work on the bike for a bit. Come get me when shit starts winding down."

"You're really not going to come in?" Grim

crossed his arms. "Girl taken, Tarzan no party?"

Taken?

Joker slammed his hand on the worktable. Grim kept talking. "There's other pussy here. You could go sample the other pieces, make your point that way and still have some fun. You've played that hand enough before."

"I don't give a damn who she's screwing!" He turned a dark look on Grim. "I give a damn if some pig in blue is using her to root around our shit. It's about looking out for you. And me. And the entire goddamn club. You're so fucking trusting—how much shit does she already know that they could use against you?"

Grim's mouth hung open. He stepped back, his fingers curling into fists at his side. "Right. Stay out here and sweat your balls off. I'll be out there with the pussy and beer."

"Send her home."

"This ain't the clubhouse. You want to be a dick, you do it on your own. And consider why the fuck you're yelling about this when we have just about every cop on retainer." Grim yanked the door open and stormed through it.

****

Ashlyn

The door crashed open, rolling a shockwave through the kitchen. Ash jumped so fast the counter dug into her back. Only Megan's quick reach kept her cupcake from hitting the linoleum.

"The hell is your—" Megan's eyes connected with Grim's scowl. Her jaw snapped shut on whatever she'd meant to say.

"He's being a bitch." Grim grabbed a beer from the fridge and headed toward the back, but stopped beside Ashlyn and put his arm around her shoulders. She glanced down, breathing out and focusing on his ink because only Grim had those marks: a mechanical arm drawn from shoulder to wrist, all steampunk gears and cogs, with the Tree of Gondor outlined on one. *Grim. Gondor.* "Sorry, hon. I tried." He added the apology so quietly she almost missed it.

"Huh? Oh. I'm sure you did." Grim's arm felt heavy. Her thoughts circled back to the way Nate woke up the night of the "vandalism" incident. *Maybe the first day back on a bike didn't go well? If it triggered something...* "What's going on with him?"

"That time of the month? Seems being cast-free takes some emotional adjustment." Grim hugged her shoulders and turned away.

"I'll go check on him. He might be nicer to people with boobs."

"Ash, I wouldn't..." Megan trailed off as Ashlyn brushed past her to the door.

"Not a great idea!" Grim called. Her steps didn't slow.

Hot air washed over her chilled skin as she stepped into the garage. Ash ignored the temperature adjustment along with her cousin's warning look, and closed the door. Two steps down and halfway across the wide concrete expanse, Joker looked up from fastening his left riding glove.

"Grim, I fucking said..." His tirade ended before it started as his brandy-brown eyes fixed on her. He wore jeans and a white t-shirt, and riding boots. She blinked, trying to accustom herself to the sight of him without casts.

Nope, I'm not Grim. Well spotted, butthead. She walked down the steps despite the knot settling into her stomach. The garage smelled like motor oil and metallic, greasy things; the breeze wafting through the big open bay door couldn't begin to dispel the miasma. It didn't do any favors for the expression on Joker's face, either. He didn't even look at her as he sat back on the bike.

So much for warmer welcomes.

"Grim said you weren't coming in, not that you're leaving." She wrapped her arms around herself despite the wasting heat. "Are you ok? Nothing else went haywire, did it? Did they order more PT or … something?"

"No. Just realized I left something at the garage."

"Can't it wait? Everybody wants to see you. And there's a kind-of surprise…"

"The slide?" He put his helmet in his lap and examined a scratch along one side. Ash's fingers dug into her arms.

"And the people."

"Most of them saw me at work already." He took a deep breath and his expression dulled from hostile to opaque. *The man missed his calling as a poker god.* "Look, it can't wait. I've gotta go." He shoved his helmet onto his head.

Right. Done with this game.

"What's wrong?" She risked taking a few more steps across the grubby concrete until she reached his front fender. "Seriously. You look like you're pissed, and 'something at the garage' is basically the shadiest thing I've ever heard you say." A half second pause, her lips thinned, and then she added, "If you're mad about the party, I promise I can help Grim get it cleaned up. You won't even know we were all here."

"Fuck." The word sounded more regretful than hostile. He glared down at the bike's gauges. "Ash, I'm not mad about the party." He lifted his foot to start up the engine and stopped. His boot landed back on the concrete as he finally looked her way. "Is Michaels here?"

"Who?" Her head canted. The name took a moment to sink in. "You mean Chris?"

"Yeah. *Chris*."

"No. I just had Grim make up the list, and I swear I would've used your Facebook if you had one, but—" Something clicked into place as all those words rushed out. Suspicion kindled in the back of her mind. "I can call him if you want?"

"He in your friends list, then?" Joker's voice made her think of rattlesnakes. He said it so quietly, but everything in his posture was *coiled*.

"Well, obviously. It's not like he took me on the world's worst date."

Joker blew out a breath. "Right. So. Guess I better say it. He's not welcome." He turned the bike's ignition. He placed a hand on the clutch and his thumb over the starter button before he faced her again, lips drawn tight. "Have a good night."

Son of a ... jealous dipshit bitch.

Logic sailed off into the wind as his bike roared to life. Ashlyn dashed forward and latched onto his arm—ignoring the rumbling engine. And that he'd already shifted into gear. The muscles beneath her hand clenched so hard she could've been holding a statue. The engine drowned out his curses but not the look on his face as he killed the bike and slammed the kickstand down. He surged off the Harley. Ash skittered back.

"Are you fucking crazy?!" The shout startled reality back into her. But not much. He ripped his helmet off. It crashed into the far wall and she got another half-step back. "You don't run up on a bike like that! *Ever*! What fucking psycho shit…"

Oh, now I'm crazy? Temper rising, Ashlyn held her ground even as he towered over her with fury in every inch of his enormous frame. "You start psycho shit, you get psycho shit."

"Don't you fuckin' lecture me. You want that cop's dick bad enough to bitch me out today, then you—"

"Shut up," she hissed. *Finally*. She forced the words out as best she could, trying to remember the calming mantras her therapist used to recommend. *I statements. Don't blame, communicate. Oh, screw it.* "You bloody coward." His jaw jutted, and his lip curled.

"Don't you *ever*—"

"You prefer pussy? You want to order my life around but—"

"Don't give me that shit, little girl," he grated as his head lowered. He loomed over her, well-armored in boots and riding jeans while she wore a sundress and flip-flops. "You got no idea what I want." His eyes glittered, hard and cold. "You know what I am. What the Crows are. It's got nothing to do with what I want or not. You're…"

"Only your friend as long as I do exactly what you allow." Her hands shook so she put them on her hips. "And you only want me until you get me. I'm aware." She wiped at her cheek, irritated all over again by her own emotions. He pointed at her head, the knuckles on his clenched fingers turning white.

"Do you even hear the words I say or do you make shit up in that crazy little skull?"

"Either I'm friends with just you or we can't be friends. Where did I hear you wrong?" She held her arms out, asking an invisible jury's opinion. Joker growled.

"I'll talk slower. You can't be friends with us and with a cop. It won't work. Never has."

"In a small town? Where half your guys drink with cops on off-weekends?" A tear slid down her cheek without interference. "Say what you fucking mean,

Joker! A cop's no threat, you just don't want me dating him."

"Stop making it out to be something it isn't."

"That's what you're doing!" She didn't have anything in her hand to throw, so she shoved his chest. Rage didn't give a shit about sizes or self-preservation. Any insult, any piece of anything to make him show something—anything—other than that horrible icy expression. He didn't try to stop her, but pushing him back on his heels was hardly the same as putting him through the garage wall. No matter how much she wanted to. "He asked me, and I went because I'm not your fucking pet!"

"What do you think we've doing the last six weeks, exactly?" He batted her hand away. She stumbled back from him, burned.

"Hanging out?"

"And that. Right there..." His tone remained as infuriating and steady as his balance. Evidently forgetting his intent to leave, Joker stepped forward, making up for her retreat. "For fuck's sake, Ash, what world do you live in that you think we'd all be okay with a cop hanging around?"

"I can meet a guy for dinner and not staple him to my bra."

"Every time I so much as hint about wanting something, you play the oblivious blonde bullshit card. But some asshole with a badge wants in your panties and you bounce right to him."

"My panties were never involved! Grandma set us up, and..."

"And how the hell do I know that? You didn't bother to bring it up in conversation at any point. What am I supposed to think? You're hiding it. And why the hell would that be, unless..."

"Because that's who I date, the ones who don't mean anything. I'll screw up anything I actually care—" The words ripped out before she could stop them. Her hand covered her mouth just a second too late. "I'm not … I'm not doing this with you." She turned away, sick with herself and the heat and the whole stupid, emotional world. The universe flickered, going high def to VHS and back, her senses overloading and emotions fraying. She wiped at her face and rushed toward the open garage door. Her Miata sat across the street, keys inside. *Megan can grab my stuff later. I'll text her.*

Three steps from the door, a large hand closed around her wrist, setting off a million crossed wires. Reflex dragged her forward, struggling against his hold. He didn't let go.

"Where are you going?" His voice rasped on the question. She didn't look at him.

"My car." *Miata. Freedom. Run. Get out. Now.* Ash tugged to free herself, but her flipflops slid on the pavement and she couldn't get enough leverage.

"No way. You can't drive like this."

"Fuck you!" She spun to him and wrenched her hand up at the same time. He finally let go, and she stumbled back, losing a sandal. Joker didn't even blink.

"Make one more move for that car, and I'll shoot the tires out. I fucking mean it. You've been drinking, and you're upset. You aren't driving."

"That's not your choice to make!" She glared at him through blurring eyes. His expression cooled.

"Ash, stop." He reached for her hand, and she jerked back. Joker's hands rose, palm out, his motions more deliberate. "I'm pissed at you. That doesn't mean I'm letting you do something stupid. Come on, give me the keys." His arm extended toward her again. Slowly.

"Give me a break. We just broke up over me

going on a date. And we weren't in a freaking relationship!" Ashlyn let him take her hand but stared down at it, expecting the rattlesnake's coils to tighten. *Or he'll lie again. Talk about things that weren't real.*

"You should have told me. People get twitchy about secret meetings with cops." His other hand moved for her purse. *Joke's on you, Joker. Ain't no keys on me. I just need to get loose...* She stayed still, waiting for the chance.

"And you don't trust me enough to ask me." She swallowed hard to keep from sobbing. "I promise I don't like Chris enough to date him. And whoever I do like, it's not your problem now. Or ever again. So let me *go*."

He winced but dropped her hand. "Ash." His eyes held an expression she couldn't fathom, so she looked away. "I just ... I need to sort my shit out. I want something you clearly don't." *That almost sounded like an apology. If snakes apologized.* She examined the whirls of dirt on the floor, eyes and chest burning until she couldn't breathe. Or blink.

"Do you?" The words escaped her in a ragged whisper.

"You have to know I do."

She risked raising her gaze, searching his face. "What if ... I wanted it so much it scared me?"

He didn't smile, or move a muscle, and what little courage she had threatened to evaporate. *This is where he laughs at me, and it's all a joke. This is where it's not real.*

"Depends. Do *I* scare you?" He reached for her hand again, slowly, like they were caught in water instead of soupy summer air. His fingers wrapped around hers in a touch so light she looked down to be sure she wasn't imagining him.

"No." She tightened her fingers around his,

powerless to resist holding on this time. She wiped her cheek with her free hand, not that it stopped the tears. "I-it's just ... easier to stay with someone who can't hurt you." *There. Honesty.* At least as much of it as she dared give.

His eyes filled with something akin to pain before he cupped her damp cheek, rubbing his thumb across a tear track. "Sweetheart." His eyes met hers. Studied her. She tried not to shrink away. *Why does he have to see so much?* It frightened her more than anything else about him. "I think being with someone safe might hurt now. Don't you?"

Did I hit my head? She laid her hand on his cheek in return, her faint smile widening as she stroked down along his stubble, appreciating his sudden, sharp breath. The heat in the garage left a light sheen on his skin, but his eyes were warmer still: perfect, drown-in-them chocolate pools.

"Are you going to ask me out or not?" *That is what we're doing? Oh, God, what if that's not what we're doing? Don't look like you're scared...* She tried, desperately, to look calm and ignore the terror careening around inside her.

He rewarded her bravado with a chuckle. His thumb stroked her jaw to tilt her head back. "Just say yes, Ash." His lips almost touched hers with each syllable. A dizzy laugh escaped her, and she put her hands on his chest, leaning in as her knees weakened. She lifted onto her toes to close the space between them.

"Yes."

The kiss started sweet, but a moment later his hand slid into her hair and he pressed for more, mouth slanting on hers and leaving her dizzy. Ashlyn's lips parted for him. She forgot the open garage door and the other people lurking in the kitchen. Nothing mattered but him.

****

Joker

She had to taste like cupcakes. His grabbed the flimsy dress, ready to rip it off. A passing car flashed white in his peripheral vision and pulled his lips from hers. *The town won't approve of killing any innocent bystanders who wander by.* His hands framed her cheeks so he wouldn't pull the dress off anyway. "We need to go in, baby."

"Yeah. It's getting too hot to be hot out here." Ashlyn's giggly voice, so at odds with her wet cheeks and reddened eyes, made him laugh even as it twisted a knife inside him. *Shit, I can't let go.* Just the thought of taking his hands off her hurt, so he swept her up into his arms. Her remaining flip-flop thumped to the floor, but Ash didn't fight him. No, she put her mouth on his neck and nearly shorted out his willpower.

Somehow, he marched through the kitchen door instead of pinning her against it. Grim and Megan greeted them with wide eyes and open, icing-smeared mouths. Grim recovered into a slow clap as Joker strode past, but no one in the yard seemed to notice—laughter and booming speakers covered whatever they might have otherwise heard from the garage. He kicked the bedroom door closed behind him, immune to Grim's shouted advice: "Get some!"

His focus didn't leave the girl in his arms. Heart rate cranking up a gear, Joker lowered Ash onto his bed without taking his hands from her body. With her green eyes darkened and her cheeks flushed, she matched every filthy dream he'd had for weeks. All he wanted was to rip that flimsy dress off and fuck her. Hard. Make her forget the goddamn cop. If he had to stay on top of her to keep her from taking off again, so be it. If he had to run

153

his tongue over every inch of her... He pulled away before his instincts shredded his intentions.

"Should I go first?" She didn't let him reply. Instead, she reached for the shoulders of her dress. The elastic around the bust kept the scrap of nothing in place so she pushed it down as well. Her eyes locked on his. He groaned. And then he saw the black strapless bra set against her creamy skin. For a moment, he didn't move, didn't breathe. Her breasts, firm and full and barely contained by that maddening lace, rose and fell, calling for his attention and torturing him with the barest hint of her peaked nipples, taunting him with their shade and shape.

If I come in my pants, I'll have to lick her 'til she can't remember. That's fair. He leaned in to taste her throat until her fingers pressed into his cheek. He drew back. Ashlyn's eyes weren't so dark, and her grip on his hip lightened. *Worry? Fear?*

"Ash?" He captured her hand to kiss her palm. *Don't say no, baby. Please, don't back out...*

"Nate, I-I want to touch you."

Thank God. If she asked him to blow up the goddamn town, it might all go sky high by morning. As long as that damn bra came off.

"What's stopping you?" His voice thickened with emotion. He pulled her hand to his chest and waited. Her fingers hovered against his skin, flexed, then slid along his pec. *Finally.*

Another hot wave of need burned through him, and he encouraged her with a kiss, forcing himself to keep still for a few heartbeats until her touch grew less hesitant. His shirt flew somewhere, and he fell back to worship her. His hands moved gently along her sides, over her stomach, up between her breasts. Ashlyn moaned and arched her back for him, so he let his lips trace her jaw and down over the delicate column of her throat as he pushed her bra away. At last. The full, perfect mounds called for his hands to cover them, dusky pink nipples pebbled and needing lips to soothe them. His mouth actually watered. He kissed his way down until he could pull the left bud between his lips. Weeks of desire flooded him, and he moaned, sucking harder. Even her skin tasted sweet.

"Too many clothes for you." Ashlyn's hands drifted lower to tease along his waistband only to stop at his zipper and earn a hard swipe of his tongue against her perked right breast. "May I?"

He put his lips to her shoulder, pushing her hair out of the way so he could let his hands run all over her perfect skin to those white panties. His cock throbbed harder than it had since he figured out how a bra worked. "Yes," he said in a rough voice. "But you first. I want to see you, Ash. All of you."

Her eyes turned up to meet his. He saw it again, the hesitation. Feared the freeze … but no! She wiggled the stretchy dress down further, taking her underwear along with it. He got a half second's unimpeded view of curving hips and thighs before she sat up and looped her arm around his shoulders, pulling him down on top of her. He let out a half gasp, half laugh, barely managing to catch his weight with his hands.

"Do I get to see all of you, too?"

"If that's what you want." Propping himself up with one arm, he claimed a long kiss before unfastening his belt and popping his fly open—as much for his own relief as an invitation. *Shit, homecoming for the first deployment didn't get this bad. Baseball, think about baseball…* He breathed out, trying to recall anything but her creamy breasts and the cute little moan she made when he kissed her throat. Except then he kissed her throat again, just to be sure of it…

"I want you," Ash whispered. "Inside me. Don't you want that, too? I'm so, so wet, Joker."

Hell yes. Speech failed, so he put his hand over her breast and teased her nipple until her fingers squeezed his dick. He swore under his breath as his vision narrowed to her face. His thoughts went primal, driven by the need to have her, fuck her, make her come until she couldn't say anything but his name. He reached to grab her hair and kiss her—hard—only to stop short. Her eyes were wide and blank…

"Or, um, foreplay?" Ashlyn's voice squeaked. He raised a brow, and her cheeks stained vivid pink. Realization dawned slow—blood wasn't getting to his brain—but it hit. He grinned. She wasn't the first one to get shy once his pants came down.

"Don't worry, baby." He thrust against her hand as he stroked her body, gliding his fingers along her ribs, cupping her breast to tease her nipple. When she gasped, he rolled the hard nub between his fingers until she cried out. "I want to fucking worship you," he whispered in her ear.

"I don't want … worship." Her hips pushed up against him, but she moved her hands to his sides. "I'm not a statue."

"No, you're all warm and soft…" he agreed, hands following her lead to her sides. *And mine.*

His lips resumed their previous path along her throat, her collarbone, and then her breast. He watched her eyes as his tongue drew a small circle around her hardened nipple before closing his lips around it. Weeks of wanting drove him to suckle, kiss, find exactly what made her squirm.

"Don't stop. That feels so good." Her legs wrapped around his. She pulled his hair at the base of his skull—not a painful sensation but one that got his attention. He met her passion-dark eyes. Light slanted along her cheekbone, catching on her pink lips and the swell of her breasts. She looked like the angel he'd once imagined her to be. "I need you," she whispered.

He lost control—and his mind—as he nibbled and sucked her breasts, moving between them at random, raking his teeth on her satiny flesh in answer. She needed to be marked. His.

"You got me," he promised with his lips against a thin, silvery-pink scar beneath her right breast. "But first..." He kissed her one more time before sliding down the bed. Lying diagonally, they had some room, but his knees reached the edge too soon. *Next check's buying the biggest mattress they got,* he decided. He pushed her legs further up and kissed her thigh. "Watch me, baby."

"Nate, you don't have to—" Her soaking wet pussy just about scalded his finger as he eased it inside her. A simple flick of his wrist softened her protest into wordless cries.

"I want. You. Coming..." He leaned in and fastened his lips on her clit before licking and teasing her entrance. Ashlyn bucked up at the slightest pressure, so he put his arm across her hips before he slipped a second finger into her. Her walls gripped his fingers—he thought she'd tightened already until she flexed for real. He groaned against her. *Lethal,* even the idea of her taking his cock. Her tight pussy pushed at his fingers, her hand clung to his hair and sweet cream slicked down his palm until she fell limp and breathless. But it wouldn't be enough. He fastened his mouth on her clit and worked a third finger into her while Ash moaned his name. Once she'd taken that much, he kissed her breasts and up to catch her mouth again. "That's it, baby. Come on my fingers..." And she did.

I need her. Now. While she panted, he settled against her, losing his breath when his cock touched her pussy—losing track of anything but his own throbbing, twitching need. He curled his fingers to stroke her again.

"Ash, look at me, baby." The words trembled on his lips. He set himself against her, rubbing his length along her wet folds while he reached for the nightstand drawer … and failed. They'd ended up at the far side of the bed, and the handle taunted him, three inches too far. "Damn it…" He put more weight on his knees to get to the drawer, instantly missing the pressure of her body against his.

"Nate? Oh." Ash touched his arm. "Hey, it's all right … if you're clean? I've got an IUD in." She tilted her hips and arched enough that his cock slid down right to her entrance. Stars ignited across his vision. "Unless you like them."

No condom? Condom? What? It took a couple seconds to catch up to what she'd said. *Skin-to-skin. With Ash. In my bed...* His answer was a savage kiss and pushing his hips forward. Ashlyn's green eyes looked straight back at him, no holding back. Her hands traced his shoulders, clenching as he drove another inch. He made himself stop. Giving her time… *Fuck, maybe I should grab one. I'm going to lose it like this...*

"Nathan?" She kept her eyes on his. He saw the worry returning. "Don't stop." She pulled her legs up around his hips, the simple movement damn near ending the game right then.

His breaths were sharp. Short. He couldn't think around the grip her body had on him. He'd started out slow for her; now pacing was the only thing keeping him in control. Every breath she took, every shift of her hips shuddered right through his dick. He put a hand on her breast, his lips hovering over hers, watching every shadow crossing her bright eyes. For once, all he saw was warmth.

Ashlyn gasped as he picked up the tempo. One hand caught in his hair, gently tugging. "Yes, Nate." Her voice broke, turned into a moan she tried to stifle. Her body got tighter—*fuck, how was that possible?*—and her hips bucked, taking him on a ride he didn't intend to survive.

"Yeah. That's it … baby, come on." He begged her in groans and half-syllables, forgetting how words worked, desperate to feel her come undone. Moments later, her nails dug into his shoulder as her body shook. Her breaths became sobs as she tried to stay quiet through the aftershocks.

"Nate. God. Please…" Random words, then just moans, and finally she was quiet again, clinging to him with shivering limbs. Even her pussy trembled. Joker held onto her hair, gripping hard as his thrusts became erratic. He'd hoped to last longer, but she kept clenching. He pushed deep as she could take him, burying himself and keeping his lips on hers as he filled her. The pulsing ache receded, leaving him near to collapse.

He rolled off of her slowly as he could. Cold air on his dick, against his chest… He closed his eyes. *Round Two may kill me.*

Soft fingertips trailed along his shoulder and down his arm while her breathing slowed. "I've been dreaming about that for weeks." Ashlyn's faint whisper stirred him from the quiet of his thoughts. He turned his head, smiling at her flushed cheeks.

"Me too." *And it's going to be so much worse now I know how good you feel, sweetheart. What you taste like. I like it when you beg me.*

Fortunately far from hearing his thoughts, Ashlyn sighed and let her head fall back on the pillow. She put her hand on his shoulder again, but this time her fingers moved in a strange pattern. Tracing the runes on his tattoo, he realized.

"Tell me your dreams, and I'll tell you mine?"

He turned his head to brush his lips against her wrist. "My dreams? Don't know where to start." He shifted so his lips were closer to hers. "Maybe all the ways I made you come with my mouth? Or about the times you made me come with yours?"

She smiled and met his kiss with renewed urgency, but she barely let her tongue touch his before she drew back. He made a desperate sound that surprised even him when she pulled away.

"I like how you think." She pushed on his shoulder. He moved at her direction, both hands going to her sides, eyes locked in a gaze with hers.

"Got a feeling I'm going to like how you think, too."

"Well, if you have any complaints, I'll take them under advisement before I kick your ass." She slipped up and straddled him, laughing, and kissed a meandering path across his shoulders. Then down his stomach. Her hand followed suit, moving until her fingertips teased his cock. She stroked him while she worked her way lower with kisses and one playful nip by his hipbone.

She looked up at him as she put her lips against his erection. The minx waited until his eyes met hers, then licked the tip of his shaft. He groaned and arched up toward her. She started licking up and down, like he was a freaking Popsicle. "You taste like me," she told him between strokes of her tongue.

"Show me, baby. Kiss me."

"I don't want to share…" Her lips blessed him in the barest touch with each breathy word. She tilted his cock down and put her mouth over the tip but didn't let him stay there—that, too, was a tease.

Everything will be, his dwindling brain realized. *She'll tease me to death. And I'm going to love it.* The hand not squeezing and pumping his dick explored his balls. Her feathery soft hair brushed along his thighs until he twitched with every breath and heartbeat. *Is she doing that on purpose, too?*

"Mm. Can I play with you? Will you come for me?"

Yes. Yes, she is.

Between her lips on his skin and her hand around his cock, he forgot his own name. He grabbed fistfuls of sheets in white knuckles while his hips lifted off the bed. Then her tongue replaced her fingertip. "Fuck. Oh, fuck." He grabbed her head tighter than he'd meant to before getting control. "God, yes." Propping himself up on his elbows, he watched her soft, pink mouth on his dick and her eyes flicked up, meeting his. Amusement, arousal— his little flirt liked having power over him. And that was hot as hell. His dick agreed. An orgasm's tight, throbbing pull crept through him. Ash must've felt it, too, because her lips parted wide and slid down over him. Sucked. Killed him. He kept one hand tangled in her hair, barely holding back from shoving her down.

Then she moaned against him.

He stiffened—hips lifting. His arms straightened, and he fell to his back, trying to breathe through his climax, fingers tight in her hair. He watched her with half-lidded eyes, hot with the knowledge of his cum inside her. Marking her. She took her warm mouth off him, licking her lips to clear away any lingering traces. "Ash, that was…"

"A normal weeknight for one of the wild Storm Crows?" Ashlyn laughed and crawled back up his body, kissing his tattoos along the way until she stretched out on top of him like a cat, her head on his shoulder so her gold hair fell across his chest. He wrapped his arms around her to run his hands over her candy-scented skin.

"A nice start. Give me a second. You won't be able to walk when I'm done…"

"That's all right. We should probably rejoin the party before Megan summons the rest of the coven and your backyard turns into an orgy." Ashlyn reached up to smooth her hair down. He pushed her hand away to do it himself. His fingers curled among soft blonde strands and he gently pulled her head to his chest. *Not getting away that soon, baby.*

A second later she pushed away and rose above him, her eyes clouded and wistful. He stopped smoothing her hair. That look couldn't lead anywhere good. *And here we go…*

"You know I'm not going to freak out, don't you? You asked me to be with you, and we did that, so it doesn't have to be a big deal," she said with an infuriating earnestness. "Just so we both know what we're doing after this. That's all." He let her words hang in the air. Waited. She stayed silent.

Joker seized her waist and turned, rolling so she lay beneath him. *Time to pin the girl down.* "Are we negotiating a contract here?" he asked as their eyes met. *No more wiggling out of this, baby.* Her smile didn't quite match her eyes, and her fingers dug into his arm.

"I … want to make sure we stay clear with each other."

"Is that what you think just happened? I picked up a crow eater, and now we're fuck buddies?"

"Um. Maybe? I just need to know which interpretation you're using so I don't, um, make things weird." She stared at his sheets so he touched her chin. She shrugged away. Joker's brows met in a scowl that might have turned into a sarcastic quip had he not felt the tremor running through her arm. There it was, written across her pale features and averted eyes. Something in her head had hold of her.

"Let me be clear, sweetheart." He leaned in until his nose bumped hers, forcing her eyes onto him. "This isn't a one-time fuck unless that's what *you* want. Do you want a one-time fuck?"

"Um. No. But I…"

"Shh." He kissed her swollen lips and lingered. "You're my girl, Ash."

"You may have to say it a lot," she admitted in a shaky whisper. "I'm sorry for that. I'm … I don't usually…" He used the hand still cupping her cheek to gently push her face back toward him, waiting until she met his eyes. Fatalistic certainty faced him.

Some asshole needs a beatdown, sweetheart. But he waited in silence.

"There's, uh, pretty universal agreement among my exes that I'm a huge mistake." She tried to turn it into a joke—he wasn't buying. "I mean, the last one picked Ebola. So … that's a thing."

Unable to listen to another deflection, he kissed her neck. "I'm not walking away, Ash. Especially not for a hemorrhagic fever."

A slow, sweet smile, offset the tearful sheen lingering in her eyes. "Careful, Joker. You get even hotter when you use big words. I might forget about your party." Her arm draped around him. "And then where would you get to show me off? The clubhouse?"

"Show you off? Do I look like I run a beauty pageant?" He skimmed a palm along her side. Her breath caught. *Maybe getting back between her legs right now wouldn't be such a bad idea…*

"I mean, hey, the internet's pretty sure I'm

supposed to sleep with half the club." Her sheepish smile didn't soften his glare.

"*Don't* believe everything you read on the internet, sweetheart." He pulled her leg up toward his hips before sliding his fingers along her vulnerable inner thigh. "You're all mine."

"Mm. I'll keep that—oh!" His hand found her clit, and whatever she might've said turned into whimpering. He took her mouth with his to catch the sounds. Some night he might want the whole world to hear her screaming, but he wanted her all to himself.

"One more time. Then we can go back…" He slid two fingers into her and grinned against her lips as she writhed. He kept hold of her hair, deepened their kiss. *All right, maybe two more times. Or three…*

Chapter Ten: June 9

Ashlyn
Oak Grove

Dark clouds building in the north and the sickly greenish tinge creeping over the daylight forced Ash to put the Miata's top up. The storm's one silver lining was that Joker planned on driving his truck to the movies tonight instead of taking the bike—meaning she could wear a dress she'd been dying to dust off. It just required a quick run to Grandpa's. *I'll be in and out in a flash,* she told herself as she sat in the driveway. She stared at the uneasy sky through a Fallout Boy chorus, a Taylor Swift song, and one commercial break before she shut the motor off. And waited some more. The car's temperature reached boiling before she forced herself out and dashed up the walk through the first sprinkling rain.

They had to find out I'm dating Nathan sometime, right? Buoyed on her own willful optimism, she swung the door open.

"And where have you been, kitty cat?" The purring, velveteen voice flash-froze Ashlyn on the threshold. An air-conditioned chill sank into her veins, creeping down to her bones.

I should have stayed in the car and driven it into the lake.

"Come in or go out, for pity's sake," Bonnie said from the other room, her voice sharp but far warmer than the first speaker. "You're letting the cold air out!"

Ashlyn stumbled into the house like her feet were trapped in lead flip-flops. In the cream carpeted living room, a familiar, petite figure sat on the pale blue couch.

"Mom." The greeting was as flat and forced as Ashlyn's tentative steps into the living room. *That storm could at least sound my doom with some ominous thunder*. Strangers might mistake Bella Tilden-Marlow's smile for welcoming, but Ashlyn saw the truth in her glass-green eyes: fury, plain and simple.

"Your grandmother's been telling me all about your adventures."

"I didn't know I had any…"

"Saving a boy on the side of the road? Going out with Megan while her biker friends are getting into some kind of shooting incident? Sounds rather adventurous to me." Bella crossed her legs at the ankles in a whisper of silk. Her lips twisted to one side, spoiling the fake smile. "If you like danger so much, why not make a tour of East St. Louis? I know quite a few businesses always desperate to find an intern or two."

Ashlyn sighed but took a seat on the divan across from Bella. Her grandmother returned from the kitchen with three glasses of sun-brewed tea on a serving tray, and a beaming countenance meant to banish the tension.

"There's never been anything like that in Oak Grove, Bella!" Bonnie chided. "You're being so dramatic."

"No, of course not, Mother." Even Bella's sniff conveyed a derisive note. "It's all very civilized here: they only kill people *outside* the city limits. Maybe inside Ravenwood in a pinch."

"Bella," Bonnie said with a touch of warning. "If Ashlyn wants to take a semester off before graduate school, I think you need to let her. It's a stressful time to enter the workforce. This mess with the state schools can't be helping anybody's faith in them. If you'd just consider sending her to somewhere closer—"

"Mother, don't change the subject. We are discussing the fact you've let my daughter turn into a biker groupie. Give it a month, she'll be trading her car for meth or getting caught in one of those 'freak fires' the sheriff's department pretends weren't started by a bunch of assholes with explosives!" Bella's cup clinked on the stone coaster. "You *let this happen.*"

"Do watch your tone of voice, dear." Bonnie remained unconcerned, adjusting the brooch on her summer-weight linen jacket as if discussing the weather. "Ashlyn is a grown woman, and if she wants to follow in your less-advisable footsteps for a few months, I don't see the harm in it."

"Her what?" Ashlyn cut off her mom's squawked protest with her own. She sat forward, staring at her grandmother while Bella leaned back. Bonnie sipped her tea with smile.

"Mother, don't you dare…"

"Dare what? Tell your daughter about *your* little biker phase? Please, Bella. She knows you well enough by now. I'm sure Ashlyn's sorted out that there's hardly an attractive man of a certain age around here you didn't … date."

"Mom!" Ashlyn stared at her mother. Bella's classic features hardened, her ivory skin paling to a foreboding alabaster. Some people seemed more human when upset; Bella looked like a murderous doll.

Her eyes leveled on her daughter. "I was younger than you, and thus excusably naive. Then I grew up and went to school. You seem to have the order mixed up."

"Mm. She dated him for about, what … three years or so?" Bonnie said, once again earning a glare from her daughter. "Quite a nice boy. He did get a bit rougher around the edges later on. I imagine you've met him, Ash. Jacob Wronski? I think his club always called him some ridiculous thing … Shrub? Maple? Something like that. Those men and their names. They're worse than Shriners."

"Tree?" Ashlyn trapped her cup in a white-knuckle grip. The twitch in Bella's temple answered loud enough. Her grandmother's arctic front room faded away. *Mom and... This is why you didn't live in a small town.* And then she laughed. "Well, that's good, Mom. Since I'm dating his son. I guess you two can get along, huh?"

Bella swept to her feet. "You're dating one of those gorillas?"

"Uh, yeah." She bit her lower lip and tried to look like she might repent.

"You aren't pregnant, are you?" Bella's voice fell several decibels. "If it's some stupid one-night stand gone wrong, sweetheart—"

"Jesus, Mom, I'm not seventeen. I have an IUD."

"Good grief, both of you!" Bonnie hissed. "Manners."

"Sorry, Grandma." Ashlyn rolled her eyes. "I assumed you knew about contraception since you only had two kids instead of twelve."

Bonnie's lips pursed, and her back straightened.

"Ashlyn Marie Davis!"

"You're the one who brought up Mom shagging half the county."

"That is not what I meant! Your mother went on a date with a variety of young men. I assume the number she engaged with in other ways is somewhat smaller."

"Oh, fucking Christ on a crucifix!" Bella put her hand over her eyes and took a slow breath. "Not that it concerns either one of you, but my mother is right. It was the eighties. People dated without screwing on the first night back then, Ashlyn. Your generation invented Tinder."

"Uh huh. And what's a key party, Mommy?" Ash pitched her voice a little higher, adding wide eyes and a saccharine tone.

"I'm sure you'll find out when your biker

boyfriend decides to host one, sweetheart."

"*Bella.*" Bonnie pointed at the seat her daughter had abandoned. "Sit down and stop insulting your child. Nathan is a nice boy. He works in that garage—the one his grandfather founded."

"The one run by his asshole father and the merry band of thugs and shitheads?"

"*Language.*"

"I'll use the language appropriate to the subject, Mother. Only vulgarity can possibly suit that echelon of society." Bella's prim tone sent Bonnie's hands into the air. Ashlyn suspected only age and a bad hip kept her grandmother from violence.

"How did I ever raise such a snob?"

"Familiarity breeds contempt. If I didn't know them so well back then, I might be better disposed toward them now."

Ashlyn couldn't resist the opening. "What happened, Mom? You catch Tree banging some chick in your car? He doesn't seem half as slimy as your first husband."

"That's a matter of opinion, sweetheart." Bella shot her an arch look. "Ian may represent slimeballs, but Tree is a mercenary son-of-a-bitch. And I do mean the mercenary part literally."

"Oh, no, not a mercenary!" Ashlyn's eyes rolled. "Half of my classmates' dads paid their tuition on contractor bonus pay. Try again."

Bella shook her head with a sardonic laugh. "Those boys are squeaky clean compared to Jacob. He joined some of the initial private contractors, long before they bothered with image consultants."

"So, he's secretly loaded? Awesome." Ashlyn waved it off, mostly to watch her mother's anger return.

Bella scoffed. "I'm sure he drank most of it. I

don't want you anywhere near him or anything he's connected to." Her expression finally softened. "Kitten, he's dangerous—more so than anyone you've ever met."

"Right." Ash's nose wrinkled, and she bit her cheek to stop the words in her throat. Frustrated, rage-born tears burned her eyes. *They never ask. They really never fucking ask. Why would they? It isn't like they want to know.*

"Nothing good comes out of hanging around with that club," her mother continued. "As much fun as I'm sure you're having by rebelling against me and society, can you please do it some other way? How about a gap year in Eastern Europe? Volunteering in a war zone? Either is less hazardous."

"Everything is dangerous nowadays, Mom. The internet's dangerous. The climate's dangerous. Sunlight kills you, the food you eat is poison. I like Nate. I like his friends, and I don't see anything wrong with the club." *You didn't see anything wrong with Bennett, or his friends. You didn't even notice. All the blood and the tears, and no one cared at all...*

"They deal drugs and weapons, Ashlyn." Bella's jaw clenched.

"Allegedly." She shrugged in a deliberate show of carelessness. "And so what if they do? Have you seen East St. Louis? Chicago? Seriously, if they deal so many weapons and drugs, how come they've existed so long without the Feds busting down this entire place? It must not be enough to get their attention, because I looked up the Storm Crows. Founded in fifty-four and barely a blip in Federal warnings beyond recognition as an outlaw club." Her eyes locked on her mother's face.

"When did young people get so jaded?" Bonnie sighed.

"When y'all invented the internet, Grandma."

Ashlyn smiled at her mother's darkening glare.

"The Crows are not just a local club." Bella snapped. "They're nationwide. Global. Like a plague."

"My point remains: Why not a lot more? Why no federal cases?"

Bella arched a brow. "I'm sure it's a foreign notion to your Millennial brain, but those kinds of cases take years to build, and longer to prosecute. Not to mention you wouldn't know where to look."

I have academic research accounts, Google, and no job. But I'm obviously too dumb to operate a search engine. She held up her hand to tick off the decades like a child. "So it's taken sixty years? Nearly seventy? What are they waiting for? Signed invitations and personalized confessions on YouTube?"

"You sound like you've given this considerable thought."

"Did you date Jett without looking up the basics on Morpheon and DevInc?" she tossed out her stepfather's two largest ventures.

Bella's fingers tapped against her cup before she sat back and rubbed her temple. "Ashlyn, come home. You can find a job in the city much more easily, and you'll have all your friends around. Wouldn't that be more fun?"

Too easy. Ash schooled her features into weary uncertainty. "As you pointed out earlier, I'm having plenty here. I like it. It's nice to have my family around. Just … let me take the summer to think about what I want to do. Grandpa's not charging me rent, I have a part-time gig and no major bills. I'll have time to get my applications together."

"Fine," Bella exhaled. "This fall, we're going to have a talk about spring registration for a grad school, yes?"

"Definitely." Ashlyn's smile widened.

Bonnie sat back in her own chair, watching the two of them with the expression usually reserved for her afternoon soaps. "Lovely! If we're all settled, how about some pie? I made a lovely peach one this morning. The local orchards are having a bumper crop this year." Bonnie stood up and waved them toward the stairs down to the kitchen. Ash and Bella eyed one another but took their cues and rose, allowing the conversation to revert to less dangerous topics.

A few months to think of something else almost counts as a win, right?

Chapter Eleven: June 15

Ariel
Ravenwood

"Hey, girl!" Karli called as the door of the clubhouse opened. "Can you—" She turned, and the cheerful greeting died on her lips. Ariel followed her gaze and found not Ashlyn but Hailey storming in, her usually perfect dark hair half-down and frizzed from the muggy summer heat. The pale, pinched look on her face chilled Ariel's blood.

"What's up, Hales?" Ariel stepped closer. Hailey shook her head in warning.

"Where are they?" Hailey's voice was higher than usual.

"Meeting." Karli pointed to the closed door on the other side of the room. Fluffy sat at a scarred wood table next to it, playing cards with Joker's Prospect, Case. Neither of them paid the women any attention. Until Hailey stormed toward the sanctum door.

"Hey, you can't go in, babe." Ariel said it even though she knew already that Hailey wouldn't listen. No woman entered the sanctum. Not even any non-board members unless they had specific business or a vote. Hailey kept walking.

Case and Fluffy looked up in time. They got to their feet while Karli and Ariel stood in frozen wonder. Fluff sported 300 pounds of pudge over muscle while Case was named for the six-pack abs he maintained like a religion, but they wore identical horrified expressions as they tried to intercept Hailey without causing any harm. Hailey didn't share their concern.

"Hales, you can't go in." Fluffy put himself between her and the door, and reached for her arm.

"Get the fuck out of my way, Fluffy." She shoved

his hand away.

"Case, a little help?"

Case scowled but obediently snagged Hailey's flailing left arm while Fluffy took her right. Ariel relaxed for half a heartbeat before Hailey managed to break their grips and dash forward. She kicked Fluffy in the shin and drove an elbow into Case's sternum as he pulled her backward.

"Hailey! The ... the hell?" Case wheezed. Hailey's frantic blue eyes didn't so much as flicker his direction. She started yelling at the door.

"Ice! Goddamn it! Ice! *Jake!*"

The door banged open, and Ice stomped out. "Hailey?!" He stared at Case and Fluffy, clearly deciding who he needed to punch first. "What the fuck are you two doing?" He shoved Fluffy back and started toward Case.

"She's trying to get in," Fluffy explained. He put his hands up as Ice growled a threat.

"Heathens!" Hailey spat at them.

"What?" Ice's eyes narrowed on his wife. "What about Heathens?" He waved the other two off and reached for her arm.

Tree, Joker, Grease, Tommy, and Dragon followed Ice out as she explained: "Star Hollow. At the stoplight. I didn't hit the brakes in time—I told you the Taurus's breaks were fucked, jackass—and then I-I started to get out but the trunk opened and they had *guns*, Ice."

"Babe, they could've been just moving…"

"A load of AR-15's?"

"Why would they have those laying around in their trunk if they were running them?" Dragon asked, bringing up the rear of the officers filing out to investigate the commotion.

Tree looked around, caught Ariel's eye and gestured to the door. Not angry, but giving her and Karli permission to get the hell out. They took it. Ariel shot one glance at Hailey but didn't let concern keep her in the room. Once the door closed behind them, Ariel stayed under the awning to open her messages and send a quick text while Karli pulled a buzzing phone from her cleavage.

"Ash, where are you?" Karli asked. "Right. Well don't rush. Church is running long and they moved out into the main room, so we're still closed for a few…"

Ariel ignored her and struggled to phrase her own message. She didn't like sending it on her phone but pulling out a burner this second would be fucking awkward. On the other hand, this sort of thing was why Brandt wanted ears here, and he might finally be convinced to get off his ass and finish off Ariel's problem. The little bitch would be good as gone after this…

Me: **Hailey's here. Saw guns in somebody's trunk. Telling the board rn. Be ready.**

She hit "Send" and let out a long breath, staring off across the parking lot to the garage. A couple of the mechanics and Prospects wheeled under cars and tinkered with bikes in the bays but her attention lingered in the recesses of her own head, with a tall VP and his sweet eyes. She waited until Karli ended the call with Ashlyn before turning a smile on her companion. Karli's bleached-blonde hair looked almost white in the sun, the roots a touch darker—Karli hadn't kept her real color once in the years since they buried Blade. "She still coming?"

"Yeah." Karli shrugged, shoving the phone back down her corset. "She needs the paycheck. Some psycho went ape-shit on her car a couple weeks ago."

"I noticed that. Joker hasn't fixed it?"

Karli smirked. "Nope."

"So ... what do you think?" Ariel twisted her silver pinkie ring. "About her, I mean?"

"She's a nice kid." Karli shrugged.

"She going to stick around or do you think it's like a summer fling?"

"Joker's nuts about her. If she makes him happy, she makes him happy. She's new to the club life, but it's not like she's some society bitch coming in and whining the whole time about how dirty everything is."

"But ... she *is* a society bitch," Ariel pointed out. "Doesn't that make you nervous? Like, she could be somebody's pet spy. You and I both know she was going out with that cop."

"Pretty sure Tree wouldn't let a chick near his VP that wasn't checking out." Karli's arms crossed, and she turned to face Ariel. "And you need to step off, babe. Whatever your history, Ash's an Old Lady. You aren't. I don't give a shit if it's you or a little crow eater bootlicker you conned into it, but those psycho texts and the rest of it stops now. If it don't, I'm taking it to Joker. Even if he's sick of her in two months, you really think he's gonna ignore it? Newsflash, honey. He'll kick your ass for it now, he'll kick your ass for it later. So knock it off, Ari."

Ariel's jaw set, and she lifted her chin. "You saying an Old Lady needs another Old Lady to take care of her shit, Karli? You suck his dick for her, too?"

Karli grunted. "I'm giving a warning to someone I count as a friend, dumbass. I'm not takin' her side, I'm pointing out you're thinking with your pussy instead of your head. There are plenty of ways to a man's heart, and high school bullshit isn't on the list."

Ariel looked away, twisting her ring again.

"I'll, um, see what I can find out. Sorry, Karli. I'm

having…" She grimaced. "It's a bad time."

"I know." The harsh edge vanished from Karli's voice. "You've been stuck on him a long-ass time, but you need to get a hobby boy. Show Joker what he's missing. It's been … a year? Two? Since Reagan bailed. He's never had another steady girl, Ari. Not one. You've been the closest he got to it. That's something. Give him space to breathe. Let him have his rebound."

"All he's doing is sniffing after her," Ariel muttered.

"Let him. And let him give her his leather, and show her the ropes: either she'll prove you right and jump ship, or he'll get sick of playing teacher. Never been all that patient, has he?"

"Good point." Ariel frowned, feeling the weight of that truth but distrusting it. She wouldn't just sit back and do nothing. Couldn't. *That damsel shit gets you walked on, not respected.*

"Much as you hate her, I can put up with a dumb puppy a fuck-load easier than another prize treasure like that cunt Tommy's licking. God help me, if Lana goes missing, don't look in the freezer." Karli drew a cigarette case from her black leather bag and selected a joint. "Just thinkin' about her sorry bedsheet ass makes me smoke. What the hell does he even do when he's fucking her? Hold on to those pointy hipbones?"

"I figured the pointy head," Ariel said with a grin. "She's gotta suck like a pool vac to make up for that voice."

"Fuckin' Chicago accent. Knew she'd be worthless the second she started talkin… Oh, speakin' of the devil, there's the puppy." The sun sparked across a vicious gash in the Miata's dusty white paint as it turned into the lot.

Ariel smiled. *I do the best work.*

"Hey, Ash!" She waved to the girl stepping out of the car. Honey-caramel-wheat balayage highlights shone in Ashlyn's long hair as she walked their direction—Ariel appreciated the work on a professional level, though she hoped the chemicals burned the brat's hair off someday. Her clothes were stupid, too—overpriced jean shorts and some bullshit Free People top. *Dressing for Coachella at the Crows' Nest. Great. I hope Brandt gets off his ass fast.*

"I know you said they were running late, but I figured better safe than sorry. I don't want to get in trouble barely out of training." Ashlyn slung her fringy leather purse over her shoulder. Ariel's teeth gritted. *I bet she smells like patchouli.*

"Afternoon shift's dead anyway, honey." Karli smiled.

"And nobody here's going to yell at a VP's Old Lady, except Tree." Ariel couldn't help herself. She had to say it, even with Karli's eyes shooting daggers. "You know you'd pretty much have to set something on fire to be in trouble."

Ashlyn's smile faded. "But wouldn't it be that much worse for a VP's girl to fuck up? I mean, if we're going to be completely feudal, then what I do reflects on him, right? Even if nobody's allowed to say it out loud. You basically end up being the Emperor's New Clothes." She wrinkled her stupid button nose. "Which has some seriously terrible connotations, equating females to clothing, but at the same time, we equate men to the value of the rings and tribute they offer so you could argue that it's—"

"Honey, take a puff." Karli offered the joint to her. "You're nervous again. It's a slow shift. Chill out." Ashlyn eyed the joint but put out a hesitant hand and took it. Ariel expected a racking cough and maybe puking, but Ashlyn sucked in and held the smoke before exhaling. She passed it back to Karli.

"Thanks." She rubbed her hand along her arm. "Sorry. Grandma made me go to lunch with my mom and stepdad. They brought my aunt and uncle for referees, but it didn't help. I considered driving off Carthage Bridge on the way over."

You need to learn to follow your instincts, brat. Ariel forced a smile. "Sounds rough. You sure you're up to working tonight? I can cover if you need a breather. The guys are gonna be in a weird mood."

A fleeting look of hope turning her into one of those wide-eyed dolls kids used to like. *Bratz, wasn't it? Fitting.* "No," she said in that stupid baby voice, glancing back at her messed-up convertible. "It's okay. You've got better stuff to do tonight. Wednesdays are ladies' nights at the Night Hawk, right?"

"My favorite." Ariel tossed her hair over her shoulder. "Text me if you change your mind. We—"

"Fuck off, Jake!"

Ariel stepped back as the clubhouse door flew open. Karli pulled Ashlyn aside just fast enough to avoid a collision with Hailey, who stomped past with a thunderous scowl and Ice's massive frame right on her tail.

"Hails! God damn it, Hailey. *Stop.*" Ice seized his wife's arm.

Hailey spun, using the momentum to bring her arm down on his. Hard. He grunted and released, drawing back in what became a feint, and caught her other arm as she rocked on her heel. Hailey yelped and stumbled. Ice captured her in a bear hug. Ariel winced at Hailey's frustrated scream, but didn't move to help the brunette while Ice hefted her off the ground. Hailey's feet wind-milled and her heel smacked into Ice's muscled thigh hard enough to buckle his knee. He recovered, cursing.

"One of you assholes want to get the goddamn car? So help me, Hailey, if I have to stuff you in a fucking pet crate … Urgh!" Another kick on his knee. "*Frog, get in the fucking car!* You're taking him home with you, Hailey. Or he's taking you in the crate. *Stop. Kicking.*"

The unfortunate Prospect came running across the lot, heading for the van closest to Ice. The other guys filed out of the clubhouse, muffling Hailey's shriek with their laughter.

"Got a spare lasso if you need it, brother!" Tree called.

"Thanks, Prez." Ice's grumbled answer ended in a grunt—Hailey's elbow was free. He sorted that out while hauling his unhappy wife toward the van Frog had fired up. The others shouted suggestions about ropes and knots.

Ariel's eyes caught on Ashlyn. Face pale and eyes wide, the little blonde clung to Karli's arm. She looked closer to fainting every time Hailey shouted. Aware of their audience, Ariel sidled toward Karli. "Ain't you never seen an old lady and her man fight?" Ashlyn's wordless, horrified expression made her smile. "C'mon, bar's clear. Let's grab a drink?"

"Baby?" Joker's voice hit Ariel like a blanket. A cold, wet one. The VP stood behind her, his brandy-dark gaze on Ashlyn. "You all right?"

"What?" Ashlyn blinked without any sign of comprehension, even though she looked right at him. "Fine. I'm good. Long drive…" Her shaky hand dropped from Karli's arm and delved into her bag.

"Karli, you got somebody to cover the bar tonight?" Joker didn't quite look at her, but Karli nodded.

"Ari's free. Aren't you, babe?"

"Totally." She grinned at Joker, deliberately moving into his line of sight to take Karli's arm. "We're good here. Ash, why don't you get home?" *To St. Louis or hell; either one.* "We'll handle it here."

"Um. I-I guess. Yeah." Across the lot, Hailey's voice rose in a fresh rant. Ashlyn winced. "I'll ... see you tomorrow, Karli." She managed a sickly smile and headed for her car with a vague, half-remembered wave.

"Thanks, Kar." Joker gave her a one-armed hug, clapped Ariel's shoulder, and breezed on past them to catch Ashlyn. "Baby, I'll take you home. Come on. You look like you need some air."

The warm summer wind carried the words to Ariel. She shivered. Joker didn't even sound like himself. Too soft. She dragged a pack of cigarettes from her purse. *Whose home did he mean?*

"I'm going back in," she told Karli. "I need a drink."

****

Joker

The trip to his house didn't allow for much conversation, but her arms sat loose on his waist and she barely bent with the curves; if he'd driven faster or had less experience, her inattention might have tipped the bike.

Joker's temper smoldered to life before they reached the drive, but he held his arm out for her when he put the stand down. She stumbled off the Dyna on her own. He dismounted after, stripping off his gloves while she struggled to unfasten the helmet—the only one he'd had with him. Her fingers slipped, then again. And again. A frustrated huff escaped her thinned lips, but she got it undone before he could offer; her eyes shone bright and hard as she thumped it onto the leather seat. He waited, but she didn't move, not even toward the door.

"You ever going to tell me what all this is about?" he asked. Her thousand-yard stare drifted from the helmet to the door. "Sweetheart?"

"Bad day." She raked a hand through her hair, displacing her silver headband and yanking it off. Her hair fell across her face like a curtain. "Can we just not talk about it?"

"No. You're missing work because of it." *Work you damn well need, and I know it.* Her mother took her name off accounts, canceled cards—he'd overheard some of the frantic phone calls, but like whatever this was, she hadn't talked to him. She might never. The thought added a barb to his voice. "Technically, so am I."

"Then go back to work!" She whipped around, face twisted in a snarl, eyes glittering with a stranger's rage. "I never asked you to leave anything. You are here because you fucking insisted on it." Her voice was low and harsh—barely recognizable.

Tale of the Body Snatchers. He rocked back, but the symptoms scrolled through his thoughts. Raging hostility. Lack of eye contact. Refusal to answer. Deflection. Panic.

So I was right. Shit. Sounds a bit different coming from a half-size Barbie doll, but that's what this is. I'd bet the bike...

Anger flaring, he turned and tucked his gloves into the saddle bag with slow, deliberate movements before shrugging out of his cut. Even in Oak Grove it wasn't a good idea to get arrested wearing colors and the way Ash looked, they might be screaming on the front lawn before all was said and done.

"I ain't biting, Ash," he announced with a calm he didn't feel. "I'm here because I care about you, and something isn't right."

"Nobody asked you to drag me home on your phallic symbol. I was fine!"

"Right. Because you sure looked fine back there. This right here is what you call normal, too, huh?"

"Smug asshole doesn't suit you. Go back to antisocial asshole."

"Baby, it's too damn hot out here to stand around. You can start a fight in there as easy as out here, so move." He kept an eye on her, calculating the odds of his guess being right. Her lip drew back, and she practically hissed at his chest.

"Oh, fuck you. Fuck your caveman bullshit. Fuck your alpha male, machismo-fueled, patriarchal dick-sucking douche nozzle crap!" She spun toward the exit, and he darted to the side, between Ash and the garage door. She squealed and backtracked, shying out of arm's reach. Joker held his hands out but didn't touch her—giving her space, though not freedom.

"Good use of your words, babe. Let's try a few more. In sentences. What the hell is wrong?"

"Don't you dare power-play me, asshole." Ashlyn edged to the side. He blocked. "Get out of my way!"

"One answer." He talked like he would to a terrified kid. "That's all you need to give, and we all calm down."

"I don't owe you anything!"

"You don't. So, you want me to start guessing?" He crossed his arms. *Might as well do it here—I can catch her before she gets to the backyard.* "See, I'm thinking it was hearing Hailey and Ice. I think something in your skull went straight to DefCon One, and you can't tell north from south. Because you damn well know Ice would cut off his own dick before he laid a hand on Hailey."

"So it's okay to throw her around like that?"

"He picked her up, babe. That's it. She needs protection, and she needs help, but when she panics, she runs. That's what she does. And she's terrified right now. When we left, she was already calming down out by the van. If you hadn't been freaking out, you'd have noticed."

"She just gave in so he'd stop."

"Ashlyn." Joker fought to remember his few counseling sessions and keep his voice level. "For fuck's sake, baby. Give us some kind of credit. We may be assholes, but we have standards. At least—shit!"

She sprinted to the right. Joker snagged her around the waist with one arm and dragged her against his side. Ash screamed. He hesitated with his ears and heart both vibrating. He could let go, and she could … *what? Run into the street? How bad is she?* He grunted as her elbow hit his rib, but heard the sob underneath the cursing. *Right. Fuck it.*

"I'm so sorry, sweetheart. We can't stand around outside screaming." He shifted his stance, hoisted her up until her feet left the floor, and hauled her flailing and shrieking into the kitchen. "Hold on, baby..." He kicked the door closed.

"You sick son of a bitch." Her wedge-clad heel hammered his left shin hard enough to bruise bone. He grimaced but didn't loosen his grip.

"I know." He adjusted his arm as she wiggled hard enough to slide down his chest. "But I'm not letting go until you—ow!—talk." Ashlyn's struggles faded as he dropped onto the linoleum, keeping her shivering body hugged to him. "Who do I need to call? Hotline? Friend? Who?"

"Nathan! This. Isn't. Funny."

"Do I look like I'm laughing?" He gentled the hold, breathing deep. *Calm. Think calm. She's not going to talk if you won't.* "We're going to sit here, like this, until we figure out what to do. You aren't getting hurt, Ash. Nobody is getting hurt. You just have to calm down, sweetheart." He kept his left arm tight around her, but chafed her chilled shoulder with his right hand.

She didn't say anything.

"Baby, you're scaring the shit out of me. Come on. I find you in the lot, white as a ghost. By the time I get you home, you're screaming and scared out of your mind. I've seen you handle bullets flying without breaking a sweat. Please."

All he got was a whimper, so he tucked her head under his chin and waited. A minute turned into five, and the shaking eased off. His leg and back ached, getting sharper while her silence stretched on. "How about we get up and go to the living room? You okay with that?" Her head moved a fraction of an inch. "Yeah? Okay. I'm gonna get up and carry you in. It's going to be all right, sweetheart."

He managed to stand, waited to get feeling back in his leg and keeping his hands on Ash's arms. She meekly followed him up, and didn't struggle when he lifted her, or during the few steps to the living room. He settled into the recliner with Ash limp and shivering in his arms. He kept an eye on the clock, and risked using one hand to turn on the television, providing a distraction via the first thing in her Netflix cue, which proved to be some chick comedian. Another ten minutes passed. She leaned against him, and her shoulders rose and fell in soft, irregular patterns. Crying. But not talking.

Who the fuck did this? Her dad? Step-dad? Ex? His thoughts continued down the list. Grim's background search hadn't turned up much beyond a couple speeding tickets, a few hospitalizations for illness, and a car wreck.

"Shh, I got you," he whispered against her hair. "You're safe, sweetheart." Ashlyn turned in his lap, burying her head against the crook of his neck—the first sign of recognition he'd gotten, so he stroked her hair. "I know it hurts. I know you're scared, and you're mad as hell at me. I get it. I know it's easier to be mad than talk, easier to run than open up. I'm sorry I dragged you inside, but if you ran out into the street like that... You scared the shit out of me, baby. If you still need to leave, I get it. It's all right, Ash. Whatever you need. Just tell me."

The sobs got louder, broken. Wrenching. She broke apart in his arms, and all he could do was hold on.

"Th-they s-sounded like ... my..." Ash's voice broke, hitched on sobs. "I came ... home ... and he was ... all over. T-threw her on the ... and ... h-he k-kept h-hitting..." Her explanation vanished into more sobbing, and he fought to keep himself from crushing her to his chest. He didn't answer until he could think enough to choose his words.

"He's not here now. He won't ever be. The army takes everybody; the Storm Crows don't." A nice version, but true: men who beat up their wives got under the DCFS scrutiny, got the cops looking their way. Caused drama. Turned on brothers to get out of that drama.

He let her finish crying her tear ducts out while the chick comedian's set finished and Netflix started up some Cable Guy special. Eventually, she stirred.

"Nathan?" Tears roughened her voice, but it sounded closer to normal. "Sorry, I—"

"Shh." He hugged her tight. "You're talking to the king of displaced anger."

"I didn't mean what I said."

"It's all right."

"It's not."

He snorted. "Last time I lost my shit, I broke Dragon's nose. You did better than me."

Ashlyn made a sound that didn't quite qualify as a laugh. "Only because you're too tall." She pinched his side. He caught her wrist and nuzzled her shoulder before pulling her hand up for a kiss.

"Next time I'll get on my knees. Sound fair?"

"But I can think of so many better things for you to do on your knees." Her words sparked a new sort of amusement, and he traced his index finger along her damp cheek.

"That's my line, baby. But if you tell me what you're thinking, maybe we can compare notes."

She straddled his hips and slid her arms around his neck before leaning in for a kiss. Her red-rimmed gaze was warm when she pulled away but another tear fell. "I can't … talk about it. Yet. I want to. I—I think I can eventually…" He put a finger over her lips and locked his eyes on hers.

"You tell me when you can. When you need to. But when you freak out, you gotta let me know. Trust me enough for that."

"How did you, uh, know?"

"I figured you were fighting something after the first couple times you froze up around Grim." He frowned. "How are you dealing with the bar?"

Her lashes lowered. "Sometimes I pretend I'm in a play when things get out of control. And I have a lot of Xanax in case I freak out. But bad days … bad days nothing really helps. The bar kind of feels normal, in a weird way."

He slid his fingers through her hair. "You know the Crows' Nest ain't nobody's idea of normal, don't you?"

"That's why it's nice," she said with a sheepish smile. "Nothing's normal, so I don't have to be either. It's ... relaxing."

"Baby, we almost got barbecued the other night. And shot."

"That doesn't scare me." She chuckled at his raised brows. "Fine, it scares me a little. Just not like ... like other things do. I know it's fucked up, Nathan. I'd rather get shot here than go back to ... to things before. Maybe it's the adrenaline-rush addiction some people get." Her red-rimmed eyes met his. "Does that make me a bad person?"

"Never." He swallowed his emotions and pulled her close. "I chose the life because I couldn't fit anywhere but the army, and I know I'm too screwed up for another tour, but you could go anywhere and do anything. With your family, and the—"

This time it was her hand that covered his mouth. "Stop," she whispered. "I've already been a lot of places, and I've lived my fair share." She blinked back more tears. "I didn't want to care about anyone because I didn't want to lie to them. Then you happened and ... and I want us to keep happening, so I'm not lying to you."

"Whatever you've done won't make me think less of you."

Her eyes bored into his as he kissed her palm. "I let someone get hurt because I was too stupid and scared to help. M-maybe more than one." Sighing, he let his hands curve protectively around her shoulders.

"I think if something was scaring you, then, baby, it had to be fucking worth being scared of."

"Maybe." Her expression was guarded—they were dancing around the hole in her head, but he couldn't stop his next question.

"Is that why you stayed with me the night I wrecked? Making it up to someone else?"

"Maybe. But it's not why I stayed with you after."

"Good." Another, softer kiss. "Because I don't care what damage you've got, sweetheart. I want you with me."

"That's your erection talking, but I'll take it." She grinned. "The compliment and your dick." Her hand slid down his chest. "Let me make that bad bike ride up to you…"

Groaning, Joker put his hand over hers, stopping her teasing descent. As much as he wanted to show her just how much better she could feel, he knew how easy it was to hide behind sex and booze. And if part of what she hadn't told him yet was about sex, jumping into bed before she was really, truly ready was a shit plan in the long run. He didn't intend to lose her to short-term thinking.

"In a little while. Let's just, uh, sit here for right now, all right?" He kissed her knuckles. "Netflix. Dinner. Then we can discuss the chill part. If you're okay with that."

Her brows drew together. "But … If you aren't mad at me, can't we…"

"I'm not mad. God, sweetheart, I am so far from mad." He covered her lips in a long, desperate kiss. "Look me in the eyes and tell me, right now, that you're a hundred percent ready to be thrown across my bed and fucked senseless." And like a charm, a shadow flickered in her green eyes. He smiled. "I can wait, Ash. My dick being hard has been a fact of life with you around, so I can wait."

This time, Ash kissed him. "And I can order pizza."

"Deal. You want to watch more *Vikings*?"

"Yes." She hugged him. "Thank you. For not telling me to get the fuck out," she added as she got up and shot from the room to the garage. He watched her go and stood up, slowly trailing her into the kitchen while she brought her phone in from his bike's saddlebag, along with his cut and two burners. He waited until she'd ordered the pizza—one with the works minus onions and one with pepperoni. Her voice wasn't quite to its usual cadence, her smile wobbly, but when she turned around, their eyes caught. She tilted her head in a silent question, and his chest finally relaxed.

"I'd miss you too much," he admitted.

"What?"

"Why I can't tell you to get out. I'd just have to go chasing after you and begging. No one needs that."

She rewarded him with a bigger smile and a pretty giggle.

"You'd never beg anyone for anything, even if your life depended on it."

"I think you might be surprised." He cupped her face in his hand and bent to give her a slow kiss.

"Player." Ashlyn sniffed as she broke away and swatted his arm. "You have to go get the pizzas in half an hour, so don't start now."

"No, *we're* going to get the pizzas. If I can't take you out, I can at least get you candy."

"Aw. It's like you know me."

"I think we've met once or twice."

This time she answered with a hug. He squeezed her tighter than he meant to, and let the rest of the tension drain away.

Chapter Twelve: June 16

Ashlyn
Ravenwood

The clubhouse's now-familiar cacophony had risen several orders of magnitude, punctuated by shouts from the pool table and calls of joy or mockery as songs changed on the jukebox. Ashlyn and Karli rushed across the worn hardwood floor, from one group of Crows and to the next, conversing in breathless words and brief smiles that didn't catch much notice. Even Karli's stunning, bustier-assisted cleavage went (comparatively) unnoticed, and if Karli's cleavage was wallpaper, Ash's clothing was an invisibility cloak. Not that Ash herself minded so much, but tips were tips—and bigger when drunks appreciated what they saw. But they definitely saw their booze, so she and Karli kept it flowing.

"Two Heinekens!" Frog called from the far end of the bar. Ash waved a hand to signal she heard. As she set the pair of beers on the bar, Joker walked through the front door. Grim, Ice, and two unfamiliar guys with Nomad patches followed in his wake.

Joker's eyes swept the room while the others kept talking, but he laughed at something Ice said and turned to the side. The hazy, smoky light accentuated his chiseled features, and transformed him into a Renaissance painting of dark and light: gleaming cinnamon eyes and white teeth, shadowy grey-black cut with the blazoned crow and badges all but shining when he turned. *Cesare Borgia on a Harley,* she thought with a wry smile before she popped the tops off a couple more beers and pushed them over to Karli. *If Cesare was blond and built like Tarzan.*

Spider called for a rum and Coke, so she filled the order and gave him a smile. He returned it but didn't linger at the bar. She spared a second to watch his retreat. Joker said she'd find her footing with everyone in time. She hoped he was right. Ashlyn shook her head and bent into the beer cooler, grabbing a Budweiser for Ice before she poured the usual Jack and Cokes for Grim and Joker.

She turned to find her boyfriend at the bar, his eyes slowly sweeping from her waist up to meet her gaze. At least someone appreciated her tank top. "Hey, sweetheart. This all for me?"

Maybe everything from yesterday is forgiven. And forgotten. Super forgotten.

"These are." She grinned and set the beer and cups in front of Joker. She picked up the soda gun and the Jack Daniels. "You guys look thirsty."

"Always." The slow tilt of his smile told her his thoughts weren't on alcohol. She looked down and prayed she wouldn't blush. "When are you free?"

"Probably whenever the VP says so, but I'd rather not leave Karli and Geiger in the lurch. Dragon's drinking with your dad already, and I'm on the schedule for two more hours."

"They can keep you for another two hours. Maybe."

"Yes, sir." She touched her forehead in a mock salute that made him grimace. Ashlyn laughed. "Tell Grim hi. And I know he's not interested at all, but Megan's 'round back by the firepit with some of the girls."

Joker nodded. He reached across the bar, but his hand angled for her wrist instead of the drinks. Before she even realized he'd caught her, he pulled her closer and kissed her hard on the lips. Her hormones went on high alert.

"Got a present for you, so don't be late," he whispered before letting her go. She watched him walking off and willed the dopey moon-struck smile off her face. The vest must've come in—the one that had "Property of Joker" on the back. Her smile widened. *I can't wait to tag Mom on that Instagram.*

Two hours passed before Ashlyn's relief showed up, but instead of manning the bar, Lana wandered into the back with a phone pressed to her ear, acknowledging Ash with the barest apologetic wave. Ash scowled but gave Lana ten minutes. Then another five. Finally, Ashlyn poured herself a drink and left Karli and Geiger to deal with it.

Karli's right. If Lana wasn't the club secretary's old lady, nobody would put up with her... God, I hope I'm not that much of an embarrassment. Megan would tell me, wouldn't she? Tree probably would. Maybe. Ash frowned as she looked around the room for Case or Jingle, or someone else to talk to.

She'd barely gone three steps when phones went off *en masse*, all but drowning out the music. A second later, one of the Prospects ran through the front doors, pushing past Crow eaters and members alike, until he scrambled out the door to the back terrace. Next came Spider. Alarm made its way through Ashlyn's tired brain. She'd never seen Spider's expression that serious.

Karli's hand landed on Ash's arm. "Better stay in here, baby girl." Ash turned a puzzled look at the taller brunette, trying to discern some answers from Karli's pin-up perfect eyeliner and blue eyes. Having been an Old Lady for years until her husband died young from cancer, Karli knew the signs of trouble better than Ashlyn.

"Why? What's going on?"

"We'll find out, or we won't. Come on up to the bar."

They both got answers a minute later when Ice and three others stormed toward the main door. Joker,

Grim, and Tree were next, and Dragon came out of the store room with two disgruntled women sulking behind. He locked the door while they reassembled their clothes and tossed the key to Karli without a word. Ashlyn eyed his would-be partners and decided they weren't the same pair he'd been with last week. *Does he have a Craigslist ad?*

"Ash." Joker crossed the room to the bar and put his arm around her waist, drawing her to him. "Stick around, all right?" He kissed her forehead before looking past her. "Karli, nobody leaves yet. Make the drinks free if you have to."

"What's wrong?" Ashlyn frowned despite the kiss. Pressed up against his side, she practically vibrated from the tension thrumming through him. His eyes held an icy edge, a glimmer of the person she knew he sometimes was. She didn't flinch when those sea-changed eyes met hers, and he didn't hide that he weighed his words before he answered.

"Hailey had an accident. We're going to check it out."

"Is there anything—"

"I'll call you." His gaze bored into hers. "Don't go home until I call."

"It's bad, isn't it?" She whispered while Karli went to inform Lana.

Joker bent close, his fingers catching her chin to tilt her head up. His lips were soft and careful on hers— light years from the way he'd kissed her earlier. "Stay." With that whisper, he left. Looking around, she realized most of the club members were out, too. A few hung back along with the Prospects—meant to keep watch, she supposed.

Dazed, Ashlyn wandered into the yard where she found her cousin. Megan stared into the flames while

Lexi and Katie barely looked up from their phones. Ash's footsteps drew their attention but not much more.

"Hey," Megan said in a hollow voice. "Better sit down, I think we're going to be here a while."

"What the hell is up?" Ashlyn demanded as Lexi made room for her on the bench. No one answered. She looked around at the circle of shifting eyes and uneasy postures. "Guys? Seriously."

Megan finally spoke. "Hailey."

"Joker said she had an accident."

Somebody coughed. Megan squirmed in her seat. "Not ... really. Somebody shot her."

Ashlyn waited for the punchline. And waited. "What?"

"Shot her," Lexi snapped. "Catch up." Her bleached-blonde ponytail caught in the breeze, and she smoothed a stray tendril while glaring at Ashlyn.

"Shot? Like, how bad shot?" Incongruous images of deer and hunting mishaps played in her head.

"Bad," Megan said.

"Deadly bad, from what my Facebook's saying," Katie added, eyes still glued to her screen.

"Fuck." Ash gulped down half her drink in one go.

Shot? That happens in hunting seasons, or Chicago, right? Sure, somebody tried to set the clubhouse on fire, but lighting stuff on fire counts as a rural tradition. Who would shoot somebody? Especially her? Hailey was the nicest of the Old Ladies she'd met so far— a small group, and one less hostile than most of the "Crow Eaters" who seemed to think (not without reason, in Ash's own opinion) that she'd stolen Ariel's rightful boyfriend. But there was yesterday's big fight that set her own issues on fire. *Was that about someone maybe shooting Hailey? A stalker? Teenage boys get weird, and she worked at the high school...*

Rather than risk saying something wrong, Ash retrieved her phone from her bag and opened a game to play, since everyone else was staring at their phones. Several levels and a few muttered curses later her text tone chimed. She gaped at the fact an hour had passed, but worse, the text...

Unknown: **2 bad it wasnt u.**

Ash shook her head and waited for her hand to stop shaking. *Of all the trolls, I had to get the persistent one.* Because the only other option... *No. He shouldn't even have a phone, and he wouldn't know what happened in Oak Grove. Not this fast. Maybe. No. Not going there. Back in the box. We don't talk about you. Never. Happening.* Her thoughts felt too raw after yesterday's panic attack and flashbacks. And she was being a lunatic while Megan sat beside her with dry eyes.

After a long pause, she replied:

Ashlyn: **Get a life, freakshow.**

Another message pinged, but this one came from Joker. Her lips thinned.

J: **Telling Case to take you & Legs to my place.**

Ashlyn: **Can't you come?**

Ashlyn: **The girls are freaked out. I'm freaking out.**

J: **Sorry. We'll talk later. Go with Case. I'll try to be back soon.**

Ashlyn: **Be careful. <3**

Ash wiped her cheek as she closed Messages. After a quick glance at Megan, she got up and tapped her cousin's shoulder. Once Megan's tearful eyes turned up to meet hers, Ashlyn nodded toward the clubhouse. "Come on. We need to go find Case. He's supposed to take us to Joker's."

"All right." Megan shrugged, but she closed her

phone case. Ash waited until her cousin stood before linking their arms together. She tried to see Lexi's screen when they walked past, but her eyesight didn't prove up to movie magic specifications so all she saw was text bubbles. Not that she'd have had time for analysis, because Case hailed them from the clubhouse door. He was closer to Ash's age than Joker's, hair still growing out of a high-and-tight cut and a Marine tattoo visible on his bare right arm.

"Hey, ladies! VP said I'm takin' you home." Joker was sponsoring him, so he'd been around the house more often than many others, and Ashlyn didn't hesitate to make a face at him.

"You and Megan aren't going to fit in my car. Did they let you bring your bike tonight?"

"We're taking my truck." Case angled his head toward the parking lot. "I won't even make you listen to the country station."

Megan ignored them both and shuffled toward the bar. Case grimaced, but Ashlyn shook her head. "Let her get a couple more shots. Not like she's driving."

"I guess." Case kept his eyes on Megan while Lana poured her a double shot of whiskey. "You doing okay?"

"Hailey was Megan's bestie. I can be not-okay later." Ashlyn sighed. "Lana, pour one of those things for me!"

A couple rounds later, they loaded Megan into Case's oversize truck. True to his word, he put on a rock playlist and didn't even mind Megan singing Joan Jett's "I Love Rock & Roll" at the top of her lungs. Everything was fine until they rolled to a stop in front of Joker's house. Megan rolled out of the passenger door and spewed an improbable amount of whiskey across the pavement.

Case retrieved the garden hose to wash off the cement while Ash dragged her semi-alert, sobbing cousin inside. The next two hours passed without major incidents. Ashlyn focused on the immediate, familiar problem of Megan's blood alcohol level, shower, and carb consumption.

"You done this a lot, princess?" Case asked as she rolled a freshly laundered Megan onto her side in the impromptu pallet of blankets he'd assembled in the main bathroom.

"The things you actually learn in college, soldier boy." Ash eased a pillow under her cousin's head. "Besides, I've been the super drunk girl. A lot. I pay it back when I can."

"How *are* you still operational?" He helped her to her feet, and she barely wavered as she walked to the front room. They left the bathroom door open so Megan stayed in view.

"Drinking was my professional calling for a while." She slumped into Joker's usual chair and stared at the television. "Can you put on a movie? I don't care what it is. Just don't make me think, okay? Thinking is bad tonight."

"No argument here, babe." He flipped on the tv.

"Actually, you want a drink? I could probably use another one."

Case gave her a calculating look but nodded. Ash left him to the endless menus and went into the kitchen. She cried silently into the drinks she poured, but it wasn't Hailey's face haunting her thoughts.

****

Joker
Oak Grove

Joker's eyes kept tracking Ice's taillight instead of the road as they all followed him into town. Red and blue light splashed along the houses on Chestnut Avenue and danced on the fog in the warm night air, but a hush hung just as thick—broken by their Harleys' roar and nothing else. *No sirens.* Joker's blood chilled. Chestnut wasn't a major street in town, but the rush of high schoolers on the cruising route should have been constant. *Another bad sign.*

A block ahead of his club brothers, Ice's cherry-red Dyna skidded to a clumsy stop before he launched himself off toward the flashing lights and milling uniforms. In his wake, the bike thumped onto its side with an ugly metallic crunch—he hadn't put the stand all the way down. While Joker and Tommy righted the Harley, Chris Michaels intercepted Ice. The sergeant was a shade under six foot and nowhere near Ice's bulk, but he put his hands out to keep Ice on the wrong side of the caution tape surrounding Hailey's silent car.

"Where is she?" Ice shoved at Michaels' shoulder and lowered his own, ready to tackle the cop.

"JC, c'mon man." Michaels used Ice's high school nickname.

"Let me see her! *Hailey!*" Ice ignored shoved again. The cop slipped a little, then regained his balance and pushed back.

"This is a crime scene. You can't..."

"Michaels, I swear to God, I will *end* you if you don't let me through," Ice growled.

Hell. Joker rushed toward his friend and the cop, with Tommy steps behind. *If anybody gets to hit that bitch, it's me.* Ariel's story about Michaels and Ash hooking up still stung. Lucky for Michaels, Sheriff Schneider got there first. Under the pale streetlights, the older cop's white hair and badge gleamed almost as brightly as his polished belt and boots.

"All right, boys." Schneider's low baritone drawl

made the words slow and unobtrusive as he sidled in between Ice and Michaels. Decades of defusing drunken brawls developed a definite skill set. "Go on, he's cleared."

"That's for the chief to decide, sir," Michaels snapped.

"Well, he's three sheets to the wind right now, and the senior officer's in Springfield for training. I'll answer to the council if shit goes tits up, Michaels."

The sergeant's chest puffed out, and his shoulders reared back. Joker nodded to Tommy, and they both sidled closer to their club brother. Joker took hold of Ice's shoulder just as Michaels grunted to Schneider. The younger cop turned on his heel and stalked off through the barricade of EMT jackets, Grove cops, and PhaCo sheriff deputies that hid everything going on across the tape.

One of the younger part-time officers, Henderson, stared after Michaels' retreating back until Schneider nodded. Henderson grimaced but lifted the tape. Ice broke into a run with Dragon and the others on his heels. Joker hung back, surveying the perimeter. *Tree cover on one side, too many people. Houses at a distance without a clear sightline. Roads going four ways. Good point for an ambush.* His palm itched to wrap around his gun, but he didn't reach for the Glock in his holster—he wanted the old, familiar curve of his service Beretta. Better yet, his M4.

Joker caught up to his brothers, breathing through his mouth to avoid the choking scents of cordite and blood. Hailey lay on the road's shoulder, highlighted by a chalk outline. A CSI guy snapped a couple more pictures before Schneider waved him off. Dark hair shrouded her face and crimson-black blood congealed across her outstretched right hand. *Splash pattern,* old training whispered. *Momentum away. She ran from them…*

An irrational hope stirred in his chest—the stupid, knee-jerk denial seeking life where none remained. Ice must've endured the same thing, but his silence shattered in a low, terrible moan. He crumbled to his knees, reaching for his wife, deaf to the voices telling him to stop. "No. No, no, no…" Ice pulled her onto his lap by her bloodsoaked t-shirt while a CSI tech scrambled to stop him and ended up with Schneider's hand on his collar. "Baby… Please, no…" He stroked her cheek like he'd wake her, oblivious to gore already on his hand. "Hailey?" A sob tore from him.

Joker looked away in time to see his father cringe. Even Tree couldn't look at the ruin of bone and brains at Hailey's temple. He let out the breath he'd been holding while his mind wrapped around this reality, stopped seeing Hailey from that afternoon—laughing and leaning on Ice's shoulder and talking about shit that didn't matter now, like going to Sturgis in August, wanting to visit that Florida Harry Potter thing with Ash and Legs next summer. Pinterest. Making dinner.

His father and Schneider pulled Ice off the corpse in a rare moment of joint forces. Grease and Geiger joined them, with Michaels and Henderson calling for an EMT while the coroner's guys moved in.

Grim stepped close to Joker. He'd aged ten years in the last five minutes. Maybe they all had. "What the fuck is this, man? Wives and kids? They kill civilians now?" Joker heard the unspoken question: *Is Diana safe?* Grim wouldn't be the only brother worrying about his kid right now.

"Guess they wanted a war."

"And they've got one. Haven't they?"

Joker rubbed a hand over his left forearm, a long-healed shrapnel wound tingling while Dragon and Tree half-guided, half-dragged Ice to the perimeter. Ice kept looking back. His green shirt was black with her blood, flecks dotted his white patches, probably covered his cut, too.

"Where's Tyler?" They assigned him to guard Hailey. *If he fucked off…*

Grim shrugged. "Hospital, I think."

"Nate." Tree caught Joker's eye and jerked his head in a "follow me" motion.

"See if anyone knows for sure about Ty." Joker left Grim to help with Ice.

Tree stalked up to the sheriff. Schneider stopped mid-sentence with one of his deputies. He exchanged a nod with Tree and joined them, walking further away from the main knots of people. Tree waited until they were out of earshot.

"Who did this?" He pitched his voice low and quiet, so the words wouldn't carry.

"Nobody's exactly clear. Nobody saw the incident, just heard the car hit the stop sign. But by then…" Schneider shrugged. "Your guy's hit. Lost a lot of blood."

Joker looked towards the car now crawling with deputies. *Disable Ty, move in and get Hailey. She manages to get out of the car. Runs. One in the head, two in the chest. Too clean for the cartel…*

"He gonna make it?" Tree asked on a sigh.

"He was awake when I got here, but he's in bad shape, Jacob. I don't know. He didn't do much talking. Not sure if it was the injury or because of the badge. They took him to the hospital. I got one of my guys watching after him in case this was the Heathens—with the shit goin' down, that's my best guess. But with this, I may have to call in the Major Case squad." Schneider pronounced the last with a strange mix of apology and warning. "I'll stall until Weatherly gets back from Springfield, but if he hounds Chief too much or the council gets their panties in a twist…"

Tree nodded and looked back at Ice, expression unreadable in the eerie, multicolor lighting. Joker couldn't tell if his father felt sad or furious. Probably both, but he wished he knew which one was winning. "Thanks, Eldon."

That didn't appease Schneider. "Look, I know how this works. You'll go pay Brandt a visit and set the cycle running. I'm asking you not to, Jacob. It's one thing if you all want to shoot up each other, but this? She's a teacher for Christ's sake. The town will be crying for justice come sunrise. Hell, probably sooner. You know how things go around here. Let us do our jobs, boys. We'll get 'em."

"We want justice same as the rest of them." Tree's nonchalance earned a suspicious glare.

"I mean it, Jacob. No meddling. Brandt will serve life if we can prove he's behind this."

"I'm aware." Tree nodded. "We won't stand in the way of your investigation." He got another wary look, but Schneider shook his hand and walked back to a waiting deputy. Tree stood straight as an arrow, his shoulders squared. Whatever he'd decided was already set in stone, but…

"What do you want us to do, Dad?"

"We'll let Schneider run his investigation." Tree nodded at Joker before he started toward the police tape. "Pick a few guys to sit watch in the hospital. If this is the Heathens, I don't want them getting ideas about keeping Tyler quiet. I've got to call Gunner."

Joker gave a sympathetic grunt. Hailey's father, now head of the West Texas charter, had never gotten along with Tree. "You want me to make that call?"

Nearby, Grease and Tommy urged Ice into Booboo's van. Their brother was in no shape to drive, but getting him to go easy took some argument. Tree watched the fight before he answered. "No. I owe him that much." Tree pulled off his riding gloves and nodded to Joker. "Be at the compound tomorrow morning. Bright and early. We'll go from there."

"Yes, sir." He resisted the urge to salute and veered from his dad's path to catch up with Grim and Dragon.

****

Ashlyn

Ashlyn woke to the credits of *Thor* and a low rumble of male voices drifting from the kitchen. The murmurs sorted themselves into familiar tones—Grim, Joker, and Case—while she blinked her bleary eyes. She uncurled from the recliner seat and rubbed at her face. It didn't help. She rubbed again. Someone said Megan's name and she turned to the hall and the bathroom, but the light was out. *Probably in Grim's room,* she realized.

"There you are." Joker stopped next to the chair, still dressed in his cut and jeans.

"Whaa—" Hardly her most seductive greeting.

"Shh. I'm taking you to bed." He sounded like he was in club land mode, so she didn't protest as he hauled her into his arms. She breathed in deep, catching the scent of leather, cologne and a sharp note of sweat or … something more chemical? She could do little more than wave at the Grim and Case-shaped blurs because Joker didn't slow his steps.

Once in his room, he kicked the door closed, set her on his bed and barely stopped long enough to get his boots and cut off before crawling in next to her. Sleepy and confused, Ashlyn just stared at him until he cradled her head in his hand and coaxed her into settling against his chest.

This is why men should have stuffed animals. Ash kissed his chest, and rubbed her cheek on his light dusting of downy-soft hair. She counted to twenty before she spoke because hearing him say everything out loud would make it real. *But it has to be real, or he'll never sort it out.*

"Are you okay?"

He didn't answer for so long she thought he'd passed out. Then, finally, "Sorry I'm late, sweetheart."

"I didn't think you'd be home early." She knew she shouldn't ask, but there were too many possibilities for her nightmares to choose from if she didn't. "What happened?"

"Drive-by."

Now she was the clingy one, hiding her face in the curve of his neck. "I didn't think those were a thing out here."

"They aren't. Shit's going sideways lately." He kissed her temple.

Ashlyn let the silence go on for a lot longer, concentrating on Joker's firm, heavy arms and muscled chest instead of what he'd said. She suspected it would take a day or two for it to really sink in. At the same time, she didn't know Hailey. Not like Joker did. Or Megan. But she knew the empty hole where a friend used to be. She bit her lip. "I ... uh, still don't know how to make lasagna."

"Hmm?" Joker ran his hand along the top of her head and down her back. Stroking. She doubted he was trying to reassure *her*.

"I need to take something to Ice. That's what you do when somebody dies."

"Oh." He brushed a kiss on her forehead. "Shit. I didn't even think about the funeral..." Ashlyn pushed away. The faint light filtering from the bathroom showed the scowl ingrained on his brow and the tight look to his lips.

"Joker. Nate. Are you sure you're okay?"

His eyes met hers, and he framed her face in his rough palms. "Just a lot of shit to get through the next few days. You good with staying here? I don't want you driving around by yourself until we know what the hell is going on."

"Is it that bad?" Her voice wavered.

"Let's go with, I don't want to take any chances." He slid his fingers into her hair and pulled her down for a slow kiss. "If anything happened to you, I'd fucking lose it."

"I'm not the one who's accident prone." She smiled for him, hoping the joke would remind him of safer, everyday things. Not knowing what else to do, she pressed closer and let him hold her, his breaths slowing while she rubbed his shoulders and sides. After long, unmoving moments, his breath hitched, and she heard it. Tears. She couldn't stand hearing him cry again, so she put her lips on his.

Their eyes met when the kiss ended. Usually, his dark chocolate gaze burned hot enough to melt her to her very core. Not tonight. He seemed almost impassive, but his touch was achingly gentle. Ashlyn brushed her lips along his cheek, ignoring the rough stubble. His warm breath sighed a caress along her ear. She understood.

"It's all right, Nathan." *Time to feel something.*

Joker's hold on her tightened almost to the point of pain. She waited for the inevitable stomachache, the fear-borne nausea, or the tears. None of it happened. Trapped in Joker's arms, she lay perfectly calm. A moment later, he crushed her mouth with his. Instinct took over before her mind caught up. She accepted the pressure of his hard body and let her hands roam over his solid chest, urging him on.

"Ashlyn…"

She opened her eyes. He watched her with some desperate, unnamed expression. Her chest hurt, and words threatened to spill out of her lips. Ones she couldn't say. He wouldn't want them. He wouldn't understand. *Words won't work, but actions might.*

Her hand glided down his stomach to his waist, fingertips ghosting over his hip before pulling at the buttons of his jeans. "I'm here," she whispered, stroking him through his boxer-briefs. He sucked in a breath, and a thrill shot down to her toes when he rolled onto his back.

"God, baby, that feels so good."

His cock twitched against her palm, and she knelt between his legs, both hands taking hold of his well-worn jeans. He lifted his hips to help her out, and his hands joined hers in pushing his underwear down with the denim. She ran her hand along his hot, velvet shaft and leaned down until her lips were only a couple inches from his.

"It'll feel even better soon," she promised him.

"I want you, Ash." His voice had a deep, angry growl she hadn't heard before. Especially not in bed. Worried, she looked into his eyes. Until she saw the heat there, the way he licked his lips. *Not anger, just serious lust.*

"You have me."

She slid her pajama shorts down, kicking free of them before he could help. His hands steadied her as she crawled over him, straddling his hips and sliding down his body until his erection rested against her. A tilt of her pelvis put him at her entrance. Ashlyn pushed down slowly, stretching herself around his thick shaft. With her palms flat against his chest, she moved in increments, coaxing herself as much as him. It took beautiful, torturous time for her body to surrender, though neither of them minded. Once he was all the way inside her, she rocked faster, tilted more. Then faster again…

He grabbed her hips and squeezed. Held. Stopped her. Ash froze. "Nathan?"

"Slower, baby." He angled hips back and used his grip to control her movements until she caught on. Then his hands moved up. He teased her nipples with slow, lingering pulls. She gasped, her eyes meeting his. Heat flooded her—too much. She was more writhing on him than riding. Nate pulled her into another ravaging kiss, and one hand teased her right breast. "That's it," he whispered. "Come for me this time. Let me see you."

His fingers threaded into her hair, holding her head back so their gazes stayed locked. She flinched, but he made a soft sound, his eyes pleading even as he kept hold of her hair. She kept moving, but true escape became impossible, in so many ways.

"Nathan…" Her eyes closed to escape the intensity in his. His body hardened, and his limbs trembled, his cock swelled inside her. The jerking, pulsing rush pressed him against something within her, setting off her climax. She bit her lip to keep quiet, shuddering until the tremors subsided.

His embrace tightened, and his lips trailed along the column of her throat as he turned them both onto their sides. "Ash, don't … don't leave."

She blinked, still lost somewhere in the haze of orgasm and kisses.

"I … can't. I don't think my legs work."

Nathan's lips claimed hers. That seemed much more important. His tongue slid into her mouth, setting off aftershocks of pleasure and need.

"Thank you." His husky whisper faded into a sigh, and his grip loosened as he fell asleep. Ash brushed her hand through his hair until the frown between his brows vanished, then settled against his side. Her dreams were warm and soft as his lips.

Chapter Thirteen: June 17

Joker
Oak Grove

A nightmare slammed him back into the world of the living. Shivering in a cold sweat, he concentrated on the soft body next to his, slipping back to the brink of sleep only to jolt himself into consciousness. Then again. And again. All the twitching and rustling stirred Ash, who murmured some wordless question. He pulled her close and chuckled as she burrowed down by his side and dreamed on. The numbers flashing across the clock got a colder welcome—he flipped his finger at them, not that it mattered. *Time to get up anyway.*

He eased his arm out from under his lady. Her eyes fluttered, their green depths dark and disoriented. He lost all track of the wider world and let his knuckles brush her lower lip. "Go back to sleep, baby."

"Mm?" She rubbed against his hand until he opened his palm, groaning when she kissed him just above his wrist. Her exact fascination with his scarred, callused, and often oil-stained hands confused the shit out of him, but it was hot as hell. "You're leaving?"

"I'll be back soon." He put his lips on her forehead, breathing in her vanilla candy scent. "Grim's on his way back. Hang out with him today, ok?"

Her hand came out of the covers and grasped his arm. "Be careful."

"Always." He gave her one more kiss before marshalling his willpower and shoving the comforter off. He dressed without turning on the bedroom light, but he sat on the bed to pull his shoe on and made the mistake of taking a last look. Ashlyn's hair fanned out across his pillow, her face turned toward him and her lips parted as slow, shallow breaths carried her back to sleep, her shirt baring one vulnerable shoulder blade with a faint pink scar. He kissed her there before whispering a last goodbye and pulling the cover over her.

Out in the front room, Case lounged in Grim's chair, attention on the St. Louis news. He straightened when he saw Joker and the Dr. Who-themed throw (Ashlyn's) he'd pulled from the futon fell to his waist, revealing a chest that every Crow Eater in three charters vied to take shots off. It would only get worse when they gave the kid his patch—Tree had intended to leave the vote until the Fourth to add to the holiday, but that would get moved up fast now they'd called in the Nomads...

"TV wasn't too loud?" Case asked in a whisper. "I can turn it down."

"Can't even hear it. You get any sleep?" Joker grabbed a box of Ashlyn's annoying vegetarian-friendly protein bars off the kitchen counter and tossed two at Case, taking one for himself and shoving another in his pocket along with his wallet. He'd have to buy stock in the damn company at this rate.

"Nodded off once or twice."

"Good. Megan?"

"Still passed out in Grim's room."

"Let her sleep. He'll be back pretty soon. I've got to head out. Stay with Ash."

"Sure thing." Case nodded, setting the blanket on the chair.

Joker hesitated at the door. "You're welcome to anything in the fridge or the kitchen, but if Ash insists on feeding you, get her to order a pizza. We don't need anybody coming down with food poisoning."

Case's smile flashed. "Gotcha." He bobbed his head in farewell as Joker walked into the garage.

The new Dyna took some time to start due to operator error. Joker sat in the saddle, taking deep, gulping breaths in and out, losing count. His nerves stopped jangling after a few minutes, and he managed to get the bike started without fumbling the keys or the clutch.

Thank God Chase's too hungry to come check on your sorry ass, soldier. Fucking nightmares. Fucking Heathens. Fucking screwed up world.

The ride out cleared his head, and he was almost to normal levels of pissed-off by the time he hit the lane to the shop. Dragon parked outside of the shop moments before Joker made the turn into the lot. He nodded in greeting and pushed his long hair back with a gloved hand as Joker pulled up beside him. "Bright and fucking early, brother."

"You should be used to it by now." Joker glanced back to the fence where Two-Bit and Blackie lounged at a convenient table, a pair of hunting rifles close by. *Sentries. Christ.*

"*I* am," Dragon said. "You're the one who looks like hell, kid."

"So I look like you? Good to know." He paused before saying anything else, but since Dragon spent the night at Tree's place with Ice... "How—" he stopped himself. Stupid question.

Dragon shrugged, not needing to hear the question to know it—Not much else on any Pharaoh Crow's mind. "Fucking brutal, brother. Blackie threatened to tranq him. Booboo got him some pills to sleep. Sort of helped." He popped his knuckles and stared into the distance. "Shit, that'd been my old lady? You'd be checking my ass in for a vacation at Chester," he admitted, meaning the mental hospital in the riverside town a couple counties over.

"Bullshit. You'd never be crazy enough to have an old lady."

"Good point." Dragon's smile vanished about as soon as it appeared.

"We'll get them for this." Joker pulled off his riding gloves and swung his leg over the bike. Time to admit they had to go inside. "You get word on Tyler?"

"He got out of surgery a couple of hours ago, but his arm's a damn mess and he's so doped up he couldn't string a fucking sentence together. We won't know what happened until he gets his head on right."

"But he's alive."

"Yeah. Guess that's something. Come on, Tree's waitin' in the shop. Said some of the girls are setting up Hailey's memorial stuff in the clubhouse."

Joker drew his lips in tight and looked forward, reaching for the door handle. Dragon beat him to it. Joker snorted but followed him in. The shop still smelled like fresh paint and sealers. The spackle on the wall didn't quite match the paint, but it didn't look like bullet holes. Tree sat at the front desk behind one of the new computers. His head snapped up when they walked in, hand already on a revolver lying in front of him.

"You're both here." Tree released the gun and grabbed a manila folder. He tossed it at the edge of the desk closest to Joker. "Got a tip. There's some exchange going on Heathen turf. Our guy's pretty sure it's headed into St. Louis. They're running protection on it, heading out along Route M. Whatever it is, take it."

Joker stared down at pictures of Heathens' personal and club vehicles, street names, maps, and times. Snapshots of known drivers. The notes on the transit went back two months.

Tree always has dossiers on the groups who hold territory around us, but this? Did he get a mole in their club?

The attacks on their clubhouse had been returned

with interest—six Heathen bikes were blown to kingdom come and others crippled for months, with serious damage to Brandt's favorite safehouses. Then Hailey caught them with weapons in Crow territory. Now she lay in the city morgue, and Ty in the hospital. The Heathens wouldn't just lose some bikes and skin for that: they would lose cargo. The Heathens were meant to be a one-trick pony, and that trick was meth—respectful payment here and there allowed their continued existence near the Crows' home base. Most of their local guys were the ones too tough to play sheep and too chicken to hang with the Crows. A little diversifying into heroin or pot was permissible to let them feel like they had some balls, but now Tree meant to cut them off. It might be their heads that went rolling next. Joker narrowed his gaze to his father's cool blue eyes.

"Just the two of us? Against a protection run?" Dragon took the folder from Joker and flipped through the pages. He whistled. "Damn."

"You two have more training than all Brandt's fucktards combined. They've only run three or four guys on the last few drops," Tree said with a careless wave. "The driver's contracted; he won't put up a fight. Even if he does, it won't make much of a difference. Get whatever they're hauling, get out."

"Where's Grease?" Joker crossed his arms. As road captain, Grease should have been running this op, and two men against a group only worked if you made it bloody. *Dad wants blood today. Grease is hitting them somewhere, and we're hitting them here. Ain't that right, Prez?*

"Busy. Think you can handle it?"

"Not a problem."

"Get this done, VP. Then we need to talk."

Oh, it's one of those days. Great. Joker's hand

clenched, ready for a punch. Tree grabbed his gun as he stood, and walked off down the corridor into his office. The door slammed behind him. Joker stared after him until Dragon cleared his throat.

"Come on. If we're quick, we can block off the road before the turn to Odessa." Joker rapped his knuckles on the desk and took the file from Dragon. He shoved it into the top drawer. "Grab some gasoline."

Dragon stopped short, eyes narrowing. "I know that look. I'm not going to like this plan."

"Probably not. Call Tommy, give him the location, tell him to keep back a mile or two with the van for any emergencies. We need two cages. Burners."

"What? Why?"

Joker shrugged. "Even the odds. This is the only way I can think of. So, unless you want to wait around with your dick in your hands, or draft six other guys in with us, better figure out which car you want to destroy."

Dragon muttered something about caged birds and feeling like an idiot. Joker ignored it and surveyed the cabinet by the desk, choosing the keys to a white Camry parked out back. Nobody would miss it—they held a collection of totaled but drivable cars, as well as the ones that wandered in from undisclosed sources for dismantling or selective part replacement. The Camry's VIN was long gone, and after about two minutes, so were the fake plates. He tossed those in the burn pit out front of the clubhouse as he went in to grab a pair of AR-15's.

Despite what Dragon had said before, none of the girls were in the clubhouse yet, so he didn't have to eject them before he pulled the guns out of the hidden back closet. He checked his shoulder piece, then took some extra ammo for it from his dad's stash in the office while he was in there grabbing det cord. Tree would hit the fucking roof when he found it missing. Joker grinned as he relocked the door. *It's the little things in life.*

Outside, he found Dragon dropping his chosen car's plates off at the pit. Joker handed him a rifle before he slid into the Camry. Dragon pulled out after him, behind the wheel of a rusted-out Jetta. It didn't take more than fifteen minutes to get around Star Hollow through the back roads and up to the north end. They drove ten more after that, well into Heathen territory along two-lane county roads until they reached the meeting point, ten miles east of the Heathens' home base in Carthage.

Checking his watch, he turned the car to face the ditch, blocking off the lane. He motioned for Dragon to block the other. Once Dragon got clear of the Jetta, Joker turned the Camry hard, running to the edge of the ditch and gunning it to a whopping 20mph. He slammed the Camry's front bumper into the Jetta's, creating the look of a wreck—at least for the first glance. The impact wrenched his shoulder but didn't set off the airbag. He checked himself for injuries, figuring the worst would be some soreness later. *Thank God. Dealing with broken ribs in the middle of this shit would suck. Of course, so does getting shot.*

Dragon poured gasoline over the vehicles, with extra around the gas tanks and fuse boxes while Joker did some quick (and ugly) work to set up a pressure trigger between the cars—if they moved, they'd blow. A professional wouldn't fall for it, but he hoped the Heathens hadn't found any pros in the last month. Once it was done, they took cover in the ditch.

Joker leaned back against the sloping ground, flipping a lighter off and on. He hadn't lit up in weeks—not since before the wreck—but the sweet buzz of THC called to him more than it had in months. *Maybe once we wrap up this shit show...*

"They're here," Dragon whispered, pointing to a

tractor trailer making the hairpin turn half a mile up the road.

Behind it, four bikers in Heathen colors pulled around, coming to a stop at the barricade. The Heathens shouted at one another, the lead guy yelling into a phone—presumably ordering the driver to slow down. Joker doubted the poor sap *could* on the steep slope.

The oldest Heathen—his patch marked him as Barker, the Road Captain—stopped first, well into the far shoulder of the road. "Get those cars moving, goddamn it!" The other two pulled off and ran to obey. The ten-wheeler's brakes screeched and wailed it to a halt. Barely. The Heathens went for the Jetta first. One stood by its back while the other reached in for its gear shift. The car rolled.

Signed, sealed, delivered.

The rigged wires sparked, hitting the fuel-soaked components and det cord around them. The Jetta ignited like a goddamn birthday candle. The guy inside was toast. The other fell back, writhing in pain and howling while his arms and front blazed. The Camry went up seconds later.

Barbecue and burning oil. Just like old times.

Joker watched the others through his rifle sights. Saw them duck, freeze, then stand up and look for the attack. *Amateurs.* He squeezed the trigger. His bullet took Barker in the shoulder. Dragon's first shot hit the remaining Heathen in the stomach as he ran to his flaming buddy. Both went down, but Barker rolled toward the bikes. The old bastard was tough enough to pull his pistol and start shooting at Dragon. Joker returned fire until the semi sputtered back to life and jerked forward. Into his line of sight.

A few yards down, Dragon rose and took aim at the cab with a .357. His second shot blew out the passenger window. The driver braked hard and pulled his horn. By the time Joker and Dragon ran up to the cab, the man's eyes were closed, his hands up.

"*Por favor*, please … don't kill me … I only drive. Only drive. *No me duele! No mate! No mas, por favor.*"

"Shut up," Joker growled, pointing the way with his AR. These motions felt more familiar than dealing with the revolver. "Get out."

"All right. All right. No shoot!" The man's trembling hands fumbled at the door but got it open. He lurched out of the cab and hit the pavement.

"Get down! Hands behind your head. Count to one hundred. *Cien, comprende?*"

Dragon had his rifle slung over his shoulder. He kept his backup piece trained on the guy while Joker climbed into the driver's seat. Dragon pulled himself up after, a Glock still aimed at the driver. Joker adjusted the seat, put the truck in gear and floored the pedals. The truck roared to life, pushing one of the cars out of the way and forcing through the obstacles in a screeching hail of twisted metal and shattering fiberglass. He flinched at the shots fired behind them but judging by the way the truck drove, whoever squeezed them off hadn't hit the wheels. Didn't matter—Dragon hung out the side, shooting back at them with a demonic howl.

"Fucker got away!" Dragon pronounced after a few more rounds. "One more throat to cut later."

Joker didn't slow down until they passed the Pharaoh county line, twisting down an old mine road where Tommy waited with another truck to transport whatever the hell they had. They cleared any signs of a tail before Joker pulled over and they both jumped out, ran to the back and threw open the trailer. Tommy joined them staring at the dim interior.

That ain't meth. Or weed. Or trafficked wetbacks. What the shit?

"Joker?" Dragon finally said.

"Yeah?"

"Think you'd call that a fuck-ton of guns?"

"Qualifies." Joker stared at racks of ArmaLite AR15's and M249 SAW's and the crates between, all stamped with fake-as-hell food labels.

"Why the fuck do those assholes have a shipment this size in *our* fuckin' territory?" Tommy looked at them both. "Why the fuck do they even have a shipment of guns any-damn-where?"

Joker scowled and hopped up into the truck. "Guess they expected to need 'em." He took a crowbar from Tommy and pried a lid off one of the crates. Ammo boxes waited under the straw. And Berettas. "Boys, I dare say somebody's day just got fucked." He lifted one and handed it off to Tommy's eager paws.

"Goddamn, son. Now that's a party favor."

"Tommy, stop cummin' in your pants and call some of the guys," Dragon said. "We're gonna need help to unload this bullshit." He hopped down and waited for Joker before swinging the door shut.

"We need to get rid of the truck fast." Joker grunted he pushed the latch down. "Get Rat and Booboo, too. We could use their driving skills. I'll feel better about this if we ditch the cases with the truck. Never know what asshole might be tracking us."

"Let's hope whatever cartel fuckstick sucked up enough coke to hire Brandt goes Scarface on his ass, and we don't have to deal with him," Dragon said cheerfully.

"That'd be sweet, brother. But I don't think we're that   lucky   lately."

Chapter Fourteen: June 19

Joker
Oak Grove

The doorbell jerked him back to earth, where the futon's lumpy mattress and metal bars set off every bruise he'd acquired the last couple days—between dealing with the weapons and busting Heathen-protected meth dealers, sleep was getting hard to come by. He rubbed his eyes, cursing under his breath. *Grim really needs to kick his damned Amazon habit.* He pictured the crates full of ammo, handguns and rifles they'd spent the last two days cataloging and parceling out to their own buyers. *Not the week to have random shit on the front porch, dumbass.* Joker stumbled to the door and opened it, mouth open to tell the UPS guy where to shove his boxes. And stopped. Stared.

Damn, UPS. You got fine.

The brunette standing on his porch was straight off a *Forbes* cover: white dress, black heels, jacket, and glittering lapel pin that probably cost as much as the gleaming black Mercedes sedan behind her. Sunglasses hid most of her face, but her red lips smiled. He swung open the screen door and stepped on to the porch next to her. "How can I help you, ma'am?"

"You must be Nathan." She sounded as expensive as she looked, the syllables spoken with a charm school enunciation.

"I am." *You better not be serving me a fucking subpoena.*

"And is Ashlyn here?"

"I hate to seem rude, ma'am, but that might depend on who's asking."

The woman's smile widened. "Don't you sound just like your father? Always so polite. I can see why my daughter's fond of you."

He cast a quick glance down at his jeans and t-shirt. *At least I'm not in boxers.* He studied his guest again. He'd pictured Bella Marlow as tall and angular, but if you got the heels off, she'd be about the same size as Ash, and while she was thin, she wasn't skeletal. He didn't see any signs of horns or forked tongues, either, despite Ash's colorful descriptions.

"You're Ash's mom? She's told me a lot about you, ma'am."

"I'm sure she did."

"Please, come in." He pushed the screen door open. "It is great to finally meet you."

"Thank you." Bella breezed past in a wave of perfume, pausing in the entryway to pull off the oversize sunglasses. Her light green eyes glanced around the interior before she looked back at Joker.

"Can I get you anything?" He noted the slight wrinkle in her ivory forehead. Which was the only one he saw anywhere on her. *What age did she have Ashlyn at? Ten? Christ, she's ... hot. Is it money or genetics?* He found himself hoping for genetics. It'd be nice if Ash was still dropping jaws in a couple decades.

"I'm fine for now. You wouldn't happen to know where she is by chance? She didn't answer her phone."

"Over in Marissa. Job interview." *With Case*, not that he would tell Bella that. Or that he didn't want Ash to get the position—Marissa was a long way out. And considering Hailey's funeral tomorrow, he didn't want her driving without protection.

"So, what has she told you about me? My daughter isn't always my most dedicated fan."

Joker shrugged and closed the door. "She knows you only want what's best for her." *More or less.*

"Very diplomatic." Bella had a pretty voice,

suited to laughing. "We've been fighting one another since she entered preschool, but I want to be sure she's doing well here. It has been rather … ah, a difficult year for her." She tucked a strand of dark hair back into her French twist with slender, manicured fingers, drawing attention to her features. Her face didn't match Ash's button nose and big eyes. Bella's was finely drawn and classic. Like Megan.

"You tried asking her? She's not one to hold back." He couldn't help watching Bella's movements. *No wonder she wins. Would a jury even notice another side to the damn case?* Bella chuckled, the sound more tired than amused. She adjusted the white leather bag hanging from her shoulder. He glimpsed the label: Coach. It looked nicer than the one he'd bought for Reagan in one of his last, failed attempts at fixing that mess of a relationship.

"Did she tell you why she came to her grandparents for the summer?"

"She listed a few reasons."

"Ah, yes: 'because reasons'. I'm familiar with that one." Bella walked further into the front room, looking at the curtains rather than him. "I suppose she wouldn't want to talk about her fiancé with you, but … poor Matt. He's going to have a nasty surprise when he gets back." Bella's eyes slid back toward him.

"Her ex? Sounded to me like he did the running." *The doctor had her, and he lost her. He's staying fucking lost.* Ash never hid that she'd bailed on an engagement. She'd explained herself one night over a bowl of cookie dough, and they'd compared notes about Matt and Reagan.

"The leaving, not the breaking up. But it wasn't about him. The problem's rather older than that." Bella's frown remained in place. "How much has Ashlyn told you about her past?"

"Considering how long we've known one another? A good deal." *Proportional to how little she tells anybody else.* He knew a lot about her school, her friends, her hobbies and viewing choices, but his patchwork knowledge of Ashlyn's family and relationships came more from things she didn't say. And those scars she kept hiding.

"Mmhm." Bella tapped her purse. "I've known your father a long time…"

"He's never mentioned you."

"No doubt. But I assume you know my profession."

"Lawyer."

She nodded. "Corporate, but I worked in defense for many years. So, I hope you can conclude I have some idea of your … lifestyle?"

"If you know my dad that well, sure." *Wherever the hell this is going, I bet I don't like it…*

"Good. Then let me explain something, Nathan. I don't particularly give a damn how you earn your living or what choices you make, save in this: my daughter does not have any place in that arena. Ashlyn isn't … she's not—" Bella shook her head.

"She's fine, Mrs. Marlow."

Bella turned away, putting her hand on her chest, over the enameled brooch. "I know this is asking a lot. I know you like her. If you want, I can see you have a good excuse for it. A job, maybe? Somewhere away from here. That pays well." Stunned into silence, he let her finish, but that last bit…

"I have a job, ma'am," he said with a harsh laugh. Her eyes shone.

"End this before she gets hurt. Because she will, and you know it." The words weren't so different from things he'd thought himself in the last four days. Yet facing the choice, having the ready excuse handed to him right here, right now…

"Maybe Ash's place isn't with me, but I won't make that call for her. She's had enough people do that."

"I'm asking you to hurt her now so you don't help her self-destruct later." Bella's words stung all the more for the lack of heat in her tone.

Joker crossed his arms to hide that his hands had balled into fists. She had brass balls to face down a member of the national charter, let alone the VP. *Wonder if she ever tried this shit with Dad?* "You and me won't be getting eye-to-eye on this." He adjusted his stance, prepared for the hit.

Bella smiled, her eyes still cool. "Try seeing my side, Nathan. My daughter is bar-tending at a location known for violence. She is dating the vice president of a 1% club whose grandfather founded the damned thing. Whose father has served in more mercenary—sorry, Private Military Contractors—than I can count. Now, if I had a daughter I thought could survive that particular milieu, I wouldn't be having this lovely conversation. But I have Ashlyn, who has obviously failed to explain a few key details about herself, and I don't enjoy knowing that I will, yet again, be cleaning up a disaster. So why don't we skip to the part where you elaborate what will help you feel satisfied with the ending of this … association?"

That's right. Keep treating Ash like she's a twelve-year-old making the wrong friends. Fuck, you'd probably wrap her in plastic and stick her in the basement. His shoulders tightened. He'd taken way too much for granted. No more.

"Sorry, lady. People worth keeping are worth fighting for."

"Good line—you've learned Jacob's little tricks

well. I expect you'll be a fitting successor to his throne."

"I'm not my father."

Bella reached into her purse for a slim-line black wallet and drawing a white business card from it. She took a second card from another pocket, this one black with white and red writing. She held both out in her flawlessly manicured fingers. "The white one's my private number. The black one is for an old friend of mine, if you reconsider the job offer. With your background, he'll always find a place for you on one of his teams." He took the cards and slipped them into his pocket without comment. Bella started toward the door only to pause a couple steps past Joker. She turned, her expression almost sad. "But if it looks like Tree and talks like Tree … eventually that is what you'll become."

"I've got too much of my mother in me. Much as I hate it." He crossed his arms. *Even if I don't bail on my family like her.*

"Don't hate it too much. Your mother wasn't all bad. She got in over her head." Bella's lips twisted in something too pained to be a smile but revealing a dark amusement. "He used to say the same thing, by the way. Always swore he'd never be his father. Look where we are now," she sighed. "Good luck with that."

He barely bothered to shrug. It didn't shock him that Bella knew his mother—Oak Grove was too small not to, but he'd never once heard his dad talk about Bella Tilden. *Come to think of it, considering Amos is around so much, why is that?* "The way I see it I have a lot of reasons to walk a different path."

"So did he, once," Bella muttered, so quietly he wondered if she knew she'd said it. He held the door open for her as she walked out. When she stood at the stairs, he cleared his throat and tried one last time.

"I get it, Mrs. Marlow. I'm not good for your

daughter. Maybe for now we can try to get along? One of these days she might agree with you."

Bella pulled her sunglasses from her leather purse, looking at Joker as she slid them on. "Tell Ashlyn to call. As I understand it, my mother intends for you both to come to the Fourth of July party. I suggest not wearing your cut and driving that truck rather than a bike."

Joker watched her climb into her Mercedes and drive off before he let the door slam shut and pulled the cards from his pocket. The white one was Bella's number, like she'd said. The black one was for some asshole at Blackstone—a security firm turned military contractor. Joker laughed. *Like Dad would let me work for the competition.* Tree still held majority share in Aesir LLC—though it wasn't nearly as large as Blackstone, the people who needed Aesir knew how to contact them. He and some buddies spent the nineties building it up, which was how the Storm Crows became an international club. And how they slid under the usual radars... Joker looked out through the storm door, and his laughter vanished.

Does she fucking know about Aesir? Was that why she offered Blackstone?

He shoved the cards back in his pocket and grabbed his work gloves off the back of his chair. Some shelves in the garage required destruction. Immediately.

****

Ashlyn

Ashlyn dashed into the house without knocking and shut the door behind her, sighing in relief at the wash of cool air while Case's truck rumbled away down the street. Blonde hair stuck to her forehead and neck, and her white tank top clung to her back. Her interview clothes were already in the blue Marc Jacobs backpack she dumped by the front door. She'd changed in a gas station bathroom while Case cussed on the other side of the door until his brother showed up with his truck and drove the Miata off to either Hell or Wronski Auto. At the moment, she didn't care which.

"Joker?" She expected him to be playing a game or on the back patio, so she continued speaking to the empty air, pitching her voice a little louder than usual—sneaking up on him wasn't a good idea. "I'm actually melting. Mind if I use your shower?" She kicked off her shoes and continued into the house. He didn't show or shout any objections, so she kept up the one-sided conversation. "My car's AC quit. Because in 95 degrees and the humidity of a fish bowl, who needs cool air? I'm sure my gills are coming in soon, right? And then it blew a tire. Because why the fuck not?"

She shucked off her green shorts by his bedroom door, and her pink bikini briefs by the bed. Her tank top came off next, and the blue bralette fluttered to the floor before she grabbed a towel and continued into the master bath with its glorious 1988 floral wallpaper and hard-water-stained brass fixtures. She glanced into the mirror as she pulled out her ponytail and almost screamed. Joker stood leaning on the doorframe, watching with darkened, appreciative eyes.

She made a face at him in the mirror to cover her blush and scrambled to get the towel around her chest. He saw too much, too many details for her to be naked in full daylight around him. Her scars were small as plastic surgery could make them, but the mark on her hip and one under her left rib remained: two pink lines that weren't as easily dismissed as the fainter one on her shoulder. And explaining them took a lot of lies.

Towel in place, Ash forced a laugh and held a hand out to ward her boyfriend off. "Don't jump me just yet. I feel like I'm going to pass out. It took an hour to get back here, and opening the windows didn't help. Turns out Case didn't charge his AC either."

He cracked a smirk and moved closer, stopping right behind her to pull his oil-stained shirt off with blackened, grimy hands. His tousled dark blond curls looked wet and his skin gleamed. *Sweat or mystery grease stuff? I should touch him... No. Wait. I should not. He's dirty.*

"Did you run the whole way?" His voice sounded deeper than normal. Her heartrate went up a notch. This close she smelled him: hot, sweaty. *And it's turning me on? Something's so wrong with me.*

"Some of us are not born heat resistant, Mr. Badass." She stuck her tongue out while she held her hand under the stream of water, waiting for it to approximate the room temperature. She didn't want a hot shower. She wanted the opposite. In fact, even Joker's lava-temperature body made her think longingly of nice, cold vampires. She glanced his way from the corner of her eye, letting herself appreciate him from a safe distance. *I must be heat sick.*

"I'll take a look at your car." He lowered the toilet lid and sat down to pull off his work boots. His muscles flexed with every motion. Not that she was staring. *Nope. Not staring. I am a totally normal, non-hormone-driven organism... Does his chest have to look that good?* She bit her lip and fussed with her towel.

"Case's little brother took it to the shop on the donut. I think. Or Case had him blow it up. You working on that loaner bike or building a time machine in the garage?" Despite his brand-new Dyna, he kept fiddling with the loaner.

"Having some trouble with the flux capacitor." He leaned back and glanced at the ceiling, apparently gripped by some internal debate. She took the opportunity to drop the towel and duck into the shower. Then, "Your mom dropped by."

The pronouncement set off stomach-dropping, just-started-a-roller-coaster pangs through her midsection. Her hand slapped against the shower wall. She turned, blood fleeing her face by the second. *Stupid me. I should have known.* Ash reeled into the back corner and pulled the frosted door closed. *Two weeks. I got two weeks with him.*

"Wow. Um. So. That's ... yeah. That had to be ... interesting."

"You got no idea, sweetheart."

Fuck it. If I faint and hit my head and never wake up, then it's the will of the Cosmos. She stepped into the streaming water. With the stall and spray between them, Joker became just a wavy outline on the other side of the glass. At least she could make her voice calm even if her face was crumpling. "I need to cool down. We can have the let's-be-friends talk in, like, five minutes."

Silence came from the other side of the shower insert. She slicked her hair back and almost got her breath to stop catching.

"Say that again?" Joker's voice was flat.

Ashlyn sagged against the wall, needing the cold tile to bring her back to reality. *Fine. Okay. I can do this naked. In a shower. This is totally fine. So completely fine. I'm so amazingly fine right now.*

"Hey, I get it. I've met my mother, too." She put her head back under the water. "I'll be, um, totes out of your way as soon as I'm human again."

The shower door clanged against the cheap metal frame. "And where the hell are you going?"

"Megan's, silly." She loofah-ed her arm and kept her back turned, then stuck her face into the water to hide any tears. She focused on evening out her breath to support her voice, keep it cheerful if a little manic. *Thank God for those acting classes.* "We can hang out today, if you want to." She turned and held out her hand, expecting a relieved smile on his end.

Joker didn't smile. He did, however, take her hand and step into the shower. The fact that he still wore his jeans didn't seem to matter. She squeaked a warning. He ignored it. Instead, he kept hold of her hand and held her in place as he invaded her space.

"Oh, we're hanging out today. And a lot of days." He bent and kissed her left shoulder, his afternoon stubble tickling enough that she twitched. "Wouldn't you at least put up a little more of a fight than this?"

"Well, you know..." She faltered and cleared her throat, thoughts still stuck on—instead of in—his pants. "Nobody makes you do what you don't want to. Including taking your pants off before you shower. Apparently." *Are we breaking up? Is that why you have pants on?*

"You're too hot to wait for." He nipped her throat in just the right place to send shivers down her back. She whimpered. The bastard chuckled and started kissing her jawline.

Right. Totally possible to have a grown-up conversation with a hot man in a shower. Yeah.

"I come with baggage. And I didn't warn you how much of it. It's justifiable to be annoyed with me." Ash slid her hand along his recently healed arm. "We both have weird lives. I realized a while ago that yours might mean that we couldn't stay together forever. But I want you in my life, so if we have to split up and be friends again ... I'll take that." *There. I said it. I'm a grown-up.* She met his eyes and tried not to look as dejected as she felt.

His left arm snaked around her waist so she couldn't miss the strange warmth of wet denim against her legs. Or that part of him was already testing the limits of said denim. "Everybody comes with baggage, sweetheart." Joker's breath whispered over her ear. "If somebody walks away from this, it's going to have to be you."

Ashlyn's laugh sounded more like a sob. *How do you explain that a man who keeps more guns in the house than ink pens, and routinely does things in total secrecy and complete illegality makes you feel safe?* Her head rested on his chest, over the tattoo of armor and Norse runes.

"You're the best boyfriend I've ever had. I can't imagine wanting anybody else for the job. Ever."

"Guess I better prove I'm qualified." He tilted her head up and reached between them. A second later his fly parted. She suspected the gesture had less to do with passion than comfort. Her brows rose as he set about the awkward process of shedding sodden jeans, and she stepped back to watch, letting the shower stream separate them. His muscles rippled as he straightened up, water trailing over six-pack abs and perfect ink. She wrapped her arm across her front, hiding the scar under her breast again. That was one detail she could live without explaining.

"You're overqualified," she informed him. "In fact, there are moments I'm pretty sure you are too qualified to ride this ride, and maybe I should've put a maximum size limit up … but I won't argue with you."

Joker's gave a wolfish grin. "You love my size."

"Mm. You're right." Her fingers teased his abs and over to his hip.

"Turn around, sweetheart." Freed from the jeans, he reached for the shampoo. He'd taken over shampooing her hair before, so she didn't hesitate. He liked playing doing it, and she liked the way her shoulders relaxed when he did. "Speaking of rides, you up for a road trip this weekend? Take the new bike, head to St. Louis, get a hotel room, get kicked out of it if I make you scream loud enough? Or maybe we could take a real vacation soon. I hear Alaska won't cause anybody heat stroke."

A low moan preceded any actual answer as his hands worked their magic, easing tension and ratcheting up her temperature. "Mm. That sounds amazing. Of course, right now you could ask me to ride a bull with you." Ashlyn giggled and reached back until her hand found his hip. His lips found her ear.

"Not the ride I'm thinking of, baby." One hand pressed flat against her stomach, holding her flush against him for a tantalizing second before he went back to working the shampoo into her hair. He put his fingers along her temples, moving in slow circles. *Manipulative, but effective.* She laughed.

"Nathan." She let herself lean into him as her nails raked lightly over his leg. Ashlyn turned around and edged back, rinsing her hair before kissing his chest. His hands fell to her back, kneading her skin while he whispered a soft encouragement. Her hands roamed his sides, pressing harder here or there, her nails skimming over his skin once or twice. She nipped at the pulse point on his throat and let her lips trace his collarbone. "I want you." Her whisper sounded as desperate as his moan. "Right now. Fuck me."

"As you wish, baby." He hooked his arm around her and lifted, half turning to set her against the shower wall, getting her level with his lips and kissing her hard as he settled between her thighs. "And I'm not letting go. Not today. Not tomorrow. Never," he said before thrusting into her. Wet but otherwise unprepared, her body stretched until it hurt, vaporizing her composure. A sharp cry tore from her, and Joker stilled with a purely male groan. "Are you…"

"Don't stop." She pushed her hips up in case he didn't get the verbal message. His thrusts evened into a smooth rhythm, and her legs wrapped around him with eager abandon. Her lips found his throat, trailing kisses to the curve of his ear. "I need you." She gasped, arching for him, reckless and stupid with pleasure. "Harder, Nathan…"

His hand held the small of her back, his hips snapping forward, pushing deep and testing her limit. He kissed her to soften the scream forming on her lips. "That's it, baby. Take it. Come for me." His grip and the angle they were in drove her down further—more than she'd anticipated—until he hit her cervix. Pain spiked through the pleasure, but where she expected the old, familiar panic, none came. Not with his voice in her ear and his taste on her lips. The realization swept her away. As much mental as physical, her climax hit her with pulsing heat and rushing dopamine until her racing heartbeat drowned out even her own desperate pleas. And some part of her, deep inside, was finally, blissfully … quiet. Even with the bruised throb already making itself known.

She clung to his shoulders because her legs shook too hard to hold her up. Tears ran down her cheeks, mixing with the shower. Joker's body trembled, too, and his fingers dug into her skin. A guttural moan wrenched from deep in his throat. The rough, erratic rhythm slowed as he came, but she reveled in the flood of warmth, and her own inescapable aftershocks from it.

Joker's heavy breaths blew past her ear until he turned his lips to her cheek. "Still with me, sweetheart?"

His whisper was velvet, soft as his touch. Passion spent, his hold on her lightened until he was cradling her instead of pinning her against the wall.

Ash tilted her head for more kisses. "Always," she answered with a smile. "We should stop the water, or Grim's going to kill us when he gets home."

Joker laughed. "Considering what he's not doing with Megan, a cold shower's good for him."

"Says the man who's never needed a cold shower in his life."

"I assure you I have. Last month mostly." But after another minute, he lowered her feet to the ground, turning her so she stood under the water. She finished rinsing the back of her neck and her hair and stepped aside to let him clear away the remnants of soap running down his luscious sides while she laid his thousand-pound pile of wet denim over the towel rack. Once he was soap-free, he turned off the tap while Ash tucked a towel around herself.

"You're the first person to endure wet jeans for me. How are you ever going to top that?"

"I'm not." Wrapping her in his arms, he shouldered the door open. "Figured now that you like me, I can pretty much coast from this point."

Ashlyn kissed his chin as she pulled her towel up another inch. "Well, *I* can't coast. I need to comb out my hair or my old man's gonna dump me for looking like a hobo."

"Baby, if hobos looked like you, there'd be a lot more charitable feeling in the world."

"I can't tell if you're being sweet or perverse."

"Why does it have to be one or the other?" He chuckled and tossed her a comb. "Get it fixed so I can tangle it up again. Before I go bust Case's ass for being a dipshit."

Her smile vanished. "He did fine, Nate. He didn't leave me alone, he called … somebody. And I thought he texted you."

"And why didn't you text me?" There it was, the edge in his voice. Testing. He slipped from Nate-posture to Joker-posture: head tilting up a little, weight shifted. Maybe it should have worried her, but it didn't. Same person, different ways of thinking. She understood that.

She crossed her arms. "Because Case already did? And my phone was dying. I figured I ought to save it for if anything went actually wrong. I'm not stupid, Joker. I know we're all in danger, and communication's important."

His chocolate eyes narrowed, and he ran a hand through his wet hair, leaving a trail of water down the sides of his face. She watched one droplet run along the curve of his neck, toward his armor tattoo. "I never said you weren't smart, baby. But this ain't exactly your world. I know you get it's dangerous, but I'm original charter VP. We're the motherhouse. Things are always going to be…"

"Weird as fuck. Yeah, I figured that out." Ash grabbed her hair product from the medicine cabinet and smiled at him in the mirror. "Everything's dangerous, Joker. Cars, bikes, terrorists, clowns, Mom…" Her voice faltered as the comb caught on a tangle. "I can be screwed up and you still like me. That's worth a few bullets. More than a few, probably. But don't get an ego about it."

"Sweetheart, don't joke about bullets right now." He took hold of her hips and squeezed. "I can't say your mom's all wrong. You'd be safer somewhere else. But I'm an asshole; I can't walk away." Joker caught her wrist to stop her comb. He waited until she looked up and kissed her. "Case tails you, and you keep that damn phone charged. Got it?"

A buzzing warmth lit up her chest. "Okay, your highness."

"Hm, say that again when you're sprawled across my bed."

Ash slapped his arm with the comb. "Get out." But she was laughing, and he only hauled her up into the air and dragged her to the bed.

Chapter Fifteen: June 20

Ashlyn
Oak Grove

Ice and Hailey lived in a small Craftsman home in Oak Grove, now bursting with bikers, Hailey's colleagues from the school, women from her book club, and countless friends, all streaming in and out to console, reminisce, and periodically try inducing Ice to eat something. Pastries, cakes, casseroles, and a banquet's worth of various dishes took up the entire kitchen counter, most of the fridge and—as Karli and two other women set about the inevitable preparation—would soon fill most of the freezer. The operational theory appeared to be that if Ice didn't have to think too hard, he might stay fed.

In the crowded front room, Joker introduced Ash to a handful of out-of-town Storm Crows, including Hailey's father, Gunner, a red-eyed, aging bodybuilder, who wore a cut with the blazon "Storm Crows Houston", and a patch marking him as president thereof. Then came several Nomads—and she'd realized that "Nomad" was Storm Crow code for "extra scary". Two of them, bearing patches marked "Chains" and "Blaze", joined into a conversation with Joker. Neither one had Joker's size, but both had a similar manner and looked a little too detail-oriented. *Like they know how many people are here and how many bullets they need to level the room. Keep smiling. Don't stare at the bloody knuckles.*

"Excuse me, gentlemen. I think I should see if Karli's got the kitchen under control yet." She slipped her hand from Joker's and gave him a one-armed hug around his waist, smiling at the two nomads.

"All right, baby." Joker touched her hair, giving a nod of approval. "We're going to step out front. Your phone on?"

Ash sighed. "Yes, my phone's on. I even added vibrate. So text if you want me to get you a beer."

"Damn, she's trained." Chains leered.

"And she carries a whole vial of Visine in her purse," Ashlyn added. "Would you like me to bring you a beer, too?" *Shit, did I just say that? I'm dead. Better keep smiling.*

"What's Visine got to do with anything?"

Blaze coughed to hide a chuckle and clapped his buddy on the back. "I'll explain it to you later, bro. Come on, let's get out of here. Too crowded."

Joker almost didn't smile. "I need all hands on deck, sweetheart. Try not to incapacitate anybody."

"Fine, if you insist on being boring." She squeezed his hand then headed toward the kitchen without looking back. Negotiating her way into the dining room proved tricky, and she ended up further toward the back of the house than she intended, but Ariel stepped in from the patio just as she had a clear route to the kitchen. They made the short walk together.

"Hey!" Ariel called over the din. "Can somebody come with me? I gotta make a beer run. I think the guys just downed a keg in the back shed. Ash? You in?"

Ash glanced at the others. "Sure. Karli, are you good?"

Karli didn't look up from shifting a rice dish into a freezer-safe Tupperware bowl. "Bring me back some rum, will ya? I need a daiquiri the size of Cuba. *Lana*! Stop putting stuff in the freezer. Wait until it's cooled down some! Christ, girl. I thought you watched cooking shows."

Orders are orders. Ashlyn retrieved her purse from the pile under the kitchen table before she and Ariel headed out the back door, avoiding the crush of people around the front.

"Where are you parked?" Ash stared out over the sea of bikes and cars lining the patched and gravel-strewn pavement. They stayed close together as they picked a path down the steep driveway and onto the street.

"About halfway to St. Louis," Ariel laughed. "I should've told you to change shoes."

Ash checked her feet, clad in flimsy ballet flats. "Hey, they're not heels. That's as good as it gets."

"You are shorter than usual." Ariel's own 5'8" height and black platform pumps put her several inches over Ashlyn. She didn't seem to be worried about walking in them. *She could probably hike Everest in heels.* "How's working at the clubhouse going?"

"Kind of awesome. I wish it came with a full-time option and benefits."

"I know that feeling." A sigh blew past Ariel's full lips. She tossed her dark hair over her shoulder. "If you're into beauty work, there's a pretty good school up in Joliet. The salons are always looking for somebody new. I can introduce you to my mom, if you come in sometime. Who does your hair?"

"A place back home." Ashlyn glanced at a blonde-highlighted lock hanging down her shoulder. *Home is a long way to go for hair. And also Mom lives there...* "What's the name for your mom's salon? I should get this mess trimmed in a couple weeks."

"Kara's Kuts, down on Seventeenth. Mom would love to book you in. Just be ready to get grilled on all the gossip your Grandma hoards."

"That sounds fun, to be honest. I don't even understand half of Grandma's news anyway."

They reached an intersection. Ashlyn looked back and smiled. The spreading trees and maintained lawns, fresh paint and classic Americana-style houses looked like something out of an advertisement, aside from the Storm Crow bikes lining the street. *I guess with them it could be a Harley ad...*

"This is me." Ariel pulled a key fob from her bag and a small white SUV beeped. Ashlyn frowned not at the car but the purse: white leather and unmistakably Coach. *Either genuine or a crazy good knockoff. Damn.*

"Gorgeous bag."

"Thanks. It was a present."

"Ooh, from who?" Ash pressed as they got into the car.

"Joker, actually." Ariel turned sheepish. "Sorry. I forgot about it when I pulled it out today. I can leave it in the closet next time."

Oh, there it is: the rulebook I don't have.

"You guys had a thing. Why hide it? But you have to tell me seriously, did you drag him into the Coach store to get that, or was it a gift card? I need to know these things. For science." *Never saw him doing big gesture gifts like that—maybe a gun or stereo, or jewelry in an emergency. Like an I-fucked-your-sister kind of emergency. But a purse? Then again, he learned to make eclairs...*

"Just a present." Ariel laughed. "My theory is a drunken eBay moment but who knows." She put the car in gear and pulled out onto the street. "You're nice, not kicking my ass over it."

"Is that some kind of thing girls do around here?" *I have got to find the Biker Girlfriends For Dummies book. Maybe Karli can write me a list.*

"Sometimes you throw your weight around to show a guy's yours."

"No thanks." Ash's nose wrinkled. "There's no point in pretending he was a virgin when I met him, and it's not like I'm putting a ring on his penis." *Ok, that would be kind of funny. I should get an empty ring box and a One Ring replica. At least Grim will laugh...*

"So you're into open relationships?"

"What? Oh ... I don't know. We haven't discussed it." The question startled her into an abrupt response, and she cleared her throat. "But it's his choice where he puts his dick, and I don't hold anybody but him accountable for it."

"You say that now." Ariel smirked. "But one of these weekends, there'll be some slut with her top off, rubbing her boobs on his crotch and begging him to fuck her on the pool table."

Ash laughed at the image. "So? It's still his choice."

"That is very ... open-minded. Most of the old ladies would be screaming pissed and breaking a pool cue on somebody's head."

"Oh. Yeah, I'd probably be kinda mad. It's just..." *If Joker was doing something like that, would I interfere? Too many variables. What kind of public persona are we supposed to maintain? Shit, I need to ask him about that... Wait. Normal girls. Possessive feelings. Sex. Jealousy. What's normal?* Ariel was waiting for some explanation. Ashlyn made a face and looked down to make sure her hands weren't shaking. "I can't explain it."

"Gosh, you take it so serious, girly. The club's a club," Ariel offered in an encouraging tone. "For all the other stuff, it's still a bunch of guys doing shit they love. We help make sure they've got ties to the community and do some good with their cash. And we get free bodywork. Speaking of: that scratch on your car..."

"Joker keeps telling me to take it in. I just ... things have been busy." She shifted in her seat, adjusting the belt on her shoulder. The estimate she'd gotten in the Carthage body shop still made her queasy. She had a couple more weeks of bartending to afford that—and convincing Joker she didn't need his help. Assuming he hadn't gotten it fixed along with her tire already. *Another thing I need to talk to him about.*

"Why date a garage guy if you can't get your car fixed?"

Ashlyn side-eyed the brunette. *Is that the point? Sex for free stuff?* Her thoughts ricocheted in another direction. "Ariel, this whole, uh, 'club girl' thing … you're okay with that, right? Like it's not, I don't know, a problem? Sleeping with people on demand or whatever?"

"What?" Ariel stopped at a sign in a side intersection and turned a wide-eyed stare on Ashlyn. "No. God, no. Seriously. It's not really like that, for one. Nobody would ever…" She laughed. "Look, if they're horny and you're into them, you fuck. It's not some kind of *Taken* bullshit. What the hell have you been reading? Does Joker even know that's what you're thinking happens?"

"Oh, no. I just … sort of heard a rumor. And I'm not judging. I mean, I'd pick a bar full of Storm Crows over an Alpha Tau kegger. The chances of your drink being roofied go way down, for one."

Ariel's brows rose behind her sunglasses. "That's actually a thing? I figured they made that up for movies."

"I wish. No, it's a thing. A really, really annoying thing."

"You sound like you're talking from personal experience."

Ashlyn rubbed the back of her damp neck. *Why hasn't her AC kicked in yet? Damn.* "My friend Kaylee, but we figured out what had happened, so we hauled her back to our suite. We were all super drunk, and we thought that roofies were like concussions, 'cause they make you kind of loopy and stupid, so you might die if you fell asleep too soon. We ordered a ton of pizza and stayed up watching movies."

"Disturbing, but weirdly cute," Ariel said with a faint laugh. "You had good friends."

"Yeah. I did."

"Where are they all now?"

Ash shrugged. "Everybody's kind of … gone. Graduation." *Yeah, that's one way to put it. Or you could say that they took the payoffs and scattered… Stop. Stop right now.* She closed her eyes and counted to five.

"Is that why you're here?"

"What? Oh. I just didn't want to stay home."

"Hold on, gotta get my phone." Ariel slid the car into park at another stop sign and reached for her purse. "Nobody's coming, are they?"

On the outskirts of town, the scattered houses and fields didn't host many cars, but she looked both ways while Ariel fiddled with her purse. *Why are we out here? Was this a Star Hollow run?*

"I—Hey, someone's here!" A white van barreled around a corner ahead, rumbling straight for them. Ash screamed, Ariel's voice joining hers. The brunette's hand scrabbled with the shifter, the SUV lurching backward as the van's brakes screeched. It stopped a yard from their bumper. If the car hadn't rolled backward…

Ariel shrieked and jammed the shifter back to park. "Get out, asshole!" She slapped a hand against her chest, trying to get her breath back. "*Out!*" Her door swung open, Ariel's legs not far behind it. They must've heard because the van's doors opened, too, disgorging four guys. Large ones. With tattoos. And two of them had beards. *Amish mafia? Bikers?* The men marched toward the SUV. Visions of Russian drive-cams played through Ash's head.

"Get the doors! Ariel, lock it! Get us out of here!"

Ariel reached for the keys. Ashlyn tried to lock her door, but it flew open. A big, ugly hand yanked Ash sideways into the sunlight with bruising force. She stumbled and cursed, scrambling to get her feet under her and escape his hold. Her purse—and her phone inside it—flew off her arm as the man shook her. The tan leather skidded on the pavement, ending half a foot from the ditch.

No. No, no, no, I need that!

Ashlyn's foot lashed out, connecting hard with her attacker's shin. He shoved her and gravel slid under her feet. Only his grip on her arm saved her balance. He used it to his advantage, dragging her toward the van. She dug her heels in, twisted against his hold, but nothing changed. He didn't slow.

On the other side of the car, a man struggled with Ariel, who yelled something while waving her free arm. The man's fist flew. Ariel's head jerked back. The brunette stumbled against her car and sank out of sight behind the driver's side fender as Ashlyn screamed again.

"Christ, someone shut that cunt up!" Ariel's assailant yelled. *Must be in charge...* Despite the chaos, a corner of Ash's brain continued operations, recording and cataloging. Survival instincts, the shrinks had called it.

The man dragging her cursed. Ash's heel connected with his shin. He cursed more but squeezed her middle and lifted. The ground fell out from under her feet. Fear spiked into mindless rage. She clawed at the leather-clad arm around her, kicking harder. Twisting. Her fingers wedged between his glove and jacket sleeve.

Her nails dug into his wrist.

"Fucking hell, bitch!" The man dropped her. Ashlyn hit the ground and rolled with her momentum, scrambled to her feet and dashed toward the SUV. *Two steps. Five! Almost there…*

A massive weight crashed into her from the back, plowing her face-first into the oil-and-gravel pavement. She caught herself on her forearms, but her sternum slammed into a rock. Air wheezed out of her lungs, leaving her choking and scrabbling for breath.

"Sorry, cutie. You got a date tonight," a vaguely familiar voice hissed in her ear.

He's on top of me. He's on top of me. No. No, no, no… Panic obliterated everything. She reacted on instinct, rolling to shove him off, gagging on the screams that wouldn't come. Pain blossomed at the back of her skull. Her gaze narrowed in on her phone, vibrating in a circle… Then, nothing.

****

Joker

Too bad he couldn't stay buried with club business. They had about enough to keep him up 24-7, with the Nomads coming in, plus Gunner and his Texas buddies. Guys from St. Louis, Missouri, and Iowa had shown up, too, and some nearby support groups who knew Dragon and Gunner from way back. A few of them were sticking around until scores got evened. Nobody was too worried about the Heathens, but if they had backers the game changed. The gun shipment hinted that the Heathens had contacts with *somebody* across the border in Missouri—whether it was one of the gangs or some bat-shit rural paramilitary remained a question.

As comforting as it was to think about the fight at hand, Joker knew he had other duties. He left Chains and Blaze with Griff, the St. Louis president, and went inside to check on Ice. He found his club brother in the finished-off basement, slouched in a ragged easy chair. He'd made the room his man cave, hung up Harley memorabilia and filled it with the furniture Hailey wouldn't allow in the rest of the house. Especially the chair Ice now occupied, in the same position he'd held an hour earlier.

Joker searched the immediate crowd for his lady—she was better at this. *What the hell do you say at funerals? Sorry for your loss? This shit went easier on deployments. You followed protocols, then didn't fuckin' talk about it. Didn't look too hard at anything, kept your head in the game...*

Ice shifted as if aware of Joker's gaze—the first sign of movement from him beyond his darting, restless blue eyes. Always looking, never focusing. Joker knew that look. Intimately. He approached with a fresh bottle of Heineken in hand.

"Mind if I sit?"

Ice shrugged and pointed to the chair next to him, a mustard yellow disaster half-covered with a sheet. Hailey had picked the sheet, Joker remembered. "Do what you want, VP." He gulped half the bottle and bowed his head. "They're talking to me like I'm a goddamn kid. Like my girlfriend just left me."

"Jake." Joker leaned in to get Ice's attention. It worked.

"Sorry. I can't fucking take it out there anymore. Idiots. Bunch of dipshit assholes..."

Joker stared into his own bottle. "Nothing about this is right. But we're here." Ash had told him something similar, more than once. After the wreck. After a bad PT day. After a nightmare. Sometimes just knowing someone else was there—and wanted to be there—helped more than the pills.

Ice breathed sharp and looked down. He mouthed numbers, counting back from five. When he got to one, he looked around again, lips turning in a smirk. "Looks like that won't be long." A telltale tremor remained in his voice, but he pointed the Heineken bottle toward a disturbance by the stairs where Grim plowed through the crowd. "Kinda looks like my dad's old pointer. Course he's usually stuck on Legs' trail instead of yours."

Joker chuckled, but his smile fell as Grim's fists curled. Uncurled. Joker got to his feet.

Ice followed suit and spoke first. "The hell's wrong with you, G?"

"Tree sent me." Grim turned to Joker. "Something's happened."

"Oh good. Thanks for being clear. Otherwise, it'd might'a been fuckin' annoying." Ice snorted and took a pull of Heineken.

"All I know is he's on the phone in the guest room barking orders, and I've gotta go find Ariel. Looks like she took off a few minutes back and forgot to take anybody with her. Stupid bitch. Now Booboo's all up in fuckin' arms that nobody shadowed Ari. Guess he's screwing Kara again... Sorry about bailing, Ice. I'll be right back."

"Hold on, I've got her number." Joker drew his phone from his jeans. A message notification blinked.

Ash: **Beer run w/ Ari! Requests?**

"Ash is with her. You sure they didn't take a Prospect?" *She promised. Unless she thought Ari counts as someone? Fuck.* Joker's knuckles paled before he typed a quick message.

Joker: **Where are you?**

"Don't think so. They're all present and accounted for." Grim tried to shrug off the concern. "It's all right, brother. I'll take a cage and get them both. I'll steal Case's keys. Tree's got him running some other errand anyway."

Joker clenched his hand around the silent, unmoving phone. *No answer from Ash.* "Give me a minute. I'll go with you once I talk to the prez…"

Ice's hand landed on Joker's shoulder.

"We'll handle the girls. I'll track down Dragon, get someone to back up Grim. You need to talk to your old man." He sounded more like himself than he had in days. *Hailey always said he was part sheep dog.*

"No worries, Joker. I'll try Ash while I'm going and call you when I got 'em. Dragon's in the kitchen." Grim waded back into the people, dislodging two of Hailey's aunts who'd blocked the stairs.

Joker lifted his chin and patted Ice on the back before following Grim, leaving Ice to seek out Dragon and whoever else he decided to pull into the detail. *They'll handle it. I'll read the fucking riot act to Ash. Of all the damned days to wander off…*

The house's short upstairs hallway led toward the back, passing a bathroom, an office occupied by a few weepy teachers, and the closed-off master bedroom. The guest room stood at the end. Inside was a cheerful space filled with antique furniture and lacy curtains. Hot pink scissors gleamed amid a sea of pastel paper and Easter stickers on Hailey's abandoned craft table. Tree sat at the edge of the frilly queen-size bed, back bowed and one hand rubbing his face. Defeated. Joker couldn't stand looking at either scene. His eyes focused on the far window, where a yellow curtain fluttered in the air-conditioner breeze.

Tree sat up, straightened his shirt collar and adjusted his cuffs. A Storm Crow pin kept his tie in place, but he hadn't worn his colors today—wouldn't don them until the ride that evening. Putting on a business suit didn't soften Tree's demeanor, nor did it banish the bruises on his knuckles, earned from beating the daylights out of a Heathen-affiliated drug dealer the night before. Tree looked at him for a moment. Too long.

Somebody else fucking died.

"Shut the door, son. This isn't good news."

"When is it?" Joker grunted. The door clicked shut, muffling the hum of voices from the living room. "What's gone wrong now? I've already got Grim chasing down Ash and Ariel." He rolled his shoulders back, bracing for the blow. He wasn't ready.

"Too late, kid. Heathens jumped them out on the Star Hollow road."

Joker's brows drew together but he kept the rest of his face still. Even with the ground opening up underneath him. *No.* He locked his legs to keep his knees from buckling. Tree kept talking. "Schneider has Ariel. Ashlyn's missing." He stood up and put his hands on Joker's shoulders.

Too late to get all fatherly, old man. Or keep me from killing somebody right fucking now.

"Son, if they meant to kill them outright, they'd be dead in Ariel's car. They're not." He paused, looking for a response. Joker swallowed his rage. Nodded. "Get your head clear, Nate. We need all hands on this." *Didn't I just say the same thing to Ash? God, where is she?*

"Only to bury the bodies."

"There'll be more of those than usual. I warned you about the Tildens."

"Worried you can't out-bribe Amos in Springfield?"

Tree snorted and let his hands fall from Joker's arms. "I'm worried an old friend may turn out to be one hell of an adversary because you couldn't keep your dick out of his granddaughter. You got any idea the favors he can call in with the wrong people? He'll have Feds crawling this county for the next twenty fucking years if shit-all happens to that girl…"

"Always preaching the same sermon: We got respect around here—hard to earn, easy to lose. If they didn't grab her, it would be some other girl. Maybe even Ari. Or Megan. You telling me you would let *any* woman hang for us with Brandt?"

"You know I wouldn't. But even I've got lines I don't cross, Nate." For a second, his expression blanked like he was looking a million miles back. "Killing Hailey meant we have to kill Brandt. Now? There'll be blood in the ditches, kid. I called in the other Nomads."

The clean-up crews. To keep Amos sweet, and make a point to whoever is backing Brandt's idiot plays. The "rest" of the nomads were out of Aesir; internationals and deep cover agents who'd earned a patch—or a debt marker. His father didn't just want Brandt, or the Heathens; he wanted their backers. Joker watched his father and didn't offer anything but a terse nod.

"I'm heading out to meet with the other leaders down the road," Tree continued. "Hailey's memorial ain't no place for this talk. You in?"

"Try keeping me out, old man."

Tree's eyes gleamed with something too dark to be a smile. "I was afraid you'd say that."

****

Ashlyn

Ashlyn woke to darkness and the bitter tang of fear and bile in the back of her throat. Rough hands jerked the cloth from her face, blinding her all over again.

"Look into the camera, dollface."
New voice, not the old one.

"Wha?" She struggled against the restraints—plastic, from the feel of it—on her wrists. The bindings held. A flash scalded her eyes, leaving her tearful and blinking.

"No, no, that's crap. You gotta look cute, or he ain't paying. Try again." The chipper male voice belonged in a level of hell.

"Fuck off." Dizzy spots haunted her vision, obscuring the camera-wielding Hellboy.

"Spunky!" Hellboy mussed her hair. "I like it. Get feisty, baby."

Ashlyn's lips curled in an outright snarl at the silhouetted jackass fluffing her hair. "If I don't murder you, my mom will, so get your fucking hands off me!" Her adjusting eyes revealed a rangy form, a muscled arm covered in ink—words she couldn't read on a banner around a scythe—and a smiling, square-jawed face.

"Seriously? Your mom?" He chortled.

I definitely hate you. Ashlyn's glare intensified. "Just tell her whatever shithead client she needs to get out of jail, jackass, and she'll get it done. You aren't the first assholes to get a bright idea—"

"This ain't about your mama."

Ashlyn sniffed at that. "Right. Is there any other reason you'd do this?"

"Who's your mom?" Hellboy's head tilted, like she'd confused him. Ash's stomach sank.

"You … actually don't know?"

"Do I look like I know, bitch?" The peevish tone and the insult told her more than he meant it to: he could be frustrated. Emotional. Ashlyn filed that in the back of her head.

Learn, explore. Think. Keep talking... She surrendered to the survival-self slipping out of its box. Three years of learning to put it away, lock the box and bury it—all for nothing. In her head, the fracturing felt like stretching, her point of view shifting to a wider angle, everything around her becoming clearer and further away. *Too late to go back now.*

"Bella Tilden-Marlow, of Crabtree, Marlow and Kane. Look, my stepdad's Jett Marlow. Is this about that merger with ZaraCorp and Morpheon? He's retired, but—"

"Ripper!" The yell echoed from outside the tiny box of a room. Hellboy grimaced.

"Whatever, doll. Sounds like the boss is getting impatient, so let's get this picture done," he said, the chipper-ness deflated. "Gotta send Joker a good one, right?"

She laughed. "You honestly kidnapped me over Joker?" Ripper ignored her and raised the phone for another shot. With the shock fading, she felt the fresh bruises throbbing with each camera snap. After one last attempt with the flash that left her seeing spots, he finally left. Ashlyn looked around as best she could. A scrap of light filtered under the door, silhouetting a cylinder she assumed to be a bucket, and something she was sitting on that might have—in a long-ago life—been a futon. Everything smelled old, dusty, and disused.

Ripper came back after a while, holding a cup instead of a phone. She sat still and watched him until he knelt to put the cup against her lips. Water. She sipped and he settled back on his heels. "I'll give you some time. You should probably get it all down, but they hit you pretty hard. See if you puke first." That amiable smile again. *Is he insane or what?*

"So … you're being nice to me before you kill me?"

"Nobody's killing anybody." Ripper made a face at the thought, like *she* was the crazy kidnapping photographer. "They might rough you up for the pictures if he's late with money or something. It's all to get him to cooperate. Killing you don't do that."

"Oh, good. Indefinite prisoner is so much better." She grimaced. "Seriously, my parents are worth way more than whatever Joker is likely to offer. Call them. Easy-peasy, nobody even bats an eyelash. They have insurance for this anyway."

Ripper shook his head but held up the cup again. She drank. *At least the water tastes like water. Wonder what the snozzberries taste like?*

"I can get you something to keep you calm if you need it." He sounded almost hopeful. "They don't want you screaming and crying all day."

Oh, the snozzberries taste like Valium. Yay?

"Am I screaming and crying?" Exasperation and panic made for an exhausting bipolar experience, she decided. "Ripper, is that your name?" He nodded, and Ashlyn smiled, hoping the bruises wouldn't neutralize the cute factor of her appearance. *I need every weapon I can get, universe.* "Look, I get the game's just business. You keep me 'til Joker does his thing. And even if he fucks off, you guys still make bank from my parents. If Mom and Jett don't work out, there's always my Grandpa Tilden. He's not on Jett's scale, but you could get something."

Ripper's eyes raked over her. "So, you're what a rich girl looks like? You sure you ain't scared?" His tone took on a thoughtful quality as he stayed in place. He hadn't touched her since he came back in—not in any meaningful way.

Let's keep it that way as long as possible: talk.

"Do you know the origin of the word 'privilege' is actually Latin for 'private law'?" His brows gathered into a confused look, so she added, "I *am* scared, Ripper. But if I get seriously hurt, my family will have Joker's balls, and the army of PIs they hire and Feds they call in favors to will fit someone's neck for a noose. So, if you're not suicide bombers, why would you kill me?"

"Maybe we hate arrogant rich girls."

"Maybe." Her words were quiet, spoken with a hesitation here and there as she modulated herself to sound meek and tired. "But I'm a rich girl who knows the score. If you let me loose and stop keeping me tied up in the dark, I'll be less likely to have a panic attack and inconvenience you." His wary hazel gaze studied her, so she gave a slight smile, thinking harmless, sad thoughts and keeping her shoulders lowered in a show of weakness.

"I'll ask the prez."

Her face remained blandly hopeful until the door closed after him. She flopped sideways on the once-a-futon, ribs protesting and head spinning. *I could leverage better if I knew whether this is business or personal grudge, but what the hell kind of business is worth this narco bullshit anyway? And how long is it likely to take? I've got 24 hours before statistics say I'm dead... Stall for time?*

The door shrieked open. A male silhouette blocked most of the outside room, but she got the impression of aging green carpet and a flash of paneled wall before he strode into her closet-cage. Ash wriggled upright and tried to look both alert and meek. The newcomer towered over her but not on Tree or Joker's scale. Maybe 6'0", decent shoulders, wearing a Heathens cut with the word "President" on his patch, and the name "Scratch". His graying hair hung long, a fang dangled from his right ear, and a shark tooth necklace showed at the throat of his worn t-shirt.

Great, I got kidnapped by Angry Biker

Moondoggie.

Then he smiled. Like he was meeting a future business partner rather than a hostage. Her blood chilled. The look, the swagger... *That's a shark wearing a people suit.* Her adrenaline kicked up a notch. *I swam with sharks before. I can do it again.*

"Got ourselves a Paris fucking Hilton, huh? Probably cuter without the bruise. What the fuck you go and bang her around for, Rip?"

"I—I didn't, Prez. Owl and them, they brought her in that way."

Owl? Megan's ex-husband, Owl? Tick another box for "personal" over "business".

"Oh well. Accidents happen." Scratch shrugged. "Just you relax, peaches. Let's talk."

"I am relaxed," she assured him. *This shark has an ego—he must have one, to go up against the Crows. Egos can be played. He wants territory, and he's made some desperate attempts...*

"Hear your mom's got some pull 'round here." He studied her as intently as she did him. Ash hoped he saw a wide-eyed, terrorized, stupid little girl. *Better to be underestimated in this trap...*

"Maybe. Sh-she'll pay for me..."

"Rich sluts don't like parting from their money."

Try harder, ass-clown. I've heard worse insults from Dad.

She raised her shoulders. "Maybe. But she'll pay for me." Something about the way his eyes moved didn't seem normal. *Drugs or insanity? A little of column A, a little of column B? Perfect.* "Ripper wasn't clear what I'm here for, so I took a guess, Mr.?"

"Scratch. Like it says on the cut, peaches. All you need to know." The man's head tilted as he stepped to the side, letting in more light. *The better to see you with, my dear...* "Not exactly Joker's usual, uh, taste."

So we're to the insult portion of the interview.

Ash ducked her head as if the assessment hit home. "He has been heavily medicated."

Ripper fidgeted in the doorway, drawing her gaze. Next to Scratch he looked young—maybe younger than Ash herself. *Either he'd be the most dangerous or the easiest target. Any port in a storm...*

"Hm. This could be a change of plan," Scratch muttered. Then he whipped around, apparently switching gears. "Rip here says you promised to behave. You good as your word, peaches?"

"What would I have to gain from fucking around?"

"The more you see, the more you risk us killing you instead of letting you go." Scratch's grin turned her stomach, but she kept the bland expression and lifted her chin.

"You run this area, right? Me showing up dead brings heat and the rage of rich, old, white men. Me alive means they open their bank accounts."

"You alive puts somebody in prison."

"But not you." She maintained eye contact. *Time to play to the audience.* "I could very well swear some crazed redneck Mexicans took me, and you rescued me off the side of some backroad. You get the money, and you're a hero. Everybody likes a hero."

He laughed. "Or you say we took you. The whore you were with probably already has." His eyes darkened in less than a blink. *Great. He's a crazy with mood swings.*

"Ariel's a club ... whatever that term is. She's not telling anybody anything on record. The story will be what I say it is. What can the Storm Crows do about that?"

"And you'd fuck over your old man? Just like that?" He meant the question to knock her off balance, but a cool detachment settled deeper into her brain.

Fuck you. Fuck your club. Fuck this whole goddamn world. You do not have power over me. She stopped fighting her survival-self, surrendering to old instincts.

"What's he got to do with some pissy cartel asshole my mom took down? I can't help who rescues me. If he wanted the credit, he should've shown up faster." She spoke with a hint of sullen irritation layered under a quavering voice while her eyes warmed toward the man in front of her. *The Crows are already in the past, a superfluous connection. I know my future lies with you. See it. See me turning. See yourself winning. I'm just one more lying whore you can convince to do anything...*

Scratch leaned against the wall. His smile widened. "Got it all figured out, don't ya, peaches?"

"I'm trying." She ducked her head in a show of uncertainty. "Would you rather I scream and cry? I could do that. I figured it wasted everybody's time and gave y'all a headache."

He stared over her shoulder, eyes fixing on some mystery point. After a few moments, he gave a slow nod. "Oh, I appreciate skipping the screaming and crying." He looked down at his cut and tugged at a wayward string from his name patch. "You've got balls. I'll give you that. But my mama didn't raise no fool. You're asking me to trust you because old, rich whities might bring the law? And you sit there telling me you can stop it with a couple a' lies? That's a fuck ton of trust you're askin' me for."

"It's the best I could come up with." Ashlyn's nose scrunched. "But I like living, so if you have a way for me to prove I'm trustworthy..." *Let me guess: I should fuck one of your minions. Or more. That boring, sexist bourgeois bullshit. Stick your dick in a girl, she's your puppet.* She bit the inside of her cheek to keep tears welling up in her eyes.

Scratch chortled with a smirk on his twisted face. "Ripper, cut her loose. Then tie one wrist to yours. She can't get far dragging your ass." Ripper obeyed his president, kneeling behind Ashlyn and cutting away the painful zip strips while Scratch continued, "This is parole, peaches. You're with us tonight. You behave, maybe I do things your way. You can come be sweet butt for our club for a while, find you a new boyfriend."

She suppressed a shudder.

"Hard to try anybody else on for size with Ripper tied to me."

"That's Rip's problem." He shot a cold look at the younger biker. "Maybe he likes to watch."

Ripper blew out a breath—she doubted Scratch heard the near-sigh. His grip on her arm remained light as he helped her stand up. "Can I *not* zip her to me? Those fucking things hurt."

"*Sasquatch*!" Scratch yelled. "Cuffs! In here."

Ashlyn maintained a calm outward expression and stayed close to Ripper as the summoned Sasquatch lumbered up to the door. *When being handcuffed to a strange man counts as an improvement to your day, you may have fucked up…*

****

The cuff kept catching on the stripes of skin abraded by the zip strip and her earlier pavement surfing. She didn't object to the pain: it reminded her of things other than Ripper's lanky frame next to her or Scratch's menace across the room. The Heathen safe house (she didn't believe for a second this was their base) proved to be a rundown ranch style farm house with a full basement, lost amid southern Illinois' interminable seas of corn, beans, and hay, with the faintest pricks of light on the horizons.

All in all, the crew included about eight guys instead of a whole club—she was pretty sure only Scratch and one other were even officers. There were three women she could see, but one of them was so doped up she hadn't moved since Ashlyn and Ripper walked out. All three were stick-figured, with irritated skin and questionable teeth. She didn't bother approaching them. Addicts didn't turn on their suppliers, and they wouldn't be any help in getting away if they did. Either no one's real girlfriend came out here, or the Heathens were a fully different breed. Neither option helped her. From what Sasquatch told Ripper, more girls were due to arrive with meth and assorted party favors, meaning more witnesses. Either she'd be dead before then, or Scratch intended to go with her idea. Not that it mattered.

I can't run out blind, lost and high onto a backroad and get away from a bunch of locals. I need a car. A phone. Something…

"*Rip!*" Sasquatch's dulcet tones reverberated in the house's mildewed air.

Sighing, Ripper led her across the yard to the door, where Scratch stood waiting. The leader pulled her and her shadow back through the front room and into a dim hallway, opposite the basement stairs that stood open, yawning like the maw of hell. She kept her eyes on Scratch.

"You're Ripper's new girl," he announced. Her bruised side sagged against Ripper's arm, but Scratch kept talking. "Anybody asks, you mouthed off and he cuffed you to him to keep you honest tonight. Ain't none of these bitches sober enough to give a shit, but just in case. You hear me?" He stepped closer, leaning in so she could see his bloodshot eyes gleam.

"Yeah."

Ripper avoided her eyes as Scratch left them for one of the bedrooms, but he helped her straighten up and walk back to the kitchen. He grabbed two red cups and poured them both a drink from a bottle of rum—even splashed in some Cola for color. He fumbled the lids on both bottles until Ash put their joined hands forward so he could use his left.

"So, what's your deal? Are you the new guy?"

"The newest they'd trust on this shit."

She let him drink first before sipping from her own cup. "Sorry. Sucks to be the hostage but sucks to be the babysitter, too." *So, Owl was in on this, but I thought he wasn't one of you yet. You're either being upstaged by a Prospect or you've both just been patched... Who sponsored you? Where are the fault lines in this group?*

"You ain't even worried," Ripper muttered. "Your rich-ass parents gonna buy you out. The prez knows we need that money. Even having you is a fucking punch right in the Crows' beak. They gotta be shittin' themselves."

"Why? The Crows are loaded, too." She let her own hopelessness leak through for a moment. "You know I'm, like, barely dating Joker. You should've picked someone else to get to them."

"Hey, now. Even if it ain't the cash, you're his old lady." Ripper finally glanced at her face. "Ain't nobody overlooking it if a VP can't keep his woman. Shit, next we'll be stealing his bike. That'd be fun."

"Well, I'm still dating him, aren't I? Isn't that all 'keeping' entails?"

"Telling me you're gonna overlook that little detail of jack-hole getting' your sweet ass kidnapped?

Shit." He took a swig of rum. "I heard you back there. You dumped his ass the second you woke up, he just don't know it yet."

"I guess that would strengthen the heroic Heathen story." Ash cocked a brow before she looked around the room, steeling herself for the next question. "So, what Heathens do you recommend I aim for?"

A startled chuckle escaped Ripper. "That's cold, girl."

"Is it? My survival depends on your club. Joker is the reason I'm in this bullshit position. Like you said, he's not the person I thought, and *you're* going to be playing my heroes pretty soon. If I'm starstruck from an orgasm, it'll help my acting. And…" She raised her cup and smiled. "Maybe this is partly revenge."

Ripper's hand caught her shoulder close to her throat, startling her into meeting his gaze. Hazel eyes. Pretty. Even his face wouldn't have been bad if she hadn't wished so hard that he was Joker, and she was a thousand miles away. "Aren't you a little scared, doll?"

Ashlyn let the pent-up fear and nerves well up to the surface and fill her eyes with tears. "Most kidnap victims are dead in twenty-four hours, Ripper," she whispered, hoping he heard over the rumbling motors outside. "I'm living like it's my last night because it is. Let me play pretend, okay? Please."

Ripper's curiosity became a frown. "No, it's like he said. Killin' you don't do shit for us."

"Revenge doesn't need logic. That's what this is, and you know it." She drank and set the cup aside so she could use her free hand to wipe her cheek. "How bad do I look? Honestly."

"Banged up. But cute." He put his cup down, too, then tucked her hair behind her ear. "Sorry we're all out of ice."

The front door crashed open and the glad yells of newly arrived revelers drowned out her chance to answer. *So that's the sound of death...*

She touched her temple and winced, waiting for the noise to die down a little. "Guess you knocked me around pretty good, huh, boyfriend?"

"What?" He reared back a couple inches. "Oh. Oh..." Chagrined, he turned to the arched doorway leading to the front room. "Yeah. Guess I did. You shouldn't have hit on that, uh, asshole at the gas station."

"Well, he was hot." Ashlyn's smile bloomed, and her eyes lit. Joining in her game meant he empathized, maybe enough to be useful. *Let's see how far down the rabbit hole we can get him to go.*

"Typical woman." Ripper grinned and reached across to pick up her drink. He held it out until she took it. "At least I can out-drink you."

"You sure of that?"

****

Joker
Ravenwood

"Joker, you need a drink. Go. Dragon, take him out there." Tree shut off the phone he'd just pried from Joker's numb fingers.

Griff, head of St. Louis, clapped Joker's shoulder while Dragon gripped his arm. "We got this, VP. Take a breather." Griff's unshakeable calm only got a glare from Joker. In his late thirties and half a foot shorter, Griff never backed out of a fight. *And he can take a punch...*

"I'm fucking fine."

"You fucking are not." With that, Dragon steered him into the main room, where Grease and a few others were distributing weapons and ammo. Ariel sat at the far side with Booboo, Grim, and Karli—a bandage on her head and one eye swelled shut—going over whatever details she could remember for the tenth time.

"Think we got enough lead to take over Panama yet?" Dragon asked, signaling the guy behind the bar for two shots. "Whiskey, Blackie. And one for Ice."

Joker didn't answer. He stared at a half-assembled M14 on a nearby table, mentally stripping it and reassembling it. Anything to get the photos on that phone out of his head. Blood on her lips, across her temple. Ivory skin turned purple and blue...

"They haven't even set up a drop point." Joker didn't recognize his own voice.

"Things take time," Ice answered. His brother Crow leaned on the bar at Joker's side, bags under his eyes and new lines on his face. His wife lay in the ground, men still filling in her grave, but here he stood.

"We're out of that." Joker drummed his fingers on the polished wooden edge of the bar. *The longer they have her...* Nausea slithered through his guts. "If we haven't moved in ten minutes, I'm going out myself."

"Brilliant plan. Assuming the plan is to get your stupid ass killed. 'Cause that'll work pretty well for you. And her," Dragon snorted.

"What the fuck do you want? This is my fault. I need—"

"Don't start with that bullshit." Ice downed his shot. "Ash knew what you were before she walked this road. Not like you called yourself a plumber or some fucking thing."

"You're right. And she trusted me."

"Stop it, Nate. Somebody's to blame, and it ain't you. It's a dead man, and you know his fucking name. We ain't losing anybody else." He reached for Joker's shot, ignoring Dragon's glare. Blackie sighed and set another on down, a few inches further away from Ice.

Blood in the ditches, Dad said... Brandt had to

know half a dozen Nomads were already in town and that other Storm Crow charters showed up for funerals—and it wasn't any secret his dad's former contractor buddies held the reins in many of those same charters. Sticking a finger in the Storm Crows' eyes right here, right now took either insanity or desperation. Ashlyn's fate lay in the hands of an idiot or a psychopath. Or both.

He pushed himself away from the bar, thankful to hear the sanctum door opening. Crow officers poured into the main room, a couple special friends of the club among them. The St. Louis leader Griff and his VP headed to the back, but Tree motioned for Tommy and Grim to join the others at the bar.

Silence passed over the rest of the PhaCo Crows while Tree poured himself two fingers of Maker's Mark before handing Dragon the bottle. Dragon didn't bother with a cup; he tilted the whiskey back and sucked down a couple mouthfuls. "Everything ready?" Tree asked.

Dragon checked his phone and nodded.

"The boys are ready to ride," Grease said as he emerged from the back hallway. "Thanks to that Heathen shipment, we're armed to the teeth."

"Well, they ain't too smart; they might not have worked that out yet." Ice pried the bottle from Dragon. Instead of starting a minor brawl—his usual response to such overtures—Dragon relinquished it and crossed his arms over his chest.

"Call Kaminski." Tree directed the order at Joker. "Let him know the stakes."

"If he calls our bluff?" Grim asked.

"If everything's ready, then it's ready."

"No, I mean … the teams are in place at the houses, but…" Grim's face paled. His eyes darted around the gathered Crows, then further out to those busy with weapons and examining tactical maps. He watched Ari and Karli walk out the side door with Booboo, then, "We're doing this? With kids?"

Ice made a low, grating sound in his throat. His eyes were all but feral. "It's not the game we wanted to play, brother, but it's the game we're in. If you're not on board, stay behind."

Tree held his hand up. "We don't have time for this. Joker, you call Kaminski and join us out in the lot. Grim. You staying or you going? Decide." His father's voice held a familiar edge, but Tree didn't follow it up with a lecture. Joker watched him leave, flanked by the others.

"Ryan..." He leaned against the bar with the weight of a planet on his shoulders. "I know it sucks. This isn't what we're about. But they killed Hailey. They have Ashlyn. We're all next on the block if they can end our alliances with her family and the towns around here. We gotta put some terror in Kaminski's soul. The sack of shit needs to taste what he's been serving."

The club's daily operations depended on the good will of those in their immediate vicinity. Fear would keep some quiet, but fear alone was a shit way to hold power: you needed respect. That meant putting things right by holding people to account when things went bad.

Grim's downcast eyes hid whatever thoughts buzzed around his busy head. Joker suspected most were about Diana—the kid was four, and already too vulnerable thanks to her junkie mother's life choices. Grim's jaw clenched. "But targeting families, brother..."

"They're already hitting ours. And we aren't hitting anybody tonight. Just trust me on this." He embraced his brother. "I'll meet you outside once I finish screwing around with Kaminski's head. With any luck, the asshole won't call the bluff."

In the back office, Joker dialed a number he'd

memorized earlier on a burner phone. A second one buzzed in his pocket. He checked it, smiling at the grainy photos and adding them to a set of texts before sending the call on his first phone. *Brandt isn't the only one who can hire a photographer.*

The line rang three times, then loud music and shouting flooded his ear. "Hold on," Kaminski barked. The mic rattled with more shuffling before he spoke again. "Yeah? Who's this?"

"Don't hang up," Joker warned. "And don't talk." He sat at the desk, his back straight as a board. "Listen hard, Kaminski. You do what I say now, or you lose your family tonight."

"The fuck did you just say?" Kaminski's voice rose again.

"Did I tell you to speak, shithead?" He hit "Send" on the second phone, displaying a whole new set of family photos: a casual picture of Goliath's wife and two kids at their current locations, with a sniper beam beside each head. The quick work of a digital editor, but Kaminski couldn't know that. "You got three texts. Look at them." *The way you fight an insurgency: brutality.*

"Fuck," Kaminski choked.

"Mayhem's coming for them, Kaminski." His voice stayed cold as his blood.

"Please…"

"Kill them all? I wouldn't blame you for asking."

"I-I never wanted this. I never wanted *any* of this."

"You signed off on two hits, Vice President." He poured his hatred into that title.

"No, I didn't. It's…"

"I don't give a shit. You owe us two lives."

"Two? I don't … the girl? The blonde one? She's alive. I swear to God she's alive."

"She going to stay that way?" The silence carried on too long. Joker had his answer. His knuckles popped as he pressed his fist into the desk, wishing it was Brandt's cock-sucking throat. "You take from us, we take from you. Call your wife. I'll give you two minutes. Then you call me back, tell me which one of them you really love. More than you assholes gave us."

"Wait! Don't hang up! Jesus, don't! Please! They … they don't have anything to do with this."

"You killed a member's Old Lady. You're about to kill a second. And you think yours gets special consideration?"

"I know. I know that. I fucking told him not to. Look, I can't change his mind. Please, give me time. I can fix this. I fucking swear it. I'll … I'll get her and I'll give you Brandt and Anubis. You want two, you get two, right?"

"How much time?"

"Give me an hour."

"Thirty minutes. If I don't hear from you … good luck." He ended the call.

Joker's eyes landed on one of the framed photos his dad kept on the desk: an awkward second grade photograph his younger self obviously hadn't wanted. He stared at his toothy, bright-eyed past. *Look where we got to, kid. Better you don't see us half an hour from now.* He flipped the frame face down, then headed out to join his brothers, phones in hand.

****

Ashlyn

"Leave her alone." Ripper stood up, pulling Ashlyn along with him. Sasquatch leered at the hem of her black sundress. She glued herself to Ripper's side, ignoring her aching ribs and bruises.

"I can share." The hairy thug's meth-mouth teeth

gleamed yellow as he licked his lips.

"Yeah? I can't. I've had to haul her ass around all day. She's mine tonight."

Ashlyn tried not to shiver. *Joker, where the hell are you?* Subtracting a couple hours of unconsciousness left her half a day to ensure her own survival. *The odds are* not *in my favor...* She canted her head toward the ancient TV in front of the sofa, where Furiosa and Mad Max rode across their post-apocalyptic desert to glory.

"Prick." Sasquatch threw the insult back over his shoulder as he stomped off.

"Thanks," Ashlyn said under her breath. She twisted her bound hand to brush her fingers along Ripper's and watched him from under her lashes.

"I ain't up for seeing that fat ass's dick tonight. Didn't think you'd be either." Ripper cleared his throat and took a big drink of rum and Coke.

"Your old lady isn't missing yours tonight?"

"Ain't got one. Easier to fuck and release." Another drink. "But I guess in this case, the whole 'release' part won't be as fast." He rattled their handcuffs with a half-hearted smile.

"The super fun part is coming when you have to go to the bathroom."

His face turned white. She tried not to laugh.

"How you feel about pissing outside? You know, in the dark?" he asked. "The bathroom's disgusting anyway."

"Is, uh, your president gonna let me outside?"

"You're locked to me, and I don't have a key. How far can you get?"

She squinted and looked him over. "About three yards? Assuming I had some momentum, and we were going downhill." Ripper had half a foot or more on Ash's 5'4" height, with a rangy build and enough clout to push

Sasquatch off. *He's probably a decent fighter. I could do worse...*

"Exactly." Still chuckling, he grabbed her cup and stood up from their spot on the ugly burnt-orange velveteen couch. "I'm making you another drink. Then we're gonna go take a leak."

"Can we lay down for a minute after? I think I'm getting kind of floaty from that last drink." Either he'd try to have sex with her or he'd end up being far more interesting than she gave him credit for. *Wonder which one would be harder to deal with?*

****

"Gotta talk to Scratch. I'll be right back."

Ashlyn roused from her alcohol-hazed slumber to nod and collapsed back into the dark. *Full dark outside. Half a day left.*

She woke to Ripper shaking her shoulder. "Come on, dollface. We're going to the bathroom." His warm breath tickled her skin. He kissed her cheek and sat up, pulling her along with him. Ashlyn considered protesting because awake felt far worse than being asleep, but the part of her still seeking escape kept kicking and screaming at the back of her head. Only once they were outside, Ripper kept walking around the back of the old root cellar, into the darkness of a country night...

"Wait. We peed closer last time. Can't we do it closer?" The flimsy ballet flats she wore weren't made for uneven ground; she hopped and kicked to get the right one back on at the heel.

"We aren't pissing."

She dug her heels in. Grass tore beneath her feet as he dragged her half a foot. "Ripper. Please. Wait. Wait, you don't have to do this..."

"Do what? Save your life?" He yanked her to his side. "You're right, ok? He wants me to put a bullet in your head and send the vid to them. Unless that's what you want, let's go."

"You're taking me out into the woods to shoot me."

"Ashlyn, I could've shot you by now if that was the plan. Don't lose your shit."

Ashlyn. Not dollface.

She let him pull her forward. "What's your real name?"

"What?"

"Your real name. I'm not trusting someone named Ripper."

"Fuck." He hesitated. Then, "Travis Cannon. Now come on. My bike's blocked in, and I can't get the truck keys off Sasquatch. There's a ride coming for us, but we gotta get to the road."

She didn't balk again. Travis knew his way around, and she didn't fight his guidance as he slipped through a half-open cattle gate, heading into the semi-darkness and down a wooded culvert that ran alongside the long gravel lane. A full moon provided more light than she'd expected, but she caught the scent of rain and the croaking rain crows. *At least one sort of crow showed up. Maybe the rain will slow the Heathens…*

Gravel crunched on the lane up ahead, and a bike revved.

Or not.

"Fuck, he put up security," Travis hissed.

Ashlyn grabbed Travis' hand. He shook his head before someone yelled: "Come on down! Takin' her for a test drive?"

"The pick-up must be running late," Travis whispered. He pulled her through the brush, his eyes turned to the lane. "If we can keep 'em busy, give it time to show…"

We're so far from the road. Ashlyn's stomach stopped lurching. The screaming engine and howling men no longer sounded like a nightmare but a distant memory, along with Joker and her mother, Megan and Jett, her grandparents, and a sea of faces she'd never see again. "You tried. That's more than some…" *One breath in. One out.* "Tear up my dress. I'll get my panties down…"

"No." His hand closed around hers this time.

"You won't do either of us any good if they think you turned."

"Too late for that, dollface. We got out of his sight. Scratch'll treat that same as turning. Listen, if they catch us, we stall for time until Goliath can get more'n a ride up here. Him and some others aren't cool with this shit. They must be late, but they'll be here. We just hang on." Ripper's free hand found her shoulder, pulling her into a hug before he dropped his phone to the ground and stepped on it. Hiding evidence of Goliath's involvement. "Come on. Least we can do is make one last run for it. Can you keep up?"

In the dark, in an unfamiliar copse of trees, in uneven ground? Anything's worth a try.

"Yes."

Travis didn't question; he just started moving. They kept low, dashing from one tree to another. Flashlight beams slanted through the trees. Crashing, tramping feet broke into the undergrowth. Ashlyn's heart pounded and her hold on Ripper's hand got shaky. They didn't have enough tree cover to hide them with ten people searching. And the field beyond was soybeans. *If only this were Iowa. There'd be a corn field in Iowa. Goddamn it.*

Another engine howled up the road. *Reinforcements or the rescue?*

Dragging her by the hand, Ripper ran. Ashlyn tripped over roots, staying on her feet by sheer force of will. Deafening cracks split the air as bullets chopped through branches. Ripper fell and rolled onto his side, catching Ashlyn's inevitable tumble. His hand clapped over her mouth, but she was too scared to scream. He smelled like mud and body wash and rum. She inhaled. It might be the last friendly scent for a while.

Splinters and branches rained down on them as more shots followed. Tires squealed, and a couple bikes kicked into gear. The revving engine from before became squealing tires as two bikes raced down the lane. More gunshots. Whatever rendezvous Ripper had intended to get to, they'd lost that chance.

"Found 'em!" A stranger yelled.

"Let's get to Valhalla, dollface," Ripper whispered, his hand still covering her mouth. She stared at him and nodded.

When he took his hand away, she whispered, "Shiny and chrome."

They raced along the edge of a dingy blacktop in a whirlwind of motorcycles and terror and rain. More shots rang, sticks and stones cut into her legs and feet, her chest burned for air. Until the bikes that'd chased off the truck formed a line across the road ahead, and three more came up behind.

****

The world fragmented. Raindrops caught in blue-white light. Gray leathers clashed with blue-grey cement. Yellow light bulbs, brighter yellow bandanas. Red—dark and terrible red—running down Ripper's cheek and into his hair from a black, sharp-edged gash in his temple.

Cinder block walls throbbed with menace—or maybe that came from the men gathered around the perimeter of their personal basement circle of hell. The closest thing she had to a friend took another blow, stumbled backward, spit blood. Sasquatch and another man clamped their meaty fists on Ash's limp, unresisting arms, keeping her ringside for the freak show. Whatever Scratch shot into his veins convinced him they needed a "trial by combat", which appeared to mean beating Ripper to death with his bare hands. The task of throwing punches belonged to the sergeant-at-arms, but it was Scratch who loomed at the far end of the circle. Only his need to punish a disobedient brother remained between Ash and a shallow grave.

Maybe he should fall. End it. They won't bother with two graves. We won't go to the afterlife alone. Frustrated screams choked her. She didn't dare open her mouth to let them out. She kept her eyes on Ripper.

"Get up, bitch." Scratch snarled at Ripper. "Gotta get your ass dead so I can make a real movie. We're gonna show the Crows how pretty their girl is on the inside."

Ripper landed a punch on Scratch that earned a retaliatory kick. He went down hard this time, and rolled to avoid another steel-toed kick to the face. Scratch was fast. And he had a knife. Ashlyn focused on the shining blade as he circled around, right toward her.

After all the assholes we escaped before, how the hell am I going down to someone like this? I won't let him control me. Not even how I die.

She hadn't moved since they dragged her down the stairs and forced her upright, so the men holding her were relaxed, their grip loose. Maybe not enough, but it didn't matter—second chances didn't come to the dead.

People yelled, and something crashed. The party continued, shouting and thumping. Thunder rolled and rattled above as the storm broke.

Thor approves. Fuck it.

Scratch stood over Travis, blade out and arcing up. She wrenched herself free, pushing off like she meant to vault the border fence. Sasquatch yelled, the other man snarled curses, but Ashlyn's bodyweight crashed into Scratch's waist. He stumbled, but Ashlyn didn't have the bulk to knock him out. Instead he turned and shoved her off, accompanying it with a sharp blow to her side and following it with another.

Ashlyn shut her eyes against him—her last defense—as a fist slammed into her stomach, cutting off her scream. Scratch's face wavered, transfigured into someone else as he hit her. The blow was familiar, his hands...

No. Wrong person. Wrong place. Everything is wrong...

She lay on the floor, fighting for breath that burned without reaching her lungs. The men around them exploded into action. Ashlyn watched their boots and denim-clad legs flicker and thump in meaningless patterns. Scratch stood above. He held a gun, black and terrible. The abyss stared down. The barrel flashed. Fired. A white sheet of pain took over her arm. Gunfire-scented air smothered her scream. Scratch stepped back, out of her sight.

More guns flashed and exploded.

Firing squad? They're terrible shots...

Ashlyn rolled onto her side, ignoring the pain. *Travis?*

He sprawled a few feet from her, blood smeared around his hands and head, trailing out of his nose and trickling down from his busted lips. She pushed herself toward him, stretching until her hand caught hold of his.

Not alone. Goal met.

She let her eyes close, waited for her breaths to stop hurting. Gunshots set her ears ringing again—so many shots—and Ice kept shouting wordless nonsense. Which was weird, since he wasn't there.

"Ashlyn!" She knew that voice, too. From somewhere.

Her eyes opened as large, rough hands grabbed her arm, apparently ripping it off and crushing it into a vise. She looked down to consider objecting. *Bandages, blood?*

Mummification? Is there a pyramid?

"Down here!"

Tree of Gondor. Blue eyes. Grim? Is he dead?

"Stop..." She tugged back, tried to free herself from the hallucination.

"Ash, quit squirming."

"No. *No!* Travis." She looked away from hallucinatory Grim to shake Ripper's arm. "Wake up. Travis, wake up!"

"Ok, ok! Ash, I'll get him. Shit, you're bleeding again. Booboo! Get the fuck down here!" He did something awful to her arm, and darkness rushed up from it. She screamed, but Grim kept moving, doing ... things. Mummifying her. Maybe killing her. "Did you hit your head, Blondie? Talk to me."

"No." Her vision narrowed to his face. "They..." The dark took her. Finally.

****

Joker

The red fog wouldn't clear his vision, and he'd lost count of his reloads. His ears rang with reverb and gunshots, and cordite burned his nostrils. Five or six bodies lay on the floor. From what he saw, it was mostly Heathens, and some junkie. He would've felt worse about the girl if she hadn't gone down as a human shield—she picked her side in this mess. Brandt's cowards were a shitty choice. Kicking in two doors revealed more cowering strangers: some tweaking Heathen club sluts and a couple of weak-ass Prospects who'd wet themselves at their first firefight. He poured his rage into his fists and one of the few conscious Heathens that Spider and Jingle rounded up.

"Where. Is. She?" He punctuated the word with blows to the Heathen's face and ribs.

"Joker!" Dragon's voice filtered through the fog. Joker drew back his hand for another punch, but Dragon hauled him off. "Downstairs." The sergeant-at-arms was pale under his streaked camo paint. "Now."

He ran.

Fresh hell waited in the damp basement: a couple more Heathen corpses, blood congealing in the fluorescent light, and a white chalk ring drawn on rough concrete. One of the nomads, Saber, bent over some unconscious kid in jeans and nothing else. A few feet away, Brandt lay face up, eyes still open. A shot between the brows, one through the neck, another through the shoulder, and his chest a mess of black gore. Hard to tell which one was the killing blow, but Ice stood a few feet away with a .35 in his hand, still eying the corpse and holding a quiet conversation.

"The fuck was going on down here?" Joker demanded.

"Nate." Grim stood up from behind Ice with something in his arms. Joker's eyes locked on the dark gold hair tangling over Grim's forearm.

No.

Joker stopped moving. Forgot how to put one foot in front of the other. Details stood out—the curve of the calf, a battered black shoe falling off a small foot… Grim kept walking toward him.

"Unconscious," Grim answered the question Joker couldn't ask. "She's all kinds of fucking loopy, brother. Said something about getting hit in the head, but I don't…"

He was down the last step and reached for her before Grim finished talking. The sheer relief of her warm, living weight almost buckled his knees. "I got you, baby. I'm right here." His voice shook.

He carried her up to the living room and laid her on the ugly orange velvet couch. Feeling the chill in her limbs, he sent Grim for a blanket and wrapped his cut around her as best he could while Booboo came up to bandage her arm. He stroked her hair, ignoring the amount of blood in the dark gold strands. It felt sticky, heavy, and none poured onto his hand. *Someone else's.* He hoped.

Her eyes opened and stared at him without any sign of recognition. "He can't die. Don't … let him." Her voice was hoarse and breathy.

He clenched his jaw. "Who, sweetheart?"

"Ripper. They kept … hitting." Ashlyn tensed up. Booboo finished her arm and shook his head at Joker.

"Hey, little girl. Look over here at me for a second?" The old medic's fingers snapped in front of her. She looked but didn't focus. He sighed. "Keep her talking," he whispered to Joker. "I gotta get some things from the truck."

"Why did they hit him?" Joker prompted, taking Booboo's place next to her.

"H-he tried to … he had a plan? It didn't work. The truck … missed it. I'm sorry, Joker…" Her voice broke and nearly took his composure along with it. "I d-did everything … to b-buy time but…"

She doesn't need your fear, don't let her see it.

He seized her hand, thumb stroking over her thin fingers. With some concentration, he managed to smile. "You did fine."

Her red-rimmed eyes stared at him from some other planet. "Can I stay with you?"

Joker rested his cheek on her bloody, tangled hair. "Always." His fingers closed around her hand, squeezing lightly at first, but it wasn't long before the hold tightened in a desperate grip. "What's mine is yours. Hear me, baby?"

"Here." Booboo rushed from door with a pill and a canteen. "Sedatives. Sorry, I had them in the van. Didn't expect shock to be on the menu, but this'll get you to the hospital."

"Hospital?" Joker stared at him.

Booboo shrugged his bulky shoulders, scratching at his greying beard. "She's lost blood, VP. I don't got a free supply hangin' around. And shock? You don't screw with that shit. I'm telling you, you need a real doctor lookin' her over. Not just for all that either, if you're catchin' my drift. Get her out. We're gonna have to evac Drifter and Kaminski's mole downstairs." Joker blinked so Booboo explained. "The kid in the basement. Tried to get her out, and they got caught, near as we can tell."

"Right. Go on. I want to talk to the kid tomorrow."

"No worries, boss. He's beat to shit, but ain't nothing we haven't fixed before."

While Booboo lumbered off, Joker leaned over Ash. He waited until she looked at him. He brought his other hand to hers and dropped the pill into it. "Just take this."

"Nate?" But instead of asking a question, she stopped talking and put the pill in her mouth with a scraped, dirt-streaked hand. He held the canteen for her, making sure she drank. His eyes caught on blood trailing down her forearm, traveled up to the weeping, bruising welts at her wrist. A glance at her other arm showed the wound's twin. *Restraints. She must have been pulling at them...*

Joker put his hand on her unblemished cheek. "I'm so sorry, Ash."

"Make *him* sorry." Behind the tears her bright emerald eyes didn't waver. "Make them *stop*."

"He already paid, baby." He kissed her forehead. "By the time you wake up, it'll all be over." With the sedative loosening her muscles and her breathing slowing, he gathered her up off the couch to get her to the cages.

His dad stood alongside an SUV, deep in conversation with Griff and the heads of two other charters, until Griff caught sight of Joker and swung the rear passenger door open.

"Thanks," Joker said as he moved in to get Ashlyn settled. She curled into the seat without waking. He touched her hair before drawing back to let the door close. "Brandt fucking shot her. Booboo says she's low on blood. Shock's setting in, but he dosed her on something." They'd usually go to the local vet since they hadn't had time to get a full mobile treatment set-up, but Joker couldn't imagine what Amos Tilden would do if his granddaughter turned up half dead and untreated on the club's watch. "She needs a hospital."

The others swore. Tree's jaw tightened, but he nodded. "We'll sort it out. Go on..."

"Prez! Tree, sorry. Joker's gotta see this." Grim ran up, holding out a cheap flip phone. "Didn't even have a password on it. Check these texts. The number looks familiar, right?"

"Where was this?" He took the phone and scrolled through the texts, brows knitting together. *There. That number...*

"Brandt's shit. The kid in the basement woke up

and confirmed that it's one of his."

Joker scrolled through a few more texts, shaking his head before he handed the phone to Tree. "We saw that number with Schneider; he found it in Ash's phone. The ones from some bitch telling her to leave."

Tree grunted. "Any idea which of your fuck toys is that flavor of crazy, son?"

"Karli thought Ariel was behind the texts. She probably bribed someone to do it—she hates doing her own laundry. That might be our rat."

Tree glanced into the truck. The bandage on Ashlyn's arm already showed a trace of pink. "Get her to the doc. Tell 'em we had a dust-up at a party. I'll have one of the boys run your bike into town. You come back when she's clear. Grim, Dragon, go find Kaminski. Maybe he has a little more to explain about which bitch got greedy."

****

He kept a protective arm across Ash's limp form from the moment Case pulled out of the dirt drive until they made it to the hospital. Each second raised another fear: she was too cold, too quiet... Was she breathing? God help him, he even put his hand on her hip, feeling the line of her panties. *If that happened—if they did that to her, after the flashbacks she had before?*

Still there. He'd take that. For the moment.

"We're here, VP." Case called from the driver's seat, sooner than Joker expected. He hopped out and circled back to roll the van door open. Between them, they levered Ash from the seat and back into Joker's arms.

Nurses swarmed their arrival, bringing a stretcher and a flurry of questions. He slipped her into the stretcher only to be stopped at the heavy ER doors.

"I'm sorry, Nathan." A nurse stood in his way.

He knew her face. A member of his high school class. *Cindy? No. Sara.* "You can't come back here."

"The hell I can't."

Case stepped up behind him, ready to force their way through. Sara crossed her arms.

****

He sat in a chair, Case across from him. They stared at the infomercial playing on a TV at the other side of the room and turned every time the damn doors opened. Nobody came.

Case's burner phone rang. The Prospect answered it, gaped, and handed it to Joker.

"VP." His father's voice was an octave lower than normal. "How's the girl?"

"Still waiting on news."

"I'm sorry, son." Tree's sigh crackled across the speak. "Get to the Heathen clubhouse. Emergency."

He almost told his father to fuck off, take the patch and shove it—almost—but the situation had to be the worst level of fucked for Tree to order him out of the hospital. Ashlyn wasn't in danger, but she would be if they didn't get their house cleaned. He hung up and turned to Case.

"Let me know the second she's out of surgery. And get Megan down here. Call her again. Send someone for her, I don't give a shit, Prospect, but she better be here." He stood up and put the phone in Case's hand. "I'll have my cell on me."

Every side street between Star Hollow and Carthage beckoned him to turn the van around, but he kept on track. Half a mile from the Heathens' base, flashing lights told him part of the problem.

"You missed him," Ice said when Joker stepped out of the van. "Pigs got here not too long ago, so Tree's dealing with them."

"That'll be expensive."

"Always is. Ash holding up?" Ice put a cigarette in his mouth and held the pack out to him.

"Yeah." Joker waved off the cigarettes. "Any idea why he called me back?"

Ice shrugged and pocketed the pack before lighting his cancer stick. "Probably has something to do with you being the VP and all..." Ice blew out a stream of smoke. "Kaminski surfaced. Last I saw, Dragon told him to wait in the office."

"If you see Tree, let him know I'm here." Joker slid his hands into his pockets and approached the clubhouse, a repurposed lodge from the good old days— OddFellows to Outlaws—mostly left to rot since the Heathens took over. Some people had no fucking pride, even in their own club. They'd even left a broken-up radio scattered across the front porch. *And this is why we don't allow drugs in the goddamned clubhouse. Fucking meth heads always break shit.*

Men wearing Storm Crow cuts covered in varying degrees of blood and filth crowded the main room. Griff stood near the bar, talking to a smaller guy Joker didn't recognize. Near them, Geiger's mud-slicked dreadlocks dripped on the filthy wood floor as he hiked up a ladder with a knife between his teeth. Joker followed his progress and smirked. *So much for the Heathens' banner.*

He passed a bathroom and turned to the back hall. The first door opened a closet full of spiderwebs and cleaning shit with labels from the 1980s. The second opened onto an actual room. A small table was jammed under a half-blocked window, hemmed in by six mismatched chairs.

How the fuck do six grown men sit there? That shrimpy guy must be one of a set.

The floor creaked as Franklin Kaminski stepped out of the far corner and slumped into one of the chairs. He stubbed his cigarette in the ash tray. "Wronski." His voice rasped, and he coughed.

"You sound like shit."

"Yeah." Kaminski tilted his head and pushed his hair back to show off a set of fresh bruises across his throat. "Sasquatch was a crazy asshole, but he was loyal to Scratch."

Joker grunted. "You wanted to talk to me."

"I do, yes. I … wanted to thank you." Another cough. "For not calling the hit."

Joker sat across the miniature table from the Heathens' VP and examined his own bruising knuckles. "I don't get hard for fucking up women and kids, Kaminski. I've made enough orphans in this life. *Your* assholes set these boundaries. And for fucking what?"

Kaminski stared at the table. "We only wanted to move our shit through. Make a profit. Then Scratch goes on some damn warpath rant, and boom. Lets that bitch Owl try scaring you. Pulls in more guns… Has this holy bullshit revelation and starts preaching this big war talk. He's got friends, he's gonna make a big play. We're all gonna roll in money."

"Back up." Joker raised a hand to stop him. "Owl? You mean Cliff Bauman?" *Goddamn it. We still can't shake the jackass…*

"Yeah. Guess Owl's been fucking around here and there with that girl of yours. They got talkin', and she spilled your route or some shit. He figured it'd show Scratch he had the guts to be one of us."

"Girl … of mine?" *Ash wasn't even here back then.*

"That hot, dark-headed one. With the legs."

Megan? Never. Grim would've noticed, for one.

And for two, she'd cut Bauman's throat before she touched him again.

"That don't narrow it much, Kaminski."

"Skinny. Face looks like my kids fuckin' Instagram bookmarks or whatever you call them things. Hashtags?"

Joker pinched the bridge of his nose, a familiar numbness creeping through him. *Ariel. She was with me that day. I left her at the house...* "What'd he give for that intel?"

"Fuck if I know. Scuttlebutt was she's sweet on you. I always figured you put her up to it, and it went wrong on your end." Kaminski cleared his throat. "But now I'm guessing I was dead fucking wrong. Or you missed your calling as an actor, son."

He sneered. "Don't call me that. We aren't old friends here, Kaminski. The only reason your head isn't flying through that fucking window is because I'm not cleaning up one more Heathen shit stain tonight."

Kaminski's hands came up, palms out. Surrendering. "It didn't sit right with any of us when we hit your clubhouse that weekend, all right? We weren't into this total-war bullshit Scratch was selling."

"Not enough for you lazy bitches to clean up your own goddamn house."

"We figured it was a one-off, with your clubhouse. But the hit on that woman? Behind our backs. Guess he wanted to go out in a blaze of glory or some shit. We ... didn't know how to stop him."

"Getting some balls might've helped," Joker snarled into the older man's face. "You handed your club to a certifiable psychopath and jacked off while he killed your brothers, innocents, your whole bitch-ass organization. The *only* reason you aren't face-down next to him in that slurry pit is the fact my girl's still breathing. So where is Bauman? I want to hear what that bitch has to say." *Right before I beat all the blood out of his fucking body.*

"Hell, I don't know. Lost track of him before shit went down. Figured he saw which way the wind was blowing and fucked off back to whatever hole he crawled out of." He let out a mirthless laugh. "I hope you find him."

Joker's eyes narrowed. "This story you're sellin' better not be bullshit, Kaminski."

"What reason would I have to lie now?"

"I think you get why I don't take your word on faith. Stay." The chair scraped against the wooden floor as he stood up. Joker didn't give the man a second glance. He found his dad standing near his Road King in quiet conversation with Dragon, a cigarette between his lips. Tree stopped talking when his eyes fell on Joker. He flicked the smoke to the ground and stomped on it.

"Any word?"

"No." Joker's eyes stuck on the cigarette butt. *God, I do need one of those.* Instead of asking for one, he slid his phone out of his pocket to check again. A text notice lit up the screen—one he'd never heard. *Fucking signal.* "Hold on." He unlocked the phone.

A bunch of texts from Case waited him. He read through them with his stomach plunging through the ground.

"Her mom showed up. Pissed as hell and stirring shit."

"Sounds familiar," Tree grumbled.

"She's out of surgery," Joker added once he got to the last text. He let that sink in for a second. "Thank God. She should be awake. I need to call..."

"All right." Tree didn't even sound annoyed—a first for the night. "Before you disappear, you learn anything from Kaminski?"

"You talked to him," he said over his shoulder, already walking. "Looks like we've got more cleaning up to do than we thought."

"That all you got?"

"Send Chains over to keep a watch on it. He'd enjoy that."

"You sure Chains is a good fit"

"If you don't want him for it, I'd say Nomad or one of Griff's guys, Prez." Joker glanced back. "Your call."

Dragon grunted. "That ain't cryptic at all."

"I'll tell you all about it at Church." Tree patted the sergeant's shoulder. "We won't keep you, son. Call your girl. I'll visit with our new best friend. Dragon, come on. You can help him with his manners."

Back in the van, Joker dialed the hospital. He asked for Ashlyn and got patched through to her room. Megan picked up.

"Hey, Joker." Her voice was rough and a little slurred—she'd probably been half drunk when Case collared her. "They brought Ash out of surgery. She's okay."

"Good. Good…" He swallowed the lump in his throat. "I'm sorry, Legs. I didn't get Case's texts until just now. Shitty reception out here. Can I talk to her?"

"She's asleep. The drugs hit her pretty hard."

"Is Bella there?"

"Yep. Making sure we got five-star treatment," Megan sighed. "I'm going to head home in a few. Visiting hours are over, but I promise I'll be right back here in the morning, all right?"

"So will I, hon. You're sure? She's okay?"

"Doctor said the bullet came out fine."

His grip on the wheel eased. "She have a

cellphone on her? So I don't have to go through the hospital maze tomorrow."

"Yeah. It's right on the bedside table. I even plugged in the charger. I'll text you the number. It's one your dad gave me a while back. Go on home yourself. You sound like hell."

"Back at you." He shut off the phone and slumped against the seat.

Time to go get this shit mopped up.

Chapter Sixteen: June 21

Joker
Ravenwood

Joker woke up between heartbeats, his body aching like he hadn't slept in days. The clock said otherwise. *Ninety-two minutes. Better than nothing.* A painful yawn helped fling him out of bed. Whether adrenaline or fury kept him moving, exhaustion didn't yet weigh him down, but he cursed the bed's short frame and the pillow that still smelled like Ash's shampoo. He reached for his phone. It rang the second his hand closed around it. He checked the screen, but it wasn't Case or Megan, so his greeting came out a flat: "Talk."

"Joker. Man, I need some help…"

"Case?"

"I'm in Carthage. State Police picked me up in the parking lot, dragged me in for questioning about that explosion outside town. Like I fucking know anything." The Prospect's voice was strained, his words short and clipped.

Joker scratched the two-days stubble on his chin and took a breath. *Don't yell.* "If you're there, who the hell's with Ash?" he asked, already texting two brothers to see who could pick up the Prospect.

"Her mother, I guess?" *Shit.* "Schneider just got them to cut me loose. He's taking me back down, VP. I… Look, there were SUV's coming in the lot as they drove me off. Black ones. If they questioned me, maybe they tried grilling Ash, too."

"She even know what happened?" *Double Shit. Did Legs tell her the cover story before she left? She knows not to tell the cops anything. God, I hope she knows.*

Case grunted. "Man, she was crazy doped up.

They won't get jack from her for days."

"Booboo's on his way. Meet me at the hospital." Joker hung up and called Tree. He answered on the first ring. "Dad, the State Police—"

"Got your Prospect. Schneider informed me. Said Major Case tried interviewing Ashlyn, but Bella put the fear of God in them." Tree sighed. "Then she pushed for a transfer. They're sending your old lady to St. Louis."

"*Where* in St Louis?"

"Don't worry about it. I got Blackie calling that girl he fucks in the admin department, and Grim's chasing the records trail as best he can. Griff's got a place for you to crash up that way."

Dad's being nice? We're in a bigger clusterfuck than I thought.

****

Joker found Case in the lot at Star Hollow General, talking with Blackie and a curvy brunette in slacks and a jacket—Blackie's admin fuck buddy. Blackie confirmed the ID by kissing the girl's cheek. The gesture emboldened her enough she managed to smile and even cast a quick wave Joker's way before fleeing inside.

"She didn't wait around to talk to me. I'm hurt," Joker said by way of greeting.

"Chicks dig scars, brother. Open wounds and fresh bruises freak their shit out." Blackie shrugged. "She might be afraid you're gonna shoot the messenger."

Joker smirked, all too aware of the bruises discoloring his face—the one on his right cheek looked like someone tried to break the bone. "Am I?" He patted the pistol waiting at his waist. "Better say it real nice, then. You ain't got her pretty lips to help put me in a merciful frame of mind."

Blackie swallowed, but Case stepped forward.

"They took Ashlyn to St. Louis."

"Tree already knew that much." Joker shrugged, hand moving away from the gun.

"Some private clinic up there," Blackie explained. "Closed records system. Tessa's been tryin' the last couple hours to get more intel, but it's a fancy-ass recovery place. They keep patient records offline. And they don't advertise. I guess it's one of them 'if you gotta ask, you can't afford it' kinda things."

"How many of those can there be? She know why they signed off on Ash going?"

Blackie and Case exchanged a look. Blackie nodded to the Prospect. "Earn your stripes, boy."

Case's grey eyes clouded, and he looked down at the fresh pavement. "Sir … VP. Me and Legs, we got pushed out of the room for a couple minutes. Mrs. Marlow said it was paperwork, but Legs got a look when she walked out. It was Power of Attorney. I'm sorry, I didn't know she'd do anything with it. Figured it was some kind of caution thing…"

Joker squeezed Case's shoulder hard before pulling the Prospect into a one-armed hug. "You did good. Whatever the fuck is going on, there wasn't anything else you could do." He nodded at Blackie, but a cool determination settled into his bones. *I find her, I get her home. That's all there is to it.*

****

At the clubhouse, a full meeting of members and their visitors assembled, celebrating the impromptu meth-lab two of the Nomads set up (and ignited) in Scratch's safe house, complete with a massive cache of weapons—Major Case and their nonexistent budget would be working it until the statute of limitations ran out. On top of that, Chains and Blaze asked to join the original charter, and were unanimously approved along with Case, Tyler, and two other Prospects. The brothers set the 4th of July for the patch party. The last vote was hardly counted when a sentry shouted from the compound perimeter: guests. The table meeting broke up, and Joker was first to reach the main room, just in time to see Megan run through the front door. She beelined right past him to Tree, who caught her into a tight hug.

"I'm so sorry. I tried talkin' him out of it. I…"

A familiar figure followed her in—tall, angular, with iron grey hair and electric blue eyes far too lively for his weathered face. Those eagle eyes zeroed in on Tree and Joker.

"It's all right, Legs." Tree patted Megan's hair before he released her. Griff caught her in a one-armed hold as she turned, and steered her toward the door to the yard. "Geiger, get her a drink. You want one, Amos?"

Grim started moving, and Joker put a hand out to stop him. Griff was her dad's best friend, and kept her at his place when her mom was too drunk to come home. Whatever reunion was happening out back didn't require an audience. Megan needed comfort from someone who didn't want her panties on his floor.

"If you've learned to keep Crown in this barbarian encampment." Amos' usual old-timey drawl faltered, but with the drink order as a peace signal, most of the club dispersed back to their own conversations and pursuits. Those who remained kept their eyes—and ears—on the exchange between Tree and the lawyer while Tree ushered Amos toward the bar. Joker stayed with them, watching every move Tilden made.

What side of the coin did you land on, old man?

"That we have." Tree nodded to Geiger. "Double, neat. Unless you like it frilly these days?"

"No. I still like things neat. I damn well *appreciate* neat, Jacob. What the hell have you been getting us all into in the last month?" The accusation started some rustling movement among the men—mostly the out-of-towners and Prospects. Everyone else knew better.

Tree straightened to his full height to stare down the slighter man—Amos had never been broad, and the decades had whittled him away rather than fattened him up. "Brandt lost his fucking mind and listened to some empty promises coming across the river. That's not on me."

"My granddaughter has a bullet hole in her. Because of you."

"Or because her grandfather has been an old friend, and someone wanted that friendship ended. You making deals with terrorists these days, Amos?" For the barest second, Tree's gaze flicked toward Joker, but he focused on Amos as the lawyer took his glass from Geiger.

"Never," Amos snorted. He sipped the Crown. "Your club still does us more good than harm. We both know it. The council knows it. And with state funds drying up we got a shitload of programs facing one hell of a funding shortfall." Amos's eyes slanted up to meet Tree's. "They've been takin' the coal companies' blood money for a hundred years. Yours spends just the same."

Saved by the Great Recession. Christ.

"And what about Ashlyn?" Joker leaned on the old wood of the bar. "You less worried about that hole in her arm than the football team getting new uniforms?"

Amos turned. The last time the old man stared at him like that—the last time they'd been this close—was old Judge Trombley's courtroom. Right before Amos suggested Trombley give Joker the "opportunity" to go to the Army instead of jail. "That's why I'm here, boy," he hissed too softly for others to hear. "I want my granddaughter the hell back in Oak Grove."

"We don't have her, Amos," Tree answered.

"Goddamn it, I know that! Her mother took her out of Star Hollow. Get her back."

"Exactly: *Bella*. Go talk to your damn daughter. We ain't in the kidnapping business."

"Don't blow smoke up my ass, Jacob. You got those fancy computer set-ups over in Aesir. Do something with 'em." He raised his glass in a half-salute.

"We might have looked already," Tree admitted with a nod toward Joker. "My son's attached to that vest he gave her."

"But don't expect a quick result either." Joker walked around the bar, ignoring Geiger to grab his own shot of Jack. He stopped across from Amos. "I figured you'd tell Megan where she was and that's how I'd find her. That place Bella took her don't keep online records. If we had some names, we could send a few boys in, shake their resident doctor upside down until something falls out of his pockets."

"The kid's a cynic, Amos." Tree's eyes crinkled at the corners. "Your granddaughter's shot, but she isn't incapacitated. If she uses one of her cards, that's easy enough. A little bit of spying on your daughter's finances might turn up where she's paying the bills. Just takes a few days' patience."

The old man nodded. "So long as you find her." With that, he marched out the back door to reclaim Megan. Once Amos was out of sight, Tree pointed Joker toward the sanctum.

"We need to talk…"

"Just a second, Prez!" Blaze sauntered through the main door with a freshly-stolen phone and a shit-eating grin. "Call me Santa-fucking-Claus, brothers."

****

Ariel
Oak Grove

Ariel reread her texts from Sara—a friend from the hospital—about thirty times that morning. Each time, her smile grew and her heart lightened. *Brandt and his numb-nut goons might be just as useless as Tree always said, but God bless rich-bitch WASPs.*

Her phone vibrated with a text alert. Ariel laughed as she tapped the screen.

Joker: **Where are u?**

Ariel: **Home. What's up?**

Joker: **need to talk. make sure ur ok.**

Ariel: **im good. But id like to see u. chains isn't so easy to talk to.**

Joker: **U ok to go somewhere? I can pick u up.**

Ariel: **Getting out of this house wd be awesome.**

Joker: **Text u when I get there.**

Putting the phone down, Ariel examined herself in the mirror. *This is the day you get back where you're meant to be, gorgeous. Let's make it memorable.* A bruise still discolored the right side of her face from cheek to temple. Her hand closed around her foundation... *No. Let him see it. Remind him that his slut girlfriend just walked out on him in the middle of a crisis.* She settled for eyeliner, lip gloss, and mascara. A quick comb through her hair, then she left it down in loose waves to complete the damaged innocence look.

This is what gets him hard these days? No accounting for taste. She stared at her reflection with critical eyes until a bike roared down the street outside.

"Hey, girl. The VP's outside." Chains—the Nomad Joker had set as her guard—called the unnecessary announcement from her living room.

A quick spritz of perfume, one last look in the

mirror, then she walked out. A six-foot chunk of muscle and attitude leered at her from the sofa. Chains's eyes were a muddy, dark color, and his face bore two ugly, ridged scars down the left side. Worse, his hair hung in a lank, river-flood brown ponytail. *He probably has to chain women up to get them into his bed, let alone keep them there.* Despite her uncharitable thoughts, she favored him with a polite smile.

"Thanks for staying last night."

"I just do what they tell me, sweetcheeks." He followed her to the door. "You have fun today. Looks like you could use some."

She shot him an acidic glance before dashing out to the street, where Joker straddled his idling Harley with leathers dark as sin, and a Crows t-shirt taut across his chest. *Wet dreams start this way,* she thought with a hidden sigh. The sun glinted on his dark blond curls as he nodded to Chains.

"All clear?" Joker called to the nomad.

"As a bell, VP. Didn't have to shoot a single idiot all night."

"Good. Get some shut-eye. Gonna be a long week, brother."

Joker met her with a faint smile and held his spare helmet out. She wasted no time acknowledging their conversation as she climbed onto the bike. Chains was irrelevant—a Nomad—called in because of trouble, and soon to be gone again. Ariel put her arms around Joker, pressing her breasts to his back. The firm contours of his thighs tight against hers warmed her smile, even when Chains looked her way with those cold, stupid eyes. *Go screw yourself, Nomad. This is how things should be. This is mine: this place, this man. Finally.*

"Where are we going?" She shouted over the roar of the bike as Joker started down her street.

"Somewhere we can talk." He sped up around the turn, racing down Main Street. She hoped people saw and tightened her hold on him.

Roughly fifteen minutes later, they pulled up to a small house well outside town, somewhere between Ravenwood and Zenobia—one of many half-abandoned old relics across the county line. She hadn't been inside it before, but she assumed it belonged to the Storm Crows one way or another—whether one of them owned it or the title-holder owed a favor. Her lips turned in a pout. A safe house meant business, and that meant she wasn't the only person he wanted to talk to.

This is only the first day. There'll be more. It's a busy time, and at least he's seeing me at all. Maybe even seeing me first...

"Come on." He tapped her thigh, cueing her to get off the bike first. Like he understood her hesitation. She swung her leg over slowly, giving him a good look at all the skin her shorts revealed.

They walked up the path together, and he held the door. She entered a small but comfortable living room with real furniture instead of the usual flea market look.

"Whose place is this?" She squinted at some of the pictures on the far wall, but no familiar faces jumped out.

"One of the Heathens. I'm supposed to meet with him. You don't mind, do you? I figured we'd knock this out and then go about our business."

Her heart thumped its way up her throat. "Um. Are there ... still Heathens? Even after all this?"

Joker shrugged. "We're patching over the ones that want to stick around. Not their fault Brandt lost his fucking mind along with his balls. They signed on to join a growing club, not a death sentence. Maybe they can make a go of it with a fresh start, playing support."

Ariel's lips drew in tighter. Being alone with the Crows VP and a Heathen patch-over didn't feel great. She had no interest in witnessing an assassination, for one. The Heathens wouldn't all be happy about this move. And they'd have to prove themselves. *Ratting me out might be a handy way to do that ... but not every Heathen knew about me. Stay cool.*

"Guess he's not here yet." Joker slid his arm around her shoulders. "Get comfortable, babe. It won't take long." The familiar weight, the welcome warmth of his big, hard body rekindled her smile.

"I heard some about what happened after they, um, they found us. Is everybody all right?"

"Dragon had to get some stitches. Couple guys had to get to the hospital over in Collinwood. Far as I can tell, we only have a couple things left to tie up." Joker touched her cheek beside her bruise. "Are you ok, Ari?"

She took his wrist and pulled his hand away, even though his touch made her blood run hot. "Better than some. Is Ashlyn still in the hospital?" His jaw tightened, and something flashed across his features. Her heart thumped faster for the glimmer of that vulnerability he usually hid so well from everybody else.

"She'll be all right. I'm only glad that it wasn't worse. Or that you weren't taken." His voice lowered to a sweet, wicked whisper. Her pussy clenched with memories of their nights together. He sounded that same way when they'd fucked each other to exhaustion...

"That's good. Guess I got lucky." *Too bad the bitch didn't die.*

"Yeah, you did." He gestured to the couch before walking to a wall cabinet across the room. He opened one side and pulled down a bottle of Crown Royal—the most expensive bottle present—along with two cut crystal tumblers. A quick shot went into each one. He handed one cup to Ariel and took the other. "I keep wondering why they *did* leave you behind." He settled onto the couch and patted the seat next to him. She took the invitation. Their legs touched, his rough riding denim tantalizing her bare skin. "They had enough intel to know your connections."

She gulped the whiskey with only a couple coughs. "I'm small fish." Another burning sip. "No rich grandpa to milk for cash, not an Old Lady, so not much use as a hostage."

"Maybe." He drank without any sign of discomfort and his gaze fixed on some distant point out the window. "Maybe it would'a gone better if neither of you was. This shit's too dangerous."

"For some, Joker. Not for everybody."

"For Ash." He flexed his left hand—the one so recently healed. Cuts crisscrossed the raw, red knuckles, matching the state of his right hand and the mark on his left cheek. The bruises and cuts highlighted his squared jaw and the cool calm in his dark brown eyes, so at odds with the obviously painful injuries. *He seriously is the only man I know who can get a girl hot when his nose is broken.* Joker rolled his shoulders like he felt her thoughts. "Been looking for places closer to the city."

Her knuckles went white on the cup. "You're … moving?"

"Maybe. Ash might need a fresh start after this bullshit, and I gotta make sure she's all right. I can link up with the St. Louis charter."

Ariel downed half the glass and studied her bare, tanned thighs. Smooth skin men would—had—begged to touch. Just not the one who mattered. "Nate, you can't just abandon … everyone. Feeling guilty about this mess can't make you forget who you are. Please, think this over." The late afternoon light ignited gold flashes in his chocolate eyes as her hand settled on his bicep.

"She's seen me falling apart, bleeding out…"

"There are ways to show gratitude without giving up your whole life!"

"You think this is all gratitude? Some Lone Ranger and Tonto bullshit?"

The Crown's pervading warmth loosened her tongue. She got a deep breath around the desperate knot in her belly. "You just said so. You're with her because she stayed around while you recovered. But you *are* this club; it's in your blood. She doesn't know the first thing about it. Sooner or later, she'll skip back to her ivory tower and let you fall wherever she drops you."

Joker's eyes flared, and then he half-smiled. "That was honest. But is it the whole truth, babe?"

"What truth?"

"I'm not blind." His Kevlar-lined jeans rustled on the floral upholstery. "I've seen the way you been acting. Did you really think you'd be able to hide it from me?"

Her hand shook as she set her cup on the chipped coffee table. She didn't meet his eyes. "I wasn't hiding…"

His smile sharpened, and a light finger touched her neck. "I'd be lying if I told you I never thought about us. I used to wonder if we would work together."

"Nate…"

"We may look good on paper, but it won't fly. We'd just be replaying me and Reagan."

Oh, but you're so wrong, Nate. I can show you.

"I'm not like her. I never was." She touched his shoulder. His body felt like hot marble beneath his cut, so she let her still-trembling hand linger. "I've *been* happy with you. All I've ever wanted was to make you happy." She forced herself to smile through the ache of a breaking heart. *Might as well push to the limits.* "Ash …

she changes you. Or you change for her. But you were perfect before."

"I haven't changed, Ari." The sharp edge on his tone pushed her back an inch. "She showed me that I can't sit around waiting for things to sort out. I gotta deal with my own bullshit, *feel* something instead of freezing it out."

"W-what do you mean?"

"You remember me breaking guys' faces so easy back in the day?" Joker ran a busted-up hand through his already messy hair. "Think I enjoy drinking 'til I pass out all the fucking time? Lighting up just to get through the day? I've been pushing down all the shit I should've dealt with since … fuck, I don't even know. Fallujah maybe."

She flinched. "I didn't…"

"Nobody did."

"But you?" Alcohol and sorrow both seared her throat as she finished off her third glass. "Why her?"

He smiled, this full, real, soft … thing in his eyes. Sappy. Stupid. And Ashlyn wasn't even in the room. "Remember that day Ice and Hailey got into it?" She nodded, and he sat back. "I got her home, and we had this fight, and I just … see it." He settled against the couch, pulling his arm away to stretch along the cushions. The loss of his touch broke her. Choking on the injustice, she took what relief she could in the Crown.

"Saw what?"

"How much better a leader—and a brother—I'd be if I dealt with my shit instead of keeping people at arm's length all the time."

"So you want to bail on … everybody. On the people who love you. Me. After everything I've done for you? For some bitch who *already left*?"

"Are you wanting a 'thank you' note for keeping

my bed warm here and there?" Joker snorted. Ariel slammed the glass on the wooden coffee table.

"I won't apologize for caring about you, or wanting more. For seeing what you can't."

"You wanted to be Joker's Old Lady. It was a power play, and you're pissed it didn't work out. You've been throwing that bitch-fit for months, judging by those texts we found on Ash's phone..."

The texts. Shit. No, don't answer.

"Joker, I know Ashlyn checked out already. She's used you as much as you *think* I used you. You can't rake her over the coals, so you're doing it to me instead."

He turned to the window. Silence stretched out for several slow sips of Crown. "I think I've quit smoking. Been trying for years."

Is that his idea of an apology? She glared down at their feet and wiped her eyes, glad she'd opted for waterproof mascara. "Bad habit, I guess."

"There are worse habits. But we gotta start somewhere, right?" Joker pulled something from his cut and dumped it on the table, right next to her glass. "You have to make a choice to remove the poisonous shit from your life. Once you get rid of one thing, it's easier to get rid of another. And then another."

"And ... you're saying *I'm* poisonous?"

"You saying you aren't?" He faced her with eyes as cold as the ice he said he'd felt. "What did you think would happen once they butchered her? Her blood would have been on *my* hands. You would have let me live my whole fucking life with that stain."

Air vanished from her lungs, and blood drained from her face. "What are you talking about?"

"I'm going to say this once, Ariel. Stop. Lying. To me." He seized her chin and jerked her head around, forcing her to look at the table. An old phone lay next to the Crown bottle. One she'd last seen in her Chevy's console.

When? How? Maybe it's a test? He had the phone, but he can't prove for sure it's mine.

The Crows don't need proof.

He let go, but the imprints burned her chin—a few more bruises to the collection. "That phone texted Scratch. He wasn't good at clearing his shit."

The hand she put on her cheek no longer shook. Or her entire body shook…

This can't be happening.

Deny. Deny it all. Everything.

Ariel started to shake her head, but Joker struck, seizing her throat, squeezing just short of choking her. She jerked back, uselessly. His flint-edged gaze bored into her. "We've got the snotty messages to Ash. He even got one right from your sorry ass about Hailey. You didn't even fucking bother with a burner."

I wanted to hurt you. For all those times you fucked other women, ignored me, walked away. I wanted to be the one…

"I would never hurt you. I wouldn't—" He let go of her so suddenly she broke off in a gasp, needing air more than justification. She coughed while Joker spoke over her.

"You were screwing Cliff way before Ash came along, so don't fucking sell me this 'all for you' bull. You're forcing my hand, Ariel."

She scooted away from him, out of arm's reach. The front door wasn't far; she could make it if she ran. "Scratch promised he'd patch Owl in," she wheezed. "Soon. Real soon … he'd set him up, send him over the river to set up a new charter in Missouri. I … didn't mean to spill your route. I was t-trying to get intel, for you. To bring back." *Or set myself up to be a president's old lady there, if I can't have it here.*

"It's bad enough I can't trust you," Joker snarled, "but what you did? They killed Hailey on *your* word. Ice knows. You want to keep lying to the one person who can stop him from ending you?"

She shot to her feet despite the room spinning. "A day ago, they were trying to kill you and the whole club. Now you're taking their words as gospel? Everything I've ever done was for the good of the club! I did hang out with Owl, but we're friends. If he ... if he used my phone or something..." Her voice trembled almost as much as her body. She was going to puke. To cry. Or scream. Ariel stumbled back from Joker, like a couple extra steps would protect her. *How stupid. Nothing's going to protect me. Nothing.* "Nate, this isn't funny anymore. You know I would never hurt you. Never. This is ridiculous. A misunderstanding." She reached the door.

"Ari, stop." He sounded so calm as he rose to his feet. "You step out that door without resolving this, and it's out of my hands."

Like it matters either way.

She looked at the door as if it were a bomb.

Knowing Joker, maybe it is...

She grabbed the handle and pulled, waiting for gunshots when she stepped out onto the porch. The outside world was silent, save for the distant chugging of a tractor and chirping summer birds. Across the road, an old guy looked up from trimming the hedges in front of his dilapidated farm house. He waved. The whole scene blurred, as much from alcohol as her tears, but she started walking.

How long before they turn Ice loose? I'm too far to get home.

She pulled her phone out. No service.

Fuck.

A familiar blue Sonata rolled over the hill. Thanking God for her coworkers, Ariel raised a hand in a frantic wave.

****

Claiming she needed time alone to calm down after getting stranded by an asshole date—which wasn't too far off the truth—Ariel pushed her friend out the door and threw stuff into the biggest duffle bag she owned. *I'll call Mom from a motel. Drive slow the first way, until this fucking buzz wears off. Make up time once I sober up…*

She hovered by her own front door for five minutes before she got up the guts to open it. A few calming breaths and then the sun was on her face again. Nobody stood in her yard. No crew of gunmen bikers waited. Tossing her bag into the back seat, she got behind the wheel and headed south toward the county line.

New start, new story. Who says those bunch of wannabes were such badasses anyway?

Chapter Seventeen: June 22

Joker
Oak Grove

Joker wiped the last of the wax from his new Dyna. The black paint gleamed damn near as bright as the mirror-sharp chrome, but he didn't *feel* it. The pride, the rush of excitement: nada. Just a vague echo deep in his chest. He dropped the cloth in a trash bag by the garage door and reached for his toolbox. A lone pack of Marlboro Reds lay tucked beneath an air filter. He stared at them a lot harder than he had the bike. *I'm fucking pathetic. It's been two days, not a week. She's barely even—*

"Nate!" Grim yelled through the open door from the kitchen. "You still here?"

"Yeah." He didn't fake any enthusiasm about the fact. "Any news?"

His roommate lumbered out of the house looking as rumpled as Joker felt: Cheeto-streaked sweats, gray t-shirt dotted with soda stains. The gym rat might even have missed a couple hours at the weights. "Sorry, man. I've tried everything. Still got a few searches running; her stepdad's accounts alone could take a week. But I was thinking it might be under her dad. I can't find shit for him, and Megan doesn't know much. You got anything?"

Joker adjusted the Dyna's saddle bag then looked outside where Grim's sat gleaming in the sun. "Guessing his name's Davis? I figured he's out of the picture."

"That's what I thought. But I can't find any—shit."

Joker followed Grim's gaze across the street in time to see Megan's blue '03 Honda Civic pull to a stop. The girl herself hopped out. She dragged a bulky purple blanket out of the back seat before running to them, cradling the messy bundle. The breeze caught her red-black ponytail and twisted unruly tendrils until she got into the garage.

"Hey, Legs!" Grim called. Daisy Duke shorts displayed the limbs in question to amazing effect—they almost distracted attention from the cleavage in her purple tank top. Almost.

"That wind's vicious. Guess a storm's coming," she said with a hesitant smile. Up close, the eyeliner didn't hide the red edges around her eyes. "I'd have been here an hour ago, but they're still picking up pieces from the wreck—kind of has the Carthage blacktop slowed down."

"They figured out what happened yet?" Grim asked with calculated lack of concern.

"Guess Ari was drunk again."

Joker shrugged, his eyes not quite meeting Megan's. She hadn't been that drunk. Ari could hold her liquor well, and he'd seen her drive way more wasted than she'd been that day. What mattered was that the coroner could argue her blood-alcohol levels were above the legal limit. Helped to make things cut and dry and meant that nobody would look too closely at anything else. Not that it mattered. Storm Crows weren't sloppy. "We all make stupid choices."

"Some of the girls at the salon set up one of those GoFundMe things to help her mom out with the funeral. I went over to help set up the fundraiser."

"That's because you're an angel, Legs," Grim said gently.

"I am." Megan's lips curved up again, and she hefted the blanket in her arms. "That's why I brought you a present, Nate."

"Oh?" Joker accepted the lavender fluff with a

dubious grunt.

"Yep." Her grin belonged on a canary-filled cat as she pushed back the blanket's edge, revealing a Dell logo on a silver plastic shell. "Ash left her laptop."

Grim stomped down the steps and pulled the computer out of Joker's hands. "Why the hell does Blondie have a gaming laptop?" He tilted it, oblivious to his companions' blank stares.

"Grim." Joker coughed.

"Could probably upgrade the storage space… Looks like solid state. Shouldn't be hard…"

"Grim!" Megan and Joker said at once.

"Okay, okay. Tinker later, hack now. She use online bill pay?"

Megan smirked. "Are you kidding? The girl lives online more than you do."

Grim started up the steps; Joker turned to Megan. "Thanks, brat."

Her dancing green eyes swept toward him, and her grin vanished.

"Yeah. Don't thank me too much yet. The next thing you *aren't* going to like."

"This ought to be good."

She held up her hands in a sign of peace. "You don't have a gun on you, do you?"

"Why is everyone concerned that I might shoot them lately?"

"If you could see your face, you'd understand."

"Let's hear it." Joker crossed his arms. "Then I'll decide if I have bullets or not."

"Right. So. Um … You-need-to-see-Uncle-Amos."

Grim stopped halfway through the kitchen to stare at them through the open door. "Jesus. Isn't one conversation with that wolverine in human form enough this year?"

Megan rocked on her feet. "Um. I was talking to Aunt Bonnie, and she sort of, uh, hinted. That I should have an idea. And maybe you should do it tomorrow, about noon. When Jett's in town." Her eyes flicked from the bike to the garage door. Anywhere but straight a Joker.

"You think she's trying to help?" he prompted.

"I think…" She tugged her ponytail and fiddled with her shirt. "I *know* Aunt Bonnie isn't happy about Ash getting sent off again, but…"

Joker's head came up. "Again? Bella's done this before?"

"About two or three years ago." Megan's nose scrunched. "Look, I was dealing with my jackass husband, and I didn't get read in on the details. Ash got super sick, and Bella didn't think the St. Louis hospitals were good enough. She sent her to some hipster private deal out west. Aunt Bonnie almost kicked Bella out of Thanksgiving."

Joker shot a look at Grim, who raised the laptop in a salute as he vanished into the house. He turned back to Megan. "Why the fuck didn't Amos share this information yesterday?"

"Maybe he thinks it's a different thing."

"Anybody else know about the last clinic?" Joker motioned for Megan go ahead. He followed her up the garage stairs and into the kitchen.

"Uncle Amos might. Jett definitely would. They all kept pretty quiet about it. Private hospitals are sort of déclassé, darling." She drawled the last words in an exasperated mockery of her extended family. "Can't have us plebes realizing how much fancier they are with ostentatious display. That's for the *nouveau riche*."

The thread of bitterness in Megan's voice caught

him up short. He stopped to look at her—really look—
for maybe the first time in years. Megan's fair skin was
the only trait she shared with Ash. Her 5'7" frame was
curvier, her naturally dark hair simply styled. Her jean
shorts were cut-offs, her sneakers well-worn, and her top
was one of those things girls made from old t-shirts. The
Crows pushed gigs her way now and then as
acknowledgment of the fact she'd chosen loyalty to her
father's club over her husband—the same lying rat
who'd sucked up to Brandt and led Ariel off a cliff—but
how often had they truly checked in with her?

"You okay?"

Hurt flashed in her eyes before she covered with a
smile. "Sick of family time. Ash is the only one who
doesn't talk to me like I'm a pound puppy they're stuck
with."

"How's your mom?" He could have guessed her
answer: rolled eyes and a shrug.

"Somewhere in Florida with some former frat
president jerkoff. I think he plays baseball." Megan
laughed. "Don't worry, she's not coming back any time
soon. Your dad's safe."

He grabbed two beers out of the fridge and
popped the tops off before passing one to Megan. He'd
probably handed her hundreds since they were kids, back
in the days when Megan was at his dad's house almost as
much as Joker himself—whether it was Tree or one of a
dozen baby-sitters watching them. They'd shared
bedrooms and toys, then beers and joints for so long that
he'd never thought much about her genetic family. The
Tildens seemed like a thing that happened to other
people, possibly on the CW shows that Ash had
marathoned on his Netflix before he set up her profile.

"Don't be too sure about that. Dad's pissed as
fuck about Bella surprising him. He might make some

Tilden-inspired bad decisions."

"Mm." She bit her lip with a mischievous giggle. "You know he dated Bella? I saw a picture of them in Bonnie's albums." Megan took a long pull from the bottle. When she tilted her head back, he caught a glimpse of her profile—one of those classic, Hollywood kind of shots. He'd forgotten how pretty Megan was. *Grim needs to get his shit together before she moves on. Damn.*

"Dad always had a thing for vicious bitches. I never understood it." Joker popped the top from his own beer and took a quick drink. His eyes cut toward her, considering. "Just to be clear: this was an *old* picture, right?"

Megan choked, clapped her hand over her mouth, and bent over the counter. "Fuu—oh my God." Laughing, she wiped tears from her eyes and beer off her lips. Joker offered her a paper towel. "Yeah, no. Waaaay before Ash. Bella was, like, barely out of high school. If that. Judging by the clothes."

"Go, Dad. Cradle-robbing bastard." He slapped her back. "You sure you're ok?"

"I'm fine, Nate. Swear." She hooked her right arm across his and leaned her head on his shoulder. "Southern Illinois, where accidental incest is a legitimate issue."

Hugging her back, he practically heard Ash in his head: "Hashtag: Small town problems?" Megan fell against him, laughing.

"Oh, honey, no. Start chugging now, or you'll be a nerd before sunset."

Chapter Eighteen: June 23

Joker
Oak Grove

The morning meeting went smoothly; Tyler's injuries would lay him up two more weeks, Drifter was in a sling, but everybody else was mobile and healing. Ariel's funeral was set. Back home, he left the Dyna in the drive, grabbed some tools off the workbench, and headed to his bedroom. Hefting a Phillips screwdriver, he eyed the king size mattress and springs blocking the closet door. The Prospects were coming by in an hour to assemble it, but... *Better this than busting someone's skull.*

Grim emerged from his own room as Joker tightened the first crossbar. "How'd it go?"

"Patch-over party this weekend. With enough booze and pussy, they'll forget and forgive." Joker snorted at his own words. "So will most of us. Add some donations to the city, and it's water under the bridge. Just gotta find Ash. Maybe do what Megan said and go see her granddad. What do you think?"

Grim leaned against the doorjamb, rubbing the dark whiskers on his chin with swollen knuckles. Joker returned to assembling the bed. Something in his expression...

"Don't." Joker lifted a wrench in warning. Ryan shifted his weight back.

"Look, Ash is great and all, but have you—"

"I said: *don't.*"

"I got to. You know I do. Your dad ain't gonna look the other way about the problems..."

"For him it isn't about Ash, it's about Tilden's voice on the counsel and his buddies in Springfield." He shifted on the carpet, getting a better angle to see Grim's hangdog, worried face. So much for a quick conversation. Joker settled his back against the upright mattress.

"You wouldn't say that so easy if your dick wasn't involved."

"Fuck if I wouldn't. I owe Ash—not as my old lady, or on Amos's account. So do you." That hit landed, and Grim shuffled his feet, shrugging.

"What if … I had some intel that she ain't who you think?"

"The computer?" Joker flipped a screwdriver into the air and caught it. "Quit the theatrics and spill."

"It's, uh, private stuff. Journal entries. Couple years old. Talks about the abusive fucker she was engaged to and, uh, look… They were into some shady rich kid shit, all right? Drugs, illegal fights, the whole nine yards. I always wondered how she took to the clubhouse so easy."

Joker nodded. "Makes a lot more sense this way. So, what's your hang-up?"

"When shit hit the fan, her mom got into it." Grim lifted a hand, palm out to ward off the questions. "This shit, it's … I don't know what a good way is—"

"Spit it the fuck out."

"I think, uh, the place Megan talked about was more shrinks than sawbones. All I'm saying, bro, is maybe we ought to just leave it. Wait. Give her some time to, uh, wherever. You know."

"Details on the clinic?"

"Nada. She called the head doctor Kublai Khan, so I'm guessing he's an asshole."

"All right. I'll try Amos." He kept his expression blank to hide the spinning in his head. Grim looked like he wanted to say something, but Joker slid back to the bedframe. He needed something he could fix here and now.

What did they do to you, baby?

Before Grim made up his mind, the doorbell rang and dispelled whatever thoughts he meant to share. Joker listened to the greetings and footsteps before he got up. He met Case and Frog in the living room and handed over the tools. "I'll be back in an hour or two. Frame's already laid out."

"Nate." Grim's voice caught him off guard. His club brother's brow creased. "You want me to keep going with the laptop?"

"Leave it. Maybe Tilden will fill in some of the blanks."

"Is Ash doing okay?" Case asked the question slowly, his eyes moving from Grim to Joker. Joker grunted. The rumors had spun out of the hospital and through the club after Amos's visit.

"She will be. Soon as we get her home."

God, I hope I'm not lying.

****

The Tildens owned a big, white monstrosity in a 1970s acid-trip of a subdivision at the edge of a pond called Grove Lake by some coke-addled developer. Joker parked his Harley on the street and walked across the freakishly green lawn, breathing in the scents of flowers and cut grass. Towering columns and a wide verandah loomed ahead. The place looked like something out of the Old South, and fit with the drawl of the aging Southern belle who stepped out into the heat.

"You must be Nathan!" she called, waving him on. "My goodness, you're tall. Come on in, honey. Don't hit your head on the door." Bonnie Tilden's silver-blonde hair fluffed around a cheerful face with full cheeks and soft green eyes so familiar that his chest hurt.

"Ma'am." He got the urge to doff a hat he'd never owned. "Megan told me—"

"That you need to see my husband and son-in-law. Come on through. I'll show you Amos's lair." She stepped back, letting him into a cream and blue parlor with soaring ceilings and a skylight, cooled to a temperature slightly above the North Pole. Ahead, polished wood steps rose to an open second story, while another set led downward. "Please, don't mind his mess in there. He won't let me or the maid near the place." Bonnie bustled away, and he followed, keeping his boots on the throw rugs until they reached the stairs.

The second story held another expanse of wooden floors, full of gleaming furniture from a variety of eras, all in perfect repair and wrapped in a heavy lemon scent. *Smells like money.* Bonnie didn't slow her pace as they passed by six closed rooms, down to the end of the hall where one door remained half-open. She knocked on the door frame, while he stared over her shoulder into a sea of bookcases and leather upholstery. At the far end, Amos Tilden sat behind a desk the size of an Abrams tank, piled with paper. Another man paced between the two windows.

"Gentlemen, you've got a guest."

"Send 'em off for today." Amos rubbed his eyes. Age spots stood out on his hand.

"It's Ashlyn's boyfriend. You remember? Jake Wronski's son." Bonnie's voice hardened.

The rangy figure turned Joker's way. He had one hand in his jacket pocket, and a phone in the other. "Nathan, isn't it?" A syrupy Texan drawl marked Jett Marlow's deep voice. Amos didn't so much as look up from his computer until Bonnie cleared her throat.

"If you don't talk to him, Amos, I will, and none of y'all will be real happy if I do. I'm not feelin' altogether charitable right now. With any of you." Amos heaved a sigh. It must have been a positive signal because Bonnie reached for the door. "Come on in!" she crooned. "Don't take his demeanor personally, honey. I'll fetch y'all some lemonade." Shooing him toward the seat by Amos' desk, Bonnie backed out. "I'll tell the maid to clean the other side of the house. It'll give you some quiet to talk."

The door closed with a hard click. He half expected to hear a key turn in the lock.

Amos squeezed the bridge of his nose. "Sit down, son. You're too tall for my old neck to go twisting around for." Joker lowered himself into in a creaking leather seat instead of arguing, and Amos continued. "Good to see you again, Nathan. I'm surprised your father could spare you. From what I hear, Tree's got one hell of a mess on his hands this week. Kidnapping, arson, shootings, the old Schumer Mine Road must be getting more traffic than it has since the seventies."

And there's the right hook from nowhere.

"I recall it was pretty busy back in the 80s, too, Amos." Jett Marlow sat on the far edge of the giant desk, his grey eyes boring into Joker. "Not to mention the 90s, when your father and his predecessor were solidifying Crow territory from the river up the I-67 corridor."

"Ancient history," Joker said without flinching. "You know why I'm here. We're running into a wall. I can't bring her back if you don't share your intel."

A tic spoiled Marlow's poker face. "No sense sharing bad intelligence," he countered. Joker's instincts went on alert.

"You already know."

"I have an *idea*, but like yours, it's taking time to trace." Jett tapped his phone screen. "I'll point you toward it: Carehall Clinic in St. Louis. Her records were there, and they'll have to transfer them to anywhere new, but…"

Joker straightened. Waited.

And waited.

The other men traded a heavy look. Finally, Amos cleared his throat. "Aw, hell. Ain't our place to tell it, but somebody better warn you…"

"About what?" Joker turned his frustrated stare on Jett. *Christ, can't anybody just talk straight today?*

Amos spoke before Jett could. "Ashlyn got into some trouble a couple years back." The lawyer's eyes fixed on a bronze horse statuette at the front of his desk.

"That's one way to put it," Jett muttered. Amos shifted in his seat, still staring at the horse.

"She was seeing a boy. Things got a bit out of hand. Ashlyn Marie had what we used to call, uh, a real bad spell. Bella had to get her some help. Took a bit of doing to get her settled."

Out of hand? Is that what you call someone beating the hell out of her?

"This isn't public knowledge, understand?" Jett's words drew Joker's glare.

"It isn't good for a girl's future to have a thing like this come out," Amos added. "But Bella may be using this whole mess to dredge all that up again… May make things delicate about getting Ashlyn home."

He closed his eyes and dug his fingers into the leather armrest. *Yeah, can't have the neighbors know you let some shithead abuse your granddaughter. They might vote you off that fucking council you love so much.* Then another thought: *Why didn't Grim find those records?*

Amos cleared his throat. "Jett, give us a minute. I need to speak with the Vice President alone." His eyes crinkled at the corners. "I'm sure he realizes I'm still on his Club's payroll. A whole dollar a month, to keep it legal."

Jett frowned, but he left. Amos waited for the door to close, then settled back into his chair with the creaking of old wood and leather. "Now, give me your version of this Gordian knot. You can play the hard ass with Jett, but I am fully aware that you all bleed like anyone else. Before I convince Jett you can help Ashlyn, I need to know the club's situation. Make sure she's not coming into an ongoing war."

Joker steeled himself. "Brandt was aiming for a takeover, but the meth got the better of his brains. He decided taking out Ice's wife and ransoming my old lady would earn back some of his merchandise that, uh, turned up missing the last couple months. Plus, maybe convince you to rethink your loyalties, embarrass us. Fucking stupid. But he committed to it, I give him that."

"Is it taken care of?"

Joker nodded reluctantly. "We're patching over the Heathens who want to join a real club. The rest are scattering or taking up a new life. We won't be facing another threat from there. They'll hold Nelson County strictly in a support role. If they aren't complete screw ups, maybe they'll become another chapter."

"All that and you still lost your old lady." Amos's brow rose. "Bad thing for the reputation of a national VP. What will the Aesir board say?"

Shit. The national part of his job description was incidental—it mostly mattered when charters called for help or a higher decision. And Amos shouldn't have known that much about Storm Crow business. *How deep does Dad let this guy in?*

"I took her back and paid the Heathens in their own blood. Ash is just recovering somewhere private. She'll be home soon enough."

Amos put his forearms on the desk. "Son, Bella

knows your world. Hell, she dated your daddy back in the 80s when we all thought cocaine was king. Blood in the backroad ditches and over the highways…" His lips twisted. Joker frowned but didn't argue with the strange route Amos's mind seemed intent on taking.

"I, uh, had some idea about that. Yeah."

"So you understand Bella's got good reason to be wary. Thing is, son, somebody in a bad way, they need people who'll stick around, and I see the way things go these days. Thinking long term isn't the way you kids operate."

He managed not to spit a "fuck you" answer. Barely. "Sir, with all due respect," *though not much is due,* "I won't be going anywhere. I'm marrying Ashlyn."

Did I just say that?

Amos's brows arched. "She hasn't said anything."

Damn it.

"Didn't want to rush her." He put his hand on his knee, flexing his fingers again and hating the tremor in them. "I wish I had." His heartbeat thundered louder, joining the grandfather clock ticking in the hall, the humming central air, and clinking echoes of glass and cutlery from somewhere. *Bonnie must have meant it about the food.*

"Well then." Amos nodded. "Jett! Come on back in, son. Sounds like this young man's got a question for you." *Like hell I do.* Joker's fist clenched as Jett strode back through the door. "How d'you feel about being a father-in-law?"

"You don't seem like the type to ask questions before the gun's warmed up." Jett's gravel voice sawed through the last of Joker's control. He surged to his feet.

"Ash will marry me or she won't. Her goddamn choice. I don't need permission from you, and I sure as shit don't want it."

Jett's gaze didn't waver. "No, you want the money in her trust fund."

"Her mother canceled every account she had. I don't see that changing. And you'll be gone in a few months, so why the fuck are you even here?" He took a step forward, ready for the fight.

"Your kind may drop your children off at the pound once they're out of the womb, Wronski, but the rest of us take our responsibilities seriously."

"You son of a—" Joker lurched forward, only to find Amos's hand on his right arm. The old man moved fast when he wanted. He snarled and shrugged the restraining grip off.

"Nathan! Go see Bonnie about that drink, won't you? I'll have a talk with Jett." Amos tapped Joker's shoulder. "Go on. No sense in you two comin' to blows when you're on the same damn side."

He glanced at Amos, but his eyes caught on a picture hanging behind the lawyer's grey head: Ashlyn smiled at him from a tree-lined walkway. The photographer caught her almost laughing, her eyes dancing—not so different from the last time he carried her to into his bedroom. How long ago was it taken? A year? Three? Was she hiding bruises and a broken heart under her lacy sleeves? His hand fell to his side, and he left the study without a backward glance.

The hidden weight in Marlow's jibe hit him at the top of the stairs: *"Your children... responsibilities." He considers Ash his kid. What if the records aren't under her name at all? He's got the cash to shift a form or two. If they hid this much before, maybe she used palms they already greased...*

He turned to wade back into the study and froze. Something was off. Changed. A door close to him stood open. Against his better judgment, he walked over to shut it, but a familiar green flip-flop caught his eye, lying abandoned a foot inside the door. *Ashlyn's*. He checked both ways down the hall then crossed the threshold.

A four-poster bed covered with pillows, heavy furniture out of some other century, and Ash's favorite sundress laid across the rose-pink coverlet. Her headbands littered the dresser, a notebook lay on the bedside table. He hadn't thought about how much stuff she'd have, all the things she hadn't brought to his place. Looking around, he filed them into his own room. She'd crowd him out of the closet and take over the bathroom. They'd have to get a new dresser... His chest tightened. He shut the door and stumbled down the stairs in a trance.

He found Bonnie in a lower level, amid a vast granite and steel kitchen. A crystal pitcher, matching glasses, and a platter of sandwiches occupied the vast stone island on either side of her. She lifted the plate. "Cucumber or turkey, dear?"

"Not hungry, ma'am."

"Ah, well then. Lemonade or whiskey?" She put the tray down and pulled a Crown Royal bottle from the cabinet behind her.

"Just a shot, please."

"Figured you might need some." Bonnie got down two glasses and poured double shots in both before handing one to Joker. "What fuse did you set off?"

"Told them I was marrying Ashlyn and they could shove their consent where the sun don't shine." Joker downed half the whiskey.

"Good for you." Bonnie took a more measured sip. "They know where she is?"

"No."

Bonnie chuckled. "Jett's accountants are busy

splitting the marital assets, so Bella can't possibly pay for Ashlyn Marie's treatment without it flagging somewhere." She said it all easily, no sign of a lie.

"He thinks I want Ash for money. Amos thinks I'm just cleaning up club bullshit. What's your take?"

"It doesn't matter," she said, rearranging the sandwiches. "You could be doing it for either reason, or both. Being with you makes Ashlyn happy, and that child needs a bit of happy just now. So, when Jett's people flag the payment trail—or yours do—I'm fetching my granddaughter home. Why don't you plan on keepin' me company on the trip, hm?"

"Amos good with that idea?"

"Sweet boy, I don't give two shits what he approves of. Far as I'm concerned, if he hadn't spoiled Bella Grace plum rotten all her life, we wouldn't have our current tribulations." Bonnie took another drink. "You objectin' to coming with me?"

"Never, ma'am." He tipped the glass to her. "Thank you, Mrs. Tilden."

Chapter Nineteen: June 24

Ashlyn
Xanadu Clinic, Nevada

Most of her existed in a fog, living in a world of silhouettes, like the start of a movie set in Victorian London. Skipping the meds for two days won her some sense of her surroundings. And a Ziploc bag with slightly-used pills stuck to the sides, hidden in her tablet case. It would probably be worth some money to the right junkie. A last-resort escape fund.

Ashlyn crept upright, counting the inches until her spine was perpendicular to the bed. No dizziness assaulted her, just the usual pain. She eased her bare feet down to the cold laminate floor. The chill seeped into her bones and lingered even after she put on the pink satin slippers by the bed. *A gift from Grandma Bonnie. But from when?* Time slip-slided around her head, memories mushing into the wrong places.

It took ten years to twist the door handle without making a sound.

She cracked the door open and peered into the fluorescent-lit hallway. No one wandered by—Xanadu resembled a hotel more than a clinic, and the halls weren't given regular patrols. Someone would be watching the security cameras, but she'd spent two nights establishing a late evening walking routine. Her doctors had all but crowed when she got out of bed instead of lying around in a fugue—she suspected knowing her motivations would spoil their day, but theirs was a frustrating existence and they deserved to enjoy their perceived victories.

Of course, what she was wandering for was a phone. Rules were rules—no patient got one without supervision. So, she had to find someone else's.

Sometimes the night-shift nurse left the phone bank unattended, but that didn't help—too much of a chance they'd see her on the camera or come in right as she dialed out. That left the orderlies and their break room. If something called them out, someone might leave a cell phone unattended. *Third night's a charm*.

She'd wandered down a couple halls before an unearthly wail echoed through the wings like a divine trumpet: the frabjous tones of an adult male howling at the moon. A big red-headed guy, gripped by some lupine dementia, ran screaming and baying into the common room. He shrieked something about spiders in the forest and tackled the tallest nurse. Ash cuddled up to the wall as curious patients and horrified staff scrambled after in a Mardi Gras parade of genuine concern and schadenfreude. Catcalls and whooping laughter, shouts for order, and demands for Wolfman's clearly superior drugs added to the galumphing chaos. Xanadu's little-used speaker system called for calm, guaranteeing further pandemonium as available staff sprinted toward the noise. Part of her wanted to go look. Join the bedlam. But she had miles to go.

At end of the next hall, a breakroom door hung open and forgotten. She limped toward it, shaking more with each step until she reached it. *Valhalla*. Half-drunk coffees, open energy drinks, and microwave-safe containers covered the tables. Here and there a book or notebook lay abandoned. So did a couple bags and several jackets with an encouraging—yet daunting—number of pockets. She scrabbled through the bags with no luck, but the fourth jacket yielded a smart phone. With a password. She put it back. Another phone, same story. She counted her breaths to stay calm.

Does no one carry dumb-phones anymore? What about unlocked phones? Tablets? Isn't somebody here a newbie? The thought no more than crossed her mind before she picked up an unlocked black Galaxy, several generations back. Thanking her stars, she limped out of the room and down the hall, the contraband device tucked into her sling.

Safely inside her room, she turned it in her free hand, her eyes glassy. *I don't know anyone's number. Oh my God, I don't know any numbers. Wait. Apps. Gotta be something...*

She signed Alex Waverly out of Facebook and logged herself in, thanking all the stars she'd chosen her email to authenticate her account instead of her phone. First message went to Megan. No response. *She's probably at work... Who else can help? Who also uses Messenger?* She ran through her contacts, sending quick messages to several without answers. Then she reached Ryan. Grim.

Ashlyn: **U online?**

Twenty seconds and several tears later, the app blipped.

Grim: **WHERE R U??**

Ashlyn: **Xanadu.**

Grim: **WTF BAD 80s Movies?**

Ashlyn: **A clinic in NV. Got a phone. Don't know numbers.**

Grim: **618-555-2648 CALL ME.**

Ashlyn stared at the number, the keyboard. Her fingers shook, but she dialed. He picked up on the first ring. "Grim?" she whispered. "I can't talk long. I stole the—"

"Holy shit it's you!"

Her mouth hung open for a second. She checked the screen. *Nope, not hallucinating.* "Um. Who else would it be?"

"Your mother's psycho minions?"

"Oh. Good point. Look, I can't talk for long." She fished the half-tab of narcotic out of her nightstand drawer and set it by the bottle of smart water the last nurse left.

"Just hang on a couple minutes. We need to track that phone. What the hell is Xanadu?"

"Uh, it's ... a sort of rehab place?"

"Fuck. We know you're under a different name, but getting into healthcare systems is a pain in the—"

"It was Ashley Marlow last time," she sighed.

"Last time. Right. Look, can you get to the Internet?"

Ashlyn crossed the room to tug the curtains a fraction of an inch more closed. With one eye on the door, she lowered her voice. "Mom's pretending her old client did something, so no outside contact. Anyway, the doctors think of it like extra detox." Grim snorted, and she didn't argue the sentiment. "So. Um. I need ... to ask something," she said, easing herself back to the bed.

"Shoot, hon."

"I—uh ... did ... am I..." The words faded. She covered her mouth with a shaky hand to feel her own breath still moving. Just not the words.

"Ash? Ashlyn? You there?"

Breathe in. Breathe out. Ask.

"I—I'm here. I, um, I just ... wondered if you knew ... am I ... still dating Joker?"

This time, the silence came from Grim.

Her stomach crawled up her throat, and she spoke too quickly, the words running together: "I know. Stupid question. I'm sorry. I didn't mean to ... it's a lot of ... the shock a-and things happened, and I c-can't remember stuff..."

"What the hell is going on out there, Ash? What do they have you on?"

"Ryan, please. Please, just ... tell me what's real, okay? Tell me." The room tilted in ways rooms shouldn't. She lay back, holding tight to the phone. Her anchor. If it disappeared like everything else, she'd be lost.

"Ash. Sweetie." His voice softened, the words slowing. "What do you think the answer is?"

"I don't know. It's all sort of ... not there." She heard Grim's breath on the other side, followed by silence. Finally, he spoke.

"You remember him taking you to Carthage?"

"Y-yes. But then he wasn't there. He left. I thought..."

"He wasn't allowed back. That's all. He wants you home."

When did I start crying? She raised an unsteady hand to find tears coursing down already wet cheeks. The dam broke. Tears took over, and the words vanished. Only the keystrokes told her the connection remained. *Maybe he didn't hear. Maybe I didn't say anything. I just thought it...*

"We ought to be setting that goddamn clinic on fire," Grim muttered.

Or I said it. I'm stupid.

When he spoke next, he sounded like a dad talking to a kid. "Ash, listen to me. I got—"

Footsteps outside stopped her heart. "I gotta go." She swiped the screen to hang up and shoved the phone under her pillow as the door opened.

"I saw your light on, hon. You sleeping ok?" One of the nurses. The nicer one, Kristi-with-an-I, who had two kids and an ex-husband. Her pleasant, round face held concern without judgment.

"No," she answered around a yawn. "The, um, screaming? It sounded bad."

Kristi nodded with a sympathetic noise. "Want me to get you something?"

"Could you? Not major. I only want to get some sleep."

"Of course." Kristi went off to get the pills. Ashlyn dragged the phone out and sent one message, wiped the call log, and signed out of Facebook before clearing the cookies as best she could. That done, she set it to silent—not even daring to risk vibrate only—and stashed it under her pillow. Next shift started in a couple hours. She could dump it in the common room during the change-over.

Ashlyn: **Tell Nate I'm ok & I'm sorry how it turned out. I'll always miss you guys. Thank you. For everything.**

Chapter Twenty: June 25

Joker
Somewhere over the Great Plains
        First chartered plane in my life, and it's the worst ride I ever sit through. Figures. Flying out to the desert: tie. Landing somewhere too loud, too crowded: tie. At least on the carriers to Kuwait and Kabul I had buddies to be miserable with...

They'd spent the last day researching Xanadu Clinic, laying plans for an extraction if one was needed, but none of it would matter if he showed up and Ash wouldn't come with him, so he had to do this the Tildens' way. For now. That meant he sat in a leather seat drinking booze a private couldn't afford if he sold his own mother, while a sweet old southern belle told him a horror story.

"Everyone always says they knew, but I swear to God *I* didn't. He seemed so damn nice, so thoughtful." Bonnie paused her narrative to stir an olive around her martini glass with a silver skewer. Her nails were well-kept but bare, unlike Bella's flawless manicure or Ashlyn's chipped, mismatched polishes. She started talking again without looking up from her drink.

"A girl doesn't want to spend her free time talkin' to her grandma or callin' her daddy. She goes out, she finds friends and makes her life. Girls have fashions: they change their hair and how they dress. I didn't think anythin' of it." The woman's faded green eyes glistened. The words must've stuck in her throat, because she sipped the martini. "'Til one day her stepdaddy Jett, he called me up in a right old state. Grumblin' 'bout how she hadn't come home in two months. And when she came home, he lit into her and she took off. Out the damn door, sayin' she wouldn't come back. My God, he was fit to be tied. I think maybe we should've known then. Ashlyn Marie wasn't never one to sass, but I told Jett to leave her be—figured she was bound to act like her mama someday. Couldn't be helped." Bonnie's head shook, and she waved a hand at the past like she was shooing out the sealed windows. "Then that dreadful fight... And poor Jenna walked into the middle of it. That was her roommate—a nice girl, but she wasn't any match for Bennett's fists, any more than Ashlyn Marie. Though Lord knows they tried.

"The law got called, obviously. End of the story, you'd think. We didn't know anything back then, Nathan." At last, Bonnie looked at him, but he wasn't sure she truly saw him. "Not 'til the psychiatrist called Bella, said as how Ashlyn Marie'd been skipping her appointments. And she lied right to our faces, talkin' how much better she felt. Then the parties. Six in the morning, comin' home and gone again by afternoon! All on pills..." Bonnie scowled. Drank. "She took too many. And thank the stars she did. Only way Bella ever got the child corralled. Took her out of school. Got her treatment."

"For what?" Joker turned his own glass in his hand without raising it to his lips.

"I suppose it's close to that Post Traumatic Stress or whatever they call it now. I never understood most of that lingo. What they had trouble with—*she* had trouble with—was this 'derealization' thing. She'd been playing pretend so long, she sort of... I don't know, got lost about what was and wasn't true. It never sank in for her that he wasn't coming back. Or maybe she told herself he never was there? Hell, I don't know what goes on in that child's head. Nobody does."

"Who? Who wasn't there?" Joker sat forward. The one thing she hadn't said yet. The one thing he needed. *Give me his last name. I can find him on that.*

"Bennett Fitzgerald. And I hope the devil knows his god-forsaken name." Bonnie drank, almost draining her cup.

He does now.

"Where is he?"

"In prison over in Farmington, across the river." Regardless of the fact they'd flown over the Mississippi and a good many other rivers since taking off there was only ever one river Bonnie would mean. "For another year or so. Wasn't much beyond that last fight we could prove, and the assault on Jenna. Ashlyn wasn't fit to testify, and nobody else knew a damn thing once his father was through with them."

Bonnie got up and mixed another martini, leaving Joker time to think.

No wonder I don't scare her.

Fuck.

He settled back in the seat, drawing a burner phone from his pocket, checking the time. Whatever else happened, a call to his father lay in the future.

"We'll have to clean you up to get you past the door." Bonnie's voice dragged him back to the moment at hand. She stood by the cabin bar, eyeing him with a freakish amount of clarity for someone who'd downed multiple shots of gin. "Bella's spinnin' tales about the cartel was probably bull hockey. But they will have access restricted. You need to look less like a biker, dear."

"I do not."

"The beard will grow back."

"No."

"Then you don't go. I'm not losing this opportunity because of your vanity."

His jaw set.

"Don't look at me in that tone of voice, young man. I'm no trained soldier, but even I know you don't spoil the element of surprise and you don't go in without scoutin' the enemies. You show up lookin' like an outlaw, you're only justifying Bella's claims, and I want my granddaughter healing with her family, not shoved off into some permanent retreat to be forgotten so Bella can mount a new political campaign without the liability."

"You're serious." *Why do I bother asking?*

"As a heart attack. Ash will become a by-line, nothing more than the reason a new candidate wants mental health reform. And that's all she'll be."

That is never going to happen.

"So you and I go in, you flash your impressive papers and Amos's contacts, drag her out and then what? Bella meets us at the door with a Marshal?"

"Hardly. When we land, I'll call Jett, and I'll call again at the clinic. He'll draw out their meeting today by at least an hour. If that doesn't work, we'll at least be in the clinic. We'll see her. Then we'll just try … something new."

Joker smirked. Only Bonnie Tilden would call unleashing a contracted group of mercenaries "something new". Thanks to the Nevada chapter's contacts, Xanadu's blueprints, schedules, and business information were filling up files in Storm Crow databases in case Bonnie's strategy failed. Tree already put Nevada's president on notice of a possible extraction. However they did it, Ash would be out within a day.

"Our guys will reroute their outbound landline calls once we arrive. They won't get hold of Bella that way. Who's next contact on Ash's file? Would her father be…"

"It's Jett." Bonnie took a drink and speared

another olive. "Since she's on his insurance…" She made a vague wave with her glass. Apparently, insurance and medical law worked in ways too mysterious even for the Tilden matriarch to master.

Not a reassuring thought. Doing all this to get tripped up by some legal hoodoo.

"Where is Ashlyn's dad? Shouldn't he be in the conversation on this?"

"Lord only knows, honey. That's another reason you're here, if I'm honest." Bonnie sat back down, martini in hand. "Jett's tryin' to adopt Ashlyn right in the middle of this nonsense. If he can push it through with Slade—that'd be her daddy's name, not that you'll hear it too often—then he'll have firmer grounds to contest Bella's choices. Trouble is, findin' Slade Davis is about like finding a needle in a stack of hay and horse shit. We can bluff today with Amos's power of attorney, and hope it holds up in court long enough to get smoke signals to that damn useless waste of flesh. Then there's you." Something of Bella's raptor quality glimmered in Bonnie's eyes. "And that pretty speech you made."

Joker swallowed the entirety of his whiskey and poured another shot. "A wedding? That's your Plan B?"

"You were already thinkin' about it. We'll be in Vegas, and I bet you already done worked out that husbands trump mamas."

"You understand if she marries me, she marries my club."

"You understand if you marry her, you marry this family."

Fair fucking point. Joker winced. *What wouldn't I do for Ash?* The list was short. And negotiable.

"Yeah, I get it. And you're not even pissed about me and the club, because it's going to torpedo your daughter's political plans."

Bonnie shrugged off the accusation. "It's for Bella's own good, much as she's going to hate it."

"Ashlyn might not be in any shape for a marriage to hold up in court."

"If she isn't, we'll handle it." Bonnie nibbled an olive. Her eyes were too innocent, her voice a touch too nice. "Amos sent his mother's ring. Resizing it won't be a problem."

Joker's balled into a fist against his leg. *What had Megan called herself? The pound puppy.*

"I'll get her a ring in Vegas."

****

Xanadu House, NV

Joker tugged at the collar of his new shirt. Despite week-old bruises on half his face and designer clothes, the half-seen reflection in Xanadu's front doors nauseated him. *Convincing men to do stupid shit must be a fucking genetic gift. I look like some limp-dick paper pusher who drinks cat piss coffee and had a rough spin class.* He glared the blue Hermes scarf trailing in Bonnie Tilden's wake as she waltzed up to the main desk.

Joker hung back by the door, checking for exits and detailing the layout. It matched the plans Grim had sent to his phone, though the reality was more intense. Around them, earth-toned tiles and polished wood shone in the filtered sunlight streaming through massive windows. Some overpriced decorator aimed for a Spanish villa and landed closer to a B-grade movie set. But an expensive bad movie.

I should've asked Grim what kind of money Marlow's dropping here.

Ahead of him, Bonnie announced her arrival with a saccharine "Why, hello, honey," to the receptionist, a skinny guy with over-styled hair who blinked owlishly at her Chanel power suit and did not leap to either action or bowing. *Poor kid.* Bonnie swept off her sunglasses and leveled a pale emerald glare at the wide-eyed young man across the blue-tiled counter.

"I'm here to visit my granddaughter, Ashley Marlow." The young man's gaze kept locking on Joker instead of Bonnie, but he made the effort to focus on the elderly, imperious woman. "Oh, gracious. Do stop staring, child. You aren't his type," Bonnie added

"I, uh, need to check her file." The young man turned beet red and rushed off presumably to find the file on a computer anywhere else.

"Is the kid gay or just nervous around oversize accountants?" He pulled on his collar again.

Bonnie rolled her eyes. "While the young man's sorting himself out, you could go looking around for the bathroom? Or we can wait. You look as if waiting is something you're ever so well-suited to."

"The bathroom?"

"If you can't find your way and get terribly lost, perhaps you better ask one of the patients for directions, hm?"

You'd think she's done this shit before...

"Yeah. Uh, yeah. Right. I'll go do that."

He started down the hall toward the sound of voices and what he assumed was a common area. That guess proved right. Instead of the standard hospital or nursing home look, he found into an oversize living room filled with people—many sporting various levels of facial bandages—talking or playing games on flat screen TVs. He approached the nearest set. A young woman, her nose hidden under bandages between two fantastic black eyes, turned his way and smiled.

"Hey, handsome." She patted the seat next to her. "Why don't you sit down and tell me about that shiner. You fight somebody for me?"

"Teresa!" Her Wii-opponent batted Teresa on the arm, laughing. "Ignore her. She's on a ton of painkillers."

"Akila's just jealous."

"Akila is coming *off* her post-surgery narcotics." Akila, a gorgeous woman with teak skin and dark eyes, smiled at him. He assumed her bandages lay beneath her silk pajamas. "You lookin' for somebody?"

"Yeah. Her name's Ash."

Teresa pouted full, silicone lips. "Figures."

"If she kicks me out, I'll come back and get your number, ma'am."

Akila chuckled. "Jesus, turn down the charm. The girl you're looking for is upstairs. Go left out of the lift and about halfway down the hall. She can't do the social hours yet—somebody said it's PTSD issues. Sweet, though. I catch her on her walks at night. She shares her chocolate stash."

He thanked them both and hurried to the back of the room, where a bank of elevators stood idle. He stepped into the first one and hit the second floor. Once the doors slid open, he repeated Akila's direction to himself. "Halfway down the hall" was vague, but he found the first likely room open and a man's voice inside yelling about day trading. The next one was closed, 212. He examined the chart outside with desperate eyes: A. Tilden. *Bella got in one last dig at Jett.*

He pushed the door open. The knot that'd taken up his chest since he left her in the hospital unraveled. A slight figure sat on a gray sofa in a sea of laminate wood flooring, ocean blue walls, and gauzy curtains. A sling and cast held her right arm, but her left hand swiped at a tablet on her lap. Pink plaid pajama pants and a loose wrap hid most of her skin and any other injuries, but…

Her posture's wrong. Broken ribs?

Ashlyn's head turned. "Carter, I don't want to—"

Her green gaze fell on him, too glassy and too dilated. Drugged. Her brow crinkled. "Joker? What happened to your *hair*?"

Of course.

"Your grandmother." He closed the door.

"Hm." Ashlyn adjusted her sling-bound right arm and sat up straighter, still frowning. "Am I hallucinating?"

The question stopped him sharp, one step from her side. He let his knees give out and slumped onto the couch beside her, then put his hand on her knee. Ashlyn's eyes followed his movements, but she didn't react to his touch. "I'm real, sweetheart." He spoke through a choked-up throat. "It was hell getting here. Combing my hair was just the start."

"What was the finale? The French cuffs?" She set the tablet aside and her fingers brushed his silver cufflink. Her hand was so close to his he didn't dare to look.

"We aren't even close to the finale." He put his palm against her cheek, waiting for her to look up. He held his breath, searching her gaze and finding little more than glazed surprise.

What the hell do they have her on?

He took her face in his hands and touched his forehead to hers. "I'm sorry, sweetheart. I fucked up with you. Should've put protection on you. I had to go sort things out with the club that night, but—"

"Don't apologize." Her whisper sounded husky. Broken. "Y-you had so much to clean up. Th-thank you. For coming. It's … nice of you." She sniffled.

This isn't her. Doesn't sound like her, doesn't feel like her.

The message she'd sent Grim twisted around his heart with vicious claws. He sat back and stared into her tearful eyes, keeping her chin cradled in his hands. "We are going home. Right now. You and me." He caught himself and forced the next words out. "If you want to go."

Tears ran down Ashlyn's face. Her eyes looked even bigger than usual. "B-but my mother... She'll make trouble. And I—"

"Shh, baby. It's handled." He brushed her hair behind her ear, leaving a kiss on her temple. "Do you want to come home with me? That's all that matters."

Ashlyn's face crumpled, and her shoulders shook with another sob. "I'm sorry. I'm so sorry I—I didn't u-understand what was h-happening in the hospital ... and I did this. To myself. I know I did. T-this isn't your fight. I s-signed..."

"Stop." He wrapped her in his arms, drawing her against his body. Wishing he could shield her, knowing he couldn't. He started to rub her back, but his hand stalled at her shoulders as his fingers brushed the edge of a bandage.

Too bad Brandt's already burned, I'd drag him up and kill him again.

"I ... I was too scared to run by myself."

Thank God for small favors.

"Your fights are mine now, sweetheart. All of them. You want out, we're going."

Her free arm slipped around his chest. Hugging became clinging as sobs wrung her out. He stayed quiet, letting the storm run its course, and watched the door. Long minutes passed before Bonnie's voice echoed from the hall.

"It's all right, baby. Whatever happens now, we're going home." He pressed a kiss to her temple.

The door flew open. Bonnie stormed through, followed by an orderly and an officious man in a lab coat. *Ah, the doctor. I've got some words for you, motherfucker.*

"Ms. Tilden! My apologies, but you can't have so many visitors at once," the orderly announced. "And these people aren't on your approved list." Ashlyn sniffed and did her best to sit up, but Joker didn't take his arm from her.

"It's my grandma."

"And who's this?" The physician glared through hipster glasses. Dr. Keene, according to his nameplate.

Knocking your face in might be worth a couple months in jail.

"I believe I explained it." Bonnie cut in before Joker or Ashlyn could answer. "Now, do stop upsetting my granddaughter. You have the revocation of the power of attorney, signed by Ashlyn this month and the new one with my husband named for her." Joker listened to Bonnie, but his eyes stayed on the two men as he gently disengaged from Ashlyn. He got to his feet and popped his right knuckles while Bonnie continued her tirade, turning up her southern drawl a notch. "You can hem and haw all you want, Doctor Keene, but you will do as we ask."

Joker folded his arms and set a cold gaze on Keene. *Do it this way, or another way. Don't matter to me, asshole.*

Dr. Keene cleared his throat, looking away from Joker's glower. "Miss Davis is aware of her, ah, delicate mental state. I have no doubt she understands her surroundings, but this is—"

Joker touched Bonnie's shoulder. "No buts, doctor. She understands, she comes home."

"I do understand." Ashlyn wiped her eyes before she stepped around him to face Keene. Her small hand caught Joker's sleeve, so he wrapped his arm around her back. "I've wanted to go home this entire time, but I was … scared, I guess." Her eyes darted up to Joker for the merest second. "I know I'm going to need help," Ashlyn continued, her voice catching. "I'll see someone. I'll sign a waiver if you want me to? Or come back if I'm not improving. Please, Dr. Keene."

"There? See?" Bonnie smiled, lifting a hand like a carnival barker showing off a prize. "She's had a terrible ordeal, but she's hardly incapacitated."

The doctor cast a penetrating gaze over Ashlyn before looking at the paperwork he held. "Very well. I'll get the discharge started, but I want you to hold to this promise, Miss Davis. If you don't feel steadier—or have another episode—you need to check back in at once. This cannot be ignored."

"I know. If I'm wrong, I'll come back." She said it with absolute sincerity. Joker's fingers tightened on her hip.

Fortunately for everyone, Keene nodded and strode out. The orderly followed him.

Ashlyn swayed against Joker's side and let out a slow breath. "I should have asked him for a something for emergencies." His fingers traced the familiar curve of her spine and continued glaring at the door.

"There are doctors back home who can do that. And his job. Before we get to them, we've got a date with the courthouse."

She looked up with a line between her brows. "For what?"

"To keep your mother from doing this shit again."

"And you're going to hire a judge for that?"

"No. It's…" He turned to Bonnie, who shook her head.

"All yours, kiddo." And with an unhelpful smirk, she walked out.

So much for the cavalry... Right. Time to do this.

Joker cleared his throat and faced Ashlyn. "Right now, I've got no way of protecting you from your mother. But if I'm your husband..." Ashlyn's eyes widened, her lips parted. He saw her expression shifting but pressed on. "Just marry me, baby."

She shook her head, wiping at her cheek. "For how long? Until you think I'm safe or you're tired of playing the white knight? A year maybe? Would that be a fair guess?"

"I was kind of hoping for the rest of our lives." He reached for her hand, knowing he sounded defensive. Annoyed. But it wasn't her fault. "Sweetheart, remember when I asked you about going on a cruise to Alaska?"

"M-maybe?"

"I meant to do this then. Some nice night, good wine, a lot of stars and music. But I've had enough of waiting. I love you." He kept his eyes on hers, hoping she'd read the truth, feel it. "I want to be with you. And if you don't want to marry me, then I'll find another way to get you clear of your mom and work on convincing you."

"I never said I didn't want..." Her voice caught again, and she lowered her eyelids, head bowing. "You're stapling me to your coattails because you're blaming yourself. And it's noble and kind and all, but if I had two hands, I'd throw that goddamn lamp at your head."

"You have to be kidding." Exhaustion hit, deflating his voice to a flat, irritated grunt. "I feel guilty as hell, but if you think that's why I'm asking, you don't know me." She winced. He held himself back from reaching for her. "Instead of focusing on all the reasons you think I shouldn't want to marry you, try to think about all the reasons I do."

Her hand covered her eyes for a second, and when she let it fall, tears followed. "That's just it. I don't know those reasons. I remember … everything with you. And it was brilliant and I never wanted it to end. But you might have a totally other memory. You might know a totally different person. Because nothing's real around me. I'm trying to hold on, but nothing stays…"

"So hold on to me. Right now. Trust me." He brushed his thumb along her cheek, and searched his aching heart for something—anything—to ease her pain. "When I say that I love you, I don't mean only when shit's easy."

"Do you know? W-what happened before? Why I'm here?" She couldn't meet his eyes, so he squeezed her shoulders, gently urging her to step closer to him so he could hug her, waiting until she folded herself against him before he answered.

"Some of it."

"Some?"

He nodded, but she fell silent. He kept his arms around her. "And knowing more isn't going to change a thing, Ash. You fit me with me, for better or worse. This is happening unless you tell me you don't want it to."

After a few heartbeats, her reddened, tear-streaked face turned up toward him. "I want a new dress." Her smile returned. "And if I'm going to be a biker princess, I get a freaking tiara."

He laughed—a real, true belly laugh. Sheer, heady relief. "Done. I'll get you the tiara when I pick out the ring."

"Then let's get going before my mom shows up with a chariot of fire-breathing dragons." She put her hand on his chest and rose onto her toes to kiss his jaw. He gave himself a second to hold her before stepping back.

He took Ash's tablet from the couch and looked around the suite. "You sure you'll be able to live in a normal house after this?"

"Says the man wearing Armani."

"This isn't Armani." He shuddered. "Shit. I can't believe I even know that…"

"You look nice," Ash said as they headed to the elevators, while Bonnie's co-opted army of orderlies invaded Ash's room to pack her stuff. Joker watched their harried faces, keeping one hand on Ash's waist, and positioning her closer to the wall so no one would jostle her or try pulling her away. "I mean, you also kind of still look like a professional hitman, so there's that?"

Still? He stared down at her as the doors closed. Her sunshine smile didn't even flicker.

"God, stop freaking out." She patted his arm. "It's not like you're the only one I've ever met."

"This is the drug talking, right?"

"Would that make you feel better, or worse?" She cocked a brow. He rolled his eyes and shrugged. *Please, let it be the drugs. Bella can't seriously have fucking hitmen over for dinner.*

****

He called the Nevada president from the car, and a minister was waiting in the Vegas clubhouse when they arrived. Bonnie spent the next hour smiling and disapproving at the same time. Ash giggled through the whole thing, but she checked out after the ceremony. Too many people, maybe too much going on—her eyes dulled, her answers got vague and short. By the time he guided her into the hotel lobby, she barely acknowledged him. They picked an off-strip place, but people crowded the foyer and casino floor, so Bonnie took Joker's cue, and the second the front desk handed him a key card, she escorted Ashlyn up. Joker smiled, telling the clerk "An extra Valium. Seemed like a great idea on the plane."

He got to the room a few minutes later as Bonnie finished taking Ashlyn's hair down, setting the tiara to the side. Ashlyn didn't seem to notice, absorbed in some brightly-colored cartoon involving ponies. *Oh yeah, Diana likes that one.*

"I gave her a Valium," Bonnie said as she stood to greet him. "Pain pills are in an hour." Joker nodded for her benefit. He'd put the schedule in his phone already.

"Thanks, Grandma."

A smile softened Bonnie's face. "Get her to bed. I'll call Amos from my room. And Bella." That idea seemed to lift her mood. "She'll be havin' kittens 'til doomsday." He stiffened as she walked up and put a hand on his cheek. "You did good today, Nathan. Welcome to the family." Then she was gone.

The door closed, and Joker allowed himself to lean against the wall. *The day needs to be done already.* He turned to the couch. Empty. *Where the hell?*

She sat alone in the bedroom, staring into a blank TV, clutching the comforter like it might disappear if she let go. He took the chance to get out of the society monkey suit while he could keep an eye on her, and stripped down at the vanity.

His eyes fell on the armor tattoo's edge, where it faded into his skin. He touched the pauldron before he pushed the wife-beater down his arm, checking the ink. Wouldn't be long before he'd need a touch up, but at least it came through the wreck. His brow creased as he traced the shapes. *Tiwaz, algiz, eihwaz,* and *hagalaz*: Honor, strength, control. *Time to live up to those ideals again.*

"We're married." Ashlyn's voice caught him by surprise, the words spoken like someone using a new language. She stared at the ring on her finger: a simple band of gold with a small, perfect emerald. Ashlyn didn't like diamonds, and she didn't want a big ring—and she had to know he listened to her. He'd chosen every feature as a message, solid and heavy. Inside the band lay another message, etched in thick block letters: Real.

"We are."

She flopped back onto the bed, dilated eyes blinking up at the coffered ceiling. Joker winced. *She can't be helping her ribs.*

"I almost got married before." She announced it with an air of authority. To the ceiling.

"The doctor who ran away to Ebola?" Joker picked the jacket off the vanity and slid it onto a hanger before shoving it into the tiny closet. *A bike. I could have a whole new bike instead of this bullshit...* He pulled his hand off like he'd been stung and returned to Ash.

"No." Ashlyn tugged at a lock of her hair and twisted it around her finger. "We met in high school. After my debut. He gave me a ring, and we had this whole stupid life planned out." She paused, and he turned to see her making herself speak the word, forcing it past her lips. "Bennett." Her nose scrunched, but Joker's hand clenched the hanger so hard he creased the idiotic shirt. "He had a plan, anyway. You always have to agree to Bennett's plan. Then things went wrong…"

His guts knotted up, flashing on Bonnie's story and Amos cautioning him. He'd assumed Ashlyn would never talk about it. Not like he talked about the shit in his head—kids vanishing into pink mist, the IED lifting the truck up ahead into the air, a sniper's bullet catching a buddy in his back. A whole list of nightmares never made it to the open air.

"Ash, you don't have to talk about it."

"Yeah, I do." She breathed out, in. Her hand

raked through her already tousled hair, but her gaze remained focused on the ceiling. "He told me to be quiet. If I'm quiet, he still calls the shots." Joker longed to argue with her, but if she was fighting the bastard… He kept back so she couldn't see his hands turn into fists. "And you should know the baggage you're dealing with." Another breath, her chest rising and falling. Joker's chest didn't move so easily.

"Sweetheart." He forced his hands to straighten and sat close to her, reaching for her wrist. *I am not going to shoot Bennett Fitzgerald; I'm going to burn him. Slow.*

She scraped at a piece of glitter on her dress. She cleared her throat, stroking the bedspread again. Her gaze drifted to the television. He practically saw her falling into her own head.

"Ash?"

"Bennett's dad cut him off a little before I started college. He'd cut the allowance that summer anyway, and Ben … he came up with this idea. Throw parties, charge admission. We had the resources, and I grew up helping plan charity stuff. This would just be wilder, you know? More fun. Maybe we'd even give some of the profit to charity…" She spoke with a vacant tone, eyes fixed on the distance. "It went pretty well. He had plenty of music connections, we had friends with cash and ways to get locations. Houses, warehouses. But Ben liked drugs a lot more than most of us. And he liked fights, you know? The real kind. The ones they don't put on TV. He met some guys, and set up fights at different parties. More drugs. Things just … you look around, and you can't even remember how you got there, or when it all stopped being fun and games, and why there's a guy choking on his own blood."

"Baby, you couldn't—"

"I wanted to stop, and Ben got mad. He got so angry, all the time … more and more. I couldn't even remember how to get out, so I stopped trying. I just pretended all day, every day, that it was all okay and fun and the bruises didn't matter, and I didn't hate every time he touched me, and…" Ashlyn's voice cracked. "He realized I didn't love him. It pissed him off more. I told him I was done. He snapped. He really hit me, and he kept going. Jenna came home. He started on her. And the cops came, and it was… They made it all go away. Poof. Never happened. All that blood, just under another carpet with other peoples' names. I couldn't remember what was real and what was their story.

"After, when he was gone … the more they said it wasn't my fault, the less it mattered." Ashlyn spoke to the television instead of the ceiling—getting closer to him, but not quite there, like she was afraid to see his face. "Until nothing mattered at all. Pills and vodka, living … places. 'Til I woke up in the hospital."

"On purpose?" He asked reluctantly.

She shrugged, still refusing to look at him. "I didn't get withdrawal or anything. I took stuff because it made me stop thinking. Once Xanadu was done with me, they put a new plan in place to get me to graduation. Put me in a new school. I was used to following plans. I didn't know what else to do." She finally looked him. Tears glistened in her eyes. "Not the wife you picked, huh?"

"You could tell me right now you're Cleopatra. It doesn't change a thing, sweetheart." Ashlyn's lips curved, and she held out her hand. He took it.

"I sort of thought once we hooked up… I never kept a boyfriend more than five minutes. They ask questions, eventually. They wanted futures, and all I could do was run from the past."

"Poor boyfriends." Joker threaded his fingers with hers. Honesty deserved honesty. "When Reagan left, I let her leave. We'd been together since high school, and she wanted me to be who I was before—the kind of guy who'd go after her. But I didn't. Figured the part of me that gave a shit about other people was gone." He closed his eyes, and his hold on her hand tightened. "Then you vanished."

I'd have torched the pearly goddamn gates to get to you. He couldn't say it. The words stuck in his heart, and all he could do was hold her hand and watch transfixed as she sat up and leaned against his side. His arm went around her shoulders without thought.

"I missed you so bad, Nathan. The clinic's better than Scratch, but not by as much as you'd think."

"It's over. You're never going back there." He set his cheek against her hair and looked toward the window, where heavy curtains blocked out the light and hid them from the world.

"How's Ice doing? We sort of screwed up the funeral, and I—I don't even know if there's a Hallmark card for that."

Joker smoothed her hair and kissed her temple. "He doesn't blame you for what happened. Nobody does, baby. They're all waiting to see you at home."

"They only care about me because you're nicer when I'm around." Ashlyn levered herself into his lap, her skirt bunching up along her thighs. Joker wished he could ignore it. Some part of him still needed to touch her, reclaim her. He caught her waist to steady her and tried not to think about all the ways he wanted to show just how much he'd missed her. "I hope you weren't too mean when I was gone," Ash whispered.

You have no idea.

"A monster." He squeezed her hips. "And I'm

going to be one again. You need to rest, so stop trying to seduce me," he whispered against her rose-petal lips and pried her hand off his belt.

She pouted. "But it's our wedding night."

"We have all the time in the world, sweetheart." Joker rubbed her lower back in slow, easy motions until he felt her muscles twinge, and she pulled her arm further forward. "Hurts like a bitch, doesn't it?"

Ashlyn's laugh was breathless and tired. "A big one. Like, Russian female prison warden size."

Joker allowed a soft, lingering kiss, pulling back before she could part her lips and tempt them both. "Tonight, you're mine, and that's more than enough. And as you would put it, 'pain isn't my kink.' I'm going to get your pills and put up with some stupid chick movie."

"Noble sacrifices all, my prince." Ashlyn giggled and nudged her nose against his. "For your generosity, I consent to a movie with only minor romance. Maybe pirates."

His resolve cracked. Joker slid his hand into her hair and captured her lips in a longer, far more demanding kiss. "God, I love you... Now get off me, brat. I'll get your pill." *And myself a cold shower.*

The pain meds and a room service dinner lulled Ashlyn to sleep in the middle of *Pirates of the Caribbean*. He let his arm go to sleep for a solid hour under her pretty blonde head before he bothered moving. Flexing his hand to work the pins and needles out, he eased away from her and tucked the covers around her shoulders before retrieving a burner phone from his bag.

He closed the bedroom door and crossed the front room, hitting dial only when he was as far out of earshot as possible. His dad answered on the second ring.

"What's the situation?"

"You've got a new daughter-in-law, if Grant

didn't tell you already." He suspected the Nevada leader would call Tree from the clubhouse, but they'd been kicking off a hell of a party on the Aesir tab.

"I heard. Congratulations. How is she doing?"

"Holding in there. You never told me she has an ex in prison for assault."

"Considering Bella's love of dramatic gestures? Figured the kid got railroaded on an unrelated issue."

"Not this time. I'm not even fucking sure she went far enough, for once."

"What happened?"

Joker faltered. Explaining the full story to his dad over the phone wasn't a risk he wanted to take, no matter how paranoid it made him. "I'm guessing the battery charges got buried under a shitload of cash and lawyer talk. He left her with a raging PTSD problem, and Bella's been doping her into silence."

"Understood. Grim already tracking it?"

"He's got some names and dates, working on finding more."

"I'll check in with him. You focus on your girl, son. We can talk when you get in."

He ended the call and went back to Ashlyn, still out cold. He flipped on a bedside lamp to check her cast and bandages before stretching out beside her. He closed his eyes and put his hand on her hair and his forehead against hers, reciting the vows he hadn't been able to say out loud.

You remind me there are good people in the world, who don't leave even a stranger to die in the cold. You saw I was hurting, when I barely understood it. You held my hand and didn't call it weak. So, wake up, Ash. Wake up and still be you. Ask me for help, I'm with you. Cry, I'll find out why. I may never understand your damn TV shows, but I will never, ever let you forget what's

real. I'm real. And I'm here until you tell me to go.
        Don't tell me to go.

Epilogue

Ashlyn

The clubhouse smelled like wood and polish, smoke and beer. And perfume, since almost all of the twenty occupants were women. Most old ladies rode with their old men on the memorial circuit to honor the fallen club brethren, especially the founding "Original Ten". Ashlyn might have, but her shoulder still hurt, and she got tired so easily that the idea of eight hours on the Harley in the July heat made her nauseous. Plus, Joker hadn't asked her. In fact, he hadn't said much about the ride at all, even though his grandfather's gravestone was among the storied ten destinations. Of course, he'd spent the last six days in Chicago, and half the week before that in Missouri. It might have slipped his mind. Patching over the Heathens had repercussions, and he had a reputation to emphasize. *Maybe he thinks I can't handle it*, she reflected as she settled on a barstool. *Maybe that's not all he doesn't believe.*

She'd half-considered asking to go back to Xanadu after the first week of worried faces peering at her and conversations dropping off when she got too close, but then Lana showed up at the house one night, sobbing and begging for help—with Megan still prostrate grieving over Hailey, Ariel dead, Karli out of town, Blackie's wife filing for divorce, and Ashlyn recovering, only Lana remained to coordinate the buffet and band for the Founders Ride, a chore traditionally handled by the Old Ladies of the Charter so all the members could pay their respects. She'd been too proud to refuse and too clueless to sort anything out.

"You don't have to do anything. Just tell me what to do, I'll get it done. I promise, Ash. Please! I'm crap at things like this…"

"You could be amazing at things! You never let yourself focus on anything but makeup and slot machines." Pain meds made Ash a little more honest than she meant to be, so she'd smiled and squeezed Lana's shaky hand. "I'll help. But if you flake out, I'm not saving you from Karli." And fear, as it turned out, was a decent motivator.

Ash glanced over her lace-clad shoulder to a groaning table loaded with homemade food from members and select dishes from the better restaurants around. A St. Louis DJ she'd had to call in a favor to book was setting up outside, and a member's son's band would follow. Food, music, a Cardinals game on the TV, and all the booze Dragon could find in three counties.

Bikes roared down the road, distracting her. The first wave was arriving.

Karli put a gently-mixed drink in Ash's hand and hugged her. "Hey! Thanks for this. You saved Lana's ass, girly. Mine, too."

"Mostly Lana's. You could have asked me at the start."

"Are you kidding? You've been through enough. I'm still pissed she bothered you."

"Don't be." She waved around the familiar room. "It got me out of my head. Reminded me I know how to do stuff aside from getting shot or being kidnapped." She hadn't thought about everything that went into an event since... *Before*. The only term she could bear to think in regard to her ex and the world they'd once inhabited.

"Well if it's chores you want, honey, we still got Sturgis, and then Memorial Day, the September poker run, Oktoberfest ride, and every dumbass winter meetup."

The sound of engines drowned out every other sound for a moment, and then a wave of mostly-male voices rose as the clubhouse doors swung open and the Storm Crows swept in—or the first dozen of them. Tree, Dragon, and a handful of others she didn't recognize but whose cuts marked them as heads or representatives of other chapters.

"Griff, 'bout time you met my daughter-in-law," Tree announced, gesturing to the lean, leonine man beside him before sweeping Ash into a one-armed hug. Her husband's father was 6'7" at least, well past sixty, and still hard as a medieval oak. Griff was a comparatively dainty six feet of muscle and beard, but he smiled easily and extended a calloused, heavily tattooed hand that Ash shook without hesitating.

"You look a lot better than last time I saw you," Griff said.

"Not being shot in the last twenty-four hours helps," Ash answered, laughing. "Legs will be stoked you made it today. She's out back." Curled into a chair and wasted, sure, but under strict supervision.

"I'll go see her." Griff was Megan's other surrogate-dad, and Ash watched him walk off with hope in her heart. She had no words to pull Megan out of the swamp she was sinking into. Losing a best friend hurt in ways words couldn't fix, and Ash's own ghosts danced in her memory too often for comfort.

"Good job on all this, kiddo," Tree whispered, kissing her cheek, his stubble brushing her skin. She blinked herself back to the present moment and offered an unsteady smile.

"Have to do something to earn my keep after all the trouble you went to."

Tree's chin tilted, but he shook his head, and his hand rested on her shoulder. "That wasn't your fault."

"Not the Heathens part. The mom part. I know it's not exactly my fault, but it happened because I'm me."

He shrugged her words off his massive shoulders and chuckled. "And because I'm me. An old, old score, sweetie. One your mom's not full settled yet."

Must be one hell of a game you two have going. But even Ash wasn't crazy enough to say so aloud. "Mom doesn't let go of grudges." She paused, sighed. "Me being with Nate probably added to it, though. Thank you for accepting me anyway."

"We'll call it probation for now, kid. Never know. He might lose his damn mind and divorce you." But he laughed.

"Tell him to ask Grandpa for a check first. At least make it profitable."

"Deal." Tree hugged her again and went off to find whoever needed his audience next. But as his giant frame moved, she caught sight of the main door. And the new arrivals. Her heart thumped. Joker and Grim stood a few feet inside, both of them grubby and disheveled from the heat. Joker's unreadable cinnamon eyes held hers. Grim vanished into the crowd of their incoming brothers, but Joker came straight toward her. He didn't smile.

She turned her attention to her drink rather than watch his last few steps. A familiar palm pressed to the middle of her back alerted her to his proximity soon enough. "What are you doing here, baby?" he asked, his voice soft as velvet. She breathed in the slight scent of sweat mixed with his cologne—she'd ridden on the back of his bike too much this summer.

"Making sure the buffet was set up and that the DJ got here. I was half worried Chains might have talked her out of it the other day." She turned, looking up in time to see the clenched tension in his jaw. *Oh. Someone isn't happy to see me.*

"And that's your problem why?"

She forced a smile. "I handled food and entertainment for tonight, sort of. Mentoring Lana. She was terrified of screwing up, lest your dad excommunicate her." Ash touched his tanned forearm just below the lower edge of his armor tattoo. "You don't look thrilled. Something go wrong on the ride? Frog told Case that his motor sounded weird yesterday."

"Nothing went wrong." He glanced down at her, clearly about to say more, but something over her shoulder caught his eye. Joker hesitated, torn between staying or going. In the end, he rubbed Ash's back and gave her what he probably intended to pass for a reassuring smile. "I'll find you later."

Ash nodded, keeping her expression pleasant until he turned, and she downed half her drink and signaled Karli for another. Technically, alcohol wasn't approved with her meds, but when your husband obviously didn't want you around anymore ... *screw approval.*

I'm being paranoid. He's busy. Maybe being married is just weird.

Or, maybe I should have kicked his shins back in Xanadu. The thought didn't make her feel better. She glanced around the room, wondering if anyone else noticed that Joker hadn't kissed her, or told her the food looked great. Or... *well, he never compliments my clothes. So that's normal, when you think about it. Yeah. He's just tired. It's fine.*

She rose to her feet and eyed the rapidly filling room. She spotted Ariel's friend, Jessica, and waved before making her way over. It seemed that, on the whole, everyone had forgiven Ash for "stealing" Joker from the former would-be queen bee. Then Jessica introduced her to some of the visiting Old Ladies, and time slipped away to somewhere else.

"Hey, you feelin' okay?" Travis's voice drew her attention from her third drink. He bore a cast on his left arm, thoughtfully graffitied with insults and greetings from his new Storm Crow mentors, and Prospect on a patch beneath his new name: Bullet. He wasn't just patched over from the Heathens like most others—he'd be a true Crow in a few months, thanks to Tree's own suggestion and Dragon's sponsorship. "You should probably sit down. You've been on your feet for hours," he said quietly.

"I've been sitting for a month," Ash grumbled. "I don't want to sit. I want to stand here and talk about stupid stuff."

"How stupid?"

"Kardashian reality show stupid."

"Could be worse." One corner of his mouth turned up, and he put a hand on her elbow, guiding her back toward the bar. "How about a tall stool instead of a chair? That's halfway to standing."

"Are you a professional baby-sitter? Because you should be."

The next couple hours spun faster, with more people coming in, and drinks flowing. Karli got shots, and then Griff and Megan showed up to order another round. Ash didn't drink much. Just enough to keep her head floaty. Then Megan requested a Katy Perry song, and somehow, they were dancing. Blaze waded in to convince them to behave, but Megan got on her toes and kissed his scarred cheek before shoving him toward Ash. Karli joined in, and by the time a slow song broke up the raucous bumping, grinding, and outrageous twerking, Ash was laughing so hard she had to hold onto Case.

"One more dance, Case?" She batted her eyelashes at him—his member patch was still shiny-new from the big 4th of July party, and she put one hand over it.

"Ash, come on. You're two weeks out from being cleared for all-night dancing."

"And then it's going to be another two weeks and another two weeks! You're a Crow now. Help me rebel against authority. It's basically your duty."

"I—" Case stopped talking, damn near stopped moving. His gaze focused with laser precision. *Ah. So that's where my husband's at.*

"Would that be my authority you're rebelling against?" Joker's voice was just loud enough to be heard.

"Um, I think I hear the Prez calling me." Case hurried away, retreating from the line of fire. *Coward.* Ash raised a mocking brow at him before turning to Joker. He stood relaxed, one hand in his pocket.

"You ready to go?" Joker asked, earning a laugh from Ashlyn. Did it sound as bitter to him as it felt in her throat? If it hadn't been such a crowded night, she might have walked off by way of answering.

"No." She pushed her hair off her face and swept it over her shoulder. "Unless you're wanting to hit that party at the Palmyra bar. I can't remember the name, but Jingle said he was heading there for a bit."

Her husband was silent for several heartbeats. "I think we should head home." His voice was strained with forced calm, but when he reached out, his fingers were gentle on her elbow. "Please."

"Why?" She didn't pull away from him, but she didn't let herself lean in either. *Say it,* she thought at him. Her jaw clenched. Their gazes locked. As far as fights went, it was quiet, and she had no intention of pushing him too hard in front of the others. But, for better or worse, Ash wasn't afraid of him, the clubhouse, or the collection of mercenaries, hell-raisers, and rebels around them. Joker was the first to look away.

"Because I'm not ready," he answered. His shoulders shifted strangely, and he shook his head. Her confusion must have shown on her face because he exhaled sharply. "I'll explain. But not here. Somewhere quieter. Sound fair?"

Her brow creased, but she shrugged. "Fine. Fair. Whatever. There's vodka at the house. Let's go." The fake-sunny smile returned. She winked at Karli and set her cup down. "My car or your bike? I'm not driving, but I think Bullet's sober if we need a DD."

"I'm sober," he said, holding his hand out for her keys. She dropped them into his palm, and he draped one arm over her shoulders, guiding her out the main doors and across the graveled lot. Members and associates milled around, but no one approached. They made it to the car in silence, save their mismatched footsteps and Joker's wallet chain jingling. She watched him over the Miata's black ragtop before getting in.

Both doors closed, muffling the endless party cacophony. Joker shoved the key into the ignition but didn't turn it. "We don't have to go." His voice startled her into looking at him more closely. She couldn't see much in the moonlight. "I wanted to make sure that you're okay being here." He lifted his hand to the steering wheel. "I'm not entirely okay with it, but I can suck it up. Figured if you needed to head out, you can blame it on me being a dick."

I'm too sober for this. She turned her head, staring out the passenger window. He'd said so many of the right things, but only one stuck in her head. "I don't want to leave. My friends are there. I missed them. I even think some of them missed me… But you're never going to be 'entirely okay with it,' are you? So, let's go."

Silence answered. Then the sound of Joker's weight shifting, his shirt rustling against the upholstery.

"Wait." He touched her arm. Usually, she would have put her hand over his or taken the cue to wind her arms around him. Tonight, she didn't move. "I get the feeling we ain't on the same page here."

"What other page is there? You don't want me here."

"That isn't... Fuck. Fuck." His palm slapped against the steering wheel, and he groaned. "I thought you were safe last month! Then shit hit the fan. The next time I see you, it's those fucking pics, all the bruises, and blood. So yeah, I'm not okay. And I don't know when I will be. But it isn't really about me." He reached over again, his fingertips brushing the back of her hand. She still didn't move. "If this is where you want to be, then we'll stick around. I was just worried you were going through the motions for—" He snapped his lips together and shook his head. "It doesn't matter. Let's go inside."

"No." Her knuckles were white on the door handle, but her free hand caught his. "We both fucked up that day."

"Ash—"

"No!" She clenched his fingers as tightly as the door. "Shut up and listen. Yeah, I got hurt. But blame the asshole who shot me, or the ones who beat me and Travis to a pulp, because you're not going to control every psycho in the universe—"

"I'd damn sure like to try."

"And you can't lock me out of your life and then say you want me in it. I said 'I do' in a Storm Crow clubhouse. I was drugged, not concussed, Nathan! Like I didn't notice I fell in love with you in a Crow war? Really? I wouldn't be letting Grandma plan a society wedding if I had any doubt I want to be with you. But if *you* don't want me with you..." She finally looked at him. Searched the hard lines of his face in the shadows.

"This *is* about you. I'm healing. I'm where I want to be. Are you?"

Joker leaned across the seat, bringing one hand up to her cheek just before his lips found hers, soft as any virgin's dream. All self-preservation evaporated in the raging heat his kisses always ignited, and a moan escaped. Instead of pulling her closer, he pulled away, but his hand stayed on her skin, stroking down the side of her neck in a lingering caress that told her he had no intention of letting go unless she pushed him off.

"I want you with me," he whispered. "Always. I love you, Ash. So fucking much. I'm sorry if I made you think anything different." That won him a solid glare. Sexy kisses or not, he didn't get to wave off the last three weeks.

"You're the one who's been gone all the time. You don't want me at the clubhouse. You don't talk to me about anything more serious than the weather. We haven't, um, you know."

"Fucked? Baby, your casts just came off this week! I was out of town. You made that rule. Remember?"

"I did not."

"Ashlyn." She could feel his eyes narrowing.

Okay, maybe I did. Shit. Ash bit her lower lip and tried to maintain her indignation. "But still. Can you see how I might be wondering if maybe you've had second thoughts? Third thoughts. Whatever round we're on now."

He bowed his head and rolled his tongue against his teeth, the corner of his mouth curving a little. "So maybe I've been a little over the top," he admitted. "I'm a pushy son of a bitch, and I never want to..." Joker trailed off in a frustrated exhale, and his fingers brushed up along her neck again. "I was so worried about hurting you, I forgot that brain of yours works overtime. I got zero second thoughts, sweetheart. Never going to. Done plenty of shit I regret. This?" The hand holding hers moved, his thumb brushed along her wedding band. "I'm not giving this up for anything. You're my life. I got no idea what I'd do without you."

"Have a much uglier house and fewer streaming channels? Less counselor appointments…"

"True. Dead guys on the side of the road don't get counseling."

She made a face at the joke and continued. "A lot more spare time and fuck buddies. No knowledge of *Vampire Diaries.*" When he looked ready to protest again, she pulled herself up in the seat enough to kiss him. "I love you, and I'm glad you're letting me totally ruin your perfect bachelor life." He grinned, his hand dropping to her bare knee. Apparently, he had noticed her skirt after all. Her legs parted just enough to let his hand slip down.

"What do you say we go home, and you make it up to me?"

Her fingers teased his waistline. "You sure you can make it home and stay on the road in that condition? Or would you rather go unlock the garage and fuck me in your office? Not that I've thought about your office in any indecent way. Or the clubhouse." She flicked the button of his riding jeans, earning a barely audible growl. "And you're making things up to *me*, VP. I haven't been with my husband since we got married. I'm not pleased…" His hand crept up her thigh, his knuckles pressing against her damp panties. His entire body tensed.

"Get out of the car," he ordered, sitting up and reaching for the door handle.

"Ooh, you're hot when you're bossy," she giggled,

all but leaping for the door. "I wonder if anyone else would believe you're the one who's anti-public sex." It was her final taunt before she took off toward the garage, knowing he'd follow more slowly, and using the extra moments in the deep shadows by the door to shrug out of her bra beneath the flowing peasant top.

He rolled his eyes, but there was no hiding his smile in the parking lot lamps. "It ain't about the public sex. Just don't need the guys seeing you naked."

"Mm. I'll believe that when you agree to sex in anything other than totally private spaces." She greeted him with her blue lace bra dangling from her fingertip. "So, did you bring the keys, or are we just going to hope Booboo didn't forget his vodka in the fridge?"

He moved in behind her, already flipping through the keys. Reaching for the hand holding her bra, he pulled her closer just so he could back her into the door until he had one leg between hers, and his erection was pressed into her belly. "I'm always prepared, sweetheart," he answered, kissing her while sliding the key in. The door swung inward, and he stepped back enough to let her breathe. "Come on," he whispered, leading her into the dark.

His kisses always hit her like a drug, and now she was almost shaking with anticipation. Months of being close to him and not with him—okay, three weeks, but that rounded up to a month, and if you added up the two weeks at Xanadu that was practically two—was a lot of being near Nathan without having sex. Considering the whole twice-a-day pattern they had going before, that was literally hundreds of orgasms missed. By the time he led her through his office door, she worried about keeping her legs under her. Had she been this nervous the first time with him? No. She'd been too mad, and then too turned on. Everything always felt so safe with him—

bullets flying or buildings on fire never mattered because all the threats were outside looking in. He would do a million bad things, and none of them would be aimed to hurt her. Unintentional? Sure. But looking in Joker's eyes and knowing she'd never see Bennett's "you're pretty when you cry" smile in them?

Oh fuck. Why did I think about him?

Ash's hand tightened on Joker's arm. He stopped, questioning eyes looking into hers, and she answered by wrapping her arms around his waist, hiding against his chest for two slow breaths. "I need you so much," she whispered. "I'm more nervous about right this second than I was the first time. Maybe we should have had a fight first."

"We did, technically." But he held her closer and kissed her forehead. "You got nothing to be nervous about, Ash. If you want to wait, we got our whole lives."

"I'm done waiting." She lifted onto her toes to kiss his throat, one hand drifting to the erection threatening to burst the seams of his riding jeans. He smelled like cologne and whiskey, and an edge of sweat that she should have cared about and completely, utterly didn't. They'd both be sweaty soon. "I need your hands on me, Joker. You've had weeks to take care of your club, but haven't made me come in so, so long." She pulled his palm toward her left breast. "You know I was touching myself when you were taking those extra-long showers, don't you?"

He grabbed her hip, dragging her up against him. "Were you?" he asked, lifting her with one arm and turning to set her on his desk while office supplies clattered to the floor and papers whooshed into the air. "Show me, Ashlyn. Show me how you touched yourself."

She didn't hesitate, just pulled up her skirt, legs

parting to reveal the boy-short undies beneath while one finger followed along the seam, her eyes on Joker's chiseled face. "Tell me what you were thinking about in the shower this morning." Satisfied by the heat in his gaze, she pushed the wet satin aside, letting her fingers run along her bared outer lips, dip to her clit, and further down.

He actually fumbled the fly on his jeans before freeing his erection. She rewarded that with a whimper, just to watch his jaw flex. "Your lips. Around my cock." He moved a few inches closer, palms settling on her knees.

"Just my lips? You didn't miss anything else?" Ashlyn reclined on the desk, weight on her left elbow while her right hand continued moving over her most sensitive places. Her right leg swung up, extending in a smooth arc until her pointed toes nudged Joker's waistline and pressed, nudging him backward

"That wasn't the question," he smirked, looking down at her foot. He caught the back of her knee, his touch light as he skimmed his hands over her calves.

"Guess I should just … get myself..." She moaned again, hips shifting against her own hand, and let her eyes close.

"I missed everything, Ash. The way your body feels against mine, your tight pussy on my dick." Still holding her ankle, his other hand shot out to catch her wrist, yanking it away. Her eyes popped open, half-playful, half-reproachful, and found Joker's dark as sin and hot as hell. "I missed the way you taste. The way your voice catches when you're about to come."

"I missed you, too, Nathan." She sat up, reaching for him. "Make me come? I'm so close. It feels so much better with you." It was almost infuriating how true that last statement was. Damn him and his pheromones.

He tugged her ankle, dragging her closer to the edge so her legs splayed around his hips while he shoved his pants down enough to keep the denim from abrading her thighs. His fingers found her clit, and his other hand slid into her hair, holding her frozen while his cock pushed at her entrance. "Hold on, sweetheart."

Ash almost screamed as he surged into her— weeks without contact left her sensitive, and unprepared for his girth. She bucked up, writhed, whimpered at the stretching pleasure-pain. Joker captured her mouth with his. The initial shock faded, and the friction of his slow thrusts washed away everything but the need for release. Her hands ran through his hair, over his cut and t-shirt, her palm pressed against his heart.

"Nathan? I'm—oh!" Her thoughts shattered, her body clenching and taut as the orgasm hit full-force, heat pounding through her veins with every movement of her husband's hips.

He kept going, rocking her higher and winding the tension deep inside. The second climax left her legs shaking, her fingers digging into his arms, and Joker circling her clit with one maddening finger. She whimpered, begged for mercy, and for more in the same breath.

Joker nipped her breast and didn't miss a beat. "One more," he whispered. "I'm close, baby."

Moments, or minutes, or ages later, her body arced from the desk. Her legs locked around him, her pussy clenched until his size almost hurt, and the rush dragged her under. She barely felt his cum spurting, anchored only by his weight and his sweet lips on her throat. His hands ran over her exposed skin as if checking for injuries, and while she drifted on a shuddering, sweet aftershock, he rubbed her hip where she felt the marks of his grip.

"I love you," she whispered. She nuzzled his shoulder and put her damp cheek to his shirt. Slow tears she didn't quite understand escaped her eyes, so she clung to him. Her fingertips traced his upper right arm, picturing his tattoo without needing to see it. "You're the only husband I ever want."

"That's good," he began, his lips brushing hers. "Because this wonderful state doesn't recognize plural marriage." And his blasted hips moved, setting off fireworks behind her eyes. She must have moaned because he bit her earlobe. "Ready to go again?"

"I figure it's not over until I can't walk, and even then, you'll probably convince me to try one more round." She ran her fingernails against his abdomen beneath the shirt, the last of her tensions vanishing like a bad dream.

"That's a safe bet," he laughed, stepping away to pull his pants up before reaching for her. "But things I plan to do to you need more than a desk."

"Promise you're home for a couple days?"

"You're not the only one wanting to make up for lost time." He bent and swept his arm under her knees, pulling her up against his chest. She should have objected, but she wanted so badly to be close to him that she didn't protest, and instead cuddled into him despite the sticky heat that the building's AC barely kept at bay.

"Time to go home and ruin one another." The words were threaded with laughter as he elbowed them through the main door and hauled her toward the car.

The End

EVERNIGHT PUBLISHING ®

www.evernightpublishing.com